# BENEATH THE STAIN

## AMY LANE

*Dreamspinner Press*

Published by
DREAMSPINNER PRESS

5032 Capital Circle SW, Suite 2, PMB# 279, Tallahassee, FL 32305-7886 USA
http://www.dreamspinnerpress.com/

Beneath the Stain
© 2014 Amy Lane.

Cover Art
© 2014 Anne Cain.
annecain.art@gmail.com
Cover content is for illustrative purposes only and any person depicted on the cover is a model.

ISBN: 978-1-63216-232-8
Digital ISBN: 978-1-63216-233-5
Library of Congress Control Number: 2014945922
First Edition October 2014

Printed in the United States of America

This paper meets the requirements of
ANSI/NISO Z39.48-1992 (Permanence of Paper).

Mary, all yours. *All* yours—I promised. I sort of wrote him just for you.

# Acknowledgments

Elizabeth North, Lynn West, Gin Eastwick, Bruce Springsteen, Muse, the Killers, and Cage the Elephant. I'm all about acknowledging the awesome.

# Author's Notes

If there is no radio I sing. If there's no one to sing with, I sing to myself. If I need to be quiet I hear the music in my bones. To everyone out there who had to make music or die, or hear music or die, this book was written especially for you.

The ocean rolls us away
And I lose your hand through the waves.


"The Ocean"
The Bravery

# You Can't Always Get What You Want

> *... from the Mighty Hunter Gazette—*
> *April 20*
>
> *And special news, our very own homegrown band,* Outbreak Monkey, *will be performing a six-song set between D.J. Boomer's dance music at the Graham Winters High School prom. The band, headed by McKay "Mackey" Sanders on lead vocals, Jeff Sanders on bass and their brother Kell Sanders on lead guitar, also features Grant Adams on second lead and Stevie Harris on drum set. All members are Graham Winters High School students and we are proud to have them play!*

THE FIRST time McKay Sanders kissed his brother's best friend, Grant, they were getting high in a burned-out car in the field behind Mackey's apartment building. Kellogg, who looked old enough to buy even though he'd just turned eighteen, had spent ten dollars the brothers didn't have on cheap Muscat. By the time Grant—whose father had money—brought out the pot, Kellogg, Jefferson, and Stevie were passed out on the old camp blanket Stevie had brought from his dad's garage.

It was a celebration, of sorts, for landing the prom gig.

The older kids had hogged all the Muscat, though, and Mackey felt left out. Kellogg kept saying it wasn't right to get his little brother drunk, and Mackey kept saying it wasn't right to drink in front of him, but by the time Kellogg was too drunk to argue, there wasn't any wine left.

Jefferson and Stevie had finished off the other bottle all by themselves—just sitting quietly, not making any waves like they usually did, passing the bottle between them.

"Boy, you two argue a lot," Grant said after Kell let out a gut-buster of a yawn and fell asleep quick as a baby.

Mackey grunted and prodded at his older brother with his toe. The three brothers present looked nothing alike. Kell was built like a tank, with rounded shoulders, a brown-eyed glare, and plain brown hair that he buzz-cut short to his scalp. He was like born practicality, which was why hoarding the wine rankled Mackey so badly. An expenditure like that wasn't going to happen again.

"He gets mad," Mackey said, letting out a sigh. He slouched back inside the shelter of the car, peering through the doorframe at the iron gray sky. "He's the one who takes care of us, you know? But not in the band."

It was true.

Kell could play guitar ably enough, but Mackey….

"You can play everything," Grant said with admiration. "You're the one who puts the songs together, figures out who should be playing what. And the shit you write on your own…."

Mackey smiled at him a little shyly. Grant had the most interesting face, with a long, straight nose, full pink lips, and almond-shaped hazel eyes. When Grant looked at him with admiration, it stopped his breath and pulled rubber bands in his stomach. "I just…." He stopped because Grant was reaching into his pocket, and he pulled out a baggie full of weed and papers. "Ooh…."

Grant looked down at the other three, who were sleeping soundly in the late afternoon chill. "I was gonna share," he said mischievously, "but Kell was a dick about the wine, so I thought you and me?" Mackey nodded, captivated by the thrill of the forbidden—and by the way that cherry-ripe mouth pulled up at the corners when Grant smiled.

"I've never, uhm…."

Grant shrugged. "Me and Kell do sometimes. But, you know, Kell's usually a good guy."

Mackey reflected on his sleeping brother. Kell *was* a good guy. For example, Mackey had a confused memory of their youngest brother Cheever's dad, the one dad they thought would stick around beyond giving the baby a first name. Cheever's dad hadn't been very patient, and he'd *hated* Mackey. Well, Mackey *was* sort of a smartass. He'd probably had that fist coming. But that hadn't stopped Kell from stepping up and hitting Enos Cheever right back. Mackey and Kell had both needed stitches after that, but their mom had kicked Enos Cheever out—child support or no child support. That was okay. Kell and Jeff had been almost old enough to work by then. They'd only needed assistance for a couple of months.

"He doesn't like it that I can boss him around," Mackey said glumly. "He… he's the leader, right? But… but I *hear* the music, and it just makes sense, you know? And… and you can't do it *wrong* just 'cause it'll hurt Kell's feelings. It's *augh!*" He was waving his hands around, trying to find words, which was funny, because Mackey actually *wrote songs*. He closed his eyes, ignoring Grant rolling a number, and tried to make a song out of it.

"He wants to keep me happy and he wants to keep me fed, he makes sure that I've got blankets and a place to sleep in a bed, but the music in my heart is like a freight train. It goes and it goes and when I stop it, it's like pain, but my brother doesn't see it doesn't hear it doesn't feel it, and all there is to do is shove him out of the way. Don't want to hit my brother with the freight train."

Mackey's eyes smarted, because the friction with Kell hurt. They were tight. They *had* to be tight, because Tyson, California, had a population of ten thousand, and it was a small enough town that the woman with the four sons and four fathers was sort of famous. They had to have each other's backs or Cheever wouldn't have survived kindergarten.

Mackey blinked and took a deep breath, then coughed.

Damn, pot was strong.

He gazed at Grant, who was staring back in awe over the glowing ember of the joint. Grant held the smoke for a minute and exhaled, shaking his head. "God, it's gorgeous when you do that," he said, his voice choked.

"Do what?" Mackey asked, not able to stop staring at him.

"Pull music out of the air," Grant said, the dreamy smile on his full lips maybe a side effect of the pot, but maybe not. Grant was sitting in the back of the car, his feet at the foot of the blanket the others were sleeping on. He passed Mackey the doobie around the doorframe, and Mackey regarded the joint with a little bit of fear.

"Just inhale?" he asked nervously, and Grant grinned.

"Never done this before?" he confirmed, taking the doobie back.

Mackey shook his head, knowing his face was flushing in spite of the iron mountain chill.

"Here," Grant murmured, taking another hit. He stood up, still holding the smoke in his lungs, and knelt in front of Mackey, so close their lips almost brushed. Mackey's mouth fell open, because, holy God, Grant was *right there*, and Mackey had been trying not to look at him like he had wanted him *right there* since he was twelve years old.

Grant took his open mouth for invitation and exhaled, right between Mackey's parted lips.

Mackey's inhale was so gentle, the smoke hardly tickled. He didn't choke or cough like he'd seen other people do, just breathed in subtle-like, afraid to startle Grant or make him move in any way. His exhale was even quieter, letting the smoke trickle out through his lips and his nose, where it stung.

He swallowed, his mouth dry from the smoke and from the way Grant was staring at him, seemingly as mesmerized as he was by those golden eyes and moist red mouth. "How's Sam?" he asked, because Samantha Peters had been Grant's shadow for the past year.

"Not here," Grant whispered, and the movement made their lips touch.

Mackey closed his eyes, because Grant started this, and Mackey was fourteen to his seventeen. Grant would know what to do.

Grant's lips on his were whisper-soft, then angel-soft, then Grant's tongue swept into his mouth, acrid with the bitter taste of weed, but something in it was sweet. Something in it made Mackey open his mouth to beg for more.

Grant took advantage, pushing him back against the seat, taking his mouth more, and more and more, until Mackey was pressed against the burned-out seat frame, his hands buried in the thick top strip of Grant's hair, his lips being bruised and his mouth plundered by his brother's best friend.

The smell of pot smoke sharpened, turned plastic, and Grant jerked his head back.

"Shit," he muttered. The joint had fallen onto the blanket at their feet, and he spent a moment stomping it out as it smoldered. When he'd killed the ember, he glanced at Mackey sheepishly.

"Got lost in your eyes," he said, and Mackey watched curiously as two red crescents surfaced on his sharp cheekbones, like disappearing ink coming to life.

"I could get lost in you a lot," Mackey confessed, feeling brave and bold, and Grant found something to look at far away.

"Mackey, maybe don't count on me like that, okay?"

Mackey had to search far away too. Well, of course, right? Two guys get high and they do something crazy—didn't mean shit, did it.

Didn't mean a goddamned thing. "Yeah, well. You know. Strong weed, right?"

"Yeah," Grant murmured. "Strong." His hand was firm on Mackey's shoulder then, and Mackey closed his eyes as he felt the rasp of Grant's chilled palm against his cheek. "Stronger'n shame."

Mackey had to. Had to see his face.

Grant was blinking hard, and they both knew he'd deny it, but one hit of pot didn't give you eyeballs that red.

At their feet, Kell gave a moan and rolled over, and that was the cue for everyone to wake up. They were headachy and sick, and it was lucky Grant had brought a six-pack of water, of all things, so they could at least rinse out their mouths after they puked.

Grant had driven them out to the vacant field in his mom's minivan, and later that evening, he stopped and let them run inside the grocery store to buy noodles and spaghetti sauce for dinner. They'd promised their mom they'd take care of groceries if she let them get away with not watching Cheever for the afternoon. When they got to the Sanders boys' apartment complex, Grant and Kell were giving each other shit in the front seat. Mackey stared out the window and let their banter wash over him, just like he ignored Jefferson and Stevie talking in quiet undertones about comic books and naked girl pictures. Jeff and Kell had best friends. Mackey had brothers—six of them, if he counted Cheever's little friend Kevin, which he did.

"So, is Sam excited you get to play at the prom?" Kell asked, laughing.

"Yeah," Grant said. For a moment he caught Mackey's gaze in the rearview, and then he glanced back toward the road. "She wants to dress pretty and dance with me in a suit."

Mackey didn't make a noise or anything, but suddenly he knew, knew like it had been branded on his skin, that Grant didn't want to dance with a girl in a dress. And that it would hurt worse than orange juice on chapped lips, but Mackey was going to have to watch him do it.

THEY WENT ambitious for the prom and planned to play all rock, with one power ballad. The power ballad was "Freebird," because, hey, you could dance to it, and because Tyson may have been in California, but there were parts of Northern California that were straight out of Alabama. Almost all the rock songs were covers—because who knew who the fuck Outbreak Monkey was, right? But Mackey had been writing songs since his mom first sent them to the church organist for music lessons, and the band? Well, they did tend to let Mackey lead—but only when he was on stage, and only when they were playing music.

"So, you guys ready?" Mackey asked before he went over the playlist.

Grant, Stevie, Jeff, and Kell all ranged around him, equipment at the ready in Stevie's dad's garage, because Stevie's dad was out of town. Otherwise they'd be practicing in the living room of the Sanders's tiny apartment, because anything was better than Stevie's dad.

Stevie perched behind the drum set his mom had bought him two years before, Jeff had his bass slung around his hips—without the amp—and Grant and Kell both had their acoustic guitars at the ready. With the exception of the drum set, this was how they'd learned to play together.

WHEN MACKEY was ten and Cheever had been in diapers, Kell had been stuck with babysitting duty while their mom was working nights. Grant and Stevie often came over to keep the boys company, both of them playing fast and loose with the truth of "Are there adults there to supervise?"

On this particular night they'd been bored—the Sanders boys didn't have an Xbox or PlayStation like Grant's or Stevie's folks—and Mackey said, "Hey, guys, want to play rock band?"

"We don't got the equipment for it," Grant said, but he'd smiled. Grant had always smiled at him, even when Kell was too grim with having to take care of the family.

"No, no—we do. Jeff, get your keyboard!"

Jeff and Stevie took orders easy. Grant liked to play with him anyway. Cheever was asleep in the bottom bunk, where Mackey usually slept. Once Mackey stood in the middle with Jeff's keyboard and played a basic hymn, he bossed everybody else into place. He knew the melody, and he picked it out for Kell on his little acoustic guitar, and he pounded out a bass beat for Jeff on his thigh. Stevie was a quick study—he picked up the beat and had fun with the flourishes on the practice pad. Jeff took piano with Mackey, too, so he understood that some chords on the bass made you happy and some chords made you sad. For "Simple Gifts" it was happy.

So they played a very basic version of "Simple Gifts."

And when they were playing it through a second time, Mackey opened his mouth and blew everybody's minds.

*I fight in the playground with the kids mouthing off*
*And I fight with the teachers when they laugh at us and scoff*
*And I fight with my brothers 'cause it's how we play*
*If I'm not fighting then I died this day*

Even Kell had been reluctantly impressed. "Keep goin', Mackey!" he'd urged, and Mackey grabbed a school notebook—their mother bought them by the case when they went on sale for eight cents a piece—and started writing, his left hand hooked at a painful angle, because that's just how he wrote. While he was doing that, Kell took them through the song a few more times, until they could play it with hardly any hitches.

By the time their mom got home, Mackey had the lyrics ready to perform. After a long night on her feet, putting up with drunks and shitty tippers and men who thought that her dating history was an insta-pass to her bed, the Sanders boys did the impossible.

They made their mama smile.

In fact, they made her laugh and clap her hands. "Oh, Mackey," she crowed, "if I've got to bail you out of school because you can't keep your fists to yourself, at least you can give me this!"

Even tired as she was, she'd celebrated by making hot chocolate for them and pulling a box of cookies from the hidden place in the pantry (because otherwise they'd be gone), as well as a box of Chicken in a Biskit crackers, just for Mackey, because those were his favorite. When Grant's and Stevie's parents came by to pick up their boys, it looked like they'd spent a quiet night at home.

The next time the boys got together, Grant brought a music book with the melodies and chord progressions of some of their favorite rock songs.

And Mackey had filled up half a notebook with lyrics.

They'd played "rock band" ever since.

The local music store let Mackey stack crates and sweep up on the weekends, even though he was underage, and in return, he got their used and broken equipment. His mom let him do it if he stayed out of trouble, which meant he had to stop belting kids for jumping his shit when he was smarter than them. He learned to use his mouth, those precious words he kept in his notebook, to keep kids off his back. It didn't make him popular, but it kept him out of fights.

"Hey, Mackey—how's your mom?"

"I don't know—how's yours? She was looking okay when I left her this morning!"

"I will fucking—"

"You will? I'd like to see that. Wait. Nobody would like to see that. Suggest something else."

"Oh God—"

"Me? I'm your god? Wow, you didn't have to! Hey! Go get that!"

"Go get what?"

"Your self-worth—I just kicked it off the sidewalk!"

"What does that even mean?"

"When you find your self-worth, you'll know! Fetch!"

The rest of the school just stopped talking to him, because, well, Mackey made a fool out of them.

But okay. He didn't need anyone but his brothers. And the band. Kell could fight for him anytime, but if he had the music to look forward to, Mackey didn't need him.

Mackey could do just fine on his own.

But he carried that *thing*, that pixilated fuck-off-and-love-me *thing* into the music.


SO HE gathered the guys in Stevie's dad's garage—praying that Stevie's dad didn't show up, because they could only bug out of there so fast with their instruments, and sometimes they had to leave Stevie behind and that didn't sit right—and Mackey told them how to play.

"We're doin' Nickelback, 'Rockstar,' first," he said, and nodded, waiting for them to nod back. "And Offspring, 'Pretty Fly'—"

Grant laughed. "Can you do the voice?" he asked. "Which one of us is doing the 'Uh-huh-uh-huh'?"

Mackey smiled lazily and shook his bangs out of his eyes. "Tell you what. *You* do the 'Give it to me baby,' and I'll do—" And all the guys joined in, "Uh-huh-uh-huh"

They laughed then, all together, and Grant winked at him. "I can't wait to see you do your thing, Mackey. It's gonna sell the show."

Mackey preened, swinging his shoulders, strutting around his little circle of godhood like he was a big man. Then he turned and said, "Nah—it's Kell and you who're gonna sell the show. We got two lead guitars—man, that's right out of Southern Fried Rock right there. You guys gotta play back and forth, 'kay?"

Grant and Kell looked at each other and grinned, then held up their secondhand Gibsons and made fake guitar battle gestures.

"Whaddo me'n'Stevie do?" Jefferson asked, all in one breath. It was how he and Stevie usually talked, which was why he never did backup vocals if there were real words in them.

Mackey smiled at him—not the flirty, cocky smile he gave to Grant or Kell when they were playing either. Jefferson and Stevie were... well, sort of special. They were quiet. In class the teachers just sort of overlooked them, and they hid in the back and got Cs and spoke an entire other language that not even Mackey could fully translate. They had the softest features, round faces, round chins, and the same sandy brown hair which they wore parted in the middle and falling layered to the sides, and they had the same faded blue eyes. They looked like cousins maybe, but Mackey and Kell had asked Stevie straight out if any of his male relatives had the last name Jefferson, and he couldn't think of one.

"Well, you're bass," Mackey said, nodding and trying to give Jeff a complete picture. "You sort of have to ignore all the rest of us here and coordinate with the drums. So Stevie's gonna be giving us a beat and you're going to be reinforcing that." He paused and saw that Jefferson looked sort of downcast. "You don't get it!" Mackey watched every performance he could find on basic cable. He stayed up late to watch talk shows that had bands in them—hell, it was the *only* reason to watch *Saturday Night Live*. "See, the bassist has *mystique*. You look totally... what's that word? Alone... no! A*loof*! You look *aloof* from all of us. The bassist always has sunglasses in the daytime, and he's just totally his own person. So Stevie's gonna be spazzing on the drums, 'cause that's his thing, and Kell and Grant'll be dueling guitars, and I'm gonna be—" He executed some pelvic wiggles and a few jerky dance moves, the kind he'd seen the rock stars do on television. "And *you*, you're gonna be too cool for all that shit."

It worked. Jeff grinned and pulled his lanky, slight body into his habitual slouch, but this time it looked purposeful. It was like Jeff *found* himself in that description, and Mackey beamed.

"So that's three songs," Kell said, frowning. "We know Nickelback and Offspring, and the Skynyrd."

"Yeah, but they're sort of old," Grant said with a wince. Well, Grant's dad could afford satellite radio. "We need something newer."

"Well, how 'bout Cage the Elephant—"

"No!" Kell commanded sharply. "Mackey, all them songs'll get us kicked outta school."

Mackey bared his teeth and started the patented Matt Shultz spazz-strut. "We don't care about the glory—"

And Grant picked up the guitar lick. "We don't care about the money, we don't care about the fame..." and just that quickly, their little garage band launched into "In One Ear" and Kell was left with nothing to do but pick up the lead guitar and join in.

The song ended abruptly, and Mackey swung his hands and his ass in time—then snarled at Kell, still wearing his stage face.

Then he dropped the snarl and gave him the stage "Am I stoned or just fucking with you" smile. "Yeah, not that one. How about the Broken Bells single?"

Grant shuddered. "Naw, man. That song gave me the creeps after I saw that redheaded girl in the space video. Can't we just do the Bravery and 'Believe'?"

And it was Mackey and the rest of the boys who all said, "Yes!" because just like the Muscat and the burned-out car, Grant really did have the best ideas.

"So, we do 'Satisfaction' and 'No Rest for the Wicked,'" Kell said, still taking care of details.

Mackey conceded to Kell's choice of classic Stones—because they'd already rehearsed it, for one—and to the "clean" Cage the Elephant song, and gave a fierce I'll-eat-your-baby smile. "Kk, guys. Jeff, give us a 3/4 rhythm, two chords, C and G, bu-*dum*-bu-*dum*-bu-*dum*—like a heartbeat, right?"

Jeff started that, and then Mackey went to his keyboard and started playing the first riff for Kell. Kell was rock solid on the beat, and he'd play anything Mackey gave him—and fast—but he wasn't much for improvising. The improv line he gave to Grant. Stevie had picked up on Jeff's thumping bass and started to keep up a dual rhythm on the cymbal and the bass drum, and Mackey nodded. Good. They had the basics now.

Into the solid sets of chords, he started to sing.

*You'll hear me screaming in the mountains and the valleys far away,*
*Over oceans over planets over moons.*
*You'll hear me tearing out my tonsils and my voice will never fade,*
*I'm begging and I'm pleading just for you.*
*I know you do not want me, not even on my knees*
*I know you want another—I got that.*
*But you can't hide away from screaming from the begging and the pleading*
*'Cause you know you coulda had me on my back.*
*A kiss is not a promise or a broken vow disguise*
*And the meaning of it's lost if you get lost inside my eyes*
*So think hard about my eyes about my hands about my mouth*
*Think hard about my stomach and the mystery in the south*
*And I'll scream to get you hard upon your back!*

The lyrics were hard-driven, borderline filthy, and everything he'd wanted to say to Grant from that moment shotgunning pot smoke in the vacant field.

But you didn't say that to another boy in Tyson, California, and that was okay. Mackey strutted in their little circle and kicked out with the mike stand and wiggled his hips, and not a girl on the planet wouldn't think he wasn't pining for her and her alone.

The first run-through was always rocky, and he finished the lyrics and let the band rattle and die to an end, then turned to them, seeing if they liked what he gave them.

Jeff and Stevie were nodding, and Kell scowled in that way he did when he was making a list of things to fix for the next set.

"Good?" Mackey asked, because this, here, this was the one place he needed approval. The band was the one place someone else's opinion mattered, and the one thing he could put in his pocket during the day with the shit-for-brains kids who couldn't just read the fucking books and stay out of his face, or with Cheever, who knew he could get any of the boys in trouble just by falling on his own toys and blaming the bruise on them.

But here, in this little circle, with his brothers looking at him, he could have something good.

"Yeah," Kell said, frowning as he continued with his list in his head. "Yeah, Mackey. I like that one. It's sorta dirty, but teachers won't be able to stop it 'cause it's clever. Whaddayou think, Grant?"

Grant was looking at him, hazel eyes like liquid, juicy lower lip worried by his teeth. "It was awesome," he said, his voice throaty and quiet. "I especially liked the part about lost inside your eyes."

Mackey couldn't hold his gaze any longer. He looked down at his keyboard and made some notations in his notebook about where the bridge fell apart and how they needed to clean that up. "Yeah, well, girls seem to like that shit," he muttered. He risked a glance at Grant then and was mortified when he realized Grant knew exactly what he meant by that. Those hazel eyes were devouring him, scolding him, and needing him, and Mackey couldn't seem to make them stop.

"Mackey, start us over again," Kell said. "Grant and I need to clean up the guitar parts or I'll never get to sleep."

"Yeah," Mackey said, his throat dry. "I'll conduct this time and work on the lyrics next time we practice."

"You do that," Grant said, his voice so growly Mackey might have been the only one to hear it.

Didn't matter.

It was more than enough that Grant knew Mackey hurt. It was Mackey's only weapon in the war they'd fight for the next five years.

PROM. HELL, it wasn't even *Mackey's* prom—he was still a freshman. In fact, although Grant was still seventeen and Kell had just turned eighteen, they didn't even think of it as *their* prom. Seniors got a ball, and since Kell couldn't afford to go and wasn't dating anybody, Grant had decided he wasn't doing it either, girlfriend or no. Jeff and Stevie were juniors, but they hadn't taken an interest in girls yet. Or, well, *apart* they hadn't taken an interest in girls. So far, their entire adolescence had been spent taking an interest in the *same* girl, one girl at a time. They didn't compete, either. They just both looked at the same girl longingly and consoled each other when she didn't look back.

The weirdest part was that nobody seemed to notice how weird it was. Mackey just accepted it for Jeff and Stevie, and that was okay, then, right?

But the fact that nobody in the band was actually *going* to the prom didn't stop everybody from getting dressed up. They assembled at the Sanders boys' apartment a week before prom, bringing their best clothes, with the intention of making sure they didn't look like shit when everyone else was going to be in tuxes.

But the Sanders boys had underestimated the bond of brothers—even ones who didn't live in a two-bedroom apartment and swap clothes until they disintegrated. Grant's and Stevie's parents could afford suits—Mackey had already figured that. He didn't expect Stevie to bring Jeff a barely worn sport coat to go over his best jeans and the collared shirt he wore to church on the rare occasions their mother still made them go. It was the same cut as Stevie's best sport coat—the illusion of their shared parenthood was even greater, but Jeff didn't acknowledge that. He smiled shyly at his best friend and stroked the arm of the nice wool. "Thanks," he said softly and then held his arms in front of him, pretending he was holding his guitar in the suit to make sure he could move when he held one for real.

Grant was slimmer than Kell, so he didn't have the pretext of lending an old piece of clothing, but that didn't stop him. He *bought* Kell a brand-new suit and lied, telling him it belonged to his dad. He'd forgotten to take the price tags off, but before Kell could look, Grant jumped in and jerked them off the sleeves without even an apology.

"I don't take—" Kell started, and Grant scowled back.

"Shut up. Just shut up. Let's see if Mackey's stuff fits." Because much to Mackey's discomfort, Grant had bought *him* an outfit too.

Mackey's outfit wasn't a suit like the other guys'.

Red superthin pipe cleaner jeans, the kind with a dropped waist even though Mackey hadn't had hair down there to reveal until middle school when his voice dropped; a tight white shirt, the kind with almost lacy sleeves and collar and the tailored bottom so Mackey would wear it untucked and flared; a blue velveteen suit coat, cut to let the sleeves and the collar spill over. It was outrageous, stunning, and could only be worn by a pixie-sized leviathan. Mackey would feel like five feet five inches and ninety-five pounds of sheer personality on stage in that outfit and knew Grant saw him that way too.

He stared in awe at the clothes pouring out of the shopping bag and then looked over his shoulder to where Grant was helping Kell on with his sport coat and trying not to make eye contact.

"Do you think…," Mackey breathed, and Grant met his eyes then. Was Mackey the only one who could see his cheeks were flushed? His eyes wide and shiny? His breathing coming a little fast?

"Yeah, Mackey, try that shit on," Grant said, gathering up a grin. He could pull his upper lip crooked, and it did something to Mackey that he couldn't even define.

"Here, I'll be back in a sec," he muttered. He was hard. His dick was *hard*. He was fourteen—he knew about wet dreams, and he'd had a few. Grant starred in all of them. And now Grant was looking at him like he wanted Mackey to star in his own private dream factory. He didn't give a shit how weird it looked to go changing on his own—he was going to have to take off his underwear to fit into those jeans, and he didn't want anyone to see.

A few minutes later, Grant banged on the bedroom door. "Mackey, let me see!"

"No!" he hollered, looking miserably at the pants barely fastened over his hard-on. The hard-on wasn't that impressive—he had hopes it would grow as he did. He'd be fifteen in a month, right?

Outside the door he heard Kell, suddenly panicked. "Cheever, goddammit, put down that fucking Sharpie!" and then some general chaos after that.

Underneath the guys screaming at Cheever and Cheever wailing, he heard Grant. "C'mon, kid. It's you and me. No one else'll see."

It was that promise—that illicit promise of privacy—that made Mackey open the door and shut it immediately after Grant snuck in.

Kell had recently moved out to sleep on the couch, so this room held the other three boys—Mackey slept on the bottom bunk, Cheever on the top, and Jeff on the twin bed in the corner. Mackey stood there, between three beds decorated with Star Wars comforters, and gestured to his suddenly adult body, swelling and proud underneath pants that showed off hair he'd barely even gotten.

Grant's gaze swept over him appreciatively, up and down his skinny body, face lighting up when he came to Mackey's crotch.

"That's some package there, McKay," he drawled, and his eyes bored into Mackey's.

Mackey's dick only got harder.

"It hurts," he confessed miserably. "And you can see my hair."

Grant licked his lips and then scrubbed at his face with his hands.

"I'll be back in a sec," he muttered. "Where's Kell keep his razor?"

"Bathroom in the hall."

Grant nodded, and almost like he couldn't control it, his hand crept out, brushed along the distended zipper of the forbidden jeans.

Mackey groaned, so close to coming he was almost weeping.

"Gimme sec," Grant reassured.

He slid out the door, and Mackey considered bending over Jeff's bed and just rubbing his dick until the ache stopped, but Grant was back by the time he figured out that bending over in the jeans hurt.

"Here," Grant said grimly. "Stand up straight."

Mackey did, holding his hands behind his head. The shirt wasn't buttoned, and it gaped across his thin chest, but the jeans loosened and so did the pressure on his cock.

Then he felt Grant's touch across his stomach, pulling the skin of his lower abdomen tight, and his cock got tight in a whole new way.

*Scrape. Scrape. Scrape.*

Mackey closed his eyes and ignored the yelling and frantic washing of something still going on in the crowded living room. He concentrated instead on Grant's fingers across his tender skin and the puff of breath across his stomach and the silky, alien sensation of going without hair.

"Mackey," Grant murmured, and Mackey was shocked into looking into those hazel eyes.

"Yeah?"

"I'm gonna unbutton your fly and pull down your pants. I want to shave lower, okay?"

Mackey moaned breathily. Oh… oh, he wanted….

"Yeah," he whispered through dry lips. He suddenly could not stop staring. Grant did what he'd said, unbuttoned his fly and peeled the jeans off his ass and down to his thighs.

Mackey's cock flopped forward, bigger than Mackey had ever seen it.

Grant made a "nungh" sound, so close to it that Mackey could feel his breath across the moist tip. Sensation fluttered across his abdomen, and Grant swept the razor a width below the line of the pants before he dropped it into the glass of water he'd been using to rinse it off.

And stayed right there, on his knees, in front of Mackey.

He sighed and then met Mackey's miserable stare. He held his fingers up to his lips and Mackey nodded, and then with his other hand, he grasped Mackey's cock.

Mackey had to bite his hand to keep from screaming.

Grant stroked, back and forth and back and forth, and his other hand made delicate dancing movements at Mackey's balls.

"Grant," Mackey whispered, "I'm gonna…."

Grant did the unthinkable. He opened his mouth and took Mackey inside, sucking his way halfway down, which was when Mackey moaned into his cupped hands and came.

His knees started to shake as he pumped jizz into that sweet-lipped mouth, and he grabbed hold of Grant's shoulders. Grant kept swallowing until finally Mackey was done. He and Grant locked gazes, and he saw satisfaction and fear. Then, when Mackey's hands were still shaking and he wanted a kiss in the worst way, Grant raised a towel he'd brought in and started wiping Mackey down.

"There," he said, and the word was crisp, but his voice was husky, his throat probably rough with Mackey's come. He cleaned Mackey's groin with efficient movements and was standing up, pulling Mackey's pants up, when the knock came at the door.

"Jesus, you guys—Cheever damned near fucked up Jeff's new suit—what the hell are you doing in there?"

"Grooming!" Grant called back. He took a step away and looked down from his six-foot height. "You ready," he asked quietly, and Mackey touched Grant's cheek. Grant turned his head and kissed Mackey's palm, then let him go and stepped away.

"Come in!" he called, and Mackey hauled at the pants again. His hard-on was gone, so they fit now, and his stomach was smooth.

Kell took him in with a scowl. "Jesus, Mackey, button your shirt. You look like a slutty girl or something."

"I didn't want him to shave the damned thing!" Mackey retorted, fumbling with the buttons—and fumbling for the lie Grant was bent on telling as well. "It's a good shirt!"

"It is," Grant said, his voice gruff. Mackey finished the top button, and Grant *un*buttoned it. "Leave it." He stepped back and nodded. "Yeah. Here, straighten your coat, Mackey. What do you think, Kell?"

Kell grinned. "He looks like Mick Jagger, only, you know, fourteen and better looking!"

Mackey grinned. *That* was the sort of compliment a boy wanted to hear before he went on stage. "So, you think people will like the music?" he asked, suddenly worried. What he *looked* like didn't really matter to him. But the music? That was everything.

"If we rehearse more than we play dress up." Kell grunted in disgust. "Now take that shit off before Cheever sees it and goes after *you* with a Sharpie too!"

Mackey nodded and started unbuttoning his shirt while Kell turned to leave. He left the door open a little, because hey—six boys in the house, who gave a shit, right?

Grant turned his shoulders to leave, too, and Mackey made a sound as he was sliding off the coat and the shirt as one piece.

Grant turned back around, and Mackey could see the shudder taking over his body. He looked down in time to see Grant adjust himself in his pants.

"What you do to me," Grant whispered. "We can't do this, Mackey, but God. The things you do to me."

And then he turned and walked out the door.

# Dancing in the Dark

THE SCHOOL had a mirror ball and some basic spotlights that the theater kids worked like crazy when the band was on stage, and they got to rehearse with those, but even then Mackey looked at the lame lights and wished for something bigger. He had an *idea* for stage effects, things that would go with the lyrics and the beat that you couldn't do in a rinky-dink high school gym.

But for now, he had the basics and he had Tony Rodriguez, theater kid, student council member, marching band member—everything Mackey's brothers picked on, Tony was it. But he'd been more than helpful this past week helping them figure out how to load the equipment in for prom. Kell wouldn't work with him—called him fag to his face—and Grant couldn't seem to get Kell to stop, but Mackey thought Tony was okay. He worked hard, even if he didn't have any guts for the sound work.

"'Kay, I got you all plugged in, Mackey," Tony said, almost pathetic in his eagerness to please. "Your amps're all set and—" His voice was suddenly picked up by the mike and the resultant feedback loop about blacked out Mackey's vision.

"Yeah," Mackey muttered, adjusting the feed and the output and then checking Jeff's guitar too. Jeff could play and maintain a bass beat, but everyone knew Mackey had the best ear for that shit. "Anything else, Tony?"

Mackey turned to find Tony right over his shoulder, body close, sweating in the gym, which was actually a little cool the Saturday morning before prom.

"Uhm...." Tony licked his lips and smiled nervously, then suddenly jerked upright. His face flushed in the cold. "Uhm, no, Mackey. No. I just.... Wait. Are you going to prom with anyone?"

Mackey squinted at him. "I'm a freshman," he said, puzzled.

"Well, yeah, but someone coulda asked you," Tony said, and then he looked away. Tony was one of *those* kids, the kind who hung out with girls constantly, the kind who always had his finger in a pie and seemed to be the center of attention. Here, in the empty gym, he was as lonely as Mackey had ever seen him.

"I don't know any girls," Mackey said, staring hard.

Tony's blush got brighter. "Well, yeah," he said, not meeting Mackey's eyes. "I, uhm, know lots of girls. I'm not taking any of them to prom."

Something about the admission shocked Mackey, made his eyes open wide, parted his lips. "You're asking me to—" he breathed, half-flattered, half-appalled. Tony was a scrawny two-bit like Mackey himself, but he had brown eyes and brown hair and brownish skin, a bold nose, and a mouth not quite as plump as Grant's.

Just that moment, it occurred to Mackey that Grant's mouth wouldn't be the only one that looked so sweet wrapped around his cock.

But Tony was shaking his head. "I'm so stupid," he muttered, almost to himself, turning toward the drum set for no real reason. "Your brother'll probably stuff me in a trash can again, and Jesus, this town just fucking sucks, and—" He looked up miserably, almost in tears, his chin wobbling. "I'm sorry. I didn't mean anything. I just—"

"I won't tell my brother," Mackey blurted, pulled out of his shock by the thought that, yeah, Kell probably *had* stuffed Tony in a trash can, because Kell wasn't real nice to anyone weaker than him. Wasn't nice, was probably just Kell.

Tony's chin wobble eased up. "Thanks," he whispered, still miserable. "I didn't mean to embarrass you."

"I...." Mackey stood up, looked at the little gym, decked out with paper flowers and streamers by Tony and his friends, and had the sudden realization that this gym would never be for him. Or for Tony, either, really, who had just spent two hours making it pretty.

"What'd you think?" Mackey asked, his voice gentle and confused. "We'd... dress nice and dance, like everyone else?"

Tony shrugged, rubbing his finger on the hi-hat. "Maybe just someone to hang out with," he mumbled, and Mackey grimaced.

"I did not expect this," he said, so startled he found the word/rhythm place without thinking. "That the person in my skin was so plain to someone else, I didn't expect it. How is it you can see the guy I've hidden mostly from myself?"

Tony was suddenly looking at him—really looking at him, his mouth parted, too, softly, like he was begging to be plundered. "Because you say things like that, Mackey," he said, half-strangled. "Man... just your voice makes me hard."

Mackey hardened his face against that want.

"So," Tony said nervously into the silence. The gym was deserted, and without the people to pad it, his voice seemed to echo, unnaturally loud. "You, uhm...."

Grant's face popped up in the dark of Mackey's vision. The angle of his jaw, the way his dark lashes fluttered across his gold-skinned cheeks, the unusually straight bridge of his nose.

The way he'd turned away.

The way Mackey would follow him.

"I...." Mackey started, and his eyes flew open when he realized Tony had moved closer, was close enough that Mackey's voice didn't echo off the walls like Tony's just had. "I can't," Mackey whispered, and he hurt inside when he saw Tony's hurt on the outside. "He's... he's got a girlfriend."

"Oh," Tony said softly. "That sucks. Straight guys—it hurts."

And because he could, because Mackey had been kissed, because he'd had Grant's mouth on his body, he had to spill this secret. To somebody.

"He's not straight," Mackey whispered, turned away. Because if Grant wasn't straight, and Tony wasn't straight, neither was Mackey.

"Oh."

Mackey busied himself looping the cords from the amp to the guitars. He knew the trick to it that kept them out from underfoot but let the guys on stage have some movement. "This conversation goes nowhere but us," he muttered.

"That's a rule," Tony said, like he was teaching.

"What is?" Okay, this cord to Grant's axe, this cord to Kell's, this cord to the keyboard….

"You don't out anyone without their permission. It's a violation."

*That*, of all things, actually made Mackey laugh. "Where do you *learn* something like that?" he asked, actually looking up from the cords.

"The Internet," Tony said, relaxing in increments. "It's the only place you can see other gay people without being hunted by torches and pitchforks."

Mackey sighed and looked around the gym. Kell made fun of prom, but he'd heard Jeff and Stevie say something quiet to each other about how the right girl wouldn't be there and it was a shame.

"I'm sorry," he said after a minute. "All this work and it's not for you."

Tony shrugged. "See, what matters is, I know there's places it can be. Two years here—how bad can it get?"

That brought Mackey up short. "I got three," he muttered. But then the logic settled in. "Three years. As long as I can play music, it's all good."

He heard a song in that, about light at the end of the tunnel, and for a moment he was distracted by the song and the quiet between him and Tony got natural again. So natural that when Tina Camden ran into the gym trilling Tony's name, Mackey actually jerked and almost dropped a guitar.

"Jesus," he hissed, rounding on her, about ready to give her a piece of his mind.

"Making enough noise, Tina?" Tony joked, and Tina laughed.

"My mom just finished making up my dress," she said. "Tony, I can go tonight!" Tina was a little plump—she'd probably needed some adjustments to that dress—and Mackey was irrationally glad, even though he didn't know Tina at all. *Someone* got to come to the gym and dance.

"That's great," Tony said. "Can Lynn and Sarah make it?"

"Yeah," and Tina's voice dropped a little. "But, you know, I was sort of hoping you and me…."

She looked up, biting her lip, and Tony winked at her.

"It'll be better in a group, I promise. Besides, I'm not really a ladies' man, honey, you know that."

Tina nodded, but Mackey could tell by her disappointment that she didn't understand at all.

"That's okay," she said, her voice picking up some of its trill again. "I just wanted to let you know. Do you all want to meet at my house?"

They made plans as Mackey finished up the sound check on his own. When he was done, he picked up the lead guitar and brushed a few chords, losing himself in that flawless communication between plucked string and air.

He played a few more notes, mumbled some words, strung them together, talked about being open inside. Like a pomegranate, all the little seeds that make you bleed.

He paused and saw Tony, down on the floor, looking at him longingly.

"That was beautiful," Tony said. "Don't stop."

Mackey smiled a little and was going to shake his head, but Tony stopped him.

"Please," he said quietly. "There's no one here. Let's play pretend. Let's pretend you're not after someone else, and I'll pretend you're playing at the prom just for me."

Mackey thought Tony had it all under control, the being gay, the hanging with all the girls, the asking and being rejected. But that right there taught him something he'd remember forever.

Nobody had it under control. Nobody had it buttoned down all the time. Sometimes all you could do was play pretend. And the people who looked at him on the stage and pretended were just as bare on the inside as Mackey, who got lost in the music on the stage for the very same reason.

"Okay," he murmured, picked up the guitar again. He played the riff a couple of times, because he had the words in his head for the singing. "Can you copy the words for me?" His notebook—this one battered and halfway done—was at the foot of the stage.

"Yeah," Tony said, looking like he always did around school, like he was thrilled to be asked to help.

"Tony!" Mackey almost panicked for a moment, remembering the personal stuff in there, wondering if he'd ever mentioned Grant by name. "Just flip to the back where it's empty, okay?"

Tony caught his gaze again, and for a minute, Mackey was sorry. Why not this kid? Why couldn't it be *this* kid? But as warm as Tony's eyes were, they weren't Grant's gold, and that's what Mackey wanted to see.

Mackey fingered the melody with delicate, dancing notes, and sang the words while Tony watched, and then he looked at the lyrics and ran through the song again and again.

He was on his fifth run-through when Kell and Grant came in to pick him up. They stopped and listened while Tony wrote the words at Mackey's direction, and when Mackey was done, they both clapped.

"I like it," Grant said. "Can we play it tonight?"

Mackey smiled and looked at his hands before he could flush. "I don't have the band set up for it—"

"You should play it!" Tony said. "That can be your last song. It'll get everyone into slow dancing again."

"The faggot's right," Kell grunted, and the moment shattered.

"Don't call him that," Mackey snarled, taking his notebook from Tony. "He's done nothing but help us and you're being a dick."

Kell rolled his eyes. "What*ever*, Mackey. See if you get to play your dumb song now!"

"Don't be an asshole," Grant intoned, and Kell, who lived and died by Grant's opinion, hunched his shoulders and grunted.

"You can call me what you want," Tony said, after shooting Mackey a grateful look. "But that don't change that if you don't let Mackey shine a little, you'll be cutting your band off at the balls."

With that he turned around and headed for the door. "I'm sorry, Mackey. You guys gotta go so I can lock up, okay?"

Mackey nodded. While he was putting his guitar in the case and grabbing his notebook, Grant walked over to Tony and shook his hand.

"Don't mind Kell—he's a dick. We appreciate the help with the equipment and the setup."

Tony nodded. "Thanks. It was worth it to watch Mackey write a song."

Grant smiled, and Mackey looked up to catch his gaze. "You got lost in his words, didn't you." And for a moment, it was the two of them alone. *I got lost in your eyes.*

"Jesus, Grant, stop dicking around with—" Kell tossed a glare over his shoulder at Mackey, like Mackey was forcing him to do something. "—with *Tony,* and let's go."

Mackey trotted toward the big heavy double door and slid by Tony after Grant and Kell. As he cleared the door, Tony stopped him with a touch on the shoulder.

"Grant has a girlfriend, doesn't he?"

Mackey turned away. "Some shit's private," he muttered.

"Yeah," Tony said under his breath. "But if you ever want to talk—"

Mackey shook his head and, conscious of Kell striding toward Grant's minivan, disentangled himself and hustled to keep up. "See ya tonight. Have fun with the girls," he said, and he meant it sincerely.

He felt bad when Tony winced, but there wasn't a thing he could do about that, was there?

HALF AN hour before they were supposed to leave, Mackey looked in the mirror, horrified.

"Jesus Christ, Mom—"

"McKay James Sanders, don't you take the Lord's name in vain!"

Mackey's hair was plain sandy brown. *Was* plain sandy brown. His mom had streaked it gently, cut his bangs, cut the sides of it around his face. He looked like… like….

"I have no idea who I look like," he said. "It's someone I saw in a television show once—what the hell did you do to me!" He had gray eyes, big ones, framed with dark lashes, and with that haircut, his eyes looked even bigger, his nose more turned up, and his chin sharper. He was already smaller than most everybody else in his grade *still*, but now, he looked like some sort of stuffed animal or Barbie or something.

His mom grinned and nodded. "You look like a '70s pop star, Mackey. With that getup that Grant gave you, it'll be perfect. Trust me."

Mackey grimaced at his mother. All he'd said was that his hair was getting in his eyes and he wished he had time to cut it before they played. That was all. And their mom, who had to find a babysitter for Cheever because she worked that night, had suddenly brightened.

"I can help!" she said, her voice full of wonder. "I can help. I *trained* to be a hairstylist between you and Cheever. I can fix that!"

"Mom?"

Their mom was young—Mackey knew that objectively, although it didn't really settle in for many years to come that if she was thirty-four and Kell was eighteen, she would have been Jeff's age when she was tossed out of the house. But now, getting excited about doing Mackey's hair, Mackey saw some of that youth in her. Her hair was always dyed blonde and black and put up in a little fan on the back of her head, and her eyes were always smudged with kohl and mascara, but when she smiled like she was at Mackey now, talking about doing his hair for the big performance, he suddenly felt it.

Their mom wanted to be a good mom. She *wanted* to be a good mom. She wasn't always there, and they spent a lot of time in charge of Cheever and a lot of time worrying about money to keep their shitty little apartment. He knew that some of their Christmas presents came from coat donation and that most of their clothes came from Goodwill, and he knew that their birthdays were usually celebrated with cake and a book—one book, new—because that's all she had. She bought school supplies in gross when they went on sale and had cleaned the church lady's house so they could have music lessons, and her temper was short when she came home late and her boys were still up.

But she wanted to be there that night. She wanted it with all her soul.

And fixing Mackey's hair was what she had.

So Mackey let her, and the results were....

"Oh God," Kell muttered, looking in. "Mom, he looks like a girl—can we just buzz cut it and let it go?"

She looked so hurt.

"I like it!" Mackey said staunchly, and she smiled almost desperately, desperate to help, to be included, to be a part of her sons' lives. "Thanks, Mom. It'll look great."

"Grant'll laugh himself senseless," Kell muttered, but he turned his solid, hunched shoulders away and barged into the boys' bedroom. "Jeff, please tell me you're not putting on makeup!" he hollered.

"I have no idea what you're talking about." Jeff sounded really confused. Mackey's mom laughed and wrapped her arms around his shoulders and kissed his cheek.

"Poor Jefferson," she said, and Mackey smiled at her in the mirror.

"Yeah. Poor me, if Grant doesn't like it."

But he looked in the mirror, at his eyes, almost inhumanly large. For a minute he thought of eyeliner, like he'd seen on David Bowie, but decided against it. Even without the eyeliner, Grant would get lost in his eyes.

"Everyone will like it," Heather Sanders said proudly. "I wish I could get someone to tape it for me, Mackey. I'm so proud of you boys, practicing, performing. I wish I could give you more time to do it, but you boys are just so good."

Mackey smiled at her, because she was proud and happy, and he didn't want to burden her with the stuff that had been roiling around in his gut since the day Grant had shotgunned smoke into his mouth and touched their lips together.

"Thanks, Mom," he said softly. "I gotta go get changed."

He'd kept his suit neatly in the closet, away from Cheever, tucked carefully in the middle of everyone's Sunday school clothes that Cheever knew he *must not touch*.

Jeff was combing his hair in the little mirror they kept by the window while Mackey pulled on his suit, and when Jeff turned around, he grinned.

"Mom knows her shit," he said proudly, and Mackey grinned back. Jeff didn't say much, but it couldn't be argued that the boys loved their mama.

Then, before Mackey could say anything, Jeff swept his eyes up and down the tailored shirt with the tails and the low-hipped jeans.

"Oh Jesus, Mackey—did you have to *shave*?"

Mackey nodded, thankful he could confide in this to someone. "I had to shave *again*," he muttered. "It was growing back *itchy*!"

Jeff laughed. "Well, if I ever have to shave my balls for music, I know who to ask!"

Mackey scowled. "Wasn't my balls, it was just… you know…."

Jeff took in the low-slung jeans again. "Well, if they'd been any smaller, it woulda been your balls. You better hope you don't get a woody or that thing'll pop right out."

Mackey stared at him. "Sometimes brothers are a real fuckin' plague of locusts, you know that?" he snapped, and Jeff laughed quietly all the way out the door.


STEVIE AND Grant arrived, and they all piled into Grant's minivan. Samantha already sat in the front, but she moved to the backseat for Kell. On one hand that seemed really gracious, but on the other, Mackey didn't give a fuck.

It was so easy to blame her.

"So, Mackey, you nervous?" she asked, and Mackey gave her his best smile, which, at the moment, was thin as January sunshine.

"Not really," he said, being honest. "I memorized that last song real good."

"The one you wrote this afternoon?" Her face was a perfect oval, and she'd done something complicated with her blonde hair, and suddenly he wanted nothing more than to rip it all out by the dark roots. Grant had *told* her about that? "Grant couldn't stop bragging about you," she said, smiling like he'd be happy about this. "He thinks you're a genius. He keeps saying about how you'll put our little town on the map, and I'm like, 'Mackey? If he's smart, he'll just forget we were ever here.'"

She winked at him, and he couldn't do it. He couldn't be mad at this girl who just wished him the same wish he'd had for most of his life.

Wouldn't it be great to not live in Tyson anymore? Live in a place with his own bedroom? Not have to deal with the daily rounds of "Hey, kid, your mom's pregnant again!"

"I wouldn't forget you," he said, surprised to hear himself saying something civil.

She laughed and patted his knee and then talked to Kell and Grant through the front seat, but Mackey wouldn't forget. She'd tried to be nice to him.

And he wasn't lying about not being nervous, either. In fact, being up on stage was….

It was like flying.

"Heya," he said when the moment came, listening for a giddy moment as his voice boomed back at him under the mirror-ball lights. He stood up with his mike, with the guys around and behind him on the small stage. Behind Steve's drum set was the DJ stand—which swung out to the side when the band wasn't playing—but in front of it?

Well, nearly two hundred and fifty people, waiting for the five boys to play.

Mackey tapped the microphone and felt a little bit of bitch welling up in his chest. "Did I say 'heya,' y'all?'" he asked, and the attitude? Oh, it caught their attention.

The swell of sound and the applause was all Mackey needed.

"That's more like it! So, we're Outbreak Monkey, and we're gonna play you some music. I'm gonna sweat some *blood* on this little stage—you all wanna see that? Wanna see some *blood*?"

In an instant they were rabid, and Mackey grinned, the same grin he'd given Grant in a burnt-out car. "Well. We'll fuckin' see. *One, two, one two three four….*"

And they launched into "Satisfaction" before the teachers could stop the show.

The kids, the ones Mackey had fought in grade school and ignored in high school, the ones who threw food at Jeff and Stevie and who bitched behind Grant's back about how Grant's daddy kept him safe—*those* kids—were suddenly eating out of Mackey's hand.

And he reveled in it. He abused them. He taunted them. He stuck his tongue out and licked their figurative balls, then shook his ass and grabbed his crotch, and they hung on every fucking word.

They'd started with six songs on their roster. By the time they were done with "Screaming for You," their original song, the crowd was foaming at the mouth. Kell hunched his shoulders and turned his back on them, eyes closed in concentration. Grant flirted with them, winking and shaking his hips. Jeff did the bass thing, just like Mackey told him to, aloof and self-contained, and Stevie kicked back on the drums, rhythmic and regular and dependable for every beat.

Mackey closed his eyes and sang. He screamed. He moved his body and opened his soul, and those kids who hated him surged, thrust, ravished, and Mackey gave it up. Everything. He gave them everything.

And they reached with greedy hands and shrieked for more.

By the time they were done with "Freebird," sweat sopped Mackey's new jacket and ran from his hair into his eyes. He flipped his head and tossed it out, and finished the goddamned song.

They screamed for more.

Mackey met Kell's eyes as they were bowing in the middle of the noise volcano, and Kell shrugged and looked at Grant.

Grant reached for Mackey's guitar, which sat on the side of the stage and brought it to him, bowing a little as he handed it over.

"Yeah?" Mackey asked, his voice below the mike.

Grant smiled faintly, his mouth moist and parted because he left sweat on the stage too. "Let them see you," he said, so quietly Mackey had to cock his head to hear. "Let them get lost like I do."

Mackey shivered and turned toward the crowd, fixing the strap of the guitar over his head and plugging it into the amp during the sudden burst of applause. The rest of the band faded back, and Tony must have done something with the lights, because suddenly Mackey stood alone in the spot, staring thoughtfully out into the sudden black hush.

His fingers started moving on the strings all by themselves. The rush of blood in his veins, the rasp of his breath, the chill of sweat, all of the symphony of Mackey Sanders wove liquid emotion through the air.

He *was* music, everybody's music, every soul's note, played on the splintered stage of Graham Winters High School auditorium.

*"Will you see me crying or would you rather see me high?"*

The song ended with a question, destruction or sadness, and the startled silence that followed his last guitar chord simply echoed their shared pain: Mackey and the audience, bound by sweat and blood as long as the music played.

The silence lasted a heartbeat, two, and then exploded, fireworks of sound. For a moment, Mackey was terrified, threatened by that neediness, alone, a child surrounded by demons, all of them screaming for his blood.

The moment passed, and he curled his lips at the frenzied students, then bowed. "Y'all can listen to my music anytime," he said.

They were still screaming his name as he walked off the stage.

He found himself whirled away, hustled off the stage and out of the auditorium while the DJ got back behind his setup and attempted to restore order. Mackey was giddy, high as a kite on adrenaline and—suddenly, uncomfortably—aware of how tight his pants were.

But he wasn't going to tell his brothers that, especially as he was engulfed again and again in their press of bodies, in the hugs and congratulations and general whooping and hollering, because, dammit, it was a *win*, and Mackey's brothers knew enough about life to know that didn't happen nearly enough.

"Mackey," Grant said, his voice low and throaty. "God, Mackey, you were amazing!"

"Hear hear!" Stevie said, and he and Jeff did a high five/down low like they rehearsed it.

"That was *awesome*," Mackey said, his voice shuddering in his chest. And then *he* was shuddering, because it was cool outside and he was sopping with sweat.

Everyone else seemed to agree, and by consensus they all wandered back inside to get some punch, because besides everything else they were dying of thirst.

Inside was the last place Mackey wanted to be.

It was loud, it was dark, it was hot. People who hadn't given him the time of day *that morning* suddenly wanted his attention, and he didn't want to talk to those people. Why would he?

So he found himself by the snack table, munching on a brownie and drinking some punch with way too much sugar in it, having stilted conversation with Tony Rodriguez.

"Are they really both dancing with Carly Padgett?" Tony asked, and that made Mackey smile. Sure enough, Carly had her arms around Steve's waist and was laying her head on his chest while Jeff whuffled in her ear from behind, making her laugh.

"I don't know if the world's quite real for them when they're split up," Mackey said, meaning it. The story was, Mackey's mom had been pregnant with Mackey himself and cleaning houses between shifts at the restaurant to pay her medical bills. Kell had met Grant, and Jeff had met Stevie while she was scrubbing their parents' toilets and getting paid out of pity. Grant lived in one of the big "dragon houses"—as Mackey thought of them—outside of town: the places of money, what usually people like the Sanderses only saw when scrubbing toilets. Later, much later, Mackey put together the cost to Grant for being friends with the Sanders kids. But when you're a kid, that doesn't really come into play. When you're a kid, all that matters is that your brother's friend is part of your life and nothing seems to stop him from riding his bike or running away to visit your two-bedroom apartment. To Mackey, Grant was like Kell, Jeff, and Stevie. Everything outside his brothers had no bearing on his life.

But Grant *was* part of his band of brothers, and Grant was being pulled away by Samantha, outside through the back door of the gym. Mackey couldn't help but watch him go.

Before the door closed, Grant's eyes sought his out in the darkness, a look of uncharacteristic bleakness on his face as the door closed behind him.

"He does not look happy," Tony murmured by Mackey's ear, and Mackey jerked back, startled.

Tony sighed and took his own step back.

"I'm sorry," he mumbled, and Mackey fought irritation.

"Man, why you gotta do that. It's not like I got any real friends, you know?"

Tony looked up at him, sudden pain aching in his eyes. "One guy on campus who knows how I feel, and he wants to be friends? *Fuck* that!"

Tony stalked away, leaving Mackey surprised at how much that hurt as well.

Fuck that? Oh fuck *this*. Home was two miles away—Mackey could fucking walk.

He found Kell, dancing in a corner with a girl whose dress was doing a worse and worse job of covering her tits.

"Goin' home," he muttered, just loud enough for Kell to look up distractedly and nod.

Good. Mackey had done his job. He slid out the same way Grant had gone, because that was the only way he could get out without six teachers jumping his shit and making sure he wasn't getting drunk or stoned or fighting in the parking lot or something. The door Grant had taken led to the dark and silent loading and unloading parking lot. Anyone who didn't want quiet and dark might have been intimidated by how black the countryside was after it cleared the circle of the one lamp the school had up back there.

Mackey wasn't. He slept on the bottom bunk, tight in the corner, ignored and unbothered. He liked it that way. The darkness reminded him of that space, private and safe, and he stuck to the shadows, letting the shaking fade as he calmed down.

He made the mistake of passing Grant's mom's car, though, and he heard it, Sam's voice, plain as day.

She was moaning, muffling sex noises against something, probably Grant's chest.

"God, Grant, please… not just… can't you…? Please?"

"Don't got no condoms." Grant's voice was harsh. "C'mon, Sam… c'mon… you can do it…."

Her repressed scream of orgasm made Mackey's eyes burn. Oh God. Really? He had to listen to this?

But he couldn't get out of it, he realized. A hurricane fence ran along the side of the school, and the minivan was blocking the gate. Oh hell.

With a little whimper, he sank deeply into the shadows, tucking himself in a corner between the gymnasium and the locker rooms, staying out just enough to be able to hear when they left.

For a long moment, there was silence, punctuated only by what must have been their breathing.

"But Grant," Samantha complained, "you didn't even… don't you want…."

Mackey had known Grant most of his life. He knew the way his voice sounded when he lied.

"No worries, darlin'," Grant murmured. "I came just getting you off."

*Sure you did. You didn't come. I don't think you even got hard.*

"Oh no! Grant—your slacks!"

"You go back inside, babe. I've got a rag in here I can use to clean up, okay?"

"You sure? Man, one of these days you've got to remember condoms, babe. We're gonna have our V-cards forever!"

"No crime in that," Grant said gently. Mackey heard what must have been a kiss, and he saw her stumbling across the parking lot, barefoot, her pantyhose probably wadded in her purse.

Mackey waited until he heard the slam of the door back into the gym before he took a step out of the shadows—

—straight into Grant's arms.

"You hear that?" Grant whispered harshly, pushing Mackey back into the dark.

"Whole fucking world heard it," Mackey snarled, hurt and horny and desperate. "You couldn't take her someplace I wouldn't hear? You *like* what that does to me? You think that's fun?"

"*No!*" Grant shoved at him, his height and the breadth of his chest enough to force Mackey back against the wall of the cul-de-sac meant to hide the guys in the changing rooms from the world. "You think it's fun for me?" he whispered, nuzzling Mackey's neck roughly, his tongue making forays against his skin, his teeth nipping Mackey's ear and his neck. "I don't want her. She's a nice girl, but I don't get hard for her. All I can think about while she's touching me is how bad I want to be touching you."

Mackey closed his eyes against the words, because they hurt, *flayed*, tore the skin from his flesh. "Dammit, how can you even *say* that to me?" He shoved at Grant's chest, but Grant didn't go anywhere.

"It's the only truth I got," Grant muttered, and then his mouth crashed down on Mackey's and there was no more room for words.

It was a brutal kiss, teeth and lips, bony fingers digging into muscles, Grant's stubble scrubbing roughly at Mackey's cheeks.

Grant's hands plundered, popping two of Mackey's buttons from the bottom of the shirt as he spanned Mackey's ribcage with his big, callused hands. Mackey clenched Grant's dress shirt, trying to stay anchored, trying to stay in control.

"I've tasted your cock," Grant muttered into his ear. "I want it again."

Mackey moaned, stunned at the words, even more stunned when Grant sank to his knees and yanked Mackey's pants down his backside.

He'd done this before. Mackey closed his eyes against the memory and yanked at Grant's hair, hard, wanting *his* turn to taste, but Grant ignored him, taking Mackey down his throat and swallowing.

"You think I don't want to taste too?" Mackey demanded, and Grant moaned against him. Words. Mackey knew words. "You think I don't want your come… *fuckin' God!*"

Grant's hand and fingers were slick with spit and Mackey's precome, but Mackey was still shocked when Grant shoved two fingers up his ass.

It hurt, was rough, but underneath the shock and the pain was an edgy dark ache of pleasure, and Mackey came, muttering obscenities under his breath.

"Come *here!*" he snapped, hauling Grant up by the hair. This time Grant moved, and Mackey lunged at him, tasting his own come before Grant swallowed and finding it bitter but sucking it off his tongue anyway.

Grant moaned, and even though Mackey was so much smaller, he let Mackey turn him around, shove him against the wall for a change, and then sink down to a squat on the cold concrete of the changing room alcove.

Mackey wanted more. He wanted to linger on Grant's body, touch his skin, take his nipples into his mouth and pull. He'd seen Grant in his underwear, in his swim trunks, hell, naked often enough, Mackey wanted time to make that skin and flesh all his.

But he didn't have time. He had this dark pocket of damp concrete, and Grant's slacks bunched up in his fists as he pulled down. His own pants were still open, his dick chilling as he squatted half-naked, but it didn't matter.

Grant was there, and for the moment, Grant was helpless wanting him.

He mouthed Grant's erection through his briefs first, because Mackey wanted to taste the spot of wetness at the tip. Through the cotton and the fabric softener it was still salty, still bitter, and Mackey would write a song about that, bitter come—but later, much later, when he hadn't just yanked Grant's underwear down and taken Grant's cock into his waiting mouth.

"Nungh...." He wanted. Wanted with everything. Straining, he shoved his mouth farther over Grant's cock, taking it back in his throat like Grant had done to him. He had no time to compare their erections or to linger over the taste of skin—Grant felt huge in his mouth, big enough to force out his breath and his pain and his thoughts. Mackey swallowed, wanting more, wanting it all, and Grant dragged him back by the hair and then let go.

Mackey shoved his head forward again, not even close to the root. He grasped the rest of it in his fist and let his spit drip, making it slick and wet. Grant spurted, salty, and spurted again, bitter, and then muffled his groan in his palm and he came, hard, dumping down Mackey's throat and again and again and again.

Mackey couldn't swallow it all, and it spilled out on his new shirt with the busted buttons, down his chin, down his throat, and he kept trying to swallow until he choked on it, sobbing for breath, wanting all of it, wanting to be good, wanting to be good *enough* for Grant to keep him, for Grant to stay.

"Shh...." Grant whispered, tugging on his sweat-stiff hair. "Shh. C'mon, Mackey, let me hold you a minute."

Oh! Of all things. Mackey felt himself engulfed, held, cuddled, all the things he'd wanted that desperate moment in his bedroom, all the things he'd needed when he'd been coming down from the performance in the gym.

He let out a little whimper, and Grant palmed the back of his head, forcing Mackey closer to Grant's chest.

"Grant...." he whispered brokenly, and Grant hushed him again.

"'S okay, Mackey. It's okay. You did good. I needed.... God. I get so lost in you."

Grant said that, again and again and again. The thing Mackey wanted to say sounded stupid. *I'm found here. You find me. You know me.*

He couldn't have spoken anyway—he was absurdly near tears.

Eventually Grant pulled up their pants and did the belts. His hands were shaking, but they felt so firm, so warm, Mackey was comforted just the same. When he was done, Grant stood up and pushed Mackey's hair from his face with both warm, comforting, shaking hands.

"Hey," he whispered. "I love you."

Mackey closed his eyes, lit up inside and torn up too. Because there was no promise in those words, just the words themselves. "I love you too," he answered, because like Grant right now, the truth was all he had.

GRANT TOOK him home a few minutes later, texting Sam to tell her that he'd seen Mackey after he'd "cleaned up" and that he didn't want the boy wandering around by himself.

Mackey was so grateful for the ride, for the small show of aftercare, that he didn't resent the lie or the implication that he couldn't take care of himself.

He opened the door to the minivan as Grant stopped outside the apartment building, and Grant risked a touch to his hand.

Mackey turned to him, uncertain.

"Mackey?"

"I...." They'd lived in this apartment complex for years, knew their upstairs neighbor, their downstairs neighbor, the people on either side. People would be looking out at them, would know the minivan, would know the people inside. There would be no goodnight kiss, no gentleness. Mackey had gotten all he was going to get in the alcove next to the boys' locker room.

"You and me, we've got... we'll find a moment, okay? That may be all it is, but... man, you're in my blood. I need to work you out."

Later Mackey would look back and wonder where his pride was. But then, later, Mackey would have a place to pull pride from.

"Anything. I need...." Mackey closed his eyes, not even sure *what* he needed, just knowing that moments in dark corners weren't doing it. "Anything."

Grant nodded and stroked the skin on the back of his hand. "Night, Mackey."

"Night."

Mackey walked up the stairs and let himself into the darkened apartment with one goal in mind.

He shed his clothes into the hamper in his room before the door even closed behind him and before he'd turned on one light. He hit the bathroom naked and turned on the shower before he hit the light switch. He jumped under the water before it was anywhere near warm.

He could smell Grant's come.

It saturated the shirt crumpled in the hamper, coated the skin of his chest, and was probably flaking off his mouth and throat. Every breath he took reminded him of the feeling of Grant's cock in his mouth, of the white-blindness of his own orgasm, of the coldness of slipping out of the car without a backward glance.

He ached with needing someone to hold him. His skin hurt with it, his joints throbbed with need of it.

He needed his own skin back.

The water froze first and scalded second, and he scrubbed hard at his face and neck, shampooed his hair twice because of the sweat and the come that had smeared in it when he'd stood up.

He wondered if anyone noticed that Grant had Mackey's come on his face.

Would Grant wash it off? Would Samantha notice? Would he kiss her good-night with Mackey's semen still on his lips, tanging his tongue, streaking his chin?

God.

The tears started when the water ran hot and didn't stop, not long after it ran cold or even after Mackey left the shower. He dressed in threadbare cotton briefs and sweats with holes in the knees and a shirt that had been old before Kell got it and then passed it to Jefferson who passed it down to him.

His hooded sweatshirt, though—that was his. That had been a Christmas gift from his mom the year before, fleecy and warm, plain, blue, and clean.

He left the bathroom light on because he couldn't make himself care to turn it off and huddled in the corner of his bunk, invisible in the dark, willing the terrifying mix of joy and awfulness to die.

He heard noises, feet on the stairs, the door opening, and then his bedroom was invaded with light. He rolled over and squinted against the light from the bathroom, grateful when his mom's silhouette blocked the glare.

Cheever was asleep on her shoulder, and from the looks of it, he'd had some night.

"Mom, what's all that on his face?" Mackey asked, surprised out of his misery.

His mom gave a muffled little squeak. "Jesus, kid, you scared me. Shh... shh...." Gently she laid Cheever down on the top bunk, then pulled the rail up into place. Cheever didn't move, his four-year-old body limp and heavy. Kell once forgot to pull the rail up when they'd put Cheever to bed. Cheever had rolled out of bed and fallen to the floor and his breathing hadn't even stuttered.

"C'mon, Mackey," his mom said, smiling at him tiredly. "Let's go watch some TV."

Mackey was the only one of them who really liked television. His mom liked comedies and movies and such—things to escape in—and Mackey could find songs in those places, so he would watch with her, especially in the summer when there was no air conditioning.

His mom kept the desperately old TV in her room, on the little dresser at the foot of her bed, and she piled the pillows high and turned it on, grabbing her own T-shirt and shorts from the dresser as it warmed up. "Lemme shower," she mumbled. "I want to hear all about your night."

He curled up on his side and watched the end of *Friends*, and it wasn't until the end of the episode when the two roommates were jumping on top of each other in an effort to get to the door that he realized he was smiling.

He could smile. Good to know.

His mom was a champion at the five-minute shower. She came back in wearing an extra-large white T-shirt that came to her knees, still smoothing moisturizer on her face, while the episode was winding down. She sat on the bed, leaning into the pillows, curling on her side like he was so she could see the television and was comfy at the same time.

The episode ended and the commercials came on before she spoke into the comfortable quiet of the room.

"How'd the show go?"

Mackey smiled a little, remembering how excited she'd been for them. He wouldn't kill that for anything. "It was great," he told her truthfully. "Kids loved it. Kids who didn't even know our name loved it. Frickin' awesome."

She laughed softly. "Good to know," she said. Absently, like she'd forgotten he wasn't a baby anymore, like Cheever, she started to smooth his hair back from his face. He let her.

"And they let us do seven songs instead of just six," he continued softly. "That was nice. We did two songs *I* wrote, Mom. They *liked* them. It was kind of sweet, you know? Like... like I had something good to give."

He huddled deeper into the new warm fleece hoodie, and although his mom left the window open at night, it still wasn't cold enough to have it on.

"It's always nice to feel like you got something to give," she said. "Did you and the boys celebrate?"

"Mmhm," he murmured. The next episode was about to come on, and he hoped it would get there before he gave too much away. "We all went out and high-fived and stuff, but we were thirsty and they had snacks, so we went back in."

"Yeah? I thought you all would have gone out after?"

"Mm. Yeah, but the prom was stupid and I was tired. I didn't want to wait for the rest of that to go out."

"Did you walk home?" she asked, propping herself up on her arm in her concern, and he shook his head, keeping his eyes on the TV.

"Grant brought me. He was going back after he dropped me off."

"Nice of him," she conceded. He'd heard her before, trying to discourage Kell from putting too much hope in Grant as a friend. Grant's dad was a car salesman—owned the only two lots in Tyson. He kept some stock on the farm and owned horses to show, but mostly he just sold cars and got rich. Too much money for the Sanders kids—she'd said that on more than one occasion.

"He's a good guy," Mackey said loyally. Stupid. Why would his mom even care?

"I know, precious," she said, smoothing his bangs off his forehead. "He's a good guy. I don't mind that you're friends. It's just... you know. That money thing. It don't seem to make a difference now, but you don't know when rich people are gonna get mean."

He grunted. "Not mean. But he sure does think different'n me."

That was the truth right there. If Mackey had wanted Tony, he would have danced with Tony, no matter what anyone said. But Tony hadn't been worth the bullshit, so he hadn't. But Grant—if Grant had asked Mackey to get on his knees and blow him in the school auditorium, well, Mackey would have done that.

As far as Mackey could see, the only thing holding Grant back was his mom and dad. It didn't feel like a reason to Mackey. He wished he could see why it was one.

"How do you mean?" his mom asked now, and Mackey shrugged.

"I never woulda thought of that outfit," he improvised. "But now, I can't think of wearing anything else on stage."

She laughed a little and ruffled his recently smoothed hair. The show came back on, so the conversation died then, but she pressed him for little details at the other breaks.

What the girls were wearing, who Kell and Jeff danced with, if he'd gotten a chance to get kissed.

"Girls are a bother," he grunted, perfectly truthful yet again. "Would rather hang with the guys any day."

"Mm," she responded.

His gaze darted up to her face and he saw nothing. She was still a pretty woman, with petite, elfin bone structure and gray eyes like Mackey's, and those eyes were far away. Then she glanced at him and smiled reassuringly, and his attention wandered back to the television. He was pretty sure they were both falling asleep.

"Mackey," she murmured, turning out the light.

"Mom?"

"Next time you feed me bullshit about girls and kissing, you need to cover your hickeys better."

She was joking as she said it—he could hear it in her voice—but he lay, wide-eyed in the dark, watching *Law & Order* long after his mother had drifted off. He heard Kell and Jeff come in, and he closed his eyes then, figuring rightly that they'd shut off the television and not ask him any questions.

When their night noises stopped, he started to fall asleep, breathing deeply from the window open at his back.

He wondered when the air would stop smelling like Grant's come.

# With or Without You

SUMMER.

As the second-youngest brother, Mackey got to watch Cheever when his mom and the older boys worked. Grant's dad had given the older boys jobs on his car lot. Kell worked on the cars, Jeff and Stevie did general work and moved them around and stuff, and Grant helped his dad in the office. On the one hand, Mackey felt left out that they all got to work together and he was stuck taking Cheever to the park with the fountain so the two of them could keep cool, but on the other hand, Mackey still worked at the music store on the weekends. He'd turned fifteen in June, so he actually got paid in money too, and not just in equipment, although the equipment was always nice.

And in the evenings, well, they still had to watch Cheever if Mom had a night shift at the restaurant, but since Stevie's dad was on business trips all summer, they got to watch him at Stevie's house, while they were rehearsing. The wind would pick up over the Sierras, and what might have been a melty, dry sort of day would suddenly smell like juniper, Joshua, and pine. Some of the red dust would settle, and Mackey could live the songs they were playing, pure as a pitch, and life held such promise. Hope was in every breath.

He and Grant were how they'd always been, most times. Grant took Mackey's direction when they were playing and made good suggestions when they weren't. Grant started looking for more gigs. They played about every two weeks, gigs ranging from steak houses to business picnics to, at one point, Grant's dad's friend's wedding. The two original songs Mackey played at the prom were big hits, and he added more to their repertoire. By the end of July, they could play an hour set, and that made them professional and everything.

But school was coming in August, and Mackey could feel it pressing against his chest like a wet blanket on the tarmac in the sun.

Mackey had no idea how Grant got time off for lunch that summer, but the first time he knocked on the door, the second week of vacation, right after Cheever had gone down for a nap, he showed up with McDonald's and a smile. "Thought you'd like some lunch you didn't have to make—"

Mackey hadn't even let him put the lunch offering on the table before pressing him against the wall and hauling his mouth down in a crushing kiss. Until that moment right there, Mackey had doubted everything, every moment they'd had in private, every touch, the feeling of Grant's mouth on his own.

Mackey needed him so much. They spent most of that afternoon with their hands down each other's jeans, and Cheever almost caught them when he wandered out into the living room after Mackey came, biting Grant's shoulder to control the moan.

They learned quiet after.

Cheever still went down for naps every day from twelve to two. Mackey lived for that time. He read every book he could find, and he and Cheever became regulars at the library, because they could walk to it and it was free. But there was always the chance, about once a week, that Grant would stop by after Cheever went down. Those days they would make out in Mackey's mom's room, with a McDonald's lunch cooling on the end table and her little television on to cover the sounds they made.

Mackey learned to kiss long and lazy, and to slow down a little, 'cause for one thing, he had to listen for Cheever, and he didn't want to be sucking Grant's dick if his little brother woke up. In fact, most of the time it was just them kissing in the whir of the floor fan, their hands roaming on each other's bodies until unfamiliarity gave way to sure possession. Coming was not the object of the lesson.

Yearning was.

At the end of July, Mackey had about enough of yearning.

Apparently so had Grant.

On the bed, Grant was moving his lips over Mackey's neck, along his collarbone, and down the narrow divide of his ribs. Grant liked this part of Mackey's body—once, after Cheever had run around in circles all morning and fallen asleep in the middle of his sandwich at lunch, Grant had gotten really brave and spent fifteen minutes just sucking on Mackey's little nipples until Mackey left a hickey on the back of his hand in the effort not to scream. It took only Grant's hand down the front of his pants and he'd needed to go change his shorts.

On this day in late July, Mackey and Cheever had gone to the library and not the park, so Cheever wasn't as tired. There probably would be no shattering, no screaming into the hand, but Mackey thrust his narrow chest out, wanting… wanting… wanting….

Grant latched his mouth over the nipple again, and Mackey whined into his palm—

Right when they heard the telltale creak of the boys' bedroom door.

That quickly they were sitting propped up on pillows, side by side, watching whatever the hell on television. Grant reached forward casual-like and grabbed his soda, wiping his mouth as he did so. Mackey pulled up his jeans and toweled off his neck with his bundled T-shirt, hoping he didn't have any marks on his skin.

"Put it on," Grant whispered, and Mackey did, seeing the purple mark around his nipple.

The bedroom door opened, and two sleepy brown eyes peered at both of them incuriously.

"How you doin', little man?" Mackey asked Cheever.

The youngest Sanders brother had curly red hair and freckles. He looked like one of those cute kids from television, especially the really old shows his mom said *she* remembered from when she was a kid, but the kid was no angel. Mackey's mom said it was because he followed the big boys and tried to be just like them. Mackey was pretty sure it was because the big boys had done so much bad stuff when they were little that God sent them Cheever to punish them early before they could have any kids of their own.

But as awful as he could be—and they didn't have a wall in the apartment they hadn't had to paint over because he'd found something to write with, and the poison control people knew the Sanders kids by their phone number—he was also Mackey's brother.

He clambered up on the bed and leaned against Mackey, pliant with sleep, and Mackey draped a hand over his shoulder in spite of the sticky heat.

"So, Mackey," Grant said, his voice so overcasual Mackey had to check to make sure there wasn't anyone else there, "how would you like to take a trip with me?"

Mackey stared at him for a minute and ran a hand over his own hair so Grant would smooth his. Grant nodded and smoothed his hair back. It was thick and would probably curl if he let it grow, so a little rumpling went a long way.

"Where'd we go?" he asked now that Grant was squared away.

Grant looked at him and then darted a glance to Cheever, who was sucked right into *SpongeBob*.

"My dad needs me to switch cars with his brother in the Bay Area," he said. With a quiet gesture, one Cheever couldn't see, he smoothed Mackey's longish hair back from his face and tucked a strand of it behind his ear. "It's a five-hour drive. Dad figured I could stay in a hotel since Uncle Davis has a little teeny house on the peninsula, and I asked if I could bring a friend."

For a moment Mackey's heart stopped, stuttered, and leapt into the sky. Then it plummeted right back down to earth. "Wouldn't Kell want to go on that?" he asked, because it was only logical, right? Kell was Grant's friend.

"Yeah," Grant said, staring straight ahead. "But it's a real shame—he's got to work that weekend and Dad can't spare him. Jefferson neither. I, uh." He looked at Mackey sideways. "I asked Stevie if he could watch Cheever while Jeff was at work. I hope that's okay. You'd have to get off work—can you?"

"Yeah," Mackey said. They mostly gave him work out of pity these days anyway. Business would pick up again in September, when all the kids started school and the music program started up. Still, although he was willing himself to not get too excited because his mom still had to say okay, his recently dropped heart began to flutter. Two days and one night—that was what Grant was talking about. Two days and one night, and a chance to be together like it was okay. A chance to pretend.

Mackey's mom let him go with a shrug and a smile and twenty dollars for food. "You work so hard," she said over a pot of noodles she was cooking for dinner. "Between Cheever and your job and the band. I think it's real nice of Grant to give you a chance to get out of town."

"Grant brings me McDonald's," Cheever said. He was standing on a chair and helping Mom put the packets of seasoning into the pot.

Their mom looked down at him and grinned, ruffling his hair. "Well, then, that's okay," she said. "That must make him a nice guy."

Cheever grinned back, and Mackey swallowed like his heart wasn't in his throat. God. He remembered his rather bold thought that he would have danced with Tony if he'd liked Tony enough. Well, those were tough words from a kid who was afraid of what his mama would think.

But the morning Grant honked his horn outside the apartment, all that fear went away. Mackey poked his head into his mom's room and said "Bye, Mama!" and before she could even mumble "Be good!" he was out on the landing, a little woven Walmart bag with his spare clothes dangling from his hand.

He pounded down the stairs, waving bye to Stevie, who was on his way into the apartment, and had thrown himself into the front of the Lexus Grant was driving almost before the apartment door closed behind him.

Grant sat with the air conditioning cranked, and laughed into the crook of his arm. "Jesus, Mackey, it's like you're escaping from prison!"

Mackey glared at him. "Fratricide, Grant. I been reading all summer—it's a word!"

"Well, I'm sure my sister has heard of it," Grant placated, backing the car out of the tiny parking lot and pulling onto the main street of Tyson. Grant's sister Alicia was away at college, and Grant had been nothing but glad she was out of the house.

"Why didn't you go?" Mackey asked. He cracked the window just to feel the breeze and checked Grant's iPod. Okay, old music—Offspring, Green Day, Rise Against, and Rage Against the Machine. That was good. Traveling music.

"Why didn't I go where?" Grant asked, and both of them squinted into the sun for a minute. Grant fumbled for sunglasses, but Mackey didn't have any. He'd just have to squint.

"College, rich boy. You had grades. Why didn't you go?"

Grant shrugged and grunted.

Mackey stared at him. "That's not a fuckin' answer!"

"My dad wanted me to stay and run the business," he said. "Take care of the property. I probably could have gone if I'd put up a fight, but...."

Under the glasses, Mackey could see his gaze slide sideways and then slip back to the road. "I didn't want to put up a fight," he said after a minute.

Mackey suddenly couldn't breathe. "Me?" he gasped, sort of stunned. "You had *college* and you picked *me*?"

"And the *band*!" Grant protested, and just like that, the laughter fell away. "And the business. And my folks."

Mackey was still having trouble taking in oxygen. "But... but... if you stayed for *me*, what are you doing dating *Sam*!"

In spite of the music, the car was suddenly so quiet, Mackey could hear Grant swallow. They were coming to the last intersection before the highway, and Mackey realized that this was the last place he could get out. If what he and Grant were going to do—if this relationship—was too scary, he could turn around and walk back home, and they'd both pretend those frantic moments on his mom's bed, needing each other like blood, with their hands all over each other, had never happened.

When Grant spoke, his voice was... young. He'd turned eighteen in July, and for the first time, it occurred to Mackey that being eighteen and out of high school was not all grown. "I'm... my *parents*, Mackey? My *dad*?"

Mackey turned to him and realized that just the thought turned his face pale and that he was sweating in spite of the chill in the car.

"Bad?" he asked. Grant seemed to be escaping his big dragon house all the time— he'd do anything to spend time with Kell's family, and Mackey got the general impression that Grant's parents were worse than prison. Which made Mackey wonder— what would his mom do? But at the same time, he had a safety in his heart. His mom tried so hard. Would she really kick him out or not love him because of something he'd done wrong? Most of him was pretty sure she wouldn't, but that little lever in him that weighed risk and reward was still choosing silence for now.

Grant's jaw clenched so tight, Mackey could see a vein in his temple throbbing. "I don't know how you do it," he said roughly. "The stage thing. You get up on stage and… and the music owns you, and you don't worry about anything. Any day now, you're going to leap into the crowd and they'll carry you." He swallowed, his Adam's apple bobbing in his slender throat. "I've always got a part of me thinking, 'I'll fall.' 'Cause I know my folks wouldn't pick me up if I did. But you—you've never had a safety net, and you think you can fly."

Mackey opened his mouth and closed it, and his brain tried to repaint and recut the jigsaw puzzle of what life was like. Failed. He was left with a pile of rubble, impressions of color, snapshots of sound, minor chords and royal blues, bright major chords and golds.

"The music owns me," he repeated, feeling dumb. "I *am* the music. I close my eyes and… I *am* that chord, or that moment, or that dance. I *am*…." *The crowd, the guitar, the mood, the lyrics, the heartbeats, the drumbeats, the guitar chords, the sweat, the muscle, the movement, the song.* "You can't fall when you're there," he said and swallowed hard.

"*You* can't fall," Grant told him gently. "I can."

Breathing. When did it get to be such a hard thing to do? "Are you saying you don't want me?"

Grant made a sound like a laugh that wasn't really a laugh at all. "God, Mackey— you made me hard just coming down the stairs. Of course I want you. I'm saying… I'm saying my plans for us are… are tonight. I don't know when there will be more. I don't know when I'll get the guts to break up with my girlfriend or tell my parents I'm…."

The silence in the car transcended the stereo, transcended car noise, transcended breathing.

"Gay," Mackey said. One of them had to. "We're fags, Grant. And we're in love."

Grant nodded. "That," he said. "I don't know if—when… I can't even say it out loud to you."

Mackey leaned his head against the window and stared sightlessly at the bleached landscape of Northern California. "Gay," he whispered. "Faggots. Fudge-packers. Cocksuckers. Fairies. Boy pussies. Fruits. Queers. Nancies. Ho-mo-sex-u-als. That's me. Mackey the faggot."

"Shut up," Grant said, his voice thick. "I'm the guy who wants you."

Mackey took a deep breath, and then another, and shoved the words back down in his throat. "Can you say it to me?" he begged.

"Gay," Grant said, so quiet Mackey almost missed it. "I'm gay. And I want you."

Okay, then. Grant, Kell's friend, who was so handsome and so mature and so self-possessed—if *he* said it, it must not be that bad.

"'Kay," Mackey said, like they'd decided something important.

They drove quietly for the next hour until finally the music penetrated the thick blanket of silence and Mackey started to sing along with "Stairway to Heaven." Grant sang counterpoint.

That was the magic line, right there. The music happened, and that conversation got to disappear. They were young and getting the hell out of their hometown, if only for a day—there wasn't anything wrong with that, was there?

They stopped for lunch in Vacaville at the BJ's by the outlet stores, and Grant paid for their burgers, which were so big they crated up half of Mackey's for later.

As they got back on the freeway, Mackey looked over his shoulders at all of the name-brand stores.

"What're you looking at?" Grant asked, his voice relaxed and warm. It was like that moment when he was scared of falling, scared like a little kid, hadn't happened.

"I just… you know. That outfit you picked for me to perform in."

"Getting threadbare?" Grant asked, and Mackey grunted.

"I have to wash it every time we perform," he said frankly. "God, I sweat like a guilty man up there."

Grant hmmed. "I've got money saved," he said quietly. "Can I buy you another outfit? For stage?"

Mackey sighed. "I… I mean, I've got some money. I could buy it." But they both knew the money the boys made went mostly to food and groceries and regular clothes and shoes. New clothes from Walmart and not used ones from Goodwill were a luxury to the Sanders boys.

"Let me," Grant said. "I don't have any promises for you, Mackey. Can I just… *do* something for you?"

Mackey laughed, low and dirty. "I thought that was the plan," he said, and Grant laughed too. But for a moment, Mackey had this fantasy, a stupid one, of the two of them walking into a store and not worrying about money, and shopping for clothes to wear out on a good night, like prom.

Grant had good taste and Mackey had a tiny body, and it would be fun to buy Grant something butch and leather and badass and slick, to go with his chest and his height. They could dress to match and laugh at that shit and dress totally opposite and see how they looked together and….

Mackey shook his head. Like all the Sanders boys, he was practical to the bone. Clothes were for wearing. If they needed something good to perform in, that was fine, but otherwise? No. Not for Mackey James Sanders.

He swallowed hard, already playing with words like *suit* and *slick* and *badass* and *hick*, his brain trotting in a rhythm of swagger and strut. *Well, why not?* the practical side of him asked, even as the other half of his brain was engaged with the song. *ZZ Top did it and no one accused* them *of being fags.*

By the time Grant pulled up to his uncle's house, Mackey had opened the ever-present notebook and written the song down, notating it with chords and basic rhythms and everything. (One of the best things he'd gotten from working at the music store was his own book on music notation. He'd known how to read it, basically, but learning the complicated stuff—time, sixteenth notes, drum rhythms—that made telling the band what to do *so* much easier.)

When he met Grant's aunt and uncle—two nice people who seemed straight out of the television with their almost coordinating slacks sets, blond-streaked hair, and long-faced features—he was able to get his head in the people space and shake hands and smile and talk and not be freakish and distracted. When Grant's uncle Davis asked them if they didn't want to sleep on the couch and the floor, he even managed not to send Grant a panicked look, because after that bitter, painful conversation on the way down, the last thing he wanted was a reason to back out.

"That's nice of you, Uncle Davy," Grant said politely, "but Mackey here has never been to the pier—I thought I'd take him and get some clam chowder and see some seals and stuff."

His aunt Ashleigh eyed Mackey's faded cargo shorts and thin T-shirt with bare grace. "Are you sure the Embarcadero is your little friend's scene?" she asked delicately. "It's sort of a… a merchandise trap, you know?"

Grant blinked at her. "It's my treat," he said evenly. "Mackey here writes all the songs for our band—this is my way of giving back."

Davis laughed, sort of over-hearty. "Yeah, your dad told me about your band. He says if those boys put half their energy into school as they put into the band, they could have all gone away to college!"

Grant swallowed and pulled out a smile that had stiff plastic edges. "Well, I *did* put that much energy into school, and Dad *still* wanted me to stay home, so I get to play in the band whether he likes it or not," he said, and Mackey wanted to grab his hand. Yeah. Money didn't buy an education, and it didn't buy easy.

Davis held out both hands like an adult to a tantruming child. "Okay! Okay, don't get testy, Grant. We're just saying, you know—"

"You're saying you expect me to run back into the gutter where I came from," Mackey said, but he batted his eyes at Davis and winked. "Don't worry, Mr. Adams, this rat knows how to find the ship back home."

The condescending smiles fell from Davis and Ashleigh like flaking makeup.

"We weren't implying…," Ashleigh said, her fair skin flushing as they stood out in the driveway in the eighty-degree day.

Mackey lowered his chin and looked out at her from under his brows and bangs. "Of course you did, Mrs. Adams, but don't worry. Grant doesn't hang out with stupid people—he knows exactly what you were saying. Are you ready to go, Grant? IHOP was a long ways away."

Grant was glaring and smirking at him at the same time. Mackey got that a lot—and often from Grant—so he figured they were okay. "Yeah, Mackey. Uncle Davis, you got the keys?"

"Grant," Davis said, his eyes darting to Mackey, who was still giving him the faintly predatory, faintly flirtatious look that he usually reserved for the stage. "You don't have to… you boys don't have to—"

"McKay is my best friend's brother," Grant said, and Mackey could hear a sort of hurt in his voice: these people had let him down. "He's my friend. You couldn't have been nice to him for a conversation in the driveway? I'll take the keys now."

Davis handed them over with a miserable look. "We'll look forward to seeing you around the holidays," he said weakly, and Grant shrugged.

"Yeah, why not." Then they got into the old car—which was almost as nice as the new car, even if it was a really lame champagne Mercedes instead of a black Lexus—and drove away.

They got back on El Camino Real, which, as far as Mackey could tell, connected the peninsula with San Francisco and hence to the rest of the world, before Grant spoke.

"God, that was uncomfortable. I'm sorry my people are such freaks."

Mackey shrugged. "I'm sorry I'm an asshole," he said, but he was chuckling as he said it, and Grant laughed.

"You're not sorry at all, you little shit!"

Mackey leaned back in the luxurious seat. "Not even a little. Can we go see the ocean now?" He'd never been to the ocean. He lived up in the mountains, so he knew trees and snow and vast sweeps of sky, but he'd had glimpses of the bay as they'd hit Berkeley and then 101, and he liked it very much.

"Yeah. You know, they have ferry rides. We've got a hotel—Dad let me book a nice one on the Embarcadero—so how about we go check in, ditch the car in paid parking, and then get something to eat. And then—"

"Ferry ride?" Mackey asked, sitting up excitedly.

He saw Grant slide his eyes quickly sideways, because of the unfamiliar traffic.

"Yeah," he said, his voice gruff with wonder. "Ferry ride."

The chow was decent—Mackey ate a hamburger that was grilled right, with bleu cheese and mushrooms and a sort of gravy he could have lived on. They ate in an outdoor area that gave him a view of the skyscrapers, and he held his face to the sun and the shade of the scudding clouds in the dazzling sky and tried to smell the ocean. It was just over the line of shops at his back, but he could feel it in the breeze. It wasn't until they'd walked the half mile down to Pier 39 that Mackey got a real feel for it, the vast and the cold ocean, looking out into the San Francisco Bay.

Grant dragged him by the hand to the touristy places first, ignoring anyone who might look, and bought him a thick fleece sweatshirt that said *I left my <3 in San Francisco*. Mackey protested, but Grant blew him off, saying it was his fault because he hadn't remembered a sweatshirt like Grant told him to. Then, still hand in hand, they headed to the ferry with the blue-and-gold insignia.

Within half an hour, they stood on the prow of a ferry, Mackey leaning against the rail and catching the spray in his face as they headed to the big golden bridge that all the songs were written about.

Mackey was cold in spite of the sweatshirt, and Grant leaned against his back, bracing himself on the rail with a hand on either side of Mackey.

Years later, when their lives had turned out very differently, Mackey would remember that moment, the freedom at his face and the safety at his back, and it would be the diamond in his mind, the one clear moment that taught him what love was all about. Even if the diamond was flawed, it was the first diamond he'd ever grasped so tight it left edges imprinted on his palm, and he would clutch it to his chest until his heart bled, sure nobody but Grant Adams, his brother's best friend and the kid he'd grown up with, could give him that feeling.

When they got back, Grant took him to a nice restaurant, one where they sat down and put napkins on their laps. Nobody looked at Mackey twice, with his tourist sweatshirt and all, and right there, while they were talking about the ferry ride and all the people who had come into the bay hoping for a new life, Grant put his hand on top of Mackey's in public. Mackey's whole body grew warm, tingled, caught fire like the pit in the center of the restaurant.

The whole day—the casual touches, the subtle possession, that giddy hour with Grant leaning against his back on the ferry while the deck pitched under their feet—that caught up with him right there, and his body remembered that it was made of hormones, and his cock reminded him that it had been half-hard all day.

Grant paid the bill and left a tip Mackey's mother probably dreamed about, and then grabbed Mackey's hand again, lacing their fingers together as they hustled toward the hotel.

Mackey's brain must have shorted out then, too glutted on the new place, on the new experience, because he came to when Grant closed the hotel room door behind them.

Slowly, like he was dreaming, Mackey turned toward the boy who had brought him here.

He was unprepared for Grant's charge, and his strong arms taking him at the waist and bearing him back to the bed, mouth fused hotly to Mackey's like he was pulling in his soul.

Mackey devoured back, shoving at Grant's pants clumsily, and Grant left him sprawled on the bed while he dropped his jeans and kicked off his shoes. Mackey did the same thing, unashamed and unafraid, wild in his need.

Their bodies, naked, skin on skin, were enough to make Mackey shudder. He started to beg, mouthing Grant's neck, his collarbone, his shoulders—

"No hickeys!" Grant said roughly, and Mackey pulled back for a minute, remembering his mom's observation on prom night.

He moved gentler then, but he needed just as badly, and for a moment they thrashed on the bed, trying to crawl inside each other's skin.

Grant took charge, rolling over, pinning Mackey. "Calm down," he growled. "Let me kiss you." He moved his lips from the corner of Mackey's mouth, down his jaw, to his neck. He didn't suck too hard or rasp his chin over Mackey's soft skin—every move was firm but not rough, gentle but not ticklish, and by the time he'd kissed down to Mackey's nipples, Mackey was crazy, writhing, sobbing, because his whole body was one bright cry for release.

Grant closed his hand over his cock, and Mackey gasped, "No! Not yet!" He wanted to cry. God, this whole day and it would be over?

Grant breathed hard into the hollow of Mackey's neck. "All night," he managed. "It's not even seven. We've got all night."

"But what if we don't...." Mackey's groin was *on fire*, he needed so bad.

Grant settled him with a light touch, not teasing but not fulfilling either. "We have to," he said, voice cracking. "I don't want to lose my virginity with Sam. I want to lose it with you."

And Mackey found himself comforting his lover, stroking his shoulders, whispering in his ear, because Grant was coming apart like Mackey was. They were young and in a bed and their hands rested on each other's cocks, but the pain slowed it down, made the sex precious. When Mackey arched his back and watched in wonder as his come shot across his stomach, Grant was in his arms doing the same thing, and the wonder of it, of giving a man the same thing he was getting, that was etched in Mackey's brain too. He'd learned two lessons about love that day, and the day wasn't even over. It had to be a good day, didn't it?

Didn't it?

Their breathing slowed, and Grant made him get up so they could huddle under the covers in the unfamiliar Bay Area chill. Mackey backed up against him and accepted the kisses on his shoulders and tried not to yell at him and ruin the night.

"Why?" he asked when his body had calmed down a little. "Why do you have to sleep with her? Why can't you just break up with her?"

Grant sighed eloquently. "She's going to tell people I'm a fag if we don't do it. She already threatened to tell my mom."

Mackey closed his eyes tight. "What would your dad do?"

"He used to go to bars," Grant said, so quiet Mackey could barely hear him. "I heard him brag to his friends about being young and going out and beating faggots up. I... I'm not like you, Mackey. You.... Music is... it's the center of you, and it's all okay there. I... I need my folks to love me."

And there it was again. That cracking voice, the reminder. Grant wasn't that much older, and Grant wasn't that much stronger, and Mackey still loved him even though he was weak.

Mackey rolled over and kissed him, and Grant opened his mouth and took. *The rest of the night*, Grant said, and Mackey had a confusing idea that they'd fall asleep at midnight with parts of lovemaking unexplored.

The fact was that from the moment of that kiss, time stopped in the little hotel room. Every kiss was forever, every touch was a brand, an invisible tattoo, marking Mackey as property of Grant Adams until the end of time.

Somewhere in the middle of that magic bubble of timelessness, Grant put both his hands on the backs of Mackey's thighs and shoved them up and performed gross, obscene, *amazing* acts on Mackey's body with his tongue and mouth. Mackey was beyond protest, beyond morality. It should have been bad. It should have been nasty. But Grant's mouth felt *awesome*, and the things he did—his mouth around Mackey's delicate balls, his tongue down the crease of his ass, dancing in his hole—were things Grant *needed* to do to him. When Grant pulled a little plastic bottle out of his pocket and used it on Mackey's asshole, all he could do was shudder and hiss.

"Don't worry about rubbers," Grant whispered, penetrating Mackey with one finger and rubbing around his rim. "I'm a virgin, you're a virgin, we're good."

"Can't get pregna—ahhhh!" Mackey's lame joke was cut short when Grant added another finger and Mackey started shaking, terrified of the tidal surge threatening to roar through his body. "Grant!" He was afraid. This was frightening.

"Sh, Mackey, I'm coming."

At first Mackey thought he meant climax and was almost reassured. If Grant was coming, then Grant could stop touching him, and he could stop shaking, stop needing. But he'd pulled out both his fingers and that terrifying pleasure was gone and the shaking didn't get any better—maybe he should keep touching, and keep touching, and....

And then Grant was there, his cock pushing against Mackey's butthole. Mackey closed his eyes and cried out. "Grant!"

"Sh, Mackey, relax," Grant crooned. "It'll feel good. You'll stretch. Just push against me and you'll... ah!"

Mackey still hurt, but Grant was right, the pushing helped. Grant kept thrusting inside and Mackey opened, slowly, painfully—so painfully he was sweating, tears slipping through the corners of his eyes. Grant kissed them, kissed him, and Mackey kept crying.

Grant pushed himself up and wiped a palm down Mackey's temple. "You okay?" he asked, his voice tortured. "Mackey, you okay? Do I need to stop?"

"Keep going," Mackey grunted, even though it didn't feel good. Grant wanted it. Mackey would give him anything he wanted.

Grant kept moving then, slowly, making low groans of pleasure, and his noises made Mackey happy. Grant felt good. Mackey was doing it right.

The ache and burn in his ass began to feel better, to work inside him, and Mackey reached down to his semihard cock and started stroking. Oh... oh yes.

That pressure/pleasure surged back. Mackey was even more scared of it now. He fought against it even as Grant groaned and sped up. Oh God, it hurt, but it didn't, and Mackey was afraid, but it felt good, so good, ouch, but good, it hurt, *so good*—

*"Grant!"*

He screamed it, and Grant's voice caught on his next moan, and his hips shifted. That tidal wave crashed down on Mackey, and he knew what climax felt like, but nothing this big. He screamed again, wordless and afraid. Grant devoured him, mouth hot on his, rabbiting his hips back and forth and—

Both of them groaned, and Grant spasmed.

Mackey felt it: hot come, jerking into his body, slick and invasive. That thought sent him smashing into orgasm, screaming into Grant's mouth until his throat was raw.

They calmed down. Grant got up, leaving Mackey cold and sprawled on the bed with his legs spread, but when Grant came back, he had a warm washcloth that he used to clean Mackey up with, and then himself. He got back into bed and touched Mackey's chest, kissed his shoulder, until Mackey turned toward him and started kissing back.

"You okay?" Grant asked, his voice shaky.

"Yeah."

"Are *we* okay?"

"Yeah." They had to be, right? If they weren't okay, then what? No more moments? No more of Grant's touches? No more of them together?

Unbearable.

"We're great," Mackey said, and he made himself believe it. Self-delusion is easy at fifteen.

It would be easy at sixteen and seventeen and eighteen and nineteen too.

But Mackey wasn't thinking about nineteen that night. All he let himself think about was Grant's body, and pleasing it. By the time they left the hotel room late the next morning, he and Grant had done everything they could think of. He'd held Grant's thighs up and done filthy, obscene things with his tongue—and loved them. Loved the taste of Grant's sweat and come and the feel of his skin. Loved the sounds he brought about, loved every act they performed.

He tried to top and was not wonderful at it. He was so greedy, so trembly, Grant had needed to take over, to direct him, to take his own pleasure from Mackey when Mackey couldn't give him what he needed.

Afterward, though, he let Mackey clean him up, wash them both, and they curled up naked under the covers. Grant turned off the light and they were alone in the dark of the hotel room, counting each other's breaths in the sudden silence.

"I wish this was us all the time," Mackey confessed, knowing it was stupid. Even if he was a girl, girls didn't get married at fifteen.

"Me too," Grant whispered back. "We'll just have to... have to take what we can, right? Be ready, all the time, to do this."

Mackey closed his eyes and breathed their sex and their body heat inside. "This is what they mean," he realized. "When they say stolen kisses."

They fell asleep in the middle of a stolen kiss.

THEY WOKE up late, with barely enough time to shower before they had to be on the road. Grant drove as fast as he could without attracting attention so he could make up time, and they ate breakfast and lunch practically on the run.

They talked during the trip home like they hadn't stolen that night together, like Mackey was Kell's little brother and Grant was Kell's best friend. But right before they hit their county, Grant pulled into a rest stop, saying he had to take a leak, and Mackey followed him, thinking he'd do the same.

Nobody was there, but Grant pulled him into a stall anyway, talking softly after the door closed. "I meant what we did last night," he said, looking into Mackey's eyes. "However this ends, whatever lies we have to tell, you just gotta know that, okay?"

"Okay," Mackey said, helpless. "I know. I know."

Grant kissed him hard and fast, and when Mackey would have gotten lost in it, Grant opened the door behind him and shoved him out.

Well, yeah.

Both of them really did have to take a leak, didn't they?

And that was how they did it. For five years, that was how they did it. Grant slept with Samantha at the end of August. A week later he showed up at the school, snuck Mackey out, and took him in the backseat, parked behind a tree by the river. Mackey went back to school reeking of come and hardly able to walk, and nobody said a damned thing.

Grant bought a van for the band's equipment, what Jeff called a serial-killer van, with no windows. Stevie hired Tony to stencil the band's logo on the side, and it looked really official, but the best part? Grant kept a stack of blankets in the back, thick ones meant to cushion the equipment so it didn't get damaged when they drove around to gigs. Mackey didn't drive, and Kell owned the other car, so it just made sense for Mackey and Grant to take the van when they went out of town. "Help move shit" became a euphemism for Mackey getting laid. The van ran like a dream, but Grant told everyone it overheated if it went too fast. Mackey got more action in the back of that van than porn stars got on set. And Mackey was greedier for it too. They had no time for shyness, for courting. The minute they had time to themselves, they were slutty, rapacious cocksucking fuckers, and both of them got pro quality at the two-minute blowjob.

It wouldn't occur to Mackey until later that speed was not necessarily what you wanted from a lover. It didn't even rank in the top three.

Outbreak Monkey continued to grow. Grant used his dad's business contacts and they played three or four places regularly, earning a steady enough paycheck for Mackey to not have to work anywhere else but the music store. Kell and Jeff moved into the apartment next to their mother's with Stevie, but Mackey could make up the difference for their mom, so it was okay that they moved out. (Mackey didn't want to tell anyone, but he liked the bunk bed anyway. If he wasn't going to sleep with Grant, the little cove kept him safe.)

Mackey made it through high school in a wobbly sort of way. His math and science scores were mostly luck, but his English and history grades were outstanding. As one teacher said, anything he could make into a song had his complete attention. For the most part, Mackey used the popularity the band gave him to stay above it all. The band played school functions and rich kids' birthdays, and the kids who wanted to hang all over him helped with the equipment.

Tony was one of those.

He wasn't annoying, though—was just, like he'd told Mackey before, entranced by the music. He never tried anything, didn't even flirt, and Mackey treated him like a friend. It was good to have friends. He played in the band with his brothers and his lover—talking to Tony about the Features or Cage the Elephant was like breathing sweet air.

Playing on the stage next to Grant with come still running down his asscrack was like breathing pot smoke until his feet didn't even touch the stage. The smell of Grant's skin got him buzzed, and the smell of his come or the musk under his balls got him high as a kite.

It gave him courage to have that stamp on his skin.

He learned to flirt outrageously with the crowd when he was still in high school. To smile that fuck-off-and-love-me smile until they screamed his name. He learned how to look right over their heads and lick his lips like he'd go down on every guy and girl in the place. When he was on stage and his heart was playing notes instead of blood, he felt like

"Hits me where I live," Grant replied, something dark and meaningful in his voice.

Mackey glanced at him quickly, because the end of the song was about leaving the river when the sun hit the shadows, and maybe never going back. Grant couldn't mean that, could he? He couldn't be thinking about making that song come true.

"Yeah," Kell said, completely oblivious to the undercurrents. "That's the one. We'll have that one as the... what's that word you use, Mackey? The one before the finale?"

"Penultimate," Mackey supplied, taking a better look at Kell because it was rare that Kell ever questioned words.

Kell had put on some weight in the last five years. He'd taken to working out, so his neck had nearly disappeared, and his guns were probably the width of Mackey's head. He still kept his brown hair buzz cut, and his Neanderthal brow had gotten, if anything, more prominent. But he'd been eating dirt for six years working for Grant's dad, and no one knew it more than Grant. Once, after what was supposed to be a frenzied moment having sex in the back of the van had turned into ten minutes of just kissing, long and slow and deep, Grant said something that stuck. He told Mackey that watching his old man peck the spirit out of his best friend was one of the things that drove him to hunt down gigs.

"My own future's cut-and-dried," he'd said, rubbing cheeks with Mackey in the sweaty closeness of the equipment and the metal siding. "That's bad enough. Watching him suck the life outta your brother.... Mackey, just don't ever stop writing songs for him, okay?"

*I don't write songs for him. I write them for you.*

"Sh, Grant. Look at the river shadows. Ain't it weird? In this light, this time of year, they look sort of purple."

"Yeah, Mackey. It's real pretty. Peaceful. Makes me want to just lie here all day."

"With me, right?"

"Not with anyone else."

So Mackey could hear the yearning in Kell, that need not to ever have to work in the garage for old man Adams again and hear him talk about Kell's thick red neck and ham hands. Kell could play old Eddie Van Halen riffs from back when Eddie was hot, and he didn't miss a note. If Kell was clumsy, it was because hatred made him that way, and Kell was angry enough as it was.

Jefferson didn't get angry—not the way Kell did. But every day, Mackey watched him sit quietly and drink beer until Stevie got home too. Suddenly he'd stop drinking beer and start talking, and the sound of his mumbling voice was like he'd forgotten how to use real words.

If Mackey really was the thing that would sell the band, he'd have to sell it tonight.

He looked at Grant and grinned. "Hey, what do you want to do if we get a big contract? Where do *you* want to go?"

Grant's brow puckered then, and his lower lip wobbled. Mackey almost panicked, because he'd never seen Grant cry in public. He didn't think he could stand there watching Kell be stupid and awkward with Grant when Mackey knew how he liked his back rubbed and how he needed to turn his head so Mackey couldn't see his face when he came apart. *If the old man calls me a fucking nancy boy behind the office door one more time, I swear, Mackey, you and me, we'll fucking run away....*

But Mackey couldn't run away. Grant knew that. His mom needed the help with the rent and with Cheever, who was less of a terror now that he'd been identified as frickin' brilliant. Tyson didn't have a good program for frickin' brilliant kids, so part of Mackey's gig money went to pay for Cheever's room and board at the school for the gifted in Hepzibah. And, of course, to bring Cheever reluctantly home to the shitty little apartment on the weekends so that their mom's heart didn't get broken without her youngest.

No. Mackey had only one way to get out, and that was up, and Grant… well, Grant probably could have gotten out five years ago, but he'd stayed for Mackey.

And told his family he stayed for Sam.

Sam was talking marriage.

Mackey knew. The first time she'd brought it up, Grant had nailed Mackey in the back room of the music store as Mackey was closing down. It was risky—risky and unnecessary. They didn't take those kinds of chances. But when they were done, Grant had collapsed against Mackey's back, soundless tears soaking the long hair by Mackey's ear, clenching Mackey to him like a child clutching a blanket.

He didn't tell Mackey what it was about then. He helped him clean up and kissed him tenderly and then took him out for what looked like a perfectly platonic steak dinner at the local tavern. Two days later, Kell made an offhand remark as they were warming up in Stevie's parents' garage.

"Sam says she gave you an ultimatum, partner. What's the scoop?"

Grant answered. "Yeah, she says next year at the latest, or she's breaking up with me."

Kell shrugged. "She's a nice girl. You could do worse."

Grant rolled his eyes—and then glanced at Mackey from under his brows. "No, I couldn't," he said darkly.

Mackey had to make the first fifteen minutes instrumental practice. His throat was too tight to sing.

But an agent? Mackey couldn't think of the money or the places they'd go or even the chance to go to school and study literature or languages or even music history or theory, all of which he could read about forever.

But Mackey could think about a chance to get out of Tyson, California, and to take Grant with him. Nobody really knew what touring was like. They'd heard rumors, of course. Everyone heard the term "party like a rock star." Maybe nobody would think anything of the two of them sleeping in the same hotel room, being together. Maybe they'd write it off like they did all those other guys doing drugs and wrecking hotel rooms. Maybe being a rock star meant you got a free pass, right? Nobody would give a shit what they thought Mackey and Grant were doing as long as the music was fucking awesome, right?

So Grant worked to get them gigs and to make sure they got paid, and Mackey worked for the vague hope that someday, somehow, he and Grant could be together, free and clear, and nobody would give a shit.

So an agent or a manager in the audience? Someone who could hook them up with a record contract and a tour? That was big fucking news.

Mackey needed Grant to smile about it, and Grant couldn't meet his eyes.

So Mackey forgot about it. He got up on stage in his jeans and a button-up silk shirt. The shirt was made with cutaway shapes—stars, moons, lightning bolts—because Grant still bought his concert clothes. The other guys didn't wear suits anymore, just jeans and T-shirts without holes. Stevie and Jefferson had taken to buying contrasting shirts, one in black and the other in white or one in red and the other in blue, both with the same logo. It was cool, because it was their thing, but it was also disturbing because, well, same brain.

Grant wore something designer and spiffy, Kell wore whatever was clean, and Mackey wore outrageous. It helped define them, and Mackey was prouder than ever that he led his brothers on the stage.

The set went *well*. Maybe it was the electricity from the crowd, or maybe it was that the guys all knew something was on the line, but Mackey could feel it. Every note was perfect, even the ones that came out as primal screams into the microphone, because some of Mackey's songs weren't gentle.

He closed his eyes and became the music, and between songs he flirted and fucked with the crowd. They played two sets, with a half-hour intermission between them. Wasn't it funny how a half hour could change their lives?

Backstage was actually *outside* at this club, and the outside had a little walled patio with a bartender who served them drinks on the house, even though Mackey was still technically underage. Mackey didn't drink until the set was over anyway—too much was riding on him not sounding like an asshole.

No one was allowed backstage between sets, so the guys got their comp drinks and kicked back in the barely faded August heat. Kell closed his eyes and honest to God *napped*, because old man Adams had run his ass off all week, making him work extra hours and shit. Jefferson was pretty close to the same state, because although Mackey had only seen him as a head by the office when he'd run by to pick the guys up, apparently old man Adams really was the asshole Grant had barely complained about during high school.

Mackey was bouncing on his toes, eyes closed, face toward the sky, running through the river song in his head, as well as "Scream" and their cover versions of "In One Ear" and "Stairway to Heaven," because they liked to pay tribute to their roots.

The tap on his shoulder sent him corkscrewing into the stratosphere, arms flailing, legs kersplanging, and when he connected solidly with a warm body, his eyes shot open and he tripped over his own feet and fell on his ass.

The guy in the suit, rubbing his jaw, was considerably older than Mackey had been prepared for.

"I am *so* fucking sorry!" Oh God. This *had* to be the agent, and Mackey had just clocked him!

"No worries," the guy said, rubbing the graying stubble on his once-square chin. "I get that a lot. I'm Gerald Padgett—uhm, is Grant Adams anywhere around? He was the one I made contact with?"

"Mr. Padgett!" Grant came from out of nowhere, helping Mackey up with one hand and shaking Mr. Padgett's hand with the other. "Oh my God—Mackey didn't mean it, sir. He just gets keyed up for a show, right?"

Gerald Padgett smiled wryly. "Yeah, well, I get that. I'm surprised you boys are doing another set, actually—that first one was a lulu!"

Mackey grinned, because he had no choice but to be Mackey. "Yeah, well, we performed a lulu so we could woo-woo, right?"

"Oh Jesus," Kell groaned. "Mackey, do you have to?"

But Mr. Padgett just waved his hand. "No, no, that's okay. It's good to know you like to play a little. Because I'm here to make sure you boys get to play a *lot*."

Kell let out a little whoop, but suddenly Mackey found he had a business brain after all. "Yeah, you say that, but who else you done this for? We get people telling us we should be famous all the time, but all they got for us is a chance to play their cousin's bar mitzvah." Until that had happened four or five times, Grant had been the only one to know what a bar mitzvah even *was*.

Gerald Padgett grinned and reached into his vest pocket and pulled out a card from his old plaid suit. "That there is a very good question. You recognize that label, boys?"

"Tailpipe Productions," Mackey breathed, looking at Grant excitedly.

"Who the hell is that?" Kell asked, glaring at Mr. Padgett fiercely. Apparently Mackey's question had hit Kell sort of deep.

"That's the company that produces Pineapple Express and Grendel," Mackey said, his eyes wide. "Kell, this guy's the real deal."

Mr. Padgett smiled gently. "I am indeed. Now, I understand you boys are going to need a new lead guitar. We've got some guys ready to audition, but once you pick one, we can be in the studio next week—"

Mackey looked at Kell first and saw his nose wrinkle in confusion, and then he looked at Grant.

Who wasn't meeting anybody's eyes.

"No," he whispered, at the same time Kell said, "No, goddammit! Grant, you pussy, you don't need to get married *that* badly!"

Mackey just stared at him. Grant... well, those eyes Mackey had always loved, those pretty, golden hazel eyes were shiny, glittering, just like the songs. Suddenly Grant grabbed Mackey's shirt collar and said, "Me and Mackey gotta talk."

He dragged Mackey back into the club, into the tiny green room by the bathrooms, then threw the door shut behind him and locked it.

"Grant?" Mackey's voice was so wobbly his knees were weak with it. "What—"

"She's pregnant," Grant said, closing his eyes.

"No." Oh God. Grant had honor. Grant wouldn't.... "You can leave her. Pay her," Mackey begged, hating himself.

Grant blinked hard, and Mackey saw his eyes, red-rimmed and glossy, spilling over. "I seen how much fun that's been for you and Kell and Jeff," he said.

Mackey recoiled. "But you can't.... Grant, you heard him. A chance to make music for a living. To go places. To *get out of our shitty little town and stay with m*—"

Grant closed his mouth over Mackey's brutally, so hard his lips rubbed on his teeth, swelling, and Mackey tried not to sob. He wanted to argue, he wanted to plead, but Grant's mouth on his had always been their best form of communication.

Grant invaded him, silenced him, then reached into his pants and stroked him, hard and without mercy. Mackey clutched at Grant's shoulders, too weak inside to pull him off and make him talk about it, too desperate not to scratch at him and try.

But Grant stayed put, jacking Mackey off until Mackey groaned for breath, aroused so hard so quickly that he hurt. Grant knew his body by now and sank to his knees, pulling Mackey's pants down in one hard yank.

Then Grant sucked the head of his cock in, and *God* but Grant was good at that, his lips so soft and sweet, his tongue so busy. Mackey clapped one hand over his mouth and screamed, and Grant pressed his free hand, the one not jacking Mackey, over it, and Mackey screamed and screamed and no one heard, because the sound was muffled in the music and the crowd and the combined force of their hands pressing his lips against his teeth.

Mackey came because there was nothing else he could do, and for a moment, the dressing room was so quiet they could actually make out the DJ warning the crowd that there would be five minutes of break followed by Outbreak Monkey doing their closing set.

Grant got heavily to his feet and pulled Mackey's pants up, then leaned his forehead against Mackey's. "You need a way to let me go," he panted into the relative quiet. "This is it. You get to go be famous, and I'll stay in Tyson and watch you fly."

"No," Mackey begged, his life opening up like a canyon under his feet, and him with broken wings and no safety net.

"Sing that river song tonight," Grant whispered. "Sing it to me. Please. I know you're gonna be pissed, but God. I love playing with you guys. Let me have one more set, and my song."

Mackey wiped futilely at his eyes. "I hate you," he moaned.

Grant wrapped those strong, load-bearing arms around his shoulders and held him. "Hate me after the set, McKay. Right now, it's the only way we got to say good-bye."

Grant left the dressing room first, presumably going to the bathroom to wash his face and rinse his mouth. He tapped on the dressing room door when he was done, and Mackey went to do the same.

He met his own eyes in the mirror as he washed his face and ran cold water through his sweaty hair. *Faggot. Cocksucker. Fairy.*

He hadn't said those words to himself since he and Grant had spent that first night together, because he couldn't say those words to Grant.

But now he was all alone, and they bounced loudly around his brain.

That is, until he was on the stage, screaming his heart out in their final set, letting Grant's riffs wash through him like prayer.

"River song last," Mackey said in the middle of the set, and although his voice was audible to the crowd, only the band knew they were making mental changes in the set list as they played. It worked fine, though, and "In One Ear" got the crowd loud and noisy and screaming for more. They did a fake stage exit then, because they'd pulled this sort of thing before, and when the decibel level got truly fucking insane, Mackey went back onstage by himself.

He picked up his own guitar, the one he didn't get to play unless he was doing the solo gig, and looked out into the crowd.

"You ever steal a kiss?" he asked them, and that vibe, that noisy, we're-gonna-burn-the-place-down vibe, turned suddenly dark and smoky, and Mackey felt reassured. Yeah. They'd all stolen kisses. It was okay. He wasn't alone. The whole world had stolen kisses, and he was playing their song.

*The river makes music just like you and I make love*
*And the sunlight cuts through shadows like a pie knife from above*
*And we sit inside the purple shade of a place we've forged from sin*
*And we listen to the river whisper 'bout the end.*

The end. This was the end. He poured his heart out into the song, lamenting for the lover who would be gone when the sun was high and the sweat poured down their necks, crying for the kisses that would never come again.

Because they wouldn't. Because Grant would be gone when Mackey left the stage, and his whole world for the next week would be moving from his tiny bunk bed in the tiny apartment into the big wide world, with only the crowd to catch him.

# Stairway to Heaven

THE NEXT month was a blur. So much of it was above Mackey's head. Someone told him and the guys where to be, when they were going, and boom! They were there. He remembered the panic of their first plane ride, the way he and Kell sat next to each other, listening to their own iPods, all the fear and apprehension and excitement theirs and theirs alone. Neither of them talked about how pissed they were at Grant. Once they got to LA, it was all *drive here* and *sign this*, and with one swipe of the pen, their world changed. Jeff and Kell let go of their apartment. Mackey bought their mom a house.

It was the last thing he did that made any sense to him. He *insisted* that part of the contract be that their mom had a house, wherever she picked.

Mackey didn't care. As long as his mom didn't have to work in bars anymore or worry about rent, or Cheever, he was happy. That moment in the Los Angeles office at Tailpipe Productions was one of the best of his life. When Gerry (as Mackey started calling him) asked them what they wanted to do afterward, Mackey said, "Go to Disneyland, of course!"

Gerry laughed and told them Disneyland was at least two hours away in traffic, but that he'd take them the next day. Instead, he proposed that they go out to dinner with the owner of the company, Heath Fowler—after they went shopping for suitable clothes.

Heath was in his early thirties, and he wore an expensive suit like he'd squirted out of his mama and right into it, and it had grown with him. His brown hair was cut perfectly, his teeth were even and white, and his blue eyes (contacts, Mackey figured) were level and steely. He let Gerry walk them through the contract and stopped to clarify stuff Gerry missed. He made sure to mention they were responsible for an album at least every two years, and to give them a loose outline of what their time would look like, provided they sold and did what they were told.

Mackey took that seriously. His mom's house depended on him putting out the albums, playing the music, doing what he was told.

"We won't let you down," he said, shaking hands after he'd signed his spot. Kell copied him, and so did Stevie and Jeff, but the fact that he was the one leading the band and all those zeroes were in his hands—that scared the crap out of him.

So while Kell, Jeff, and Stevie nodded, fine with being dragged in this current like fish on hooks, Mackey recognized the shopping trip for what it was: part of his duty to the band. Had to look the part, right? He trooped along with them to the outlet mall in the LA burb he couldn't remember, even the next day, feeling more like he was being inducted into the Marines than making his dreams come true.

It hit Mackey then—hard—that their cleanest T-shirts from Walmart and their least-worn Wranglers were no longer adequate for whatever life they had signed into. He'd have to pick out his own clothes, and someone besides his mom would be bleaching his hair, and Grant wouldn't be there to keep him from acting out in public.

In the middle of the big dressing room with four mirrors surrounding him, Mackey's hands started to shake. He longed to be on stage, where *he* was the mirror, because the punk kid reflected back at him was small, scrawny, badly dressed, and unprepared.

"You okay?" Gerry said kindly.

Mackey shrugged, swallowing down nausea. "It's… I mean, it ain't Walmart." He played up the twang in his voice, figuring he could get away with more if people thought less of him.

"No." Gerry patted his shoulder. "Here, kid. Let me get you some clothes to try on and a glass of water. What are you, a twenty-eight in the waist and a—"

"A twenty-six," Mackey replied, grimacing. "And a twenty-eight inseam."

Gerry shook his head. "Son, in a town where a small waist is a prize, you're gonna be so small you fly under the radar. Jesus, you're scrawny. But that's okay. Room to grow." The look in the older man's eyes was sympathetic, and he rubbed his hand over his stubbled cheek and then along the back of his neck. He didn't look well either, Mackey thought. He was sweating, even in the seventy-eight-degree day, and his eyes looked bleary, like he still hadn't woken up. But he'd walked them through the contract in Mr. Fowler's office using language so simple even Kell could follow along. He'd included the caveat for Mackey's mom—the band's only caveat, actually—and the provisions giving Grant part of the profits for the songs he'd helped to develop instrumentally. Kell had argued against that, because he was still pissed, but Mackey insisted.

Grant got them there—and Mackey wasn't going to let him bail on a guilty conscience like he'd bailed on his brothers.

The thought made Mackey a little sick to his stomach, and he started sweating even more. He had to get out of there!

"You know, I think I need a little air. If you let me go outside, I can get—" He thought maybe he could run out of the store all the way to the airport, and catch a plane back to Sacramento. He could be in Tyson before his mom even picked a new place.

Gerry shook his head. "No, kid. Here. The girl'll be in with the water in a sec. Take one of these—it'll calm you down."

Gerry pressed a Xanax into his hand, and Mackey clutched it for dear life. It came from a doctor's bottle, right? Couldn't be any worse than weed or wine, right? Just something, anything, to make Mackey feel like he could deal with having someone other than Grant pick out his clothes, and go to dinner in a place that wouldn't take the jeans he had on.

The girl—a skinny thing with a minidress and no tits—came in and smiled with big, straight white teeth as she handed him a glass with ice and a bottle of water. Mackey managed a weak smile back, and he washed down the Xanax while she was watching. She didn't bat an eyelash, and he wondered what the hell kind of town this was.

The water helped, though, and he sat down on the leather benches and finished it off. By the time Gerry came back in, his arms full of choices, Mackey had stopped sweating and was mellow, able to smile at jeans that would actually fit.

"Fuckin' awesome," he muttered, winking at the salesgirl. She simpered and left so Mackey could change.

"You feeling better?" Gerry asked. Mackey grinned, fuck-off-and-love-me. Gerry nodded, reassured. "Well, now we know the magic little ticket," he said. "Here, Mackey—you got any water left in that bottle? Time for Uncle Gerry to take his own medicine."

DISNEYLAND DIDN'T need Xanax—Disneyland was a drug all its own. They went on a weekday, from early in the morning all the way until it closed down, and Gerry went with them. He bought them T-shirts, bought them stuffed animals—even shipped most of those back to Mackey's mom and Cheever—and then took them back to the hotel room, exhausted and happy. Stevie had been to Disneyland before, but only with his aunt, who got sick on all the rides. The Sanders boys had never been, and Gerry laughed at them kindly as they raced, as eager as eight-year-olds, from roller coaster to roller coaster. Even the Pirates of the Caribbean had its own sort of magic, and Mackey was entranced by every detail. (Kell was not. Kell muttered all the way through that one, saying it was stupid. Jeff and Stevie murmured happily to themselves like bees in the seat behind them, and Mackey wished heartily for his mom or even Cheever, who wouldn't have tried to crap all over Mackey's parade.)

That night, Gerry told them to sleep tight, because the next day they'd be auditioning guitarists.

Mackey didn't hardly sleep a wink.

He lay there in that strange hotel bed, listening to traffic noises from too many cars outside, wondering why he needed a queen-size all on his own, while Kell snored in the bed next to his. If Grant had come, he found himself thinking resentfully, he would have at least kept Mackey company as he floundered on soft white sheets that didn't stay stuck under the mattress.

When Gerry came in at eight, Mackey was mostly asleep in the corner of the hotel room between the bed and the wall, wrapped up in the comforter. At Gerry's "Howyadoinkid!" he stood up, bleary-eyed, dressed in one of his old T-shirts and the tighty-whities he'd packed for the trip to LA, and Gerry sighed.

"C'mon, kid. Put on some of your new duds and I'll get you coffee."

Mackey smiled at him gratefully. By his third cup of coffee, he felt like he could face his day.

By one o'clock the four members of Outbreak Monkey were about done. They'd sat in the control room of the record studio and listened to more than ten lead guitarists, most of whom were better, skillwise, than Grant had ever been, but not one of whom looked like someone they could play with. Mackey had a headache that wouldn't quit.

Gerry was there with two ibuprofen to help him out.

The next guy up was Blake Manning, sort of a whip-thin kid, not as small as Mackey, but with a gangly, liquid grace all his own. His hair was too long and not sculpted or trimmed, and he sported a scraggly goatee/beard hybrid that mostly looked like he couldn't afford to shave. He was wearing pretty much what the Sanders boys had worn coming down to LA: worn jeans and a T-shirt from Walmart.

He opened with an acoustic version of "Backstabbing Betty," and he wasn't the most fluid of the guys who had played for them, but Kell grunted as he spat out the word "motherfucker," and Mackey harmonized with him when he went into the high-pitched scream.

He finished playing, and the guys looked at each other.

"Him," Kell said, and Mackey nodded, letting Kell know he approved.

Gerry grimaced. "Him? Eduardo, the guy before him, had faster fingers—"

"Feed this guy," Mackey said decisively. "Feed him. Give him a stay in the hotel room. Let him practice with us tomorrow. We might not hate him."

"Blake?" Gerry spoke into the microphone. "Could you meet us outside the sound booth, please?"

That night they stayed up late and talked, the boys and Blake and Gerry. Gerry brought them good liquor, Cuervo Gold and margarita mix, which they drank until two in the morning. Mackey didn't say much—Kell did all the talking, really, but that was fine. Mackey didn't have to love the guy, just had to be able to give him directions, and with Kell to translate, well, that would work. When it was time to pop up at 8:00 a.m., Gerry was there with the coffee and some ibuprofen for everybody, and when Mackey had to run outside to throw up from a combination of nerves and hangover and sadness for playing with someone who wasn't Grant, he was there with the Xanax.

Blake, it turned out, had grown up in one of the tiny desert towns over the Grapevine. So close to LA and so far away? It had left him with the acrid ozone bitterness of the smog that never quite left. He fit right in with the boys from Tyson. He got Mackey's jokes, but he was cynical like Kell. The second time they all went to Disneyland, Kell and Blake refused to go on the Haunted Mansion, and Mackey sat with Jeff and Stevie, listening to the secret murmur of their own language, jokes they got with half a word, references Mackey hadn't been present to catch. He lost himself in the fantasy instead, but at the one curve of the ride, when the crystal ball was floating with the face of the fortune-teller encapsulated inside, for a moment, he didn't see the fortune-teller at all. Instead he saw a long road, blank and white, and himself, a tiny black figure standing alone.

That night he had his first panic attack, shivering under the comforter on the floor by the bed. Kell yelled at him to quit his fucking whimpering, and Gerry showed up with a magic pill and a glass of water. Mackey slept after that, but the next morning, he needed more than coffee to wake up.

Gerry gave him that too.

By the time they were done cutting the album, Gerry had a tour booked with a kickoff performance in a club in LA with over a thousand people. Mackey refused the Xanax for that. The crowd was his place, his safe haven, his harbor, and he rode their applause—screaming applause, because after six weeks in the studio, every song they performed was diamond-cut perfection—for the rest of the night.

But they had to be up to fly to Chicago at four the next morning. He needed a little pick-me-up to haul his ass out of bed. Gerry wasn't there—it was the guys stumbling around on their own, trying to figure out how to pack five times the clothes in the same amount of luggage—and Blake pulled out the tiny vial they'd seen him use sometimes when coffee wasn't good enough for him either.

"Here," he whispered to Mackey in the bathroom, as Kell swore up and down the damned room. "Just a little snort—all it does is wake you up, I promise."

God, anything. Mackey couldn't function this fucking tired, could he?

The powder burned the back of his nose and dripped into his throat. *Pfaugh!* World's *nastiest* taste. *Never again*, Mackey vowed as he sat jittering on the plane, bouncing on his asscheeks alone, so high his heart rate had nowhere to go when the unfamiliar engine noise picked up, and he was lifted into the air for only the second time in his life. *Never fucking doing this again.*

By the time they got to Europe, Gerry had gotten him his own prescription for Xanax, and he went through ninety tabs a month. Blake could find a dealer in an igloo in Alaska if he needed to—he'd been living on the streets of LA for three years, bussing tables and mopping floors before he'd landed the gig with Outbreak Monkey—and he kept Mackey supplied. A little bump to wake him up, some Xanax to stop the shaking hands, some alcohol to help him sleep at night.

Their first night in London, Tailpipe held a contest. Twenty lucky winners got to come in and party with Outbreak Monkey and the band they opened for, Tiger Bright. By the time Mackey was done with the set, he was ready for a shot of vodka to calm him down. As he was kicking back the shot glass, he noticed the fans, who had all grouped by the catering tray and were timidly pecking at the little canapés and shit as the band talked about the set and who fucked up and could Blake maybe try to keep up with Kell and did Jeff really need to wear his new sunglasses on the stage?

He kicked back another shot of vodka and smiled at them tiredly. "You all enjoy the show?" he asked, because he needed to hear it.

"Yeah, Mr. Sanders," said the bravest boy. He was maybe Mackey's age, with a long face and a few blemishes still, and hair shaved on the side and spiked orange.

"Call me Mackey." He winked then, and the boy blushed.

And opened his mouth slightly, and licked his lips.

Mackey shuddered. God. He *knew* that look.

At that moment, Tiger Bright came in and the fans got hyperactive, screaming and chattering among themselves, but the kid with the orange hair looked at Mackey and then darted his eyes toward the hallway leading to the bathroom.

Mackey—well, his body was flooded with alcohol and Xanax and the cocaine from that morning, and still high from the set, and all he could think was how good it would be, how *great* it would be, to get off, to be touched, to be *fucked.*

He grinned—fuck-off-and-love-me—and sauntered by the fans. "You'd better have a rubber," he whispered to orange-haired gangly boy with spots, right next to his ear.

The kid looked at him with predatory eyes and nodded.

Mackey wandered down the hall until he heard footsteps, and then he dodged into one of the dressing rooms they'd used before the show.

The door hadn't closed behind him when it was thrown open and shut again, and Mackey found himself pressed face-first against the mirror on the far wall.

The dark was reassuring. He couldn't see his own face in the mirror, much less the guy behind him slobbering in his ear, fumbling with his pants, grasping his cock. At one point he heard the words "Such an honor to be jacking you off, Mackey Sanders," and the *sincerity* almost crumpled his boner right there.

It didn't matter. The condom was lubed, and all Mackey had to do was bend over. Bend over and close his eyes and spread his ass and hope the kid could get him off, make him come, because maybe when his vision went white and his body shot into the stratosphere, maybe everything but the crowd, the music, the song—maybe everything else could go the fuck away.

# Your Own Worst Enemy Has Come to Town

YEAH, TRAVIS Ford was *sitting* in Heath Fowler's fancy LA office for Tailpipe Productions, but for once, he couldn't focus on business.

*"You're home early," Terry said, looking appalled as he opened the door to their little apartment in West Hollywood.*

*"You said we needed to talk." Trav had served in the military for eight years. He didn't believe in bullshit, and he didn't believe in the coy beating-around-the-bush looks Terry was giving him.*

*"I said we needed to talk last week!" Terry protested, looking at him in disbelief. "Last week, when I was* crying *over the phone, I was so lonely!"*

*"I was on a trip, Terry! There's not much I could have done about it." Trav shoved his way inside the apartment, seeing the pizza on the coffee table and frowning. "Did you eat in the living room? I thought we agreed—"*

*"Well, yeah," Terry said, half laughing. He hadn't shaved in a couple of days, and his curly brown hair and brown stubble looked unkempt in a way that had always turned Trav off, and he was wearing little more than a white tank top and basketball shorts. Trav could tell by the way he was swinging around in the shorts that he didn't have anything on underneath. "Yeah, we agreed not to eat in the living room," Terry said bitterly as Trav tried to concentrate on what was going on around him. "But we also agreed that you'd cut down on trips, and we also agreed to listen to each other when we were talking!"*

*"I heard you!" Trav protested. "I'm back three days early, aren't I?"*

*The shower in the bedroom was on, he realized dimly. The shower in the bedroom was on, Terry was half dressed, and Trav had walked into the classic scenario. "And none of that is an excuse for cheating!"*

*Terry's lower lip quivered. "If you'd even said you were coming home," he said softly. "But you just kept telling me to get over it. I'm not a robot like you, Trav. I don't start relationships so I can be home alone."*

*Robot? He didn't feel like a robot. He felt hurt and betrayed. But he ignored that part. "So you went out and found someone, for spite?"*

*Terry shook his head and rubbed his stupid stubbled face with a shaking hand. "For spite? You would think that. I was crying in the damned bookstore, looking for one more book on how to fucking communicate, when a goddamned kid comes up and tells me I look lonely. A stranger, Travis. Walks up and says I look sad. I've been telling you that for* months, *even* before *you left for Vancouver, and you couldn't see it, but this kid walks up and just... nails it. I started to cry—again—right there in the fucking bookstore. Do you get that?"*

*"I get that you took him home and fucked him," Trav snarled, and to his surprise, Terry slapped him. Terry, the gentle artist who apparently couldn't hear a daffodil drop without crying, actually* slapped *him.*

*"You don't get to talk ugly about him,"* Terry snarled, no longer gentle. *"You say what you want about me. Tell me I'm weak—I get that. I can't change it—"*

*"You don't want to!"*

*"I can't! Tell me I'm weak, tell me I'm a cheating fucker, but don't say anything ugly about that kid who gave me a hug when I fucking needed it, do you hear me?"*

*Trav stared at him, rubbing his cheek. "I came home early,"* he said, feeling helpless. *He wanted to howl and be angry and hit him back—but eight years in the military, six of those years in the MPs. Six years of being stoic and thinking fast and not ever once letting his temper get the better of him, because he had a big fucking gun and a lot of fucking power and people depending on him to think. Six years after that, business school, cutthroat competition, becoming a consultant in personnel relations and how to keep your company from being ripped off—Trav knew nothing if he didn't know discipline. He* couldn't *hit Terry back. He couldn't.*

*"I came home early,"* he said again, closing his eyes. *"You sounded sad."*

*"You couldn't call me up and tell me that?"*

*Trav breathed hard through his nose. "I came home early."*

*Terry touched him on the shoulder, gently. "And I let you down."*

*Trav had dropped his suitcases—expensive gray leather luggage with the smooth rollers—at the front door. He turned around mechanically and retrieved them.*

*"Take my name off the lease,"* he said, keeping his voice even. *"Box my stuff up and put it in the storage unit downstairs. I'll get it when I have a place to stay."*

*"Trav?" He sounded so surprised. "That's it? You're just going?"*

*Trav didn't even look over his shoulder. "Why should I stay?"*

*"Because we love each other?" Terry's voice cracked, and in the background, the shower went off.*

*Trav turned back around and grimaced. "Maybe, but I'm not ever gonna let this go. Better I leave now, and then we can both move on with our lives."*

*Terry started screaming at him, his voice half-hysterical, his words—well, it was probably best Trav just forget what he was trying to say.*

*It wouldn't change anything, would it?*

"Trav? Trav, are you paying attention?"

Heath Fowler was one of Trav's oldest friends. They'd survived boot camp together, and MP school two years later, and six years in the MPs together in the Middle East. Heath had opted out of the military first, because he had a friend in the music industry and he wanted to take advantage of that, but the minute Trav had cleared college, Heath had offered him a job.

Trav had taken it, actually—his first two years out of business school, he'd managed Pineapple Express and had loved it.

"I'm always paying attention," he said, and he meant it. "Poor Gerry Padgett dropped dead while Outbreak Monkey was getting ready to record their new album, and now *you* need a Management Monkey, and hello, you know I'm between gigs!"

Heath shook his head and scowled, and Trav sat up a little straighter. "Be nice," he snapped. "Gerry was a friend—"

"Gerry was a pill-popping disaster—"

"Yeah, but he was a nice guy. I sent him to Outbreak Monkey on purpose, do you get that? Man, one look at those kids on stage—three of them are brothers, right? No dad—not even the same sperm donor, and they've got the ripped jeans and the hungry eyes and the fucking attitude, and I'm thinking, 'Heath, if these guys make it, this business is going to ruin their lives.' So I send them Gerry, thinking that he's going to be good ol' Uncle Gerry, and he'll sort of take care of them, right?"

"Wait—you say kids. How old are they?"

Heath grimaced. "Let's see—I've had them for fourteen months, and Mackey— that's the youngest—he turned nineteen just before he signed, so, he's twenty, Jefferson and Stevie are twenty-one, and Blake and Kell are twenty-three."

Trav rolled his eyes. "That's hardly children in a salt mine," he muttered.

Heath scowled again. "You liking the corporate apartment, Trav? The one I gave you with an hour's notice because Terry fucking left you like he should have done years ago? So you're an adult—you're thirty-fucking-five years old, and you need a hand up. These guys are kids, and they've never had money in their lives, and now they've got it and they don't know what to do with it. I mean, some of it they're shoving up their noses, but most of it just sort of sits there. Gerry had to make them buy clothes, and he kept them on tour, so I don't even think they've got a place to fucking sleep that's not a hotel room. They're here in LA for the next three months with one goal—"

"Put out the fucking album. I'm not stupid."

Heath grunted. "Not businesswise, no. But sometimes I think the reason you became an MP was because you knew people would hate you anyway, and that way you had a patch on your arm that gave you permission to be an asshole."

Trav must have made a sound then, some sort of pain grunt, because Heath sighed and looked him in the eyes.

"Trav, I'm sorry. Man, I don't want to be *your* asshole. But these kids need more than a manager, okay? I thought Gerry could do it, but he was in a lot of pain himself, and I didn't see it. He died—I had to get the kids to the funeral, do you know that? They had no idea what to even wear. I mean, Gerry didn't have a family—there I was, two days before the graveside, and I'm taking five stoned kids to buy black suits because the only thing they had close was from their first gig as high school students and none of that shit fit." Heath looked away. "And Mackey's shit was too goddamned big because I think he's been living off of Jack and Coke for the last year." Heath shuddered and looked at Trav with naked pleading in his eyes.

"We sign them up and then work their asses off to make money for us, Trav. This industry—man, it chews the kids up and spits them out, and we both know it. And these kids... I mean, Mackey's got more talent than any kid I've ever dealt with. You know how Bruce and Bono and Madonna are like, *old* now, but they keep making damned good music?"

Trav nodded. "Wrecking Ball" had been playing in his temporary apartment since he'd walked away from Terry. God save Bruce Springsteen.

"Well, this kid could be that guy. He's got so much inside him. But it's not going to happen unless someone gets him to rehab and makes his life regular and shows him how to fucking survive, you hear me?"

Trav sighed. "Babysitting?"

Heath glared at him. "You remember Private Banneker?"

Oh God. Trav swallowed against a sudden dry mouth and the memory of eyes popping out of a swollen face and the haunting swing of feet four feet above the ground. He'd checked. Goddammit, he'd *checked* to make sure Banneker was clear, didn't have any goddamned thing to harm himself with inside his cell.

Fucking kid had ripped his fatigues on a rough spot under the bunk and found a way to hang himself.

"Horrible fucking memory," Trav breathed, trying to clear that image from behind his eyes. Stupid kid. It was a three-month offense, max. Three months and a demotion. He couldn't live through three months and a demotion? Trav had learned after that. Learned to talk the prisoners down as he locked them up. Learned to make it practical, a thing they could handle instead of the end of their lives.

"Yeah?" Heath asked, rubbing his face restlessly, his own voice shaking. "Wasn't great for me either." Heath had been the one to find Banneker. They'd bunked together then, and Trav had been the one to help him through the nightmares.

"You're saying this kid's gonna—" Trav couldn't even make himself say it.

"I'm saying someone needs to hold this kid's hand for a while."

Heath looked Trav square in the eyes, and for once, he wasn't wearing the contact lenses he called his Hollywood Blues. Trav found the honesty in his plain, average brownish eyes refreshing.

"Babysitting," Trav said, but he winked as he said it and stuck out his hand to shake on the bargain. "When do I start?"

"Tomorrow morning," Heath said, taking his hand. Square and firm and trustworthy—one of the reasons Trav had stayed friends with Heath through the military and beyond.

"Let them know I'm coming," Trav warned.

Heath grimaced. "Frankly, I don't think it's gonna matter."


THE WEIRD thing about the Burbank Hilton was while from the inside it looked over the entertainment industrial town of Burbank, from the freeway it looked sort of gracious in a tacky West Coast way.

The best part of the view from the fifteenth floor was the swimming pool almost directly below the window from the hallway.

Trav sighed and put his suitcase down next to the bed. The boys were in the suite across the hall—they did not yet know he was there. The *hotel* knew, and had politely asked if he'd be able to pay for all of the damages incurred by the other members of his party.

He'd been politely surprised that the charges were under $5,000.00. The nest of stoners (as he'd been calling them in his head) had lived there for nearly a month, and apparently poor old Gerry had died there. Trav had actually seen worse.

Now he was standing at his window, looking at the swimming pool, wondering which would be worse: answering the text Terry had just sent him before he went in to face down the pack or saving it for the cherry on the shit sundae when he was done.

With a sigh, he figured he'd never been good at putting unpleasant things off. Rip-off-the-Band-Aid was his favorite school of thought. And of course as soon as he thought that, his phone buzzed again.

*You don't want the chess set?*

Trav closed his eyes. They'd met playing chess. One of the clubs Trav used to belong to had held some sort of tournament, and he'd been between jobs. Terry had been fun to talk to, spontaneous where Trav was not, flirty and funny. A simple dating progression: dinner on the first date, movie on the second, the park on the third, bed on the fourth. Somewhere in there had been an exchange of medical information, a decision to use condoms, and then an informed decision to go without. Six months of that, and they moved in.

Terry had bought the set—something nice, with pretty blue and red stone pieces and a marble board—for the one-year anniversary of the day they met.

Which had been about three and a half years ago.

*No thank you. You keep it.*

*God, that's fucking cold.*

*Was there anything else you needed?*

*Yeah. I need to know if you ever loved me.*

Trav closed his eyes for a moment, remembering the way they'd wake up slowly on Sundays, maybe make love, maybe not, then gravitate to the kitchen and bowls of plain old oatmeal from a packet in Trav's blue stoneware bowls. They'd sit and play chess in their pajama bottoms, and Terry's dark hair would fall in his eyes when he was thinking. Trav would push it back, and Terry would smile at him shyly, as though he was aware he lost time and place when he was concentrating.

Oh God.

*Wow. It's taking you a long time to answer.*

*Yes.* He took a deep breath after he sent the text and then typed the next one quickly. *Yes, I loved you. That's why we need to do it this way. I can't see you face-to-face while we do this.*

He was breathing hard, and he forced himself to stop. Just stop. This was irrelevant.

*Trav, I'm sorry.*

*Fuck you. Contact Heath if you have any questions.* Terry knew Heath—they'd had him and whatever girlfriend over to dinner more than once.

Ruthlessly he turned off his phone, tucked his key in his pocket, and left the room.


HE KNOCKED on the door and was not particularly surprised when a girl opened it. She wore cutoffs and a red-striped spaghetti-strap tank top, no bra, and her skin was the pale copper freckled variety of the true redhead. Her hair—thick and layered around her face—hadn't been dyed or gelled or messed with, and she smiled winsomely with full lips.

"Hello," she said softly. "You must be the new guy, right?"

"I'm Trav Ford, the new manager. Are the boys—"

"Jefferson?" the girl called behind her. "Stevie? Your new guy is here. The one to take over for Gerry."

From behind the girl, he heard two male voices. "No, goddammit, Kell, don't you go—"

A big, battered, meaty hand wrapped around the girl's arm—not rough, but it wasn't the touch of a lover either. "Move, Shelia. This shit's important."

"Okay, Kell," Shelia said. "Don't need to shove, I'm moving." She smiled sunnily at Trav while she stepped aside. "Pleased to meet you, Mr. Ford. The boys will be happy to start playing again." She sauntered into the hotel room, which was sort of cavelike, with the lights dimmed and the strong smell of pot smoke and patchouli, and Trav was left face-to-face with the oldest Sanders brother.

"Mr. Ford?" Kell Sanders said, shaking his hand. His grip was strong but sort of spread out, but maybe that was because his paws were massive. Trav wondered how he managed to play guitar with such a mighty claw, but this wasn't the time or the place. "Pleased to meet you. Come in. We, uhm, tried to clean up and all. I mean, the maids have been real nice helping us, but, well, Mackey sort of lost it when Gerry died, and that's why they needed to replace the table and the window. But come in, 'kay?"

Of all the things, Trav had not been expecting *that*.

He took two steps into the room and looked around. The coffee table in the middle of the conversation pit held beer cans and a recently cleaned ashtray, as well as a couple open boxes of pizza in the middle. Ah, lunchtime.

The end tables held the bongs.

Dirty food containers, beer cans, wine bottles, and the occasional dime bag lined the counters. A faint scatter of green herbal powder ringed the edge of the garbage disposal, making Trav think they'd cleaned up just a little too quickly, and there weren't any dirty needles in the sink, but there weren't any clean glasses either.

Trav grunted. *Could be worse.*

"Pleased to meet you, Kell," he said after a pause that he'd *calculated* to go on too long. "Is everyone else here?"

Kell had a huge head and buzz-cut brown hair, a few moles around his mouth, and eyes that reminded Trav of a landed fish—sort of suspended open. He was wearing an Outbreak Monkey concert T-shirt, well-ripped in the armpits and around the neck, and jeans that had no ass, just a series of frayed strings, wearing thin, where the ass used to be. When he turned around and looked back into the living room and paused, Trav honestly believed he was counting people.

"Uh, I think Mackey's still in his room," Kell said. "Uhm, this here's Blake." A kid with a wispy mustache, scraggly brown hair, and an addict's skinny build raised an unenthusiastic hand. He was dressed a little better than Kell—his shirt was some sort of store brand, and he wore a matching vest with his newish jeans, but his eyes were bloodshot and at half-mast. Awesome.

"And my brother Jefferson, and his friend Stevie."

Jefferson and Stevie were sitting on the love seat together, and Shelia had just taken her place between them, burrowing like a bunny into the back of the couch. She laid her head on the shoulder of one young man and wrapped her hand around the thigh of the other, knocking Trav for a loop. That relationship did not look usual, he thought before mentally smacking himself away from judgment. The boys themselves were dressed in contrasting shirts—the one on the right wore yellow and the one on the left wore green— but the logo on the front, another expensive store brand, was the same. With their matching round faces and matching sandy hair, they were weirdly twinlike.

"Nice to meet you, Mr. Ford." The twin on the left kissed Shelia's temple, and she scooted fluidly into the other twin's lap. "Here, I'll go get Mackey." The young man stood up and turned to his twin for a sec. "Stevie, do you know if he's got anyone in there?"

Kell grunted. "I think he was stoned enough to be gay last night."

To Trav's surprise, the twins met eyes grimly.

"Yeah, Kell," the one who must have been Jefferson said, his mouth flat, "that's why."

Kell darted a look at Trav and grimaced. "When he's sober, he's with girls," he said defensively.

Jefferson and Stevie shook their heads in tandem.

"C'mon, Mr. Ford," Jefferson offered politely. "You can help me get him up."

Trav was surprised enough to follow Jefferson to the room at the far end of the suite. "When he's sober, he remembers to ask girls to beard for him," Jefferson said quietly. "Kell doesn't like fags."

"Fan*tastic*," Trav muttered savagely, not even sure he could put words to what he was thinking. "He calls me a fag, I'll break his fingers."

Jefferson's shoulders slumped, and right there Trav had a sudden moment of sympathy. His sister was a little older than he was, but he also had a brother, a younger one, who had gone to college on scholarship and had shortly thereafter spawned the first of the requisite children to make up for the brother who probably wouldn't have any, and whom Trav saw once or twice a year. They loved each other. They talked. They hugged at Christmas. They called or texted or e-mailed every week or so. How much would Trav love Heywood if they worked together, lived together, partied together, knew the cracks of each other's asses like the backs of their hands?

"Don't break his fingers," Jefferson begged, like he believed Trav meant it. "Break his jaw if you want—he doesn't sing a lot of backup, we'd be okay without him there— but Mackey don't need to find another guitarist. It'd kill him."

Trav blinked at Jefferson with real confusion and wondered what he'd find on the other side of the door.

"Mackey!" Jefferson banged on the door. "Hey, Mackey! You ready to get up? The new management guy is—"

The door was opened by a tall, thin, dark-haired boy with guyliner smudged heavily over brown eyes and mascaraed lashes. He was wearing a leather jacket and, as they talked, belting a spiked belt around his waist.

"Sh," he said, squinting at Trav and Jefferson. "He's sleeping."

"Who are you?" Trav asked.

The guy shrugged. "A fan. No one you'll see again. Just—" The kid shrugged again and looked away. "Don't wake him up, okay? He doesn't sleep good."

With that the boy pushed past them, through the living room, and out the door.

"Bye, faggot," Kell muttered under his breath as the front door closed, and Trav sighed. His jaw—that was right. Break his *jaw*, not his fingers.

The boy had left the door open a little. Trav looked at Jefferson, deciding the guy didn't look too scary—a little red-eyed and sleepy, but not scary—and said, "'Kay. You wake him up, I'll throw away whatever he's getting stoned on, okay?"

Jefferson looked away. "Man, I wouldn't want to be you."

Together they ventured into the room.

At first all Trav saw was the pharmacy and the mirror with the powder on it next to the king-size bed. His first thought was *Thank God no pipes!* The coke mirror was nasty enough.

His second thought was *Where the hell is Mackey?*

The bed was rumpled and well used, with little spots of blood on the far side. The trash can by the bathroom held dime bags, used condoms, an empty bottle of gin, a bloody needle, and a dirty spoon with a sponge in it, but no Mackey. No Mackey in the bed, no Mackey in the bathroom, no Mackey in the closet. Trav made himself busy, pulling housecleaning gloves from his back pocket and using them to pick up the coke mirror and two mostly empty bottles of vodka, all of which he threw away, while Jefferson looked in the bathtub and under the bed. He started going through the pill bottles, surprised when he saw that about half of them had *McKay James Sanders* on the side.

"Xanax, Percocet, Valium… and look. Three different doctors."

"Huh?"

Trav looked over to where Jefferson was rooting through the comforter that was stuffed between the bed and the wall. "The prescription drugs," Trav said. "They're not legit—"

"Sure they are," Jefferson said, nodding. "Gerry got those for him. He got real wound up when we had to perform, and the traveling—couldn't sleep, couldn't sit still. That shit helped. Isn't that right, Mackey?"

To Trav's surprise, the wad of comforter started to move. "Yeah, Gerry got that." The comforter moved some more and Trav got his first look at the elusive Mackey Sanders.

He looked about twelve years old—an underfed twelve at that.

Messy hair, bleached blond at the ends and growing out from sandy-brown roots, fell in his eyes and across his mouth. He was wearing a pair of plain white briefs, the kind you bought at Walmart, and they didn't look all that clean. His chest was narrow and his arms were stringy. His skin was marked with sex, and grimy, like maybe sweat and come were the only liquids that had touched it in the past couple of days. Trav could smell his unwashed body from the far side of the bed. He had a few red marks on his arms, Trav noted clinically, but no hardened track marks—not yet.

Who needed needles when you had all those lovely pills?

"What'd you do with the coke?" Mackey asked, squinting at Trav. "Who are you, and what'd you do with the coke?"

"I threw it away," Trav said patiently. "I'm your new manager, this band is officially drug-free, and the coke's in the trash can."

Mackey squinted some more and stumbled to his feet, holding the once-white comforter over his shoulders like a cloak. "If you're our manager, don't we have to go to the studio today?"

Trav nodded patiently, figuring that with the state of the room and Mackey's bloodshot eyes, he was probably *way* too stoned to make any sense. "You'll have to go tomorrow," he said, his voice short. "Today we're going to lay down some ground rules."

Mackey grunted again. "No coke?" he asked, like he was making sure. He glared at Trav again, but his eyes were covered by hair and barely open. Trav couldn't have recognized him on the street if he saw him awake and sober. "So I don't have to get up and do anything? And I can't have any drugs?"

He was staring at Trav like maybe Trav just made this up for fun, so Trav kept his asshole teacher voice. "No, Mackey. You *can't* have any drugs."

"Okay," Mackey mumbled. "Jeff, move. I'm going back to sleep."

"'Kay, Mackey. We'll shut the light off when we're done cleaning up."

"We'll do *what*?" Trav's chin actually dropped, even more so when Jeff held his finger up to his lips.

While Trav was standing there, wishing for a breath mask so he didn't have to smell Mackey's unwashed body and the stench of sex and drugs and booze, jaw unhinged, Mackey sank down into the soiled comforter, curled up into a little ball, and covered himself with that once-fluffy blanket. Jeff walked to the end of the bed and stripped it, then shoved the sheets and the clothes that littered the floor—mostly jeans and T-shirts, no store brand, like Kell—into a fabric laundry hamper, which he dragged to the door.

"Bring the trash out," Jefferson said. "We can ask for maid service and a new comforter—he'll sleep right through it. Gerry used to do it all the time."

"But we need to wake him up! Dammit, he can't—"

Jefferson sighed and looked around the room, his eyes unfocused. For the first time, Trav noticed the stack of notebooks—the cheap spiral kind—sitting on top of the desk in the corner of the room and the well-used acoustic guitar leaning against the wall. A few empty cans littered the area—soda, not beer—and the occasional cheeseburger wrapper. It was like the room was divided in two parts: Mackey the hardworking musician, and Mackey the hard-partying rock star.

"What're the notebooks for?" he asked after a moment.

"Writing songs," Jefferson said, surprised, like Trav should know this. "He was up until four in the morning doing that." He glanced at the bed and shrugged. "Whatever he did with that other guy, that only lasted 'til ten. Mackey's got an album to put out, and our mom's got a house we bought on credit. You don't think he'd forget that, do you?"

Trav looked at his watch, feeling old. It was ten o'clock in the morning. No wonder the kid had asked for coke to wake up. "He's got two hours," he said, trying to sound like a hard-ass.

"Yeah, okay," Jefferson said, but he was still looking around the sterile hotel space. It wasn't a bad hotel room, but in the end, that was all it was. "Mackey used to have rock posters all around his room, do you know that? There were three of us in there, and he had all these free posters he got from the music store, and every one of them had someone great. Michael Hutchence, Jimi Hendrix, Jim Morrison. I sorta miss those posters. Stevie says when we get a real home, we can put up framed pictures. I'm looking forward to doing that."

Jeff's lips quirked up at a sudden cacophony of voices in the front room, and Trav realized he was going to have to change his tack.

He'd take care of the rest of the band first and *then* deal with Mackey. Heath had been right—whatever obscure warning he'd been trying to give Trav, he was right.

The Sanders boys weren't kids, but they were special. He was going to have to pull out his dusty people skills before he got military precision out of *this* bunch.

# Not an Addict

SOMEONE YANKED the comforter off of him, and he was *fucking freezing.*

"Give it back," he mumbled. "Kell, gimme the blanket back, I'm fucking cold."

"You're in withdrawal," came a flat voice, and Mackey groaned.

"Fucking shakes, man. I didn't even need the coke, but where'd you put the fucking Xanax? I need that shit." Mackey dimly remembered waking up to pee and coming back to the freshly made bed, only to see his stash had been leveled. He'd gone back to sleep—*God*, it had been so long since he'd been able to sleep—but then he'd been yanked rudely awake, and the pills were still gone.

*That* time, the fucker who'd taken his drugs had dragged him into the bathroom and shoved him under the fucking shower.

That was confusing. Someone had *bathed* him, rubbing his hair roughly with shampoo and scrubbing at his back and between his legs with a washcloth. It had been awful and invasive, but at the same time sort of comforting. When was the last time someone had taken care of him?

But that didn't mean he wanted douchemonkeys washing him without his permission again.

Mackey sat up in his little corner, clutching the suddenly clean comforter to his naked chest. "I'm fucking sick," he snapped. "Can't I just get one lousy fucking pill?"

"No, but you *can* get one lousy fucking trip to rehab," snapped the douchemonkey who'd forced him into the shower.

"I don't need rehab!" Mackey shouted, standing up in his space, the holy country of Mackey. "Just give me the fucking drugs!"

The guy was sitting by the side of the bed, one hand on the concierge phone. For the first time, Mackey got a good look at him.

He wasn't bad, really. Short brown hair, maybe a little red in it. Brown eyes. One of those long faces with a long jaw, and a strong nose—not a pretty face, but a hard-ass face. You'd follow that lantern-jawed bastard into hell.

Apparently Mackey was doing just that.

"Don't worry, Mackey," the guy said in an absurdly gentle voice. "They'll help you clean out in rehab. Sedate you until this shit's out of your system."

Mackey laughed a little, even though his skin felt like it was being pierced with a thousand tattoo needles. God, all the other guys had gotten inked, but not Mackey. Mackey wasn't sure he knew what he wanted on his body for permanent yet. Nothing that was his. Nothing real. So maybe what tattoo needles *would* have felt like—myriad pinpricks on exposed skin—and his joints ached like he had a fever, and his chest hurt, and his head. A wave of black nausea washed over him, and he bent double.

"Man, I'm gonna puke," he muttered, and before the next wave swept him, a firm hand was supporting his back, lifting him so he could hang his head over the trash can.

He finished, and the guy disappeared, leaving Mackey blessedly alone to die in peace. He was *not* pleased when the guy came back and wiped his face with a wet cloth and made him rinse out his mouth. He was even *less* pleased when strong arms—hella strong, like tree trunks—lifted him off the floor and laid him on the bed.

"Let me back down!" he protested, feeling feeble. God, he could barely roll over. "Man, I hate this bed. Too big. Too fucking big. Don't need a bed this big."

He wrestled with the comforter, which disappeared with a jerk only to float back down on top of his body. He clutched it to his shoulders again and huddled, freezing and sweating and wishing he could die.

"One fucking pill," he muttered. "All this asshole needs to do is give me one fucking pill. Goddammit, I need to fucking write."

He struggled to sit up. "Don't you see that I need to fucking write? I need to write, motherfucker! We're not gonna get the album done, and then there goes our contract, and I gotta have the music, man—what else'm I gonna fuckin' do?"

"Sh, sh sh...." A washcloth, warm and not freezing, wiped at his forehead. "Mackey, I swear, you haven't lost your contract, okay? Could you just calm down so I can call the rehab clinic? They'll send an ambulance, get you an IV—it'll be fun."

"That there is a bald-faced lie," Mackey said bitterly. "That don't sound like fun. That sounds like a fucking hospital, but worse because there's not any fucking Xanax!"

The washcloth kept wiping. "Mackey, do you really want to need the Xanax this bad? Do you want to need *anything* this bad?"

Mackey whimpered. "Music," he muttered. "Music. It's all I need."

"Good. I'll bring your iPod, make them play it all you want."

Another wave of shudders wracked Mackey's body, and he was too tired to fight. "God, who the fuck are you?"

"I'm Trav Ford, your new manager."

And Mackey remembered Gerry, face blue, tongue distended, a puddle of vomit and pills next to his face. "Hell. Can *I* die this time?" he muttered. "I don't want to see Gerry die again."

"Yeah, kid," the guy—Trav—said, smoothing back his hair. "I mean, no. You can't die. But we won't make you see anyone else die, okay?"

"'Kay," Mackey muttered. "'Kay. Whatever. Just... God. Put me to sleep. Anything. But it hurts. It hurts and I need it."

"Yeah," Trav said. "Music, Mackey. Remember that. Music."

A sudden shaft of humor penetrated Mackey's misery. "She don't lie, she don't lie, she don't lie," he sang.

The only thing that got him through the next couple of hours was Trav's voice, off-key and sardonic, singing the chorus.


HE DIDN'T remember much about the hospital. Mostly it was like the hotel, but his iPod was on shuffle in the background and the people giving him the sponge baths were not half as memorable as Trav.

He did a lot of sleeping—he remembered that. And when he woke up, clean and confused, a nice man in a very expensive sweater vest and tie was sitting next to his bed. He had neat gray hair and a goatee and a sort of patronizing smile.

"How are we doing, Mr. Sanders?"

"We feel like a weasel crapped in our mouth. Who are you?"

The guy blinked. "Why a weasel?"

"'Cause it sounds funny. It's a funny animal. Nothing rhymes with weasel. Who the fuck are you?"

The patronizing part left and only the smile remained. "I'm Dr. Cambridge. You're in a rather exclusive rehab facility in Beverly Hills, Mr. Sanders. I'm going to be your tour guide on the way to recovery."

Mackey narrowed his eyes. "How long is this tour supposed to last?" he asked suspiciously. "And what stops is it supposed to take?"

Dr. Cambridge smiled, oh so gently. Mackey was reminded of all the times he'd gotten kicked out of school for fighting. Not all of the kids he'd beaten up had been mean. Some of them had been missionaries or counselor's kids or kids trying to start a club. All of them had smiled *exactly* like that.

# I Should Have Known

TRAV'S FIRST order of business after getting Mackey to rehab was getting the guys out of the fucking hotel room. No, they couldn't record without Mackey—and Kell and Blake complained bitterly about the decision to send Mackey away for that very reason. They shut up, though, when Trav emerged from the bedroom, Mackey in his arms, so Trav could take him downstairs to the waiting ambulance.

Trav didn't want to think about how thin Mackey was, his emaciated ankle and absurdly large-boned foot sticking out of the covers. Trav had carried children who weighed more out of war zones.

He didn't want to think about a lot of things relating to Mackey, actually. He didn't want to think about his pathetic insistence that he had to work, and he didn't want to think about the way he'd sung, everything from Eric Clapton to Foo Fighters, as withdrawal cramps racked his body.

He didn't want to think about the surprising, darkly funny bursts of irony from a guy he'd had to throw in the shower because he couldn't stand the smell anymore.

Or the fact that Mackey James Sanders, who had a multimillion-dollar recording contract and six Les Paul guitars, had three personal items in his room besides his laptop. He had his iPod, his beaten-up Walmart brand kid-size guitar, and his notebooks.

That was all.

God. Trav had actually bought him underwear so he'd be able to send some clean clothes to the rehab center.

He took some deep breaths and shored himself up. He'd co-opted Mackey's room in the suite and given up his own room. He hadn't even unpacked. As soon as he'd walked into Mackey's room later that first afternoon and heard him moaning while stinking in sweat, he'd realized that this was not a hands-off operation. God, he'd never seen anyone look that bad and live.

He shuddered.

He could still hear Mackey croaking out "Cocaine," making fun of himself while he felt like death. He still remembered Mackey's scrawny body in the shower, the annoyed way he'd batted at Trav's hands, and the totally helpless way he'd snuggled into Trav's arms when Trav had wrapped him in a towel.

As Trav sat at the desk and wrote in one of the few unused spiral notebooks Mackey had stacked in the room, he tried really hard not to let himself wonder how long Mackey could have kept going like that, from gig to gig and fix to fix, before he just stopped.

*Years*, he thought with a surprised snort. Kid was fucking tough.

The phone at his ear clicked, pulling Trav out of his weird obsession with the lead singer of what was now, admittedly, *his* band.

"Yeah, Daphne? Yeah. Trav—I'm with Tailpipe again. What do you got for me in a modest mansion?"

Daphne purred happily and started listing various properties up along the canyon, and Trav mulled on the length of the drive to the recording studio in Burbank and rethought that.

"Maybe not," he muttered. "Okay, maybe North Hollywood—it needs to be closer?"

Daphne always sounded like she was in high school, but she must have been in her thirties at the very least. "Oh, absolutely, Trav. We've got some nice houses in North Hollywood. Like twenty minutes from downtown Burbank—or, you know, before six in the morning and after eight, because otherwise...."

Yeah, in LA, there was only one way to finish that sentence. "Traffic," Trav muttered. "Okay. Let's go with one of those. Which one can I have in a week?" he said. In a month, when Mackey was out, they could have it all set up, and he could pin up some posters or buy his own goddamned duvet or something. "Yeah, two weeks at the mo—" He broke off when he heard a disturbance in the front room. "Daphne, you have my info—Heath Fowler is taking the expenses for at least the first six months—but I've got to bail."

He hung up without even a good-bye and strode into the living room.

And almost plowed over Mackey Sanders.

"Oh my God you're short," he said reflexively. "And what in the hell are you doing here?"

Mackey had seemed small before when he'd been jonesing and sick, but now that he was walking on his own power, clean, with his hair pulled back in a ponytail out of luminous, overlarge gray eyes, he was *still* only five foot six.

"Looking for my spot," he muttered. "I'm fucking tired. Man, they tell you that you have to recover, but you just don't buy it, you know? *I* didn't buy it. *I* thought it was a crock of shit, but no. I'm fucking wiped out. I need to fucking sleep. Where's my spot?"

His voice was singsong and sarcastic, and for a moment, all Trav could do was stare at him. "Are you *high*?" he asked in outrage.

Mackey shot him a look of pure disgust out from under sandy-blond eyebrows. "After the last four days, are you *shitting* me? I don't ever wanna be fucking high again. Fucking *Jesus*, do you know what that detoxing thing is like?" He looked at his brothers and bandmates and Shelia (an odd, indefinable quantity Trav was not ready to discuss). "It's *horrible*. Jefferson, you and Stevie, don't never start doing the pills, guys, 'cause I know you don't touch them, but they're *seriously* bad for you." He nodded gravely. "Blake, man, give up the fuckin' blow." He yawned then and turned around to Trav. "Now where's my spot? I need to sleep."

Trav had to remember to close his mouth. "Mackey, I thought you'd be in rehab for a while. I sort of took over your room."

Mackey shrugged. "I just need to sleep next to the bed," he said through another yawn. "I'll be out of your way." And with that he brushed past Trav into the room, the little knapsack of goods Trav had packed for him hanging on his back like a high school student's.

Trav watched the door swing shut and tried to remember how his life had gotten completely out of hand.

"He's not staying," he said to the mildly surprised band.

Kell snorted. "That's what you think," he muttered and then turned back to his own room. He had a girl in there, but Kell and Blake didn't really talk about their girls. Living with the band was like living in a frat house, except with maid service. And except for the fact that Shelia stayed with Stevie and Jefferson, in their room. Hell, she had her own dresser.

Blake snickered. "Was he fucking serious about the blow? Jesus, what a fuckin' moron." And with that he turned to the kitchen, probably to make himself a drink so he could couch. They had an Xbox and a Wii, and Blake was reigning champion.

He was going to get fat, Trav thought meanly, watching as Jefferson, Stevie, and Shelia made plans for Shelia to take them shopping.

God, that was almost normal. Trav sighed and reached into his pocket. "Here," he said, pulling out his corporate card. "Get some shit for Mackey—shit that fits. Go to the kids' department if you have to, but try to make him *not* look twelve years old, okay?" He paused. "And *don't* get any more of those damned crackers!" Every time somebody went out—Kell, Blake, Jefferson/Stevie/Shelia—they came back with a giant box of those Chicken in a Biskit crackers. It was like this weird obsession—they had six boxes of them, and as of yet, nobody had opened *one* of them.

Shelia smiled sunnily. "Yeah, sure." She took the card and handed it to Stevie, who seemed to handle day-to-day matters for the three of them. "Here, hon. You sign for stuff. Me and Jeff'll pick it out."

Stevie smiled at her, his average brown eyes lighting up. He kissed her forehead tenderly. "You guys are real good at that," he said sweetly, and together, the three of them trooped out, like magical elves or fairies or wizards or something.

Trav sighed. Mackey, he thought, almost with relief. He needed to talk to Mackey.


MACKEY WAS asleep. Mackey was asleep for the next two days.

True to his word, he'd walked into the bedroom, found a space between the wall and the bed, taken off his pants, and curled up with the comforter. Trav had ordered another comforter from housekeeping and slept in the bed. Mackey barely breathed hard, much less snored—he hadn't been kidding about it being like no one being there.

Trav did his work around that huddled, sleeping form in the corner—and his first order of business was to talk to the guy Mackey was *supposed* to be "touring" rehab with.

"You just let him walk out?" Trav said after he got the guy on the phone. "All that money to have him bussed there and he just *walked out?*"

"Rehabilitation is a voluntary thing," Dr. Cambridge said unapologetically. "Mr. Sanders was going to attend all of his classes, all of his programs—we had a deal—and then, the second day, he was sitting in my office for a single session. I asked him a few personal questions and he got up and walked out. And apparently caught a cab to the hotel."

Trav grunted. Mackey had paid with his corporate card. It had been a $200 cab ride.

"But… he's not cured!" Trav sputtered. "He's an *addict*. They need *treatment*, not just detox!" God, everybody knew that!

"I agree," Dr. Cambridge said mildly. "No. He may not be high, but he's definitely not clean and sober yet. The first trigger, the first sign of stress, he'll be using something as a crutch, even if it's just a beer. The very little I know about him tells me that, and everything I know about rehab confirms it. Mr. Sanders is going to have to come back here. But unless he's court ordered, we can't make him stay."

Trav grunted. "Can we sort of reserve a place for him?" he asked, wondering if Heath would recover from the bills the boys were racking up. "I mean, I know you need to fill his spot with people—"

"I give it two weeks," the doctor said, his voice dry. "I'll keep a space open for him for the next two months, but he'll be back here in two weeks. I'm sure of it. You only need to pay for the time he spends here." The doctor's voice grew growly. "I am going to get another crack at this kid's head if I have to crank his music at top volume for the whole two weeks."

Against everything Trav knew about himself, he found he was laughing. "Oh God," he muttered, trying not to just lay his face in his arms. "He got to you too."

"He's a very original young man," Dr. Cambridge said defensively. Trav couldn't really gainsay him. Damn *it, Mackey, could you just make things easy?*

"Well, I'm sure you'll be seeing him soon," Trav muttered. He'd live to regret those words.

THE THIRD day after Mackey came back, Trav found a house—six bedrooms, attached baths, and a music studio, because LA was where musicians came to party. Heath okayed the lease for a year, and they'd be able to move in the next week. Mackey at rehab or Mackey with them, the band was getting a home, and a studio, and hopefully a little closer to getting their shit together.

Trav remembered managing Pineapple Express. The guys had spent ten years working clubs before Heath signed them on. They'd had their own homes, they knew how to live on the road, and sure, they'd gone out and partied plenty. Trav had even kicked back a few drinks with them. They knew how to stop and they knew how to work, and they knew how to treat it like the world's greatest job but a job just the same. He'd decided to go into consulting because he wanted a chance for a relationship, for a home, not because managing for that group had been too intense, or too painful, or too much of a pain in the ass.

They'd thrown him a going-away party, with a cake and a silly plaque that had been one of the few things he kept after the breakup. He'd felt needed and competent and like he'd done a good job—but he hadn't been too closely intertwined with their lives. Sure, he knew who was dating and who broke up and if someone needed some chicken soup and some cold meds. He'd canceled a week's worth of concerts once because the lead singer and the lead guitarist had picked up the flu and he hadn't wanted them to perform when they could barely stand. He'd flown in a girlfriend and a wife from across the country to care for them and even hired a babysitter, because the guitarist's wife kept squirting out babies like a fish and she didn't want to haul them all cross-country.

But he'd never been their family. *His* family was in a nice house upstate, where he visited his perfectly normal, repressed, WASP parents, and his brother and sister, who got him off the hook for the childbearing thing and generally dealt with the world in a sane, rational manner.

He did *not* room with five balls of testosterone and angst in a hotel room in Burbank, dammit!

Somehow, rooming in a house in North Hollywood sounded better.

The second night after Mackey returned, Trav woke up to the sound of music. The light was on at the desk, and Mackey sat there in a new white T-shirt and a pair of the briefs Trav had ordered, playing the guitar gently and making notations in the last clean spiral notebook. He'd obviously been up for a while, because a few empty cans of soda sat on the desk, and a once-full box of Chicken in a Biskit crackers. Trav stared at the box for a minute and felt an absurd little punch near his spleen.

All those people he didn't understand, buying those stupid fucking crackers. Even Kell, whom Trav wanted to blame for half of Mackey's problems, had bought the stupid fucking crackers.

For Mackey. Even when they thought he was going to be gone.

Mackey was picking out a melody, something harsh and astringent interspersed with something seductive and sweet.

Trav listened to it for a moment and waited until Mackey put the next bit on paper.

"The harsh part," he said, propping his head on his hand and squinting into the light. "That's the part where you do the primal screaming and the guitar cacophony, right?"

Mackey looked up at him and smiled, and Trav realized that he had a fox's face. His cheekbones were supposed to be sharp, and so was his chin. But with his hair scraped back from his face in a queue, his eyes were huge, probably because he weighed less than mouse shit and there was so little flesh in his thin face.

Even in the lamplight, Trav could tell he had freckles, fading with adulthood, but still faint.

And his smile was like a little boy's.

"Yeah," Mackey said with deep satisfaction. "Gonna be a good song. If I'd known rehab would gimme such good shit to write about, I would have done it months ago."

Trav was no longer sleepy. He sat up, crossing his legs under the sheets. He was wearing pajama bottoms and a T-shirt, but suddenly Mackey's youth and vulnerability made Trav feel… inappropriate.

"Well, yeah," he said, hating to bring this up. "But you've only been through detox. Rehab's a different fish, Mackey."

Mackey stopped making the notations for a minute, then frowned and kept working. Trav wanted to argue with him—he did. But he'd lived with Terry for three years. Terry made a living with his paintings, and Trav had seen it firsthand. Interrupting that kind of concentration was cruel. Trav could wait.

Mackey kept working for a few moments, then set the guitar down and turned toward Trav like he'd just asked the question.

"Why?" Mackey asked, pulling his mouth up. "I don't want the shit anymore. My body don't need it. I just need some sleep and I'll be—"

"Addicted," Trav said flatly. He'd seen guys get addicted in the Army. The boredom, the stress—it'd do it to you every time. Tracking those guys down had sucked. They'd been absolutely sure that if they explained why they *needed* the drugs, all would be forgiven. "Just because your body doesn't need it doesn't mean there's not stuff in your *mind* that needs it, Mackey. You were open to it. It's not like you took one pill and got hooked. Not even one hit of coke. It's that it happened again and again."

Mackey shrugged and thought about it. "But I know how it happened," he said, absolutely sure. "It happened 'cause I was stressing 'cause of the business. I'm not stressing anymore. I know how it works. Know what I'm s'posed to do. I'll be fine." He grinned. "I mean, once I get on stage, it'll be great, you know? Once we start recording, it'll be all sunshine and fucking roses. I don't need no drugs when we're making music. It's better than Disneyland."

"Yeah." Trav foundered. "But Mackey, music can't be all you are!"

And for the first time, he saw a crack in that "fuck you, I'm fine" thing Mackey had going. "Of course it can," Mackey said, thrusting his lower lip out. "It's who I am!"

Trav frowned. "No—it's a *part* of who you are, but I'm pretty sure you're more than the music."

Mackey shook his head, serious as a fifth grader swearing a blood oath. "No, I'm not," he said. Irrelevantly, Trav noticed that his eyelashes were blond with dark roots, like a baby's. "Just ask my brothers. It's all I've ever been."

"Well, it doesn't *have* to be!" Trav laughed, trying to make the moment lighter. "Mackey, don't you want... I don't know. A house, a family, a cat? Don't you want to take trips that have nothing to do with work or learn another language or get a degree in something?"

But it was no use. Mackey's face had shut down at the mention of *a house, a family, a cat.* "Man, lookit me. I'm not cut out for a house or a family—"

"Just because you're gay doesn't mean you can't have those things!" Trav burst out, and then *really* wanted to kick himself.

Mackey didn't even get angry—that would have been better. At least it would have been honest.

Instead he just grinned and winked, and Trav could see him making that expression on stage as part of his act. "I'm not gay, brother," he said, pulling his squirrel cheek back and making his dimple pop. "I'm only bi when I'm high!"

Trav's jaw dropped. "Jesus fucking Christ!" Heath had taught him that blasphemy. His parents would be appalled, but Trav had learned to love it.

Mackey laughed for real and played idly with the strings on the guitar. "You know, my first song was a church song that I twisted for purposes that were definitely not on Our Lord's agenda," Mackey said wickedly. Then he launched into a very charming version of "Simple Gifts" that, it was true, had probably never been sung in a church.

Trav laughed bitterly when the song was done. "Was that you?" he asked. "Were you fighting all the time?"

"Of course it was." Mackey smirked. "You've known me for three days and you probably wanna smack me. Imagine living in the same fucking town!"

"It's not funny," Trav rasped—partly because he *did* want to smack Mackey and partly because that would be a hell of a thing to grow up with. "'Only bi when you're high' is a perfectly good reason to get high, isn't it? How're you going to have a relationship when you're not jacked on pills, Mackey?"

Mackey grunted and shifted his gaze left and right quickly, like he was searching for an answer. "Maybe I'm just not a one-woman man," he said with a tight swallow. He played with the strings some more and sighed. He'd obviously lost his momentum, but Trav couldn't make himself feel bad. The room was silent, and Trav stared blindly out the window, seeing Mackey's reflection against the darkness. His head drooped against his chest, and he rubbed the back of his neck restlessly with long, obviously roughened fingers. His hair fell out of his ponytail, straight and halfway down his cheekbones, but he didn't brush it out of his eyes. If he wasn't a junkie, Trav would have recommended an ibuprofen or something, but he was, and Trav wouldn't bring it up if Mackey didn't.

"How long can you tell yourself that?" Trav asked into the heavy quiet. "I mean, if it's just your ignorant brother—"

Mackey snapped his head up. "You don't say shit against my brother," he snarled. "You don't know fuckin' nothing, Mr. Ford. I *hate* that you even think you know as much as you do. I *hate* that you saw me naked and sweating and helpless. So you don't make no fucking assumptions about what you *think* you know about me and mine, you hear?"

Trav gasped, shocked by his fury and a little hurt.

For a moment there'd been an intimacy between them. For a moment they'd almost been friends.

"Sorry," he muttered. "My bad. I'll just keep that bus to rehab all warmed up for you, okay, Mackey? That'll be my job. I'll get paid a fucking fortune to carry you down to the fucking ambulance because you can't tell the fucking truth, even to yourself."

"You do that," Mackey muttered. "Man, I'd rather be the body than *find* the body, so that's just fine with me." He clicked the light off savagely and set the guitar down in the corner, then stalked to the bathroom to brush his teeth.

Trav lay back down and pummeled his pillows under his head. Mackey returned to the bedroom and threw himself in the tiny space between the bed and the wall, wrapped up so tight Trav wasn't sure he could breathe.

The only sound in the darkened hotel room was their harsh breathing, and then Trav remembered something he should ask.

"Mackey, when we move into the house, what kind of bed do you want? I mean, you can't sleep on the floor in your own home, even if you only stay there between tours."

"I don't know, man—get me a fucking coffin. That way you'll be all ready for it when I finally OD."

Trav buried his face in his pillows and growled. "Jesus fucking Christ," he said, because it really was an all-purpose blasphemy, especially with Mackey. "You're right, you know that? You're so goddamned lucky you never got beaten to death I can't even think of *words* to tell you how lucky you are. How in the hell did you live to adulthood?"

"Kell," Mackey said succinctly. "Him and Grant kept us alive in that shitty fucking town. Don't say nothin' mean about either of 'em."

"Well, if he doesn't stop using the word 'faggot,' I'm going to have to hit him myself," Trav groused.

"Why?" Mackey muttered. "Why you got such a vested interest in Kell not being mean to faggots?"

"Because *I'm* gay, you obnoxious little turd," Trav snapped. God. Look at what this kid made of him. He was a *professional*, for sweet heaven's sake!

"Oh," Mackey said, taking the wind out of Trav's sails.

"Oh?"

"Yeah. Don't worry. I'll make him behave. He'll back off if I tell him to."

"Then why don't *you* tell him to for *you*?" Trav asked, out of patience.

Mackey took a breath, and then another. In the darkness, they rattled against the wads of comforter wrapped around him. "See, he don't like people weaker'n him," Mackey said at last. "I just don't want him to decide I'm one of those."

"I could take your brother out in my *sleep*." Trav would go do it *right now* if it would make Mackey see sense.

"Yeah, he probably knows that." There was a beat of silence, then another, and then Mackey spoke again. "I couldn't," he said at last, apologetically. "I'm scrawny. All I got is my mouth. It won't be enough if Kell don't love me enough."

Oh. "Oh." Trav wasn't even sure he said the word, but it seemed to echo between the two of them. Trav's eyes had adjusted to the darkness, and he rolled to his side, trying to make Mackey out in his little roll next to the bed. "You're stronger than you think," Trav said, because that was what people said when they were trying to give pep talks.

"Don't bullshit me, babysitter," Mackey said dismissively. "If the only thing you're good at is truth, then that's all you should do."

Trav felt a burst of shame. Mackey was right—the truth really was his only strength.

"Okay, fine," Trav muttered. "I have no idea how strong you are. But you don't either. Maybe have a little hope for yourself, you think?"

Mackey laughed, low and sleepy. "Ten million people bought my record last year," he said, his voice full of pride. "Ten million people singing my songs, screaming them out loud with me. You think that don't give me hope? It's the only hope I ever had."

Mackey's breaths grew deeper and more even, and Trav figured he'd gone to sleep.

Which sucked, because Trav was left with those words rattling around in his head.

*Hope for more*, he thought, the words so insistent he had to say them out loud, even though it was four in the morning and Mackey was already asleep.

"Hope for more."

"I'd need to see a picture," Mackey mumbled. "I don't even know what that looks like."

And *then* he fell asleep, leaving Trav staring into the darkness until the gray horizon made the windows glow. Trav got up and shut the blackout curtains so he could go back to sleep, but the whole time he was wondering, what would he put in Mackey's picture? What would attract Mackey Sanders enough to make him want to stay?

MACKEY HAD enough songs that they could make some forays into the studio while they were waiting for the house. Trav knew recording would be interrupted—*knew* it wouldn't be complete—but he couldn't justify just sitting on his ass while he took a gamble that Mackey was going to disintegrate like a dandelion. Figuring they could at least get their rehearsal time in, Trav booked a room in the recording studio and stood on the other side of the glass to see what they did.

Watching Mackey work turned out to be a revelation.

They walked into the studio to find their equipment all set up and in tune, but that wasn't enough for Mackey. Trav sat behind the glass with Grayson Holloway, their producer for this particular work, and watched Mackey pull out his spiral notebooks and set them on the music stand. Then he started talking to the band as he walked around and played a few chords on everybody's instrument, tightening a string here, playing with the keyboard there, making sure the drum kit was exactly to Stevie's spec. Mackey put his hands on everything—he didn't let one bit of the band's equipment go without his own personal sound check.

For a moment Trav expected the band to object—it was their shit he was groping. But they stood there and listened to Mackey's instructions. When he was done, he sat on the little stool they'd placed for him and picked up his guitar.

"Okay," he said, "so here's how this first song goes. It's called 'Tattoo,' and it's about detox, so it's gonna be pissed off. Kell, gimme some pissed-off minor chords in a standard progression, canya? Quick-like—2/4 time."

Kell picked up his guitar, without the amp, and started softly playing what Mackey asked for. Mackey nodded. "'Kay, Blake, same thing, but half an octave higher. Same progression, at least for the hook. We're gonna do about fifteen bars of hook before lyrics, so you guys get that squared away." Mackey listened for a second. "Blake, half an octave higher does *not* mean in a different fuckin' key. Man, get it straight."

"You didn't tell me the key, dammit!"

"Well, learn to fuckin' hear. Minor chords—at least go F# and take a fuckin' guess." He listened for a second and grunted. "Clean up the progression and it might not suck. Jeff?"

"Yeah, Mackey."

"'Kay, I want that whole thirty-second/sixteenth syncopation thing going. That bump-buuump, bump-buuump, like a heartbeat gone wrong. It's gonna be hard—you and Stevie'll have to read each other's minds or you'll speed us up off a motherfucking cliff, right? Stevie, heavy on the bass, heavy on the high snare—leave all that other shit out. You gotta be the cleanest one of us or the song'll get fucking cluttered."

Stevie nodded, and started, and the song was on.

Mackey picked up his own guitar and picked out the riff, then put it down and started them all over again while he conducted from the center. After those first fifteen bars, he began to sing.

*Needles rip my skin but I ain't bleeding I just sinned*
*Now I'm paying for my roller coaster screaming can you hear?*
*My heart is playing pain as it thunders through my veins*
*Like a tattoo of my bane can you all hear me screaming*
*COCAINE!*

Mackey gave the signal at that last word, and the band broke up into complete chaos—or that was what Trav thought at first. Then he realized each player was just going off of the riff Mackey had given them as he played and making up the bridge from the riff as they went along.

The players quit, and Mackey turned to each one and told them what to do and whose lead to follow and generally aligned them with military precision into which instrument should play what where. He was matter-of-fact with Kell, sweet to Jefferson and Stevie, and a fucking dick to Blake.

When he was done, he started them off from the beginning.

Trav turned to Grayson when they'd gotten to the end of the song, and shook his head. Gray echoed the gesture.

"I was here for the last album," Gray said, scratching at the brown-and-gray stubble he let grow when he didn't need to be seen. "Man, watching that kid turn those bozos into a band is one of the joys of my fucking existence."

They weren't really bozos, Trav thought, watching them. When they were all in the room, playing the song, they were a unit—every guy in that circle was as driven as Mackey, and they all had talent, either God-given or earned by sweat.

But Mackey was their key, their epicenter, their heartbeat. God, Trav thought, remembering that quiet nighttime conversation from three days earlier. When he was in the center of his band brothers, he was stronger than strong enough. No *wonder* he needed help when he was dealing with the everyday. Trav would find day-to-day a letdown too, if he had this much magic in his veins.

But Mackey wasn't a saint—not even close. Trav watched them interact for a few more minutes.

"Is he always such an asshole to Blake?"

Gray hmmed and adjusted his keyboard. "They started out not bad. But Mackey kept expecting Blake to read his mind, and Blake? If the boys hadn't taken a shine to him, studio musician was as high as he was going to get. I mean, the boys"—Gray gestured to take in the Sanders brothers, and Trav was starting to understand that Stevie counted as one of them—"they've been playing music since, hell. Mackey probably played it in his mom's stomach. But Blake? He just wants to be a rock star. That's all he's got. Mackey isn't patient with him."

Trav watched Mackey rip Blake up again, and was a little saddened by the repressed hurt on Blake's face. And the disappointment on Mackey's. "Why do they keep him? I mean, you'd think Mackey would ask for another guitarist—"

"Kell likes him," Gray said, like that was all there was to it.

"But Mackey—"

"Man, haven't you been living with them? That's not what families are like!"

Trav shook his head. He *really* needed to visit his parents for the holidays, because apparently he had missed something big. He wouldn't have put up with Blake in the band or Mackey as a boss for all the love in the world.

By the time they were done rehearsing that day, they had the song in rough but usable shape. By the time they were ready to move into the house, they had almost the whole album outlined and were ready to cut the first track.

Of course, by then, Dr. Cambridge's two-week prediction had just about run its course. It was a shame Trav forgot that, because he'd never forgive himself for what happened next.

# Rape Me

OH GOD, Mackey was so not ready for fan interaction.

He glared at Trav accusingly from across the crowded studio canteen, and Trav grimaced. Well, Trav hadn't been ready for it either, apparently. It certainly hadn't been planned. One minute they were .breaking up from a really good rehearsal and talking excitedly about moving into the house in North Hollywood. None of them had seen the house, but Trav assured them it would be better than a hotel room, so, well, excitement, right?

And apparently that was when Trav got the text.

Trav came into the studio hesitantly, wearing one of those frowns that said his plan—whatever it had been—was not going to be followed.

Trav got a lot of those looks. When they left the hotel late because Shelia forgot her feminine protection, when Mackey ended up in the cab with Stevie, Jefferson, and Shelia instead of the one with Blake, Kell, and Trav, when the guys decided to order pizza when Trav had reservations someplace that would make them eat salad—all of that shit made Trav's eyes narrow in the corners and little divots appear in his forehead.

This time, the plan had been more than interrupted, it had been fucked to hell.

"Look, guys, word's got out that you're in town. It's apparently a big furry deal, especially that you're getting ready to record again, and the PR girl booked a little meet and greet without me. High-profile fans, some executives, that sort of thing—Mr. Fowler apologized for the inconvenience, but he'd like us to attend. They've got snacks and drinks in the canteen, some photographers. It shouldn't go on for more'n two hours, but I assume you know the drill?"

Kell laughed. "Yeah, make nice and try not to get caught if you're banging someone in the bathroom."

There was general laughter, and Kell and Blake went in for the fist bump. Blake looked tired—Trav had been throwing away his stash too. Blake might not have been as strung out as Mackey had been, but it was getting harder and harder for him to buy. At the news of the meet and greet, though, he perked up. Of course he did, Mackey thought sourly. Someone was *always* there with some free blow.

Which Mackey really did not fucking want.

He'd heard Trav's words about how detox was not rehab—and as much as he'd blown them off that night, they'd sort of whispered in his ear for the past week and a half. He didn't ever want to go through detox again, which meant he didn't ever want to take drugs again, and here they were, faced with two hundred people, and maybe a hundred of 'em would sell their grandmother to get Mackey fixed up.

And Mackey—who'd been happy rehearsing with his brothers for the past ten days, getting the next album set up, playing music, creating music, *being* music—suddenly wanted a Xanax so bad his hands shook. All those people and no dodging out of talking to them. God, at least when they'd done prom and dances back at home, he'd been able to hang with the guys and let them talk. It was like the older he got, the bigger the crowd got, the more exposed and alone he was. With that pretty little pill in the palm of his hand, he could deal. And now he couldn't.

Suddenly that conversation in the dark of the hotel room made so much more sense.

Mackey wanted to find Trav, tell him how much sense it made, because he'd been a little hard on the guy for thinking he had all the fucking answers. But now Mackey was surrounded by teenaged girls—the daughters of someone big in the business and kids he'd actually met before—so he needed to be as personable as he could. In the back of his mind, he heard Gerry telling him that making nice was what let him make the music he wanted. Gerry had been good about breaking it down like that. "You do this, kid, and then you can do that." Of course, some of that "doing" had been the pills, but they'd been Gerry's problem too, so Mackey couldn't hold that against him. He'd learned at his mother's knee, whenever she'd had to go to work and leave them with Kell because a babysitter would have bankrupted her, that you did the best you could, and the mistakes you made were part of the best you could do.

"So, Mackey, you're so skinny! How do you do it? I can't lose weight to save my life!"

Mackey looked at the nineteen-year-old girl with bleached-blonde hair and a little minidress sheath that probably cost the rent for *both* the shitty apartments his family had lived in that last year.

It was a mindfuck. It wasn't any easier to do now than it had been a year ago.

"It's the drugs," he said, smirking so it looked like a joke. "It's like the song says— we all stay skinny 'cause we just don't eat."

The girl cracked up, her laugh brittle like ice, and he wondered how many times *she'd* been to rehab, because it sounded like she knew it wasn't funny.

Her little sister sniffed. "Well, I like a man with some meat on his bones," she said.

He grimaced at her. Sixteen, and she'd probably had as many men as he had. "Don't you mean with a boner of meat?" Mackey cracked, and both girls giggled. He winked at them and took that as his exit line, looking for Trav again. Trav was talking to Heath, his drill sergeant's face compressed into those lines that meant he was being earnest.

Which was always.

Mackey paused to watch him, liking the way his shoulders stayed square and he didn't break eye contact. He had nice eyes—brown, with brown-red lashes, and Mackey had been surprised at the gentle, sneaking attraction that hit him at the oddest times these past weeks. There was something solid about Trav. Something *unyielding*. Even when he was making Mackey crazy with rules like "Everyone has to eat breakfast, dammit, even if it's only a protein shake!" and "Yes, there's a curfew until you prove to me you're not fourteen, and *yes*, I can and will impose penalties because thank God it was in your contract!" He was watching out for them. What Gerry had done with rewards and cajoling and gentleness, Trav did with lines in the sand and an army to make sure they didn't cross them. Gerry had been a nice guy, but Trav—Trav would fight them to make them take care of themselves. Mackey wasn't so young he couldn't appreciate the difference.

His musing on that tight military form was broken by an unfamiliar arm slinging around his shoulder and steering him to the corner of the room leading to the hallway.

"Mackey Sanders—it's a wonder we've never met."

"Speak for yourself!" Blake snapped. "Kid's not *my* responsibility. You're the ones all overwhelmed with this brotherhood shit. I'm just the hired hand, remember? He wouldn't hardly *talk* to me because I wasn't the almighty Grant fucking Adams."

"Who?" Trav asked. He wanted nothing more than to hold Mackey close until the roofies wore off and Mackey could fight him, argue about being held, tell Trav he could do it himself.

"Our first second lead," Jefferson muttered. "Kell's best friend. We grew up with him, but he knocked up his girlfriend right when we were signing on with Tailpipe."

"Oh," Trav said. The name meant nothing to him. Nothing. There would be a day when Trav would *yearn* for Grant Adams not to mean a goddamned thing.

TRAV HAD to relinquish Mackey into Kell's arms for a moment as they were getting out of the limo, and he resented the hell out of it. Kell held his brother easily, like maybe he'd been used to holding children once, and he didn't get grossed out at the smell, but Trav couldn't help it. Kell wasn't good enough to hold Mackey, and he couldn't change that.

He snatched that limp, unprotesting body back as soon as he could stand, and shouldered his way through the front doors of the ER. The nurse at the registration desk met him. Apparently Jefferson had done a good job at giving Mackey's info, including his insurance number and his birthday, but as the nurse nodded Trav to a waiting gurney, Trav caught her eye.

"I need to talk to the doctor," he said grimly. "Alone."

He didn't stay to hear the reaction from the rest of Mackey's people. He stretched Mackey out on the gurney and charged through the double doors with the doctor and nurses waiting for him. They got to a prepping area and Trav pulled the doctor aside, sacced up, and said what he needed to.

"He's been raped."

The doc jerked back and frowned. "How do you—"

"I found him. He's been drugged and raped—you'll see when you do the rape kit. This kid is in the limelight—we'll talk to the police, report to whomever you need to, but do *not* make a lot of noise, you hear me? When he wakes up, let me talk to him first—"

"And you are?"

Trav swallowed. "I'm the one person who knows his last HIV test was negative," he said, thinking about getting that little nugget when Mackey was in detox.

The doctor narrowed his eyes. "Aren't you a little old for this kid?"

"He's twenty," Trav said and tried not to be defensive. "And we're not lovers. I'm just saying that I know things his brothers don't—including that you need to do a rape kit. We can't change that I know that, but I can keep it from getting out to the rest of the world."

The doctor wasn't giving an inch. "A title, Mr....?"

"Ford. I'm his manager. And"—God, this was such a fucking misnomer—"and his friend."

The doctor nodded and turned around, dismissing Trav, and started giving orders. Trav thought he'd go back into the waiting room then, go back to the brothers, reassure them, tell them not to talk to anyone, but he paused.

Mackey was flat on his back as they cut off his clothes, and his full lips were blue in his pointed, white face.

Trav pulled out his phone and texted Jefferson instead.

*Stay put. He's going to be fine. Don't talk to anyone not in the band. This includes Blake. I'm getting backup to take you home and help you handle the press if it comes to that.*

*They're already here. Security kicked them out of the waiting room.*

Fuck.

Trav backed out of the curtained enclosure and speed-dialed Heath.

"Trav? What the hell is going on? Allison from PR says the whole band just disappeared—you were supposed to give a thank-you speech or—"

"Heath, just shut up and listen. We need a handler for the band at the hospital here, and we need everybody involved to sign nondisclosure agreements. We need a liaison with the police department, and we're going to need to give a press release. Are you ready?"

A stunned silence buzzed on the other end of the line. "Yeah, sure. Give it to me straight."

HEATH PERSONALLY did the announcing—after ten minutes on the phone with Trav, he said, "Look. I'll handle the press. You get a hold of yourself—Jesus, Trav, I actually saw you take a bullet with less freaking out!"

"He *trusted* me!" Trav snapped, wishing he had a wall to pound. "He *trusted* me, and I fucked him over."

Heath's voice was almost gentle. "No, Travis. He trusted you and you kept it from being worse. You found him before he could be flashed all over the press, passed out in an alleyway."

Trav let out a horrible sound, a sound he didn't even want to own as his. "Heath... man, we've got to go to the cops ourselves. I can't have his... this violation smeared all over the fucking press. Whatever you've got to do to keep this shit Mackey's and my secret—"

"What about his brothers?" Heath asked doubtfully. "They're pretty close, aren't they?"

*Only bi when high.*

"Yeah. They're claustrophobically close. We need to give him some fucking privacy or he's going to come unglued."

Heath grunted. "Yeah. Okay. I'll contact the cops—the doc probably already has the rape crisis officer on his way. You handle Mackey and the boys. I'll send an assistant there to get them to the hotel when they're ready to leave, okay?"

Trav tried not to sound as upset as he felt. "Thanks. I appreciate it." Then he grimaced. "And Heath? Man, you're gonna have a helluva cleaning bill for the limo."

Heath's laughter came from a dark place. "You think I don't know *exactly* how much it costs to get vomit out of a limo? Don't worry about it, Trav. Man... these kids. *This* kid. Just keep him from self-destructing, okay? Just... just keep him together. It's...."

"It's, like, moral," Trav said, feeling stupid and naïve but feeling right too. "It's not... not *moral* to just fucking leave them on their own."

"Almost poetic." Trav could hear top-priced scotch hitting a crystal tumbler even as Heath spoke. Well, he was going to need it.

"You're the one who put me in a box with rock stars," Trav said bitterly. He thought about those quiet moments in the middle of the night, watching Mackey in his underwear assembling beauty with an acoustic guitar and cheap spiral notebooks. "What did you expect?"

"Not this," Heath sighed. "I'm so sorry about this."

"Me too."

There wasn't much else to say about that, so Trav hung up and watched some more as the doctors worked on Mackey.


TRAV AND Jefferson watched the announcement from Mackey's bedside later that evening. Mackey was still out of it—whatever had been mixed with the roofie to make it knock him out that quickly had been bad shit, and it had *not* played nice with the Rohypnol.

The doctor told Trav privately that if Mackey hadn't been brought in, he might have stopped breathing within hours of passing out.

"He's just so small," the doctor said, shaking his head. "And I take it he just got out of detox? He had very little fat reserves and no way to metabolize what was in his system."

Trav swallowed, and the word "rehab" assumed epic proportions in his head, lit with gold, neon, and sparklers. Mackey's body couldn't have taken much more of what he'd been dishing out. This thing with the Rohypnol? That was just icing on the "Mackey needs to clean up his act" cake.

"I hear you," Trav said, his voice sounding unfamiliar, his throat feeling like a cat box, full of sand and gravel and shit.

"And thankfully, that's all he'll need to worry about," the doctor said clearly. "The specimen we collected was negative for HIV."

Trav had been fighting the urge for the past five hours, and fighting it so successfully he barely recognized what it was until he lost. His eyes filled up and he blinked hard, willing himself to get his act together.

"That's good," he said. AZT was a bitch. Heath had gotten bitten once by a perpetrator who'd gotten away. Trav had been in the infirmary, recovering from a gunshot to the shoulder, and he and Heath had deepened their lifelong attachment to each other playing chess between Heath's bouts of violent vomiting. *Mackey, thank God, there's your fucking break.*

The doctor told them he wanted two days' observation, and Trav said he'd be there for it. Heath's promised assistant showed up, a dapper, crisp woman in her fifties named Debra, with short gray-blonde hair and cheekbones that spoke of an early career modeling. Jefferson elected to stay after a hug from Shelia and one from Stevie. Debra rounded everybody else up into a new town car, complete with a promise to stop somewhere to eat on their way to the hotel.

Trav's last thought of the bunch of them was to remind them they were moving their shit to the new (and newly furnished) house the next day, so they should pack. He quietly gave Debra permission to pack his stuff, and to gather Mackey's as well.

"He shouldn't have anything untoward," he said, grimacing. "We got rid of his paraphernalia two weeks ago." Besides lubed condoms, there shouldn't be a damned thing that would make her blush, and given what she did for a living, Trav was pretty sure the lubed condoms were tame. "If you could have some clothes sent over when Jefferson needs picking up—jeans, underwear, shower shoes, a clean button down, clean T-shirt—I'd sure love to shower and change."

Debra nodded briskly, not batting an eyelash. Trav wondered if she'd raised a football team or something, because the woman had a poker face that would put most MPs to shame.

She left and Trav was alone with Jefferson, leaning back in the hospital chairs and scanning the (many) news channels for Heath's press release. Mackey was positioned on his side, one arm stretched out over his head, the other hand tucked under his cheek, like a baby after prayers. His hair fell in his pale face, and every so often, he shivered. Trav pulled up the covers as close to his neck as he could.

Jefferson played on his phone for a while. When he broke the silence, Trav was actually relieved. It felt like his entire being had been focused on watching Mackey's thin chest move up and down.

"Mr. Ford?"

"Yeah?"

They were whispering.

"Why didn't they turn him on his back?"

Trav took a deep breath and looked at Jefferson. Was it an idle question? Did he suspect?

Jefferson was looking directly at Trav, his blue eyes open, gnawing on his lip with slightly prominent teeth. He was probably the plainest of the boys—he and Stevie tying for least attractive—with his round face and completely average cheekbones and chin.

But those eyes were direct and honest.

Trav couldn't lie to those eyes, and he'd lied to a lot of criminals and bureaucrats in his day.

"Why do you think?" he asked, trying not to be bitter.

Jefferson swallowed hard and took a deep breath. "What's Mackey going to say about that when he wakes up?"

"I don't know. What are *you* going to say?"

Jefferson laughed softly and closed his eyes. He leaned forward and rested his weight on his elbows. "Me and Stevie, we're damned good at not talking, yeah? We're like a... a cul de sac, you know? Nothing goes straight through. All the cars and the houses and the people just sort of get caught at the end. That's me and Stevie with secrets. We tell each other, and that's as far as it goes. It's the telling each *other* that matters."

Trav closed his eyes, then opened them. "What about Shelia?" he asked. This seemed the time for it.

Jefferson's smile grew sweet. "She's getting to be our other house, you know? Like every cul de sac has three? But me and Stevie, we got some secrets older'n her, and she knows it."

"Secrets like what?" Trav asked, suddenly hungry for them. What made these boys? What secrets forged them, their loyalty and indifference toward each other? What made a Mackey James Sanders?

And that sweet smile shuttered. "Take your pick, Mr. Ford. I can tell you why Mackey don't like Blake and who kept Mackey supplied with coke. I can tell you why Mackey didn't go home for Christmas last year and why the whole family thinks Stevie and I are related. I can tell you why Stevie's mom ain't talked to us since we left home and why Stevie's dad wants us to come back real fuckin' soon. But I wanna know what happened to my brother, so you better pick a good question."

Trav took a short breath and then a longer one. "So much to choose from," he muttered. Then: "Okay. I'll tell you what happened to Mackey, and you tell me which thing I most need to hear."

"Fair enough," Jefferson said calmly.

Trav closed his eyes and said it in his head. He'd had to tell Banneker's parents that their son had killed himself. This moment should not be that hard.

"Your brother was drugged—*hard*—and raped in an alleyway. The rapist left DNA—and was, blessedly, HIV negative."

Jefferson nodded. "That's a motherfucker. You gonna tell Kell?"

Trav didn't even think about it. "Nope."

"Good. Kell does his best, but he's not real bright. Until Mackey makes nice with Blake, he ain't gonna listen much."

Okay, all those questions. Now was his chance. "Why doesn't Mackey like Blake?"

Jefferson grimaced. "'Cause he ain't Grant. That was a weak try, Mr. Ford. I coulda told you all sorts of stuff."

Trav smiled in spite of himself. "I'll just have to ask Mackey himself," he said softly. His hand, which had been resting on the bed near Mackey's head, suddenly twitched all on its own, and he used the movement as an excuse to push Mackey's hair out of his eyes.

It occurred to him that Mackey wasn't the only one with painful secrets.

He looked up at Jefferson, suddenly curious. "So *are* you and Stevie related?"

Jefferson grinned delightedly. "There ain't a state in the union that wouldn't let us marry, if we were a boy and a girl."

Trav snorted, amused. "That's not saying much. Most states will let first cousins marry."

Jefferson kept grinning and nodded. "Yup. That there is true."

Trav suspected he was being played. "I'll bet a thousand people have asked you and you haven't given any of them a straight answer."

That playful grin on those crooked teeth was as innocent as a sociopath's. "You'd win that bet, Mr. Ford. Kell and Grant came closest. It's the name thing, you see? All us boys have our daddy's last names as our first names?"

Trav's jaw dropped. "I had not heard that!"

Jefferson shook his head in disgust. "Everybody's heard that. It's why Mackey's name is really McKay."

Oh. Well, hell. "I had not heard that either," Trav said, feeling stupid.

Obviously Jefferson felt the same way. "You ain't done your homework, that's all. But Kell and Grant sat Stevie down alone and asked him if anyone in his family had the last name of Jefferson."

Trav narrowed his eyes. It was a child's game, and the boys had played it to perfection. "Does somebody *outside* his family, who is still related by *blood*, like a half brother or a bastard brother or someone born out of wedlock, have the last name of Jefferson?" he asked, grimly amused.

There was no grimness in Jefferson's amusement. "You figured that out right off, Mr. Ford—you 'bout got the whole town beat!"

Mackey's hair was rough under his fingers, but Trav was okay with that. He'd let himself be distracted. "Well, no offense, Jefferson, but I've talked to Mackey, and that doesn't sound hard to do."

That fast, Jefferson was serious and sober. Trav felt bad. The boy—and Trav couldn't delude himself anymore, they were *all* boys—had been proud of himself for a moment, happy and free. One mention of their hometown and all that went away.

"Wasn't hard to fool the town at all, Mr. Ford. Fool them about knowing who your daddy was, about so and so's mom fooling around and so and so's dad wanting to touch your ass when you didn't want it touched. Fool them like Mackey did in a thousand different ways—wasn't a hard place to fool. But it's a damned hard place to get out of your head."

Trav nodded. "Yeah. I believe it. Well, Mackey's going to have to leave some of that stuff behind if he wants to move on with his life, you know?"

Jefferson snorted. "You still don't know shit. But you asked more questions in half an hour than Gerry did in a year. You might not be a total asshole."

Trav had nothing to say to that, but that was okay because in that moment, Heath's announcement came on the television.

Trav turned the volume up, and Trav's oldest friend announced to the whole world that the person responsible for Mackey's aggravated assault (as the police were calling it to the press) had been captured. Trav turned down the television and sighed.

"What's that mean?" Jefferson asked, subdued and not nearly as cocky as he'd just been.

"It means Mackey's going to have to make a decision when he wakes up."

"What's that?"

Oh, this was such a shitty choice. "It means he can tell the cops to press for assault and maybe get two years from it, or it means he can tell the cops he was raped and this Charleston Klum can get fifteen or twenty years. But it's going to have to be Mackey's call."

"I'm picking the thing that has me move the least," Mackey slurred.

Trav turned to him, relief washing his body cold. "You little shit—how long have you been awake?"

"I heard, like… your last sentence."

"Oh. That's bad." Trav didn't have any words for how bad that was. "I… I'm so—"

"How come I don't remember?"

"You were drugged out of your tiny little body, Mackey. I bet your head aches like—"

"Like it was popped off my tiny little body and used for soccer."

Trav laughed helplessly, because it was a funny image and because the tightness in his chest, in his stomach, was so overwhelming that if he didn't laugh soon, he'd throw up or forget to breathe or both.

"Yeah," Trav said when he could talk. "Yeah. Sorry about that."

Mackey grunted. "Jefferson?"

"Yeah, Mackey?"

"Go away."

Jefferson squeezed Mackey's shoulder, then Trav's, and turned around to leave the room. "I'll call that Debra person—she'll send the car for me."

Trav pulled up a chair and sat eye level with Mackey so he didn't have to sit up.

Mackey squinted at him. "I don't want to think about it," Mackey murmured. "I feel like shit and I don't want to think about it. How bad is that? How bad is that gonna fuck me up?"

Trav swallowed. He'd once imprisoned a woman who had taken out five guys in her platoon with her weapon. Only two of them were responsible for assaulting her repeatedly, but by the time she picked up the gun and released the safety, that hadn't mattered.

"Really fucking bad, Mackey. I got no words for how bad that'll fuck you up."

Mackey whimpered. "I got... man, how do people deal with all that shit in their head? I got all this shit in my head and I can only write so many songs—how do I deal with all this crap?"

He closed his eyes then, and helpless tears slid through the creases. Trav stroked his hair again, because someone should. Someone should comfort him. It was all Trav had.

"You go to rehab," Trav said, his voice shaking with conviction.

"I didn't take anything!" Mackey struggled to sit up and then whined in pain and fell back down. The IV tube in his arm bled a little.

Trav flicked him gently on the forehead. "I know you didn't," Trav snapped, hating everything about life at this moment, including Mackey. "But you took the damned beer from a stranger, and that left you open. And your body was stripped thin from detoxing two weeks ago, and that made it worse. And if you and me hadn't made eye contact about five seconds before that guy got to you, you would have laid in an alleyway, choking on your own goddamned vomit, for an *hour*, because your band would have thought you went somewhere to get high and get laid. You *need* it, Mackey. You talk to the doctors about all this shit in your head, all the shit that made you get high, all the shit that's in there now. You talk to them and you yell at them and they tell you the things that help make it better—"

"Oh, how would you know?" Mackey demanded, his voice thick. "How would you know? How *excited* would you be to have your insides all spread out and messy? Isn't it bad enough the whole world's got a microscope up my ass right now as it is?"

Trav snarled. God, he was trying to *help*! "How would I know? Do you think I came back from the Middle East all happy fine?"

"I didn't know you'd been there," Mackey said, his lower jaw still thrust out. "How in the fuck would I know you've been there? Two weeks, and it's all 'Mackey, go here,' and 'you need to eat' and 'don't be a dick to Blake.' I don't even know what Trav stands for, unless it's 'cause you travel all the time, and I doubt you got parents, 'cause I think you were named for a goddamned truck!"

Trav laughed a little, but his hand never ceased that gentle motion. "Yeah, well, I get that too." Hell—he'd buy a Ford Trav, right? Sounded like a solid SUV. "It's short for Travis. My parents live in upstate New York in a nice suburb, and they both teach, so they don't have too much money. I joined the military right out of high school to pay for college, and I joined the MPs for six years out of eight because I liked the idea of being a badass and my peers pissed me off. How's that? Do you need a bigger résumé than that?"

"Yes," Mackey mumbled, "but not now. My head hurts. You saw a shrink?"

Trav sighed and paused his stroking of Mackey's hair. "I've seen bad shit," he said simply. "Heinously bad shit, Mackey. And I was in the military during Don't Ask, Don't Tell, and I didn't have a soul I could share that with." Trav grunted, because the memory hurt. "Not even a one-night stand, in case I got caught."

Mackey made an indeterminate sound in his throat. "Keep doing that thing with my hair," he said after a minute, and Trav resumed. "What made you leave? You like being a badass. I can tell."

Oh Lord. Trav wasn't going to tell this story—he wasn't. But looking at Mackey, curled on his side, he realized he'd seen this kid naked and bleeding—and Mackey hadn't seen any part of Trav.

"I do," Trav said quietly after a moment. "I like it when life makes simple patterns and I can understand them. But...." He stood and stretched and sat down again—and resumed touching Mackey intimately, gently, because Mackey needed it.

"But what?" Mackey murmured, obviously determined that Trav didn't get to delay the game.

"I was lonely," he confessed—a thing he hadn't even confessed to Terry. "A bunch of us—Heath included, and Heath knew, because he's smart and knew I never looked at girl porn—were on leave. We were walking down this street in Paris—and it's a beautiful city. All the things they have in those pictures and posters? Yeah. It really is like that in places. So we're walking down this little street with cafés and bistros and flower vendors, and there's this kid...." Trav examined the memory for a moment so he could get it right. "He was drawing chalk pictures on the sidewalk—probably about your age, you know? But I was only twenty-six, so it was okay. But he was pretty—so pretty. He had big brown eyes and curly brown hair and these full lips—"

"Stop it, Trav, you're giving me a woody." Mackey's voice dripped with irony.

Trav tousled his hair gently. "Yeah, well, I think you're just sort of naturally horny," he said, knowing sex was the last thing on Mackey's mind. "But all my buddies were going to get laid, and I was going to—I don't know. Sleep in the hotel. And this kid and I—you ever make eye contact with a stranger and know it'll be phenomenal?"

Again that self-deprecating laugh. "Man, I think that's the only kind of sex I've had for the last year."

"Has it been?" Trav asked, wanting him to be honest.

"Has it been what?"

"Phenomenal?"

Mackey pulled in a deep breath and let it out slowly, like sand trickling off a table. "No," he admitted after a moment. "It's sort of sucked. I mean, I used to think sex was... never mind. Sex sucks when you're high. You can barely remember it and you don't give a shit who you're with. Go on with your story."

"This would have been phenomenal," Trav said. He still knew it in his bones. "Whatever he saw, he wanted me. And I... I nodded to him and just walked on by. Because I wasn't supposed to be gay in the Army."

"That sucks a whole lot," Mackey mumbled. "And that's why you quit?"

"Well, it took two more years—I had to let my tour run out. But yeah. And when I got out, well, living in the States was hard. My family believes in shrinks—"

"Rich and educated, right?" Mackey asked, and since there wasn't any censure in his voice, Trav answered him.

"Middle-class—not enough money to pay for college, but lots of expectations that we'd make it through."

Mackey laughed a little. "Yeah. I hear you. Took me a while, you know?" It sounded like he was growing tired.

"To what?"

"To realize that rich wasn't just the way you spent money, it was the way you think."

That had never occurred to Trav before he started doing the books for and management of Mackey's band. "Yes—well, I'm starting to think you're right." He sighed and made himself more comfortable, wiggling back into the chair. He couldn't stroke Mackey's hair from this angle, but he kept his hand there, fingertips touching his head. He felt weary deep in his bones, and he figured he was going to fall asleep in this uncomfortable hospital chair. Well, Mackey was okay, so he didn't mind.

"So that was it? You saw a guy you couldn't have—"

"I saw a guy I might have loved." Might haves. Painful might haves—Terry was becoming one of those. Trav hadn't seen Mackey for five minutes, and he'd panicked. But he and Terry had been split up for almost a month, and it hadn't occurred to him that Terry wouldn't be where Trav had left him. Yeah—Trav hadn't learned much from that encounter in Paris, had he? "Anyway, I realized I wanted that for myself. I wanted to love. I mean"— Trav's laugh rasped in his throat, bit into his tissues, poisoned his bones—"I'm not very *good* at it. I've had some really false starts, but I want the job and lover and the home. It's what people get when they live well, you know?"

Mackey didn't say anything, and Trav wondered if he'd fallen asleep. Then Mackey pulled both of his hands under his chin, being careful of the IV needle. "What's that have to do with rehab?" he asked when he was comfortable.

Trav sighed. "I had to be honest with myself about what I wanted before I could get it. You want drugs, Mackey, and you can't let yourself have them. You need to be honest with yourself about why you want them, and that second part might be easier."

Mackey made a sour sort of gurgle. "I'll think of a good argument for this tomorrow," he said. That sounded pretty wise. "Heath said they had the guy in custody— can they get him for drugging me without the whole...." Mackey's voice skewed and clattered. He didn't want to say it. Trav didn't blame him.

"I'll talk to the police tomorrow," he said gently. "I don't know why he targeted you—"

"'Cause I'm easy ass. Everyone knows that." God—no apology, just frank admission. Trav's heart hurt even more.

"Well, you don't have to be," Trav muttered. "But that's another discussion. We don't have to mention the rape, to the press or anyone else. But you should know…." Oh hell. Trav had seen court cases destroy as many victims as perpetrators. As an MP, he'd always thought the cost was worth it, but here, in this hospital room with a kid whose whole life had been a case of coming up from behind, he wasn't sure. But Mackey wasn't a child—hadn't Trav maintained that from the beginning? He was old enough to make his own decisions.

"He'll get less time," Mackey grunted. "Yeah, well, more power to him. Can we get a restraining order? If he comes anywhere near us, you can kill him?"

Trav's shoulders shook. "I may do that without court approval," he said, not entirely sure he was kidding. "You're rambling, Mackey. Now go to sleep and think about what I said, okay?"

"'Bout what? You talked a lot."

Well, he had. "About rehab. I want you to take care of yourself."

Mackey closed those big gray eyes and yawned into his hands. "Thank you for the story. The one about the boy, in Paris. It was pretty. Like a song."

A few moments later, his breathing changed, and Trav was left in the hospital room feeling wrung out. *So much to talk about, Mackey. So much you got wrong.* But who was Trav to talk? Trav had let him down too. Trav was about to room with his band because he was so fucking lost. Who did that? Sure as shit, *Debra* wasn't going to sleep in the hotel room or the new house when that came around. Debra probably had her own home and her own spouse and a bunch of boys who played on the football team or something, but Trav?

Trav was staying right here, next to Mackey, next to his brothers and his band.

Because apparently that was where Trav belonged.


TRAV FELL asleep just after Mackey, leaning his head on the mattress.

He awakened just a few inches from Mackey, close enough to smell his sweat and the faint patchouli of his body wash and the antiseptics from the cleaning the hospital had given him. Mackey still slept, and Trav had spent moments just looking at his small, peaked face, the pointed cheekbones, the slight overbite, the slightly darker freckle that rode the crooked bridge of his nose.

Trav couldn't explain the surge of protectiveness, of reluctant admiration, that knotted his stomach when he watched Mackey sleep. He was defenseless like this, every bit of sarcasm, sass, and fire shuttered behind closed eyes. Trav *had* to protect him when he slept—who else would? So far the world had done a *stunningly* poor job of taking care of Mackey Sanders. Kell had Blake. Stevie and Jefferson had apparently always had each other. But Mackey?

Mackey couldn't even protect himself from himself, although God knew he tried.

For that vulnerable moment between sleeping and waking, Trav hadn't been able to protect himself from Mackey either.

Attraction, unwanted and uncomfortable, wormed its way into Trav's consciousness and settled in his gut. It left a host of uncomfortable realizations behind it.

*That* was when Trav sat up, used the bathroom, splashed water on his face, and tried to scare up some breakfast in the cafeteria.

He couldn't. Not the breakfast—he had a piece of fruit and some milk. No, it was the attraction he couldn't do. He would *not* acknowledge it. Impossible. This kid depended on him. Trav couldn't let him down.

He came back into the room and Mackey was sitting up eating eggs, the blanket loosely draped over his bare legs. Trav could make out one of those big donut pillows under his hips, and he sighed.

"Yeah," Mackey muttered. "Hiding this shit is gonna be hard."

"You know," Trav said, feeling like a dog with a bone, "there's a place where people are really fucking anonymous, and where you could heal your body and your soul."

Mackey glared at him. "Rehab," he muttered. "Yeah, yeah, yeah. All roads lead to rehab. I'm hearing you."

"Do you hear me enough to go from here to rehab without passing go?"

Mackey thought about it and munched on some toast while his eggs and sausage congealed on the plate. Trav looked at the food getting ready to be wasted and sighed.

"Will you think about it more if I go get you a donut?"

Mackey looked up and just emanated sunshine. "Really? They have donuts? You'd get me one? Really?"

Trav swallowed hard. "Yeah, Mackey. I'll go get you a couple—any preferences?"

His smile widened, pushing his cheeks up until his eyes squinted. Trav could see his overbite, and the crowding on the bottom, and the pure vulpine beauty of his features. "Apple fritters," Mackey said, nodding. "Not pastries or danishes but fritters—do they have those?"

"I'm pretty sure—and if they don't, I'll go down the block, so I might be a few, but I'll be back."

That smile, sunshiny and surreal, stayed in place. "That's awesome, Trav. Thanks!"

Trav nodded. He had to get the hell out of there, because he was suddenly not comfortable in his own skin. He tried to remember Terry, a grown-up, sitting across from him and eating cereal in his pajama bottoms and socks, but he couldn't. There was too much sunshine in his eyes to see anything but Mackey.

"You're welcome," Trav said and practically bolted through the door. He had a sudden thought when his hand hit the frame, though, and he turned around. "Just, uhm, don't go anywhere, okay?"

Mackey rolled his eyes. "My ass fuckin' hurts, Trav. Where'm I gonna go?"

Great. There was some cold water right there.

"Yeah. Yeah—I'll be back."

He actually *did* have to go to the donut shop down the block, and he came back with a dozen since he knew Mackey's brothers would be by later. Jefferson—apparently the Trav/Outbreak Monkey liaison—texted telling Trav they'd be by to visit around noon. Trav asked for him to bring some of Mackey's clothes—new ones, he specified, because he was tired of seeing Mackey ignore the new clothes on his own and go for the stuff that

Kell had probably worn in the ninth grade—and then asked if Kell or Blake suspected the rape. He didn't ask if Stevie or Shelia knew—he was going to assume they did.

*No. But Blake is stoned already. Maybe him and Mackey should be roomies in rehab.*

Trav grimly thought he'd have a look at Blake's contract and see if he could force that issue. For one thing, putting Mackey and Blake in the same room for some deep soul-searching might be a way to keep Blake in the music business. Trav was pretty sure that without the family support the Sanders boys had, Blake wouldn't last long if they kicked him out.

Trav refused to analyze his lack of regret at that thought—why losing Blake as lead guitarist didn't pluck a single guilt string while having Mackey descend into the pit Trav had just pulled him out of annihilated him.

When he got back, Heath was there, carrying a suit bag for Trav and a knapsack for Mackey.

"God, did you just buy me clothes?" Trav asked. He set the pink donut box down so he could take the bag from Heath. The price tag still dangled from the hanger.

"How many old friends from the service do you think I have?" Heath muttered. "Now do you have a place you can clean up? Debra sent you a kit last night, but the nurse said you were too out of it to put on your jammies and brush your teeth. I can't believe you went out like that. You look homeless."

Trav groaned. He didn't even want to look—he was pretty sure Heath was being nice.

"*Animaniacs*," Mackey said, clearly delighted as he opened the knapsack and took out a brand new pair of pj's. "Fuckin' awesome! I ain't seen these guys since I was a kid!" He took the pajamas from Heath and swung his legs around to stand up. A look of discomfort crossed his face, and he settled back up on the bed. "I'll change into these after I eat my apple fritters," he said, like he was fooling anyone. "Trav can help me into 'em—I'm feeling sort of weak."

Trav met his eyes then, and the world stuttered. Weak, sore, and vulnerable. Trav nodded. Yeah, he understood. "Yeah, okay, Mackey. Let's hear what Heath has to say while you eat, okay?"

What Heath had to say reflected pretty well on the LAPD, actually. For one thing, the recording studio had security cameras everywhere. The cops had a great shot of this Charleston guy drugging Mackey's drink and another of him guiding an obviously out-of-it Mackey into the hallway. There weren't any pictures from the outside of the building, but that didn't matter—they had the guy's DNA, and that was all they had to say before he'd called lawyer and the lawyer called deal.

"What's the deal?" Trav asked grimly.

Heath looked at them both. "The deal is, you come down and sign as Mackey's proxy—it's in the contract you can do that for just such emergencies, so don't worry, all real. And this guy goes in for three years, aggravated assault, and nobody breathes the rape charge—not him, not his lawyer, not anybody. But we've got his DNA on file—if he does it again, we've got him dead to rights."

Mackey exhaled unhappily. He put his half-eaten apple fritter down on the little portable table. Trav wanted to sit there and feed it to him, bite by bite. "God. I hate that thought," he muttered. "I hate it, like I'm a big fucking coward, taking the back door out." He laughed grimly at his own pun. "Man, what kind of waste of fucking skin am I, I can't fight on—"

"Shut up," Trav said gruffly. "Eat your fucking donut and thank God the justice system runs on wheels greased with money. Mackey, I've seen these trials, you understand? I've seen women up on the stand facing down their whole fucking platoon— and neither of the lawyers are on their side. The whole world wants them to think the worst of themselves, and by the end of the trial? They do. If you were in prime fighting shape? I'd say go for it. If you'd already come out to the press, were clean and sober? Yeah. You cry rape and get this guy hanged for a scumbag. But right now they're going to try the victim, and Mackey, I know you're innocent, but—"

"You what?" Mackey said, staring at him.

"I know you're innocent. Heath knows you're innocent. We know you were on the wagon and trying but—"

"You know? You believe me? You...." Mackey floundered. His mouth opened and closed for a minute, and then he pulled a piece of his apple fritter off and ate it. "Fucking imagine that. Yeah, fine. Pep talk over. Bored now. Go put on your suit, Mr. Ford—you gotta look all shiny and shit."

Trav stared at him. "You're giving me orders?"

"Well, you've got barf on your shoes. I didn't want to say anything, but you might want to wash that off."

Trav fought the temptation to smack him. "Yeah, McKay, I'll do that."

"Yeah, Travis, you just fucking go ahead." Mackey looked at him sideways and stuck his tongue out to lick some sugar glaze from the corner of his lips. He was being a shit on purpose, Trav knew that, but that tongue—that was innocent provocation right there. Trav was too strung out to be provoked.

"Back in a minute," he muttered, and Heath followed him out.

"He doing okay?" Heath asked, darting a worried gaze into the hospital room. Mackey crammed the last of the fritter down his gullet and followed it up with a little carton of milk he must have kept from breakfast.

"Mackey?" Trav asked sourly. "Someone could nuke SoCal and Mackey would come back, glowing with radiation, with super spider powers, and get on the stage and sing."

Heath laughed and shook his head. "Those kids are tough," he said, his voice full of wonder. "Man, they grew up in a two-bedroom apartment, can you believe that bullshit?"

Trav grimaced. "It makes more and more sense to me every time I talk to him. So I get to go sign and this guy goes away. That fast?"

Heath shrugged. "Mackey's going to rehab after this?"

"Says so. Why?"

Heath had a wide, almost florid face. In another ten years he was going to *look* like the fat-cat record producer—all he'd need was a trophy wife and a three-olive martini. The almost paternal concern might have seemed smarmy and self-serving, except Trav had known Heath for a while, and he was anything but. He'd once carried a kid across twenty miles of desert, on his back, to get him to medical care, while wounded. Trav had carried the kid's wounded sister, who had been tinier but had taken a shine to Trav. They'd spent the entire forced march singing rock and roll, telling the kids about the video games the soldiers would let them play when they got to the hospital. Heath, with his family connections, had come through with a couple for the kids to keep.

That was Heath. He liked having money—liked spending it—and didn't understand people who might not have had it growing up. But that didn't mean he didn't want to share.

"Because I saw the tape," Heath said gently. "He was on the verge of a five-star freak-out, and then he spotted you and calmed down a little. And then Charleston Klum gave him a beer, and everyone watched him take that beer and give thanks to a merciful god. If that kid doesn't go through a program, he's going to go home in a box."

Augh! "I knew that," Trav muttered. He'd known that. He'd *known* that.

"Well, yeah. But now you can fix it."

"You're giving me too much credit," Trav muttered. "Stay with him until I get back."

And then he went to change.

# Going Back to Rehab

TWO DAYS after Trav went in to sign paperwork, the limo came to take Mackey from the hospital to rehab. Trav sat with him, like he'd sat with him through most of the time in the hospital, and Mackey was a little disgusted. It wasn't like he was going to take off, was it?

Okay, well, yeah, he'd thought about it, but seriously—in the hospital, they were giving him pain meds. Why would he leave that?

But sure enough, the pain meds were a thing of the past by the time he got gingerly into the limo (and onto the waiting donut pillow Trav had set down for him) and discovered he wasn't the only one going to rehab.

"What in the fuck is *he* doing here?" Mackey snarled. Blake flipped him off from the other end of the car. His suitcases were next to him, along with Mackey's, and suddenly Mackey laughed. "Heh, heh—did your last blow, huh, Blake?"

"I don't even want to fucking talk about it. Do you know I've got a *sobriety* clause in my contract?"

Mackey blinked and stared at Trav, who was waiting for him to get in.

"I don't got one of those," he said, sliding next to him. My, that man looked mighty fine in his suit. Of course, Mackey was starting to think Trav looked mighty fine in anything. He'd looked mighty fine in khakis and a polo shirt the last time Mackey had seen him, and that was usually the least attractive getup in the history of anybody, as far as Mackey was concerned. Mackey moved restively, grateful for the stupid donut pillow, and sighed inwardly. The last thing Trav needed was a fuckup like Mackey hanging on his pockets.

"Nope," Trav said in response to his question. He looked up from his laptop and gave Mackey a grin that was all teeth. "We assumed *you'd* be a good boy, McKay, and go on your own."

"Which one of my stinking brothers told you McKay was my name? I want to kick him in the 'nads."

"How come I didn't know that?" Blake asked, surprised. "Man, I lived with you people for a fucking year. I bought your coke, I ate your shit—"

"You got on the party bus and you and my brother did *everybody's* drugs," Mackey snapped, unsettled again. "Man, why you gotta get mad at me? You and Kell hung out for a year. You had a grand ol' time. Now we both gotta clean up our shit or that goes away. It's a job like anything else, Blake. You don't pull your weight, you get fired."

"Yeah, well, I don't see anyone threatening to fire you. Poor little Mackey Sanders—"

"He writes the songs, moron," Trav said from behind his computer screen. He looked up. "And I think maybe whatever you two have against each other needs to get worked out in rehab. That's why you're going together."

Mackey pouted and crossed his arms. "Did you bring my sunglasses?" he whined, obnoxious and not particularly caring. "My head feels like a giant split it like a melon with a mace!"

Trav laughed a little, because he got that shit, and Blake rolled his eyes.

"You couldn't just say 'headache,' could you, Mackey?" Blake snapped, but it was an empty sally, and everyone in the limo knew it.

Trav handed him sunglasses—obviously *Trav's* sunglasses—and Mackey sighed.

"Naw, Trav, I won't take your shit from you so I can be a diva. Just—"

"Take them, Mackey. I'll get more. Now before we get there, I need you guys to touch the screen here, and here, and here—"

They spent the next twenty minutes signing paperwork. Mackey was honestly surprised when the limo pulled up in front of the now familiar beautiful garden grounds with the giant flower bushes and the fountains and the building that looked like a retirement home for active seniors.

The limo stopped there, idling, and Mackey stared moodily outside while waiting for the driver to let him out.

"You'll make it happen this time," Trav said, but he sounded more hopeful than sure.

Mackey grimaced. "I only need to make it stick once, right?" he asked, trying to sound insouciant and breezy.

Trav's gentle hand on his shoulder made him want to cry. "That's right, Mackey. Only once."

"Speak for yourself," Blake said. "I plan to get my blood replaced like Keith Richards until I'm too old to go on stage."

Mackey would have bitten his head off, but he sounded nervous too—and besides, it was funny.

"Yeah, just remember that having the blood of an eighteen-year-old girl *in* you isn't the same thing as being inside an eighteen-year-old girl," Mackey returned, and he could tell by Blake's reluctant snicker that it was the right thing to say. Well, good. As much as Blake got on Mackey's nerves, Kell seemed to like him, and God, wouldn't it be a pain in the ass to have to train up another lead guitarist. Mackey fought a shudder. No. No more new lead guitarists. Trav was right. He'd have to make his peace with Blake and make it stick, and this was the place to do it.

Mackey was reaching in to grab the suitcases when his phone buzzed. He set the cases down and leaned against the limo to answer while the driver got a porter from the rehab place.

*The press says you got hurt. Kell says you're going to rehab. I'm sorry.*

Grant. Oh God. Mackey had gotten the phone the day after they'd signed, and sometime in the past year, Kell had passed Mackey's number on. For the most part, Grant left him alone. In fact, this made three texts total.

*Wish me well, McKay—I'm married* had been the first one. He'd gotten it the morning before his first one-night stand.

*Her name is Katy, after McKay. Don't hate me—I had to have a memory of you* had been the second, accompanied by a picture of his baby girl. Mackey had saved the picture, but he hadn't replied.

But this one—this one he had to answer.

*Don't be. You're not the dumbass with the pills.*

*Don't let me off the hook that easy, McKay. I thought I was doing you a favor.*

Oh God. Oh, Grant—don't do this.

*God save me from dumbasses doing me favors. I gotta go.*

He pulled Trav's sunglasses over his eyes and pushed off of the car with a grunt.

"Was that your mom?" Trav asked, squinting at him perceptively in the California smog glare.

Mackey grunted again and shook his head. "She called this morning—saw the press release." Mackey had calmed her down—as, apparently, Kell had been unable to. "I told her I was going to a... whatstheword?" God, his brain had seized up, a rictus of remembered pain, as soon as he'd seen Grant's text. "Retreat. Yeah. I'm going on a 'restorative retreat.' Some bullshit. Fuckin' LA—it's like shrink city here, you know that, right? The shrinks have shrinks who have shrinks who have kids who buy our records and tell us they're just as fucked-up as me and my brothers are. It's insane."

He rambled—he knew that. He did it on purpose, because letting his brain just spew forth with whatthefuckever was an easy way to dodge the hard shit.

Apparently cutting through whatthefuckever was Trav's best talent. "So if that wasn't your mom, who the hell was it?"

Mackey glared at him through the glasses. Nosy fucker. "The ghost of Shannon Hoon. Whatsit to ya?"

Trav narrowed his eyes, and Mackey took perverse pleasure in the thought that Trav was squinting against the sun because Mackey was wearing his sunglasses.

"Whoever it was made you look like you wanted a fucking Xanax, Mackey. Tell me who it was so I can block the call, or I'm taking your goddamned phone. I'm not shoving you into rehab so you can get cozy with your dealers all over again."

Mackey's throat shriveled up. "You've met my dealers," he said, shoving the phone at Trav and grabbing his suitcase. "One of them is dead and the other's going to rehab with me. Happy now?"

"No," Trav said shortly. He took two steps forward and shoved Mackey's phone in the back pocket of his jeans. "Here. Keep your damned phone. Text me if you need anything. And whoever that was who texted you—man, stay away from them. That look on your face just now—that was a bad thing."

Mackey stayed still as Trav pulled his hands away from his hips. For a moment under the orange sky, everything stopped—the wind, the birds, the whirr of the engine. Mackey cursed the suitcases in his hands—he wanted to lift his sunglasses and look Trav square in the eyes. Trav had nice eyes. That redhead's brown definitely suited him.

Trav took a deep breath and slowly raised the sunglasses, then set them on top of Mackey's head. Mackey took a deep breath and smelled... Trav. It had gotten so that Trav's smell, his animal, had pervaded Mackey's sleeping and waking in the past few weeks. Suddenly Mackey was comforted and turned on at the same time, and he was *so* not ready to deal with that.

Slowly he licked his lips, still captured by Trav's brown eyes. "This," he said, too softly for Blake to hear, "is for boys who don't have to go to rehab."

Trav nodded slowly. "You won't always have to go to rehab, Mackey. But you do now."

Mackey took a step away and turned toward the entrance. Blake was already halfway up the walk, and Mackey expected that he'd just walk in by himself, like that.

He was surprised and unsettled when Trav fell in stride next to him. "I can do this by myself," he muttered.

Trav bent and took his largest suitcase from him. "You don't have to now."

Somewhat reassured, Mackey kept walking.


THEY CHECKED in, and, thank *God* and maybe thank some of that money they had rolling around, they got separate rooms. Mackey was both relieved and a little spazzed out about that, actually. His room was small, with a bed, a dresser, a desk, and a chair—much like most of the nicer hotel rooms he'd ever been in, except with fresh flowers and no minibar—but Mackey wasn't used to sleeping alone. Most of the time, he'd slept in Gerry's room, and on the odd times they hadn't roomed together, well, Mackey had found ways not to be alone.

The first morning, his phone went off at six, all the better to start the day with some good old-fashioned PT. He hit the Dismiss key with every intention of getting up, and then fell back asleep in the little spot between the bed and the wall.

When the administrators—Dr. Cambridge included—came in to wake him up, he was fast asleep and nobody had seen him. If his phone hadn't buzzed insistently in his hands, he could have stayed happily like that until noon.

"Wha'?" he answered, remembering to hold it to his ear.

"Mackey, where the fuck are you?"

"Trav? I'm in rehab. You walked me here, remember?"

"They're looking all over for you!"

"I'm asleep."

"I can hear that," Trav replied with some humor in his voice. "*Where* are you asleep?"

"Same place I'm always asleep. Why?"

"Never mind."

Trav hung up and Mackey went back to sleep—for a whole five minutes. This time Dr. Cambridge alone came in to get him.

"Hi, Mackey—what are you doing down there?"

"Is this a trick question?" Mackey squinted up at the top of the bed, where the nice doctor with the sweep of gray hair and the matching goatee was lying on the bed, peering over the edge.

"Nope. First of all, I think we need to apologize."

"Wha' for? I overslept."

"Yes, but until your manager called us, I didn't realize you probably weren't up for PT anyway."

Mackey squinted some more. "So *maybe*," he said pointedly, "you could *let me sleep!*"

Dr. Cambridge smiled patiently. "No, Mackey, I think it's best if we start you out in the same schedule as everybody else. The rest of the residents are out taking a morning walk—or run, if that's their preference. How would you like to have a cup of coffee with me?"

"Caffeine is okay here?" Mackey asked guardedly, trying to make sure it wasn't a trick question.

"Just fine," Dr. Cambridge assured him.

"Great. Lemme take a shower, okay?"

"Fine, Mackey. Make it quick?"

"Yeah, all right."

Mackey was a champion at the quick shower, and he soon found himself in the dining room, eating apple fritters (the ones Trav had brought him were better) and drinking coffee with Dr. Cambridge, who explained the stuff he'd been too tired and in too much pain to remember from the day before. He wiggled on the chair, grimacing, as Dr. Cambridge explained about the schedule, the therapy—both group and individual—and the trust and self-help exercises he'd be doing.

He narrowed his eyes. "Trust? And self-help? Seems to me that sort of cancels shit out, doesn't it?"

Dr. Cambridge sighed and poured himself another cup of coffee. "No," he said shortly. "If you can have faith in your fellow human beings, you can have faith in yourself."

Mackey hmmed, shifted on his sore ass, and then made a sorry little sound in the back of his throat.

Dr. Cambridge eyed him sourly. "And speaking of asking for help, Mr. Ford said something about letting you have ibuprofen on doctor's orders?"

Mackey felt pathetically grateful as the man pulled out two tablets and let him have them with his coffee. He chuckled evilly as he washed them down. "Gotta say, Doc, you're not filling me with a lot of confidence here. Trust everybody but help yourself? No drugs but wash down your muscle relaxants with your stimulants? Telling ya, I think your theory's a little cracked."

"You're very funny," Dr. Cambridge said in a voice that indicated he didn't think Mackey was funny at all. "With lines like that, you should do stand-up instead of music."

Mackey grinned and pulled his sunglasses down to cover his eyes. "Where's the fun in that?" he asked, all swagger. "Doesn't everybody want to be a rock star?"

"Not particularly. Now I'm going to give you some time to go get gum from the little gift shop. Trust me, by the end of the day, everybody wants gum. Gum or cigarettes. Stock up."

Mackey nodded, thinking that gum might take up some of his body's boredom if he was going to be sitting around talking so much, and then looked hard at Dr. Cambridge. "Thanks for the advice, Doc. Now what did I say to piss you off?"

The doctor grimaced. "You pointed out what you felt to be contradictions—which is fine. But the fact that you did it? Makes me pretty sure you're set to find reasons for the program to fail. You find reasons for something to fail, Mackey, and it's going to live up to every bad expectation you have."

Mackey sighed. Yeah, well, couldn't argue with that. But he couldn't let the doc think he was whipped either. "Man, you have no *idea* how bad my expectations are here. So far I've been pleasantly surprised."

Cambridge shook his head. "I only wish *I* had been. Go get your gum. First trust exercise is at eight o'clock, down the hall and to the right. It'll look like a big living room, with coffee, water, and snacks."

"And flowers," Mackey said, making Cambridge blink.

"Yes, we do have them—"

"*That* is a good thing, Doc. My mom used to say flowers made everything better. We'd bring her handfuls of them—dandelions, mustard flowers, poppies before she told us they were illegal to pick." Mackey shrugged and stood, picking up his coffee. "I mean, we send her big bunches of them now when we get the urge, but looking around here? She's right. The flowers are a nice thing. Make sure you keep doing that."

He left, aware that Cambridge was staring at his retreating back and not giving a fuck why.

THREE DAYS later Mackey had about had it. This whole rehab gig was such an endless repetition of questions. *Why are you here? What different choices can you make? What are your triggers? Who have you hurt? How would you make it up to them?*

Mackey didn't feel like answering any of that shit.

And the trust exercises made him roll his eyes.

"So lemme get this straight. You want me to fall into Blake's arms and see if he catches me?"

"Yes—you can see everyone else is doing it."

Mackey surveyed the room with deep suspicion. So far he'd met starlets, bankers, producers, and agents. Everyone was too pretty, too made-up, too rich, and too obsessed with being pretty and made-up and rich.

The girls were falling into men's arms and getting all happy and clapping, and the men were heartily shaking their own hands for daring to trust their bodies to women who spent more time in the gym than Mackey probably spent sleeping.

"Yeah, Doc, it's a laugh riot, but me and Blake don't have to do that."

"Why not?" Dr. Cambridge asked, looking at Blake to see what he had to say.

Blake shrugged and Mackey rolled his eyes. "'Cause he's my lead guitar, that's why! If I couldn't trust him to catch me, I'd never cut the band loose for a bridge! Of course he'll catch me, watch!"

And without preliminaries, Mackey spun himself around and fell backward onto Blake, who caught him and shoved him back to his feet none to gently.

"Now see? Blake, c'mon. My turn."

Blake did the same thing, with a lot of insulting looks backward and an apparent expectation of being dropped on his ass.

Mackey caught him—even though Blake was a lot taller and weighed a lot more—and then used his shoulder to help him stand up. "See? This ain't no big thing."

Blake was looking at him with a quivering lower lip, though, and eyes that watered. "Not big?" he echoed. "Not big? That's fucking *huge*, Mackey! Oh my God, you couldn't fucking tell me you trusted me someplace *not* in rehab?"

Mackey stared at him, one side of his mouth curled back. "How could you think I didn't trust you, dumbass? You're in the fucking band, aren't you?"

"Oh yeah, right. I'm in the band with the almighty fucking wonderful Mackey Sanders, wunderkind and fucking musical genius. We all know I'm barely a backup musician, Mackey."

Mackey threw up his hands in disgust. "Oh, bullshit. You're Kell's fuckin' bestie. You're in the fucking band. You're in the band, you're a brother—just get over yourself and deal with it. If you want to quit, fine, but don't blame me if you don't like it here!"

"I'm a *brother*?" Blake asked, his voice dripping in sarcasm—and, if Mackey had to admit it, hurt. "I'm a *brother*? Since *when* have you made me feel like a brother? When have *you* welcomed me? Man, I did everything for you—I bought you coke—"

"You got me addicted to it!" Mackey snapped, not particularly mad. "I mean, yeah, I could have turned you down, but you're all 'I've got this great way to wake up!' and I was just trying to get us off the fucking ground, you know that, right? I mean, you were fucking new, the rest of the guys were scared shitless—hell, we hadn't even been on a plane before we came down to LA, and suddenly we were going to play in Europe? And you don't even fuckin' practice!"

"Why should we practice, Mackey? We're on stage for two hours a night!"

"That's different—dammit, Blake, you whine about not being good enough. Don't you know what you have to do to be good enough? You have to *work* for that shit! You have to practice, and try and create. You think I just wake up and sprinkle some fucking cocaine like fairy dust and suddenly shit out songs? I'm up to fuckin' three in the morning writing that shit, and I can't get you to play it for me. I *know* you can. We get up on stage and you pick up every cue. But off stage, all you want to do is couch with Kell and do blow!"

Blake stopped, his mouth open. Mackey hmphed in disgust. He looked around and realized that Blake was not the only one looking at him. The whole *room* was looking at him.

Mackey bared his teeth at the world in general and glared at Doc Cambridge sourly. "So see," he said, trying for dignity, "we trust each other."

"On stage," said the doc. "But that sounds like it's a lot more of your day than his. Why is that?"

Mackey glared at him. "You don't get it, do you? We bought our mom a *house*. Our little brother is in *private* school. Kell, Jefferson, Stevie, me? We had to work our way through high school, but we're sending Cheever to some sort of art school. Mom's got a car, and she's got friends, and she don't have to work unless she wants. But I'm not stupid, Dr. Cambridge. I read our contract. If we don't put out something that sells, they *drop* us. No nice house, no fancy cars, no super-nice hotel stay in rehab. Yeah, I did all the fuckin' drugs, and I'm not saying I didn't. But I did the pills to calm me down and the coke to wake me up and the booze because it made that other shit work better. I don't got no patience for a guy who doesn't work to pull his own weight."

Blake sniffled a little and ran a hand under his eyes. "Man, all I wanted to do was play the damned guitar."

Mackey sighed and pinched the bridge of his nose. "Well, you do a good job of it when you're not stoned. And Kell seems to like you just fine. I'm not planning on firing you, coke or no coke, so maybe just fucking relax."

"But why don't *you* like me?" Blake asked, sounding pathetic. "I swear, I was so excited to work with you—man, I'd been playing your single for *months*, do you know that? I landed that audition and I was like, 'No. Way. Outbreak Monkey wants *me*!' And then I met you all, and Kell and Jeff and Stevie, they liked me fine, but you—the guy with all the ideas—you only talk to me when we're recording, and I'm stuck not knowing what I done. Man, I bought you the drugs so you'd fucking *like* me, do you get that?"

Mackey made a puppy-dog sound and then sat down on the floor next to the coffee table and wrapped his arms around his knees. "Well, sorry," he said frankly. "But you were Kell's. Kell fuckin' loved you, and there you go."

Blake sank shakily into the chair behind him. "But why couldn't *you* love me, Mackey? Man, what was so wrong with me that I had to be the brother you liked least?"

God, Mackey's ass hurt like this. His ass hurt and his heart hurt, and he'd been a dick to this guy for a year, and it turned out he just wanted to be friends. Mackey sighed and stood up.

"It wasn't your fault," he said, not wanting to tell Blake why he'd never be good enough to play second lead guitarist. "You just took over for the wrong guy. Can I go now?"

Doc Cambridge looked at his watch in surprise. "Yes, yes, of course. You all have an hour before dinner!"

Mackey bit his lip and walked away. He walked straight to his room, packed his suitcases, and then walked straight outside, calling for a cab while he went. He remembered to use his own card this time so he didn't charge the record company for fare. This so obviously wasn't their fault.

# Communication Breakdown

"TRAV?" KELL knocked on the door to his room/office. "There's somebody here to see you."

Trav looked up and smiled. In the four days since they'd moved, everyone else in the little band seemed to have settled down and actually appreciated the change. Stevie, Jefferson, and Shelia spent their time decorating and ordering new furniture not just for their room—the room with the really big bed, which confirmed every suspicion Trav ever had. For some reason that calmed him down about the three of them. Just *knowing* they were in a threesome (Trav assumed Shelia was the middle of the cookie sandwich, given how Kell felt about "fags" and "weakness" and how much Stevie and Jefferson seemed unaffected by all of that) and were totally low-key about it made it easier to manage. So far the press hadn't asked, which meant whatever magic Jefferson and Stevie had that made people not notice them, it was powerful hoodoo. Trav was starting to be a believer.

Kell, on the other hand, had been... different.

Without Blake to impress or Mackey to be at odds with, Kell had turned into—well, the perfect son was the only way Trav could describe it.

He asked if people needed help, he did the dishes, he didn't even *ask* about getting high, and Trav hadn't seen a girl in his bedroom in a week. If Trav had been in an uncharitable frame of mind, he would have said Kell just didn't know how to get from downtown to his own house, but he knew that wasn't true because he'd been out with the others and had come back just fine.

The well-dressed, cleaned-up young man currently playing Trav's butler was a far cry from the disgruntled stoner Trav had met nearly a month ago.

Trav squinted at him now, wondering at the change. "Did he give a name?" Trav asked, heading for the door. His own bedroom/office had a bed and a computer table. Shelia had picked out the bedding—something in green, which surprised him, but it wasn't bad. Between that and a *really* nice area rug in green and brown, Trav sort of liked the place—especially after Shelia had the wall without the window painted green too. In fact, he wanted to see what she did with Mackey's room. The other boys had been so excited about their own rooms and decorating and painting that he sort of liked the idea of making that kid a home.

"Terry," Kell said promptly. He bit his lip. "He seems sort of like a... uhm, I mean, gay."

Trav grimaced. Well, it was an improvement, right? Of course, Trav had heard the row Kell had had with Mackey when they thought Trav was in the shower. *Trav* wouldn't have wanted to be on the side of Mackey's vicious tongue, but then, he wouldn't have wanted to be Mackey when his brother was using "fag" like the new black, either. Either way, between that fight and Mackey being in the hospital—and probably Blake going to rehab—Kell seemed to be trying to clean up his act.

Well, Trav approved.

"He is gay," Trav said now. "In fact, he's my ex."

Kell wrinkled his nose and then the lightbulb went on. "Oh fuck," he muttered. "Goddammit, Mackey. He coulda fuckin' told me. Just suddenly he's the voice of God, and 'you can't fucking say this word, Kell,' but no why I can't say the word or I might piss off the new manager if I say the word, just you can't say the fuckin' word!"

Trav stood up reluctantly. "Maybe he thought that not being an asshole was reason enough," he said dryly.

Kell shook his head. "I don't try to *be* an asshole," he muttered. "I'm supposed to keep 'em safe, right? You can't do that if people think you're weak, right? I mean Anus Cheever wasn't going to back down if I was weaker'n him, right?"

Trav swallowed. "Who in the fuck is Anus Cheever?" It *had* to be Enos, right?

"Cheever's dad. For a bit we thought he might stick around, but man, he *hated* Mackey. Couldn't let him beat on my little brother, right?"

Math, Trav thought miserably. He needed to do math. "How old was Mackey?"

"Well, ten, eleven—the guy left when Cheever still looked like a boiled potato, so not that old. And tiny. Man, he looked like about six. But that mouth...." Kell shook his head. "Mackey can get under your skin in under a minute, and he didn't give that guy a rest. But still—you don't go beating on my brother."

"Of course not," Trav said numbly. Little pieces of Mackey were fitting together in his head. He heard a noise from out in the living room/dining area and grimaced.

Well, hell. He might as well deal with Terry now, right?

And then it occurred to him that Kell was still looking at him mutely, begging for some sort of absolution. Trav suddenly needed some Tylenol and a comfort movie.

"I'm sorry," he said, feeling like an asshole. "When Mackey went missing—I was really hard on you."

"I let him down," Kell said back, looking away. "Not just that day. This whole last year."

Trav sighed. "Well, it's not like you ever had a childhood anyway," he muttered. God. Fucking Sanders kids, Stevie included. This fucking band. He looked back at Kell and made sure the young man made eye contact. "Kell, we can talk about this later, but for now? Just... you're going to have to make peace with yourself. I'm sure Mackey has some regrets too."

Kell shrugged and looked away, and Trav wasn't sure which option sounded more uncomfortable: finishing the conversation with Kell or finishing the relationship with Terry.

Trav excused himself and found Terry in the open kitchen, sitting on a stool in front of the counter while Shelia made him a smoothie.

"And I'm putting protein powder in it," she said soberly. "Now Stevie says it tastes like Play-Doh, but Jefferson says it actually adds some sweetness without sugar. Did you want orange juice or milk as a base?"

"Orange juice," Trav said dryly. "He's lactose intolerant. And put lots of fruit in there, Shelia." He shook his head and patted his stomach. "The protein powder makes the damned shakes binding if you don't have enough fruit."

Terry nodded and smiled, and they shared a moment of benevolent amusement for the girl in the bright yellow tank top and short-shorts who had greeted a perfect stranger with a smoothie.

"Hi, Trav!" Shelia said with a smile. "Would you like a mango/pineapple with juice?"

"Sure," Trav said, more to be companionable than anything else. "Thank you, Shelia—you know I didn't buy that thing so you could wait on us."

Shelia grinned. "Yeah, I know. But I never had a chance to entertain before. I'm like lady of the manor here—besides being the only girl!" Her smile was all sunshine.

Terry turned bemused eyes to Trav. "She's adorable—did she come with the new digs?"

Trav shook his head. "She came with the new band. She's, uhm, Jefferson and Stevie's... uhm... they're together."

He'd tried to speak below the wheeerrrm of the blender, but she cast one of those brilliant grins over her shoulder and Trav knew that she had not only heard but she had no problem with it. He still didn't know how to explain it to his parents.

Terry raised his eyebrows and quirked up a corner of his ripe mouth. "That's funny. I've never met a real ménage before."

"Well, check it off the bucket list."

Shelia came forward with two smoothies in the little cups with the tops, moving around the island and kissing Trav on the cheek. "You two have a little talk," she said sweetly. "I'm going to go help Jefferson put up posters. He's like a little kid, you know?"

She disappeared and Trav watched her go, hoping the twins (as he'd started to think of them) appreciated the hell out of her. He knew *he* was starting to, and he'd never seen himself living with a girl.

Terry took a sip. "That's not bad," he said. Then Shelia rounded the corner of the kitchen and disappeared. Both of them dropped their public faces and looked at each other soberly.

"I brought your stuff," Terry said. "There's a couple of boxes that I set outside in front of the garage. I know you said you'd come by and get it, but I wanted to see the new digs. Nice." He looked around, indicating the multilevel house. The kitchen and living area had a wraparound window that looked onto the acre's worth of front yard. Apparently Daphne at the real estate office had some *very* nice connections, and Heath meant what he said about making sure the boys were treated right.

And, well, owing Trav for that whole saving-his-life thing that Trav tried to forget a lot.

"I'm earning it," Trav said soberly. "The boys need a lot of help—and I haven't even started booking their tour. But it was nice of you to bring by the stuff."

Terry dropped his gaze. "I brought the chess set—"

"I told you—"

Terry held out his hand. "Think of it as a peace offering," he said. "Dammit, Trav, I just need to know it meant something. Because the way you left—man, that was cold."

Trav hated the misery roiling in his stomach, hated it worse than poison because he liked to think he was over this bullshit. "Well, I'm a cold bastard," he said through a thin smile.

Terry looked at him hard.

Then his face softened and his chin quivered. "Yeah, that's you. Cold to the bone," he said, but his lips were playing with a bitter smile, and Trav knew he hadn't hidden as much of himself as he'd wanted to.

"How's the kid from the shower?" Trav asked, hoping that topic at least would pull them both back emotionally. God, *something* needed to.

"Working at the bookstore, waiting for me to get over you," Terry said simply.

Trav put his shake glass down with a thump and slid off his stool. "Well, go take him out for wine or a soda or something. You need to be over me, water under the burned bridge or something. I wasn't good enough, I was a fucker who didn't listen, I'm just a fucking soldier who can't read a poem or look at a picture or—"

"Stop!" Terry begged, rubbing a shaking hand in front of his eyes. "Stop—I'm sorry I said that shit, okay? Do you want me to beg? I'll beg. I'll fucking beg for you to come home, quit this job—"

"Quit this job?" Trav stared at him, appalled. "Quit this job? This isn't a *job*, Terry— it's a... this thing I'm doing is *important*. These guys *need* me. Like I thought I needed you, but I was wrong about that. I'm not wrong about this. The whole fucking world has walked out on these kids—"

"This isn't a musician's foster home for burnouts!" Terry snapped.

Trav literally saw red. "Get out, or I will hurt you."

Terry took a deep breath. "I didn't mean—"

"You slapped me in the face, Terry. Do you remember that? And I didn't fight back, because I could level you. Well, I'm *begging* you—walk out the door. Do you understand?"

Trav's jaw was clenched, and he could feel a pulse throbbing in his eyes. He was violent, when he'd never been violent unless the situation called for it. You didn't just walk into this house with the cute girl and the bewildered brothers and the broken, healing camaraderie and say it wasn't important. You didn't call Mackey James Sanders a burnout. You just fucking *didn't*. Not when you knew what Trav knew. Not when you knew the boys like Trav was coming to know them. And it didn't matter that Terry didn't know it—Trav couldn't forgive him anyway.

God*dammit.*

A red haze still threatened his vision and he turned around. "Just go."

"I'm sorry," Terry murmured. "Please—at least keep the chess set."

"Go."

"But I just got here."

Trav whirled around just in time to see Mackey Sanders walk in before Terry walked out, and for a moment he wondered if it was possible for your jaw muscles to constrict so hard you strangled yourself and died.

"Holy fucking mother of fuckity fuck fuck fuck—*Jesus Christ*, Mackey, what are you doing here?"

Mackey turned around and watched through the glass panes in the entryway as Terry walked toward his car in the long shadows of the early autumn evening. "That guy was crying. What'd you say to him, Trav? I mean, you don't got a lot of poetry in your soul, but I didn't think you made pretty guys cry."

"That guy was the shitty part of my day," Trav said, taking in the kid's appearance as he tried to breathe. "The *good* part of my day was supposed to be that you were in rehab, getting better."

Mackey was still thin and still pale. His hair wasn't back in a ponytail, though, it was hanging in his eyes, and looked like he'd dragged his hands through it about six thousand times. His eyes were red-rimmed—not like he was high, but like Terry's had been before he'd walked out—and his goddamned new jeans were hanging off his hips.

"Why's it gotta be rehab?" Mackey asked, and his chin quivered like Terry's had too. "I'm sorry I interrupted your... breakup or whatever, but why's it gotta be rehab? Man, I don't know those people, and I'm supposed to be talking to them, and it's like everything I say there hurts. Hurts Blake, hurts... hurts to say. Why can't I just not do drugs? Just not drink? C'mon, Trav, whatya say? How 'bout I just don't do the bad shit?"

Trav wasn't a cuddly guy. He barely hugged his parents. The best thing about having a boyfriend had been the uncensored touching of skin, but even then, it had been all about sex.

But Mackey was standing here, his suitcases at his side, which meant he'd probably taken a cab right out of rehab and packed his own shit, and Trav had the most absurd urge to hug him like he'd hugged Terry sometimes, and just hold him until it was better.

He was so raw from the talk with Terry that he almost didn't trust his own voice, his own hands, his own body, to even give this kid a hug.

"Mackey?" he asked helplessly. "How bad do you want a pill right now? Or a shot of vodka? Or a snort? Tell me straight up, what would you give for something to make your hands stop shaking or to blur whatever is buzzing around in your pointy fucking head *as we speak*."

Mackey closed his eyes and dropped his bags. "Shut up," he begged. "Man, I just want to crawl in next to your bed and—"

"Sleeping in a corner isn't going to solve it!" Trav snapped, mostly because he envied Mackey's corner at this very moment. He wanted it—*craved* it. "Whatever's in your head, it's not going to get better until you tell someone. You need to get it *out* of your head, make it stop hurting—"

"Well maybe I don't wanna do that!" Mackey snarled, pacing in the entryway.

Trav heard some restless movements on the stairs behind him and wondered if the brothers were visible or just listening. Probably just listening, because God, who wanted to be there for *this*?

"Maybe I just want to stay here and fall off the fucking wagon and—"

Trav's blood ran cold. "Mackey, could you not fucking say that shit? You know the statistics and the names and the histories—probably better than I do. Do you want to be another face on the memorial wall?"

Mackey nodded, his fuck-off-and-love-me smile firmly in place, his slightly crooked teeth showing, a full-fledged panic sweat seeping through the underarms of the new jersey he was wearing. "Yeah! Yeah—why the hell not? I could be like fucking Jim Morrison or Shannon Hoon—Jesus, I could go out *proud* like fucking Kurt Cobain, 'cause that motherfucker didn't just *go*, he went with a *blast*—"

*Crack!*

Trav stared as Mackey, all 110 pounds of him, flew back against the coffee table, thrown there by Trav's right hook.

"Oh God."

Mackey stared at him, rubbing the rapidly reddening spot on his jaw. "Holy crap, Trav—you just hit me."

"Jesus." Trav couldn't stop staring. "I don't hit people. I don't hit people—I don't. Jesus Christ, Mackey—I don't fucking *hit people*. Man, just—"

Mackey grinned at him, working his jaw gingerly. "That was fucking *awesome*. I haven't been hit that hard in ages! And I had it coming—I mean, you gotta admit I had it coming."

"I don't hit people," Trav said numbly. "I don't—"

Mackey laughed. "Man, Trav, I had no idea I could make you freak out like that. Which part was it?"

"Mackey, you've got to go back to rehab, you fucking hear me?"

Mackey's smile dimmed. "Trav, really? Do I have to? Doc Cambridge is nice and everything, but I mean, you were in the room with me for five minutes and you decked me—"

"That wasn't your fault." Trav couldn't seem to blink. The coffee table Shelia had just picked out had collapsed like cardboard, and Trav could hardly see it. "It wasn't your fault—"

Mackey shook his head. "Yeah, yeah, it was. I'm an asshole—I mean, a complete waste of skin. Why the hell would you want me to talk to a shrink and dump all my shit out there in the world—I mean, I've hurt people, you know? Blake? I've been hurting him all year. How do I make that up? How do I tell my mom...." He closed his eyes. "Everything," he said, his voice cracking like glass. "I know it's coming, you know? How do I tell people—"

"You have to tell people," Trav said, numbly echoing what he just said, feeling stupid. "You have to tell people I hit you—I'll have to quit—"

"*No!*" Mackey screamed. "Jesus, Trav, aren't you hearing me? I'm not worth it! People will find out who I am, and I'm not worth losing your job over, or Blake feeling like shit, or what this is going to put my mom through. I mean, Kell won't love me anymore if I talk, won't be my big brother. You... you wouldn't even care enough to hit me if you knew all of me. I'd rather go out now, be the found body, than be left all a—"

Trav's heart was going to burst through his skin and turn his bones to shrapnel.

He turned toward the wall by the staircase and screamed, "Jesus fucking Christ, Mackey, just go to fucking rehab!" and hammered the blank accepting space with his fist.

And then crumpled on a muffled shriek, because he'd hit a stud in a load-bearing wall and broken three bones in his wrist and hand.


KELL DROVE them to the hospital. Mackey sat in the back, holding an ice pack over his wrist. The silence in the car was overwhelming.

"Kell, could you put on some music or something?" Mackey asked plaintively, and Trav puffed out a laugh through the black haze of pain in his arm.

"No," Kell muttered. "Mackey, you sure he wasn't beating on you?"

"Absolutely," Mackey said, nodding sincerely.

Trav thought about rolling down the window and throwing up. "I'll call Heath and resign," he said, his lungs like lead. "Obviously I'm no good at—"

"Shut up," Mackey and Kell said together, without heat.

Then Kell spoke up. "Mackey?"

"Yeah?"

"Don't make me find your fucking body, okay? Don't make me have to tell Mom we let you overdose or shoot yourself or whatever the fuck else you've got in mind. Don't fucking make me. I mean, I ain't been the greatest big brother on the planet, but dammit, Mackey, I fucking deserve more than that."

Mackey tried not to whimper. "Kell...." He closed his eyes, and Trav found he needed to look at him, *needed* to see, get a glimpse of whatever was going on through his head. "Man," he whispered. "If I had a bottle of Percocet, I'd take the whole fucking thing. Trav was right about that. I need it. My insides... what's inside my head...."

"Then get it out!" Kell yelled.

They pulled up to the ER, and Kell stopped short. They were all thrown against their seat belts, and Trav howled like a wounded badger as he jostled his hand.

It didn't even put a hitch in Kell's stride. "Get it out," Kell repeated, not screaming. "Go talk to the doctor. Talk to Trav. Talk to *someone* if you can't talk to us, but don't make me find your fucking body. I swear to God, Mackey, I can't do it. You've got all the words in your heart—what kind of words do you think will be left in mine if that's what I've got to see in my brain every day? Whatever you've got to fucking do, you do it, do you understand?"

Mackey took a breath, and another. "Let's get Trav to the doc," he said, his voice thick. "One thing at a time, right?"

He slid out of the car and ran around to open the door, and Kell met agonized eyes with Trav in the rearview mirror. "Please, Mr. Ford," Kell said. "I don't want you hitting him anymore, but could you please talk some fucking sense into him?"

"It's going to be hard to do when I have to resign," Trav said honestly.

Kell snorted in disgust. "Resign? Are you shitting me? It's like you don't even *know* Mackey if you don't want to hit him."


MACKEY WAS surprisingly competent with the details, and when he was done talking to the nurse, they sat side by side in the little ER cubicle, waiting for X-rays. They had given Trav some pain meds, which he took, and he was aware and more than aware that Mackey watched him hungrily as his throat worked, washing the pills into his system.

"Why'd you leave?" Trav asked quietly, leaning his head back against the wall and closing his eyes.

"There's too much stuff I don't want to talk about," Mackey said, just as quiet.

Trav sighed and reached for his phone, working a one-handed dial to Heath's office.

"Who are you calling?" Mackey asked incuriously.

"Heath—I need to tell him I'm resigning."

And just that quickly Mackey yanked his phone out of his good hand and threw it against the wall.

"You *can't!*" Mackey begged.

Trav opened his eyes enough to see tears starting at the corners of those luminous gray eyes. "Mackey, I *hit* you—"

"Everyone wants to hit me—"

"But I *did*. Man, do you even *know* how far under my skin you've got to be for us to be here? But we are. And you won't even... won't even talk to the doc in rehab, and what's going to happen to me? What's going to happen to Kell and Jefferson and Stevie when you break loose and get high and your body just fucking can't take it anymore?"

Mackey hugged his knees to his chest and took a big, shuddering breath. "I'm trying to keep it together," he confessed brokenly. "But how am I going to tell people? How do I even *look* at Kell when someone else knows? Or Mom. Or Jefferson or Stevie?"

"Knows what?" Trav asked gently. He sat up and gingerly moved his good hand to rub a soft circle on Mackey's back. It wasn't hugging, but it seemed to calm him down.

"And they're not even the worst part," Mackey went on, like he couldn't keep it back but like Trav wasn't even there either. "How do I tell that baby—he named the baby Katy, do you know that? After McKay. So she's out there in the world, and how would I tell her that I never wanted her to be? Or if she was going to be born, that I wanted her daddy to leave her? I *know* what that's like—how can I even look at them if they know that's what I wanted? And he knows I'm in rehab. God, what if Kell tells him about all them guys? But he was married and I just needed to be touched so bad, and Kell won't even look at me if I tell him I'm a fag, and I wouldn't even care, but he left. You see, he left, and he'd always taken care of us, but he left to go get married and I hate him and it's just all... just all...."

Trav managed to haul that slight, unresisting body against his and to hunch his shoulders over Mackey's. When the doctor came in, Trav waved him away and had to wait another hour for his X-ray, but it didn't matter.

It wasn't until he'd waved the guy off and gathered a sobbing, repentant Mackey Sanders into his arms that he realized that he was crying too.

God. He'd only heard one name in their past—one. They all knew one guy who stayed home to get married and have a kid. Kell only had one best friend he was pissed at for leaving. And Mackey only had one heart to break, and it had been broken for over a year, and he hadn't told one person—hadn't wept, hadn't vented, hadn't grieved.

Trav hadn't expected this. Of all the sins and all the demons, a simple broken heart hadn't been on his list. *Oh, baby boy—did no one teach you how to have your heart broken? How long has this been a secret sorrow, held close to your heart until you were consumed?*

"Mackey?" he asked hesitantly, *needing* to know. "How long were you with this guy?"

Mackey was sobbing so hard Trav almost didn't hear. When he made out the words "fourteen" and "seventeen," he had a physical sense of dislocation. *They're hardly children in the salt mines.* Had he actually said that to Heath? Children. They were children. Mackey was as fresh and as new to the world of broken hearts as a newborn bunny to a wolf's den, and he was weeping, savaged, because this whole time he'd thought he was a wolf.

The storm passed—all storms must—leaving Mackey exhausted and helpless, leaning against Trav as they perched on the bed in the ER. Trav had wrapped his good arm around Mackey's shoulders, and every now and then he could feel shudders of breath shake their bodies.

"What was his name?" Trav asked in the sudden silence. He knew, but he needed Mackey to say it.

"Grant," Mackey whispered. "Grant Adams. He and my brothers were friends since the third grade."

Trav swallowed, then swallowed again. He closed his eyes and saw the colors of rage, and then opened his eyes and tried to breathe. A part of him, the rational part, told him that Kell wasn't that much older than Mackey. Mackey was precocious as hell—there was no real abuse here, just kids getting it on.

The part that was in the ER with an aching wrist and a devastated, emotionally stunted rock star wanted to hunt Grant Adams down and put him in a room with the guy who'd raped Mackey in an alleyway.

*Not the same thing.*

No, it wasn't. Grant, with his heartache and his baby daughter and his leaving, had probably done more damage to Mackey than his rapist. The assault was par for the course, as far as Mackey was concerned. One more proof that everything in the world was out of control, including who you loved and what you could do to make them stay, or who took advantage of you when you were passed out in an alleyway.

But it couldn't be fixed now, not while Trav's wrist was swelling exponentially and Mackey was probably running probabilities on leaving the hospital high. Trav saw the orderly coming and dropped a kiss on Mackey's hair.

"Time to go," Trav said reluctantly. God—all this time hoping Mackey would break, and now he'd broken and it was Trav they were putting back together.

"Don't quit," Mackey begged, whispering through a clogged throat.

"I'll make you a deal," Trav said, standing up gingerly to wait for the wheelchair. "I won't quit *if* you go back to rehab. And make it stick."

Mackey wiped his cheeks on the knees of his jeans. "Tomorrow morning," he said. He hopped off of the ER bed and waited for Trav to sit himself wearily down in the wheelchair. After the orderly grabbed the handles, Mackey moved to the side with Trav's good hand. "I'll see you through this first," he assured him.

Trav breathed through his nose and squeezed Mackey's hand. "It's a deal," he said.

Trav had been shot before—more than once. He'd been beaten and knifed, and he'd been through the hospital just fine. His parents had freaked out, and he'd gotten the best care packages in Afghanistan while waiting for active duty, but he'd never been scared and had never needed reassurance. Life or death, Trav was steady. He knew right from wrong and he knew to enforce one and not to tolerate the other, and he was happy living and dying by that.

But he didn't say a word of this to Mackey. Mackey stood by his side, clutching his good hand, while they X-rayed him and set his wrist in a splint with a promise to put it in a cast the next day. He clutched Trav's hand while they got his pain meds and then called for a town car and were driven home.

It was late when they walked back into the house. The others had left dinner out for them—some sort of health-food casserole from Shelia—but neither of them ate. They went without speaking to Trav's bedroom.

If Trav was hoping for approval, he was disappointed. Mackey looked around the bedroom with dead, exhausted eyes, kicked his shoes and jeans off in a puddle, and then grabbed the coverlet from the top of the bed, wrapped himself up in it, and curled up next to the bed, by the end table. He fell asleep before Trav could get back with more blankets.

Trav lay in the darkness, listening to him breathe as he slept, and wished he could do the same. The feeling of that lithe little body, limp and sad next to his in the ER, seemed to be imprinted on his skin, etched into his muscles. He started doing math in his head. Mackey was twenty-one, right? Mackey was almost twenty-one? Trav was thirty-five. That was fourteen years. That made Trav a pedophile. He was worse than Grant Adams, the kid who'd loved Mackey and left him. He was Daddy—Mackey had obviously never had a daddy. Mackey was impressionable, and Trav had left a big impression.

No. There would be no relationship. There could be no relationship, because it would be based on every sort of wrong.

That was what his brain was saying, the part of him that had walked away from Terry without a backward glance.

But another part of him, a quiet part of him he didn't listen to much, had started to whisper.

*He's an adult. Wait until he's cleaned himself up and he'll be able to make his own decisions. Look at him. He's walked out of rehab twice. If he makes it through this time, that means nobody* tells Mackey Sanders to do something he doesn't want to. It's not like he respects authority anyway, Trav. If he wants you, he wants *you, not the authority, not the daddy, just the man. You're the only one he can trust. Can you trust anyone else with him?*

That last question made him bury his face in the pillow and growl. No. No, he couldn't trust anyone else with Mackey. The world had done a shitty job for Mackey James Sanders so far. Trav could do things right. Trav could take care of him and help him take care of himself and keep him clean and make sure nobody, not even Trav, not even Mackey, ever hurt this kid again.

*You clocked him in the jaw, you bastard. Not hurt him? Mackey's in danger from the people who love him most.*

Trav lay on his back, squinting into the darkness, tears of anger and frustration slipping down the creases of his eyes.

"What's wrong, Trav?" Mackey mumbled, and Trav was too exhausted to hold back. How had Mackey kept that terrible secret so close to his heart for so long?

"I hit you, Mackey. I don't think I can forgive myself for that."

"Man, you're too rough on yourself," Mackey said. "Fucking up don't make you unforgivable—just makes you human. I totally deserved it."

"Nobody deserves to get hit, Mackey."

Mackey shifted and popped up over the edge of the bed. "People don't deserve to get beat," he said after a minute. "They don't deserve to get bullied or assaulted or abused. But you didn't hit me thinking I was weaker and you could get away with it. You hit me thinking I was your equal and a pain in the ass." Even in the moonlight coming through the big open window behind them, Trav could see Mackey's teeth glinting in a smile. The bruise on the jaw, Trav couldn't see, but that smile was plain as day. "Besides—you pulled that punch. We both know it."

He dropped out of sight then, leaving Trav alone in the darkness, but Trav found himself laughing bitterly.

There you go. He was an equal and a pain in the ass. Trav was going to have to let Mackey make his own decision, and maybe have to live with the fact that he was human after all.

And Mackey was right. Trav knew himself. He'd pulled the goddamned punch. If he'd hit Mackey as hard as he'd hit that wall, Mackey would have been the one getting X-rayed.

It would have to be enough.

THE NEXT morning, bright and early, Trav called for the limo. He needed to go to the hospital afterward anyway so they could take off the splint and put on a cast, but nobody but Mackey had a reason to load themselves into the limo.

But the entire household got in anyway.

This time when Mackey got out, everybody got out with him. Shelia started it with the hug, and then Stevie and Jefferson and Kell.

And then Trav.

The kid had slept in his corner, between Trav's bed and the wall. Trav gathered him into a one-armed hug that wasn't even pretending to be distanced or professional or even platonic.

"Be good," Trav whispered. "Come back. We're all pulling for you, kid, okay? Don't be afraid of us. We love you."

Mackey jerked back and grimaced. "Not possible," he said. Then he grinned that same cocky fuck-off-and-love-me grin that had sent Trav over the edge. "But remember, I only have to make this stick once."

And he grabbed his suitcases and sauntered up the damned sidewalk alone.

# When the Levee Breaks

*Stefan Olsdal,* Trav texted.

Mackey rolled his eyes. *Duh.*

*Billie Joe Armstrong.*

*Really?* Mackey was surprised.

*He's bi. Says it shouldn't be a big deal.*

*Note to self: Buy FOREVERLY.* Mackey owned everything else Green Day had put out. Why not?

*It's already on your iPod.*

*Oh.* He couldn't remember. *I must have been high.*

*I am shocked. Rob Halford.* Trav wasn't letting up.

*Who?*

*Judas Priest, you heathen.*

*Seriously?*

*Duh!*

Well, how do you like that? Mackey had no idea.

*Michael Stipe,* Trav pursued doggedly.

*I am not surprised.*

*Chuck Panozzo, from Styx.*

*I know who Chuck Panozzo is.*

*You didn't know who Rob Halford was!*

Mackey let out a breath. *I'm not big into the Satan metal, okay?*

   *\* sigh \* Heavy metal was my one rebellion.*

*You mean you didn't just squirt out with a crew cut?*

Mackey laughed as he texted, thinking that you never did know about people. He never in the world would have suspected Trav capable of anything resembling a rebellion.

*It was all the way past my ears in high school,* Trav texted, and Mackey could hear Trav's dry, deadpan sort of humor.

*So was that before or after the Internet and the invention of the cellphone?*

*Shut up.*

Mackey laughed, enjoying the idea of giving him shit. *Make me.*

There was an uncomfortable silence, and Mackey rolled over to his stomach on his little bed. It was "contemplation time," which meant that they had about an hour to themselves to read, play on the net, call their dealers (yeah, Mackey knew a few not-so-clean-and-sober folks in rehab), or generally fiddlefuck around. The doc said the idea was to give them time to get used to being by themselves. Mackey figured it was just impossible to structure everybody's day down to the last fucking nanosecond while they tried not to think about their drug of choice. Right now, as Mackey wondered if he'd crossed the line, gone too far, poked the one guy who texted him with impunity in this human desert too hard for him to text back, he sort of longed for a Xanax.

*Please don't give me shit about that,* Trav texted, and Mackey stared at his phone for a minute. It was just so damned honest, really.

*I'm sorry.* He wondered when the last chance he'd had to say *that* had been. *I crossed the line. I'm sorry.*

*I will never be okay with that, do you understand?*

Mackey sighed. This here was a fundamental disagreement. *Then you will never be okay with me.* And wasn't *that* scary? He wanted to take it back. He had been *anything* for Grant, would have done *anything* to make it so Grant would stay with him and not Sam. When he'd been high, he'd been like an in-and-out drive-through of ass. He would have bent over for Satan if he'd had a condom.

But he wasn't high, and he wasn't a kid. This... this *attachment* he had to Trav—it was not going to be worth anything if Trav couldn't deal with Mackey James Sanders as God made him. Mackey could change for the better—he could learn to say "I'm sorry" and try not to piss people off quite so much—but he would never believe that people were meant to be perfect.

Trav apparently believed *he* was meant to be perfect.

*Not so serious,* Trav prompted.

Mackey cocked his head, smiling a little. *What in the hell does that mean?*

*It's not a philosophical disagreement if I think what I did was wrong.*

Mackey laughed. Okay. So they were going to debate—that was okay. A debate was good—it was bickering, bantering, whatever. Mackey could deal with that.

*Do you MEAN to contradict yourself? Should there be a sarcasm font I can read?*

*I don't want you to forgive guys that hit you, Mackey.*

*Trav, if I hadn't been losing my fucking nut, do you think I wouldn't have hit you back?*

*If you hadn't been losing your fucking nut, I wouldn't have hit you in the first place!*

*So think about it like a really hard bitchslap. I had it coming.*

*This whole conversation is making me violent.*

*That's hilarious. It's cracking me up.*

*Just promise me, okay?*

*What?*

*Nobody gets to hurt Mackey Sanders. Not even me.*

Mackey looked at the words for a moment. Wow. A promise not to let himself get abused. Did that extend to mental abuse? Did it extend to not letting himself get dicked around by someone who said they loved him but didn't follow through? Did it mean not letting himself get called a faggot, even by his stupid brother? Did it mean telling Trav when he got too tired or was spazzing out, and maybe have something happen besides another pill or a bump of coke? Did it mean not lying to his mother or the press or *his mother, goddammit* when they asked him about girls?

Did it mean letting someone close enough to love him?

One little goddamned sentence and Mackey's whole world crashed to a halt.

*Mackey?*

He swallowed.

*Believe it or not, that is really fucking profound.*

There was another long pause, this time on Trav's side.

*It should be a simple truth.*

*Yeah, well, so should not getting high to get out of bed. Doesn't mean it's not new to me.*

*Yeah. I get that.*

*Okay, how's this. How 'bout you promise not to abuse me and we both go from there. Sort of like I'm promising not to do drugs anymore.*

A few seconds ticked by and Mackey realized his brows were knit and his eyes burned. Suddenly this answer really mattered to him.

*That's a deal. We can shake on it on Sunday.*

Sunday would be his first visiting day, which meant his stint in rehab had gone an entire week. Go Mackey—only three more to go. Well, he hadn't walked out yet. That was something.

*Deal,* he texted, and then Doc Cambridge walked into his room, so he signed off.

"Sorry," Dr. Cambridge said, looking at Mackey with some anxiety. "I didn't mean to interrupt. That looked personal."

Mackey felt the oddest thing. His face got hot and his hands went clammy and *oh my God,* was he *blushing?*

"Well, I didn't think so," he said, distressed, "but now I'm starting to think it was!"

Cambridge opened his eyes really wide like he was trying to figure out what to say next. "Well, who were you talking to?"

"Trav," Mackey said, turning off the phone.

Cambridge frowned. Mackey had mentioned "a fight" with Trav, and, well, he had a shiner and a bruise on his face—it wasn't rocket science. "Is he putting pressure on you to—"

"To never let anybody hurt me? Yup. He's damned insistent." Mackey raised his eyebrows a couple of times and watched as Cambridge readjusted his thinking.

"Was he the one who hit you?"

"Doc, how many times have you wanted to hit me this week?"

The day before, he'd been playing his guitar in his room, and Blake had come by with his own. They'd sat and played for about a half an hour, Mackey giving Blake pointers and Blake, for once, listening. It had been a decent moment, but then, as Blake stood up to take his guitar back to his room, Mackey's inner demon reared his ugly head.

"You think that's all, don't you?"

"It's almost dinner, Mackey! They don't let us stay up and eat like in the hotel room!"

Mackey glared at him and shook his head. Food didn't matter. Hell, taking a *piss* didn't matter, not when you were on a run like that one.

Blake stomped away, and Cambridge came back ten minutes later. After a heated discussion, Mackey outlined his philosophy for rehearsal times and basic human maintenance, and Cambridge threatened to take his guitar away if he didn't— Cambridge's words—get his scrawny ass into the goddamned dining room and eat some fricking food.

Mackey glared and rolled his eyes and thought of all *sorts* of awful things to say, but he stomped off and kept them all to himself, because he was trying not to be too bad of an asshole in general and not just to Trav in particular.

But there was no doubt about it. Cambridge had wanted to rip himself a piece of Mackey Sanders, same as anyone else who had to deal with him on a regular basis.

Dr. Cambridge narrowed his eyes now—he had a really impressive set of white eyebrows. Mackey almost wanted to pull on them like a kid to see if they'd stay on.

But he nodded sagely instead. "See? You're counting the times, aren't you? And you're a *shrink*. Trav's a manager—he's like, a permanent member of the sphincter police. You think I didn't light his fuse, you ain't been paying attention."

There was a heavy sigh from the doctor's direction. "For now, I'll let it go," he muttered, apparently not convinced that Trav got a get-out-of-jail-free card because Mackey was a complete dick. "So what are you two texting about?"

Mackey shrugged. "Gay rock stars." Because seriously—not a big deal.

"Why is that a thing?"

Mackey sighed and swung his legs over the edge of the bed. "Because he's trying to convince me that coming out wouldn't be the end of the world—wait. You have to keep it quiet in case I decide not to, right?"

Dr. Cambridge's eyes had gotten big. Like, the size of *bowling balls* big. And his mouth was slightly parted. And he looked like he was going to cry.

"What?" Mackey asked, unnerved. "I mean, you're a shrink, right? Being gay can't possibly be the worst thing you've ever heard, right? It's just the whole press thing, and it's gonna be a big fucking hassle, and Blake doesn't even know, and—"

Oh my God! His shrink's lip really was wobbling. Mackey gaped at him.

"What?" Mackey asked again. "Seriously, what's the big deal? This place is no faggots allowed? 'Cause I've got to tell you, you've got a couple of orderlies here who are giving it to each other in the supply closet, and them fuckers are *loud*! So only me? I'm no—"

"No," Dr. Cambridge said, seemingly coming out of some sort of weird trance. "You're fine, Mackey. Your secret is safe with me, which is good, because we'll probably be talking about it a *lot*, but don't worry. This is totally a safe place, and you don't have to worry. Nobody in rehab will judge you—"

"Then what were the googly eyes and the drool all about?" Mackey demanded. He slid off the bed and started rooting under it to find his moccasins. They made you wear clothes and shit to dinner, but so far moccasins seemed to fall under "casual footwear," and since they didn't require socks and went with pajama bottoms, Mackey was a fan.

"I... I mean, I used to think I was good at my job," Cambridge said. It didn't really sound like he was talking to Mackey. "People would ask me, I'd say, look, there's the degrees, I'm making some money, rich people pay me to unfuck their lives, and yeah, I'm decent...."

Mackey found a moccasin and slid his foot in. Ah, yes. Something about warm feet made even the jitters of not working and not fixing a little more tolerable.

"What in the hell are you talking about?" he demanded bluntly. "I'm lost. Am I, like, a mark on your record or something?"

Cambridge glared at him. "I'm supposed to *know* these things, Mackey. Being a closeted gay rock star has fucked up more lives than you can possibly count. It's important information to share about yourself, do you understand?"

It sounded like he was enunciating carefully because Mackey was stupid.

"Nnoo." Mackey enunciated just as clearly. "Why in the fuck would you care that I'm gay?"

Cambridge cleared his throat. Several times. "Mackey, you've sat in group therapy for three days. You've heard people talking about their children, their boyfriends, their girlfriends, their mistresses, and the stranger they banged who gave them HIV, which is when they decided to go to rehab. Do you know what these people have in common?"

Mackey grimaced. He remembered the poor girl who had woken up with HIV and a hangover. "Their judgment is as shitty as mine and they need to wear rubbers?"

"They're *human*, Mackey. The people you fall in love with are part of what makes you *human*. They're also the same people who might send you screaming for Percocet and whiskey, so *yes*, who you love is really important to the rehabilitation process!"

Mackey rolled his eyes—and fought off a coldness in his chest. It was exactly what he'd thought when he'd left. He was eventually going to have to talk about Grant. *But Trav knows, and he said he's pulling for me.*

And he'd given Mackey a hug there, at the end. A real hug.

"Okay, then. So I'm gay. Now you know. And nobody else does. And there we are."

Something funny happened to Doc Cambridge's face: his eye started to twitch, for one thing, and Mackey laughed and pointed.

"You're thinking about it again," Mackey said slyly. "Tell the truth. You're thinking that there's a boxing ring in the gym and you're gonna put my last publicity shot on the big bag and beat that fucker to dust, right?"

Cambridge took a deep breath, but he didn't deny it. "Mackey, we're going to talk about this more later—I swear, we really are. But right now, I want to ask you something that you don't have to respond to right away. Just think about it, okay?"

Mackey nodded and toed on his other moccasin. "Shoot, Doc, but hurry. We're running out of time for me to go push my vegetables around."

"Why's it so important that you piss people off? Why do you work so hard at it? Why?"

The doc's voice cracked a little, and Mackey sighed. Yeah, sure, he *said* Mackey didn't have to answer him right away, but Mackey thought he'd pushed the guy enough, and it was only right.

"'Cause when they're pissed at me, at least they know I'm there," Mackey said. "You spend enough time with a town that wants you to disappear, you realize that you can't do that when someone wants to slug you."

With that he turned and sauntered to the dining room. They were having some sort of lettuce with protein today—God knew he didn't want to miss it.

*How was dinner?* Trav asked, right before lights-out.

*Lonely. Blake's got friends, and I piss people off.*

*Yeah? Who'd you piss off today?*

Mackey laughed a little. Well, Trav knew him and didn't hate him for it. *Blake, for one. The shrink.*

He took a breath. This one hurt. He hadn't meant to do it. In fact, for once in his miserable life, he thought he was helping.

*Who else?*

He sighed. Why not?

*Some girl. Bitching about her father not being there. I told her the one time we got our wish for a dad to stick around, turns out, he liked to hit. Maybe she should fix her own life and not worry about who was watching.*

There was another break, and he winced. He'd said it *nice*, though. He'd been trying to give her something, some wisdom, one of the few things he thought he really knew.

*Sounds like good advice.*

He closed his eyes. God. *Someone* got it.

*I think I sounded like an asshole. Made her cry. For once, I wasn't even trying.*

The silence between them stretched long, and for a moment, Mackey almost put the phone down and started packing. God. He couldn't cut it here. He'd been a total wash in school, and he couldn't even *remember* how he'd functioned for the past year. Social skills—he sucked at them. If he could piss people off or toss away one-liners at a press conference, he could manage. If his relationships consisted of a cock in the dark, he was great. But talking to real live people—or, hell, texting them for that matter—was just....

*You were trying, Mackey. You were trying to be a good guy. Don't worry about it. I bet a lot of people cry in rehab.*

Mackey couldn't decide whether to laugh or, there in the semidarkness, let the burn in his eyes take over.

*You're not shitting around about that. Whole fucking world cries. BLAKE cried—something about his dad calling him a fuckup.*

*But not you.*

*I cried on you. Jesus, what do you people want from me?*

*We want you to live to thirty—and maybe even longer!*

Mackey chuckled, the sting in his eyes receding.

*Good luck with that,* he texted. *I don't know if anyone expected me to live THIS long.*

*Please don't.*

Mackey frowned.

*Please don't what?*

*Please don't joke about that, Mackey.*

*Sorry—that would be one hell of a mess, wouldn't it?*

*It would leave a fucking big hole, asshole.*

*Are you kidding? I'd be immortalized. I'd be a GOD!*

Suddenly the phone buzzed—not with a text but with an actual phone call.

"Jesus, Trav—you're calling me? Who does that?"

"It's why phones were invented, genius. Take it back." Trav's voice was uncompromising—and God, but it sent a shiver of joy and want down Mackey's spine, where it detonated in the pit of his stomach.

"What?"

"Would you really rather die young, leave a good memory, all of that rock star glory bullshit you were just saying?"

"It was... I don't know. It was a joke!"

"It was a shitty one. Now promise me you're not thinking that way, or I'll never get to sleep."

Mackey sighed and closed his eyes. "Yeah, sure, whatever. I'll live forever. I'll be Bruce Springsteen or Mick Jagger or something."

Trav made a considering kind of sound. "You promise?"

"I can't promise that bullshit—hell, have you never seen *The Buddy Holly Story*?"

"We can't control helicopters and ice, Mackey, but we *can* control your damned suicidal impulses. Promise, or I'm driving down there and sleeping on *your* floor for a change."

Mackey shifted uncomfortably. He gave up showering three days ago and he'd spent the past four days in his pajama bottoms with his hair in a pile on top of his head. It was nice—no dressing up for stage, for press conferences, for shuttling from one place to the next—but he knew he stretched the boundaries of casual, and he liked it that way. It sort of helped him relax if he thought of this whole thing as one big vegetation day on the couch. He really hadn't gotten any of those when they'd been on tour.

"I, uh, I don't know, Trav. I sort of don't want you to see me this way." Oh God. How did that sound? Did it sound as bad as he thought it sounded? "I mean, you know. I just... it'd be nice if you saw me... not awful, sometime. You know?"

"I don't think you're awful." Trav's voice in the dark suddenly doubled up on the shiver quotient. "I think you're a great kid—"

"I'm not a kid." *Crap. Crap crap crap crap crap.*

"No." Trav sighed heavily. "No, but you're—"

"I can be a grown-up, Trav. I mean, I can do rehab and get clean, if that's what it takes to be grown up—"

"Lots of people who don't get clean are still grown-ups. I just think I'm a little old for what—"

"Not old. Not too old. I'm not a kid and you're not too old, okay? Just, you know. I'm in rehab. See? We're talking on the phone. It's not a thousand miles away. Just don't write me off as a kid, okay?"

God. Because he sounded like such a man here, didn't he? Oh hell. Texting had been *such* a better option.

"Lights out, Mackey!"

Mackey looked up at the orderly—a sweet-faced little guy who liked to bottom, if the adventures in the broom closet were anything to judge by—and nodded, smiling. "I gotta go, Trav. I'll text you tomorrow."

"Yeah, text you tomorrow."

"When I'll be older."

Trav's laugh was nice. Low, growly, grumbly. Mackey was suddenly a fan for life.

"So will I," he said.

Mackey stuck his tongue out at the phone and then hung up.

Trav's text buzzed not ten seconds later.

*I saw that.*

*That was a very adult reaction to an irritating person*, Mackey texted primly.

*Goodnight, Mackey.*

*Night, Trav.*

Mackey wanted to say something else. Something deep and profound and at least more attached than "Night, Trav."

But he couldn't think of a thing that didn't scare him silly. And would probably make Trav quit.

He fell asleep thinking about it, and hadn't reached a solution in the morning.


THE NEXT day, during his individual session with Doc Cambridge, he thought Trav really might have to come out and camp on his floor to get him to stay.

"You want me to...." He squinted, and Doc Cambridge helped him finish his sentence.

"Write letters, yes."

"I've got a phone! Can't I just call them up and—"

"No." Just one syllable and a whole lot of attitude for a guy who was so goddamned flamingly nice to every other person in the fucking facility.

"Why in the fuck not?" Mackey snapped. "Are all shrinks men?"

"No—there's a whole lot of female doctors in this facility. Why do you ask?"

Mackey shrugged. "I don't know. I was just thinking you looked an awful lot like my mother right then, that's all."

"Well, since your mother might be the one person in your life who hasn't let you down, I'll take that as a compliment. Now about writing the letters—"

"Yeah. Why can't I just call people? I mean, you know, technology and everything? Easy." Mackey pulled his phone out of the pocket of his hoodie and mimed punching in numbers. "Just, you know... beep boop bop...."

Cambridge glared at him through the gap between his finger and thumb. Every so often, he pressed them together like he was popping a zit.

"You're squishing my head, aren't you?" Mackey asked, grinning.

"Yup."

"Well, answer my question if you want me to shut up. Why letters?"

Cambridge sighed and cast Mackey a weary smile. These one-on-one sessions hadn't been easy for either of them. Cambridge asked questions, Mackey dodged—like a game, except Mackey was using the diversion to not think about all the things he'd like to take to not think about *anything*.

"For one thing, you can't dodge the subject when you're writing a letter."

"And for another?"

"Jesus, kid, would you just let me finish? For another, you can't piss them off accidentally." Cambridge's voice softened. "Look, I know you were just trying to help Kimber the other day, okay? You wanted her to know that it was okay if she wanted her father's approval, but she had to learn to live without it. I get that. But you're so used to telling people to go to hell while you're smiling in their faces, that's what's coming across."

Mackey sighed and let his face sag into the lines of unhappiness that he'd been fighting all day. He picked restlessly at a cuticle for a minute, thinking his guitar calluses were going to go away if he didn't practice more.

"I didn't mean to make her cry," he said at last. They'd talked about this subject the entire morning. All of Mackey's fucking problems, all of the things he should really be working on, and somehow it all came down to making one stressed-out socialite cry. He hadn't meant to do it. He'd been trying to be a nice guy and he'd failed. Why should he even try?

"I know you didn't," Cambridge said, his voice gentle.

Mackey didn't want to look up. He didn't think he could do this if Cambridge was still trying to squish his head.

"What would I say in these letters you want me to write?" Because letters? Wasn't that archaic? "I pretty much say whatever the hell I'm thinking anyway."

"Really?"

The skepticism made Mackey look up. Cambridge wasn't trying to squish his head, but he wasn't agreeing with Mackey either.

"What's that supposed to mean?" Mackey shifted uneasily, wanting his guitar. His stomach hummed softly, somewhere between his spine and his groin, a restless itch he hated noticing because he could never get rid of it without music or drugs.

"Fine, then. Let's start with a few questions that *I* am curious about. If you can answer those without wanting a shot of whiskey—"

"Vodka," Mackey said seriously. "Or gin. They don't taste as bad."

"Okay, if you can answer those without wanting a shot of anything, I shall take it all back."

"Woot! And that'll be winning the lottery right there," Mackey snapped, dripping acid.

"Oh yeah. I'll throw in a gold watch for free." Cambridge was a sarcastic shit too— Mackey grinned at him raggedly, approving.

"Then shoot." Mackey pulled out his best fuck-off-and-love-me grin so the doc knew that nobody was getting under his skin.

"How old were you when you knew for sure you were gay?"

*Grant softly breathing smoke into his mouth, and all of those things he'd been silently yearning for singing through his skin....*

"Fourteen."

"How did you know?"

*The almost soothing pungency of marijuana, the lower tones of cut grass and rain, Grant's aftershave and his body surrounding Mackey....*

"I was kissed."

"By whom?" Doc's eye was twitching again. Good. Mackey's whole gut was clenched into cannon shot.

"My brother's friend."

"Did your brother know?"

*Grant dropping to his knees in Mackey's bedroom, shaving his crotch so he could wear those damned pants, taking Mackey's cock in his mouth while Mackey's brothers ran around in circles in the living room....*

"No," Mackey said softly. In spite of himself, his breathing started to quicken like it did before a fight or after a fix or in the middle of fucking.

"Did he ever kiss you again?"

*Grant showing up with the McDonald's bag and need in his touch, face alight as he took Mackey's ass in the back of his mom's minivan after Mackey had cut school; the feel of his shivering body after that first time in San Francisco; stolen kisses; hands in the dark; the sound of the river; the full lips, golden eyes, straight-bridged nose, self-loathing smile....*

"Mackey?"

Mackey ran a shaking hand over his mouth and yearned—*yearned*—for a Xanax, or the bitterness of coke on his tongue, or the burn of liquor, or his guitar in his hand.

"Mackey?" Cambridge was no longer sarcastic or irritated or kind. He was firm and relentless and—

"Can I get my guitar?" Mackey begged, a cold sweat popping out over his chest and his back.

"No," Cambridge said, and he meant it.

"I've got to pee—can I go pee?"

"No." His voice got a little softer, but not less adamant.

"I really gotta go," Mackey complained. "I mean, I'll wet my pants—"

"Good, then you might change your clothes and shower."

Mackey cringed. "I was trying for casual," he muttered.

"Well, the effect was 'depressed and recovering from addiction.' I've seen your concert footage—it's not your best look."

"You've seen my concerts?" Mackey smiled, feeling pathetic. Oh God. Suddenly it was really important to him that this guy who wanted to know all his secrets had seen him when he was all together and fucking dominating the stage.

"I own your CD too," Cambridge said gently. "I owned it before you showed up on my door. Now answer the question."

Mackey stood up and paced. "I...." He laughed, because it was true and he felt stupid. "I honestly can't remember—"

"How long did you keep kissing this guy that your brothers didn't know about?"

Oh.

"Five years," Mackey said. He started bouncing, clenching and unclenching his ass muscles, making his stomach hard as a rock—anything to try to stave off the need.

"Wow!"

Mackey glanced at him quickly, looking for judgment, and saw nothing but honest surprise. "What?"

"That's a long time to keep something secret when you're—what? Fourteen through nineteen?"

"Yeah," Mackey muttered. "Felt like my whole life." And then it ended.

"How old are you now?"

Mackey glared at the guy. "Turned twenty-one in June. Why?"

"Because you were really young. How old was the boy?"

"Ahh...." Mackey's hands were sweating, and he prowled over to the wall. "Kell's age." God, how old was Kell now? "He'd be twenty-five in September."

"So not much older. Why'd it get broken off?"

Mackey closed his eyes and simply dropped to the floor, hugging his knees to his chest and shaking. "Do we have to?" he asked, talking into his knees. "Is this—I mean, it's stupid. I—"

"C'mon, Mackey. See this through!"

"He knocked up his girlfriend and couldn't follow the fucking band. Happy now? He knocked up his girlfriend, we had to get another second guitar, Blake took the job, and there you are. We're all fucking caught up. Good? Do you need to know anything else after that? Who, how many, cock size?"

"No," Cambridge said, crouching down by Mackey. "Because really, they're all the same guy, aren't they?"

*Cocks shoving into his asshole with pain, the rubber not always lubricated, the strange mouths on his cock, the smug looks on their faces, all of them thrilled to take a piece of Mackey Sanders, the guy they'd just watched thousands of people eye-fuck on stage....*

*Grant. Grant, whose hands had trembled on his shoulders, who had buried his face against Mackey's back and wept....*

"Yeah," Mackey admitted, because his voice would stop it—stop the weight of the memories pressing him to the floor, detonating in his stomach, making him shake and heave and yearn.

"What was his name?"

"Grant." His voice was a whisper, a gravel slice of pain. "My brother's friend Grant Adams."

*He's beautiful. So beautiful. And hurt. And he needed me, I know it, and he let me go.*

"Have you spoken to him since you came to LA?"

Mackey reached into his back pocket and fumbled for his phone. He looked up Grant's text messages and then shoved the phone at Cambridge, hoping that would be enough. For just a minute, he didn't have to answer any questions, 'cause all the answers were in the phone.

The doctor raised his eyebrow and then sighed. Creakily, he settled his middle-aged bottom in front of Mackey, crossing his legs.

"Succinct," he muttered, looking at the text. "Is that a thing with you guys?"

Mackey glared at him. "It's not Los Angeles, Doc. Do you know what people in my neck of the woods think about shrinks? Wanna take a guess?"

"No need," Cambridge said dryly. "I'm grateful you graced us with your presence—"

"What the fuck ever," Mackey snarled, in pain and needing. "I could have been fucking Grant on the sly for my whole life if we'd stayed at home. But no—he's got to get us a fucking contract and run away like a pussy, because his girl's knocked up and he can't fucking tell them all to go to hell. Graced you with my presence—my whoring fucking ass." God. He was crying. He hated crying. It left him raw and stripped, like a kitten without skin, and he knew, just knew, he'd never be warm again.

The sob that escaped him was as whipped as that kitten's, and he couldn't find a way to stop it.

"You know what?" he whimpered, trying to keep it together, keep it together, keep it together.

"What?" Cambridge put a warm, soothing hand on Mackey's shoulder, and for once, Mackey couldn't find the wherewithal to shake it off.

"I would literally spread my ass for a gangfuck right now if I could get some fucking Valium."

That hand didn't move. "You are *so* not allowed to go to the bathroom," Cambridge muttered.

That did it. Mackey started to laugh semihysterically into the hollow of his body. His stomach muscles ached, they'd been taut for so long, and his shoulders screamed with tension. The laugh rocked him, careened through his bones, veered out of control, and began to slam him back and forth. He rocked in the fetal position on the floor of the shrink's office as his sobs ripped him apart.

He couldn't stop. He tried. He deepened his breaths and got a stitch in his side. He counted to ten, and counted to ten, and got lost at eight.

He tried to recite all the lyrics to *Led Zeppelin IV*, and actually *forgot* the words to "Stairway to Heaven" and had to start all over again.

He leaned into Cambridge's arm and begged for Trav.

"T-T-Trav'll fix it," he sobbed. "Trav'll m-m-make it stop."

"C'mon, Mackey, just deal. Don't make it stop, just feel it."

"Aw, *fuck you!*" he shouted and spent the next few minutes catching his breath. Then he sobbed some more. "*F-f-f-uck th-th-thissss....*"

"Stop fighting," Cambridge whispered against the side of his head. "Just for once, stop fighting."

"Aw *hell!*"—and he went limp with it, let the pain wash over him, let it burn under his skin, immolating his resistance in grief. No memories of Grant existed in that white-flamed holocaust, no need for drugs, just the need to follow one breath with the next, and another, and another, heedless of the choking, inarticulate word-shit that fell out of his mouth.

Eventually he stopped cursing.

Eventually he could breathe.

And eventually he was still, curled into a ball, breathing in quiet puffs into the cream carpet in the shrink's office.

For a moment he just stared at the carpet and realized the light had changed from the long shadows of a late September afternoon to the artificial light of Doc Cambridge's lamp.

"I've missed dinner," he said dully, and he was surprised by the little half laugh from Cambridge, who was sitting somewhere behind him.

"So have I," he said. "And my wife was making something special."

"Your wife cooks for you?" For some reason this was a good subject to talk about. "That's nice. My mom never had the money. Lots of Top Ramen and hot dogs and peanut butter and jelly."

"There are nice things about money sometimes," Cambridge said. He was still touching Mackey's back, and his hand moved for a moment and then resumed its desultory, soothing stroke.

"Trav got us a house," Mackey told him. He wasn't sure he'd mentioned that before. "When I get out of here, I'll live in a house for the first time in my life."

"You looking forward to that?"

For once Mackey didn't have the strength to resent the probing question. "Maybe he'll let me get a bunk bed," Mackey said, suddenly interested. "I'll text him and tell him that. I want a bunk bed. I'm tired of sleeping on the floor."

"I'll bet that won't be a problem." Cambridge sighed and leaned forward, groaning a little as he stretched out his muscles. "Maybe the first step is getting off of this one, you think?"

"God." Mackey pushed up on an elbow and stood up, wiping his face on his shoulder as he did so. The fabric of his T-shirt was a mess—snot and tears and spit—but he thought that maybe the doc was right, and it was time to change anyway. "I don't even care about the food. I need a shower." That long-ago shower when he'd gotten back from prom echoed in his mind, but right now all he could remember was how the warm water had relaxed him and not the pain he'd tried to wash away. He reached a hand out and Doc Cambridge grimaced, trying to push himself awkwardly from the floor.

"Oh c'mon and take my hand," Mackey snapped. "I'm not a little kid."

Cambridge grabbed his hand and Mackey hauled, shaking his head when Cambridge came up easily.

"You're right," Cambridge said, smiling a little. "You're stronger than you know."

Mackey shook his head in disgust. "I'm gonna go shower. I *feel* like I smell bad."

"I'll have my wife bring us leftovers," Cambridge said. "Bring dinner to your room."

Mackey looked over his shoulder, surprised. "That woman must really love you," he said in wonder. "You should definitely keep her."

"Yes, well, third time's the charm."

Mackey giggled. He stopped for a moment to make sure this time he *could* stop, and then started again.

"What's so damned funny?" Cambridge called after him.

Mackey just kept giggling, shaking his head.

Yeah, he dressed nice and everything, and the white hair was all distinguished and shit, but money or no money, the guy was as fucked-up as any pot-bellied homeboy in Tyson.

Mackey turned around and grinned, walking backward for a few steps. "Man, you are just regular people, you know that?"

And then he trotted to his room before anybody could come out and ask him why he missed dinner.

THAT NIGHT, after Cambridge came by, good to his word, and served him some damned fine London broil with bordeaux sauce and vegetables, he texted Trav.

His conversation with Cambridge had, surprisingly, been about music. Cambridge had been a fan of Led Zeppelin, who had been big when he'd been in grade school, and was also a huge fan of some of the classics—Def Leppard, Tesla, Guns N' Roses.

"Yeah," Mackey said, picking at some bread Cambridge had stolen from the cafeteria. "Old Axl could really tear shit up. It was a shame what—"

"What he let the booze and the drugs do to his talent," Cambridge said with meaning, and Mackey felt a particular wrench at the words.

"Yeah, well, I guess they don't all go out in a blaze of glory, do they?" He took a bite of London broil and closed his eyes. "You know, it's like food tastes better now that I'm not doing coke anymore. Is that right? I mean, the coke tasted *nasty*. Fucking nastiest shit on the planet. And all I can think right now is that must have been some rush if I was gonna give up food that tasted like this."

Cambridge nodded and made a "mmf" sound through his own food. After he swallowed he wiped his mouth. "Yeah, I remember coke—drug of choice in the eighties, when I was going through college. Taste was bad, but it could definitely keep you up all night."

Mackey stared at him in surprise.

"What?" Cambridge asked before taking another bite. "You think just because we're doctors here doesn't mean we haven't done some of the drugs?"

Mackey thought about it, thought about everything he'd learned. "Were you an addict?" he asked carefully.

Cambridge shook his head deliberately. "Good question," he praised. "No. I finished grad school and stopped buying coke. I was done." He grimaced. "But my first wife, who finished the same year I did—she wasn't so lucky."

Mackey nodded, hungry for some poetry, even if it was from his shrink. "What happened?" he asked seriously.

Cambridge sighed. "We started working for an HMO, and she put most of our salary up her nose, and when we couldn't afford it anymore because we were paying off our student loans, she started stealing from the hospital."

Mackey listened, enthralled—and at the same time sympathetic. "Hard," he said, reasoning it through. "Watching someone do that to themselves."

"You think?" Cambridge said dryly.

If Mackey wasn't so relaxed, so hollowed out by his breakdown in the office and the damned decadent forty-five minute shower he'd just taken, he might have flushed. "How'd she stop?" he asked, not wanting to talk about himself anymore.

"She got busted by the hospital and got arrested," Cambridge said, grimacing. He wiped his mouth with his napkin and set it on top of his little foil-insulated lunch box. "It was before hospitals were so generous about sending people to rehab—she lost her job and her license and did two years in minimum-security prison."

Mackey was aghast. "That sucks," he muttered. "Man, that shit is just so *everywhere*, you know? You forget it's illegal until someone wants to remember."

Cambridge nodded. "Yeah. That's the truth. I know Kristin was pretty damned surprised—and so was I. I mean, I don't know why it was so much easier for me to stop. *Professionally* I do. I know about genetic studies and personality profiles and the differences in the way people respond to stress. But... but in my stomach, I don't. It hit me, how really damned lucky I'd been, to just be able to walk away. She couldn't, and it never seemed like her fault. I mean, we *bonded* doing blow in the bathroom when we were doing our clinical rotations. It was 1987—who *wasn't* getting high? But...." He sighed, and Mackey realized his voice had gotten really impassioned.

"I'm sorry," he said, his mouth dry. "What happened to her?"

Cambridge smiled. "She got out, rehabilitated. Got a job in retail. But she... she was angry with me. We both knew it was irrational, but the situation was difficult. It was as though I'd gotten away with something. Doesn't make for a long-lasting marriage," he said, twisting his lips. "I understand she met a nice man and is working on grandkids right now, but we were never the same."

Mackey nodded thoughtfully. "It can fuck shit up," he said, picturing Trav.

"It can indeed," Cambridge agreed. "It's how I found my calling, though." He smiled at Mackey's surprise. "Yes—you heard me. That's why I'm here. Penance, sort of. But mostly it felt important. A real reason to practice healing."

"Craft is important." Mackey nodded earnestly. "If it's... it's a *real* thing you love to do, you want to do it your best."

Mackey was starting to hate that thing Cambridge did with his face, the thing where he wrinkled his nose and squinched up his cheeks. "And *that* discussion is for another day," he said grimly. With that, he stood up and started gathering plastic plates and throwing everything in the lunch bag his wife had brought him.

Mackey had a thought. "Hey, Doc?"

"Yeah?"

"Where's your wife right now? The one who brought you the food?"

Cambridge smiled. "She's eating dessert with the nurses. They know her here."

Good. "You guys riding home together?"

"Yup. She'll drop me off in the morning."

So the guy had stayed there for him, special. That was nice. "Doc?"

"Yeah?"

"'Kay, even if I fall apart and fuck this whole thing up? This was nice of you to stay here, bring me dinner. This was a real good moment. Thanks."

Cambridge looked suddenly bleak. "And that's something else we'll talk about," he said softly. "Here's hoping you have a lot of good moments to come, okay?"

Mackey nodded and gave the man his Tupperware. "Yeah, well, if I have them, they're going to have to be without Grant."

"Maybe they can be without anyone for a while," the doc said meaningfully.

Mackey grimaced. "Well, right now, I wouldn't mind if they were with my friend."

And that was why he texted Trav after Cambridge left.

*Trav?*

*Yeah?*

*Are we friends?*

Pause.

*At least. Yes.*

*I've never really had a friend,* he confessed. *Only brothers.*

*Friends are brothers you can pick.*

*Fucking profound.*

*I was trying to be wise.*

*Leave that to me. I've got the ass for it.* Mackey cackled a little as he texted.

*Why are you asking?*

Mackey sighed, took a deep breath, texted again. *Good friends are harder to lose than boyfriends, aren't they?*

*Depends on the friend and the boyfriend.*

*I mean... if you think of me as a friend, you might be more inclined to stick around.*

*Ah.*

Mackey scowled. *Ah what?*

*You're right. Being friends might be easier if you want me to stay.*

Mackey felt a solid ping of loss in his chest. *I do want you to stay. Maybe... maybe the friends thing has to come first. Maybe.*

*Maybe it does.*

*But that doesn't mean you can go out and bang someone and think I don't care.* His breathing had quickened as he typed it. God, he sucked at this.

*Backatcha, Mackey.*

*Great. Friends who are celibate.*

*Until you find someone your own age, I guess so.*

*And deluded. Deluded friends. Awesome. Healthiest relationship I've ever had.*

Mackey's eyes were closing—he had to type that last word six times.

*We're coming in two days. Anything you want us to bring?*

*Yeah—furniture catalogs and stuff. Don't I get my own room?*

*Yup. We were bringing those anyway. Anything else?*

Mackey thought about the dinner he'd just had, and suddenly he had a craving. *Chocolate cake. I want some, bad. The kind with pudding in the middle, and fudge frosting.*

There was a long pause, and Mackey wondered if someone had just walked in.

*Done,* Trav said in a minute. *Anything else?*

*Just thank you. Seriously. Thank you.* Mackey closed his eyes, thought that Trav and his brothers were waiting for him, and was profoundly grateful.

*Thank you.*

*Night, Mackey.*

*Night, Trav.*

Lights out.

# My Baby Sent Me a Letter

THIN, PALE, and tired.

Trav grimaced. Mackey was right—Trav needed to see him not awful sometime. He'd probably be stunning.

But Mackey didn't seem to care about how sad he looked. His hair was scraped back in its queue (his brown roots were beginning to show—he'd probably need a touch-up when he got out), and he was halfway through the gourmet chocolate cake Trav had ordered the minute Mackey had texted.

"Thmfh iff mrrelly fckkn gdd!" he garbled.

Blake, who was working on the other half from the other side, looked up and nodded.

Both of them swallowed in tandem, and Blake spoke up. "I didn't know 'til Mackey pointed it out, but coke really fucks up your taste buds. Man, it's like chocolate cake is seeing in *fucking color*, you know?"

Mackey nodded and made sincere eye contact with Stevie, who was sitting next to him at the little picnic table. "Don't ever start doing it," he said. "You know how you love cherry freezies? That shit all goes away."

Stevie looked appropriately horrified, and Jefferson put a comforting hand on his shoulder. Shelia had been making him cherry freezies since she got the damned blender—it was part of her mission to feed them better through Ninja.

"Yeah, well, we're not as driven as you," Stevie said apologetically.

Mackey paused in the middle of a bite. He chewed thoughtfully and swallowed. "Well, that's not necessarily a bad thing," he said after a minute. "I mean, you guys got each other, got Shelia—can't do that shit if all you do is play guitar." He wiped his mouth then, and Trav noticed his hand was shaking.

Apparently that idea was pretty close to the bone too.

"Mackey, you done there?" Trav asked quietly.

Mackey nodded. "Yeah. Blake, man, you can have the rest." He smiled quietly, his shadowed gray eyes lightening up for a minute. "Trav, that was damned good. Where'd you get that from?"

That whole text message about just being friends sat uncomfortably in Trav's lap.

"I, uhm, ordered it special," he said, because he'd started punching it into his computer the minute Mackey asked.

"Special?" Kell snorted, rolling his eyes. "It was delivered to the house *this morning*, and I swear the delivery guy looked like he was from the secret service. I don't think diamonds or rubies got as much red-carpet treatment as your chocolate cake, Mackey."

Mackey looked up at his brother and smiled, and for no reason Trav could think of. Then, without warning, as he was looking at Kell, Mackey's eyes got really red-rimmed and shiny and he blinked.

Trav decided he'd had enough. "Hey, Blake," he said kindly, "do you want to show everyone the facilities? I was going to show Mackey the catalogs for his furniture, okay?"

Blake nodded and scooped the last of the cake in his mouth. Trav noted with satisfaction that they had demolished it. Blake had shaved since he'd gotten to the facility, and even put on five or so pounds in the past week. He looked a little tired, but it was clear whatever his addiction issues were, they weren't as tough as Mackey's.

Mackey watched them all go with a haunted smile on his face. "They look good," he said, smiling quietly at Trav.

Trav nodded and slid into the spot next to Mackey at the picnic table, pulling out his briefcase with the furniture catalogs. His cast bumped the table, and he grimaced. God, that thing had been awkward this past week, and, yeah, a little painful. He refused to complain, though. He'd wanted this to be a happy thing—he really had—and he'd marked all of the bunk beds and the pages with the bedding, just to make it less of a pain in the ass.

"They look great," Trav said brightly. "I've got them running in the morning—we're almost like a little track team—and Shelia is cooking for everyone."

"That's not right!" Mackey said, suddenly passionate—Trav thought that was a plus in his favor.

"Yeah, I know. I hired a cook-slash-housekeeper to help her out. Astrid does the shopping and helps with the clean-up. She doesn't speak much English—"

Mackey squinted. "We're not... uhm, you know. Exploiting her or anything, are we?"

He seemed so concerned, and Trav reminded himself that Mackey's mom had worked service jobs for most of Mackey's life. "No, Mackey—we're paying her top wage and providing her with transport as well."

Mackey's tension eased a little, and Trav felt him relaxing slowly against his body.

Trav needed to give him strength. He just seemed so weak, so quiet.

So not the Mackey who had fought Trav for nearly two months.

Trav wrapped his arm around Mackey's shoulders, a little alarmed when Mackey leaned against him, sort of like a three-pound disaster of a stray cat.

"Mackey, how you doing?"

"Tired," Mackey muttered. "The cake was really good, but... I'm talking a lot to the shrink and it's wiping me out."

"Yeah, I'm getting that. Do you want to look at beds now?"

Mackey shook his head. "I want to just sit here like this," he said, and Trav tightened his arm. "I can't, though. I need you to do something for me."

"Anything."

Mackey reached into the pocket of his hoodie and pulled out a notebook that had been rolled up inside. "I wrote these letters—the doc said I could communicate with my family this way. I need you to read them for me... you know, proofread them?"

"But aren't those... private?"

Mackey straightened just enough to look at him. "You get what I'm trying to say and when I don't want to piss people off. I need that here. I don't want to piss people off accidentally. Can you make sure I don't?"

Trav nodded. "Yeah, Mackey. No problem. Right now?"

Mackey leaned his head against Trav's shoulder again. "Yeah. I was supposed to write one to you, but I wrote a song instead. It's like, I don't have the same secrets with you that I have with anyone else. And, well…." Trav felt Mackey shrug.

"Well what?" he asked, opening the notebook. Mackey had brought six or seven to rehab, and this one had scraps of lyrics in it as well as musical notations and even doodles.

A pair of eyes that looked suspiciously like Trav's glared at him on a number of pages, and Trav could only be grateful Mackey had progressed enough beyond fifth grade that it wasn't his penis instead.

"They're all near the end," Mackey said softly, looking at the notebook too. Trav's cast was getting in the way, so Mackey reached out and flipped a few pages, stopping at one of several pages that had been dog-eared.

"Got it," Trav said, his mouth dry. It hit him like an express train that this was a big, painful deal to Mackey. He wasn't going to fuck with that. "Okay—Kell's first?"

Mackey shrugged. "If he doesn't get it, the band falls apart," he said.

Trav figured that was pretty sound reasoning for an addict.

> *Dear Kell,*
>
> *I'm gay. At first I thought I didn't have to tell you, and then I figured you'd realize it all by yourself. But you didn't, and you started saying "Only bi when high," and I figured if you believed that, I wouldn't break up your world.*
>
> *But every time you use the word "faggot," I die inside a little, and I've spent most of my life wondering if you'd still be my big brother if you knew I was gay. And I'm weak and sad and an addict, but I think some of what's killing me is the not knowing. If I knew, even if you didn't want to be my brother anymore, at least I'd know where I stood.*
>
> *You're still the guy who didn't want me to get beat up and who didn't want me to overdose, and I love you for that. I hope you can love all of me too.*
>
> *McKay*

Trav swallowed. Aces. This was McKay James Sanders, the real Mackey. The articulate young man who let his emotions out in lyrics and who swung a wide berth around anything personal, anything private, anything that let anybody in.

Trav felt something escape him, a sound, a sort of nonverbal violence, and his eyes burned.

"What?" Mackey asked, his voice shaking. "Bad? Was it bad? Is it gonna piss Kell off? Man, it's gotta be—"

"Calm down," Trav said, and he dropped a kiss on the top of Mackey's hair. It smelled just washed, something masculine and sharp, and Trav liked it. "It's great. I'm just… just being stupid because I'm so glad. Something this honest, Mackey, and I know you mean it. You're working on it for real this time. Trying to make it stick."

Mackey grunted. "Yeah. It really hurts, you know that?"

Trav breathed hard out his nose and tried to still the shaking in his hands. "I'm so fucking proud of you I can't stand it. Let me read the other one."

> *Dear Mom,*
>
> *I'm gay. I think you might know already, but I've been trying not to tell you, not to give you anything else to worry about. But I'm in rehab, and things got really bad before I got here. I wanted to take care of you so bad, Mom, but I don't think parts of me ever got taken care of first. It's not your fault—don't ever think it is. You did your best. You loved us all. You fed us when there wasn't any money and kept us dressed and made us do chores. I really admire you for that—you should know that. I think parts of me were just needy. That's nothing you did. But I love you and I hope you still love me too, even though I'm gay, and I'm an addict. I worried so hard that you wouldn't.*
>
> *McKay*

Trav wiped a shaking hand over his mouth. God, this must have gutted Mackey. Must have ripped him inside out. It hurt Trav just to read.

The next letter sort of let him off the hook.

> *Dear Jefferson and Stevie—*
>
> *I didn't want you guys to feel left out by not getting a letter, but I don't have too much to write, really. You guys just always accepted me. I love that about the two of you. I want you to know that I accept you and Shelia too. Don't let anyone give you crap about being three people. You're happy. I'm just so damned glad that kids I grew up with are happy, I wouldn't care if Shelia was a whole other rock band fucking in your bedroom. I'm glad she's not though—that would be loud. But I love her—she's really nice. If she makes you happy, she's even more awesome.*
>
> *McKay*

Trav laughed a little.

"Jefferson and Stevie?" Mackey asked, his voice taking on some animation.

"That was a nice one."

"The next one…." Mackey sounded, if anything, more pained. "I'm not gonna send it. I can't. I told Cambridge it would do more harm than good, and he agreed with me. But it felt good writing it, you know?"

"Good in a good way?" Trav asked, looking at the name on the top.

"Not really," Mackey admitted, his voice clogged. "Just read it."

*Dear Grant,*

*I'm pissed. I'm really pissed. For most of my life, you were what love was all about, and you just ripped that away from me like skin. I try not to hate you, though, because it couldn't have been any easier for you than it was for me. We both had shit we had to do, responsibilities that about crushed us after we split up. I hope your baby girl gives you joy. I hope you find it in you to love your wife. It's taken me a fuckton of drugs and nameless men and pain to realize you were not the end-all and be-all of my life. But someday I will be over you, and I'll be able to forgive you, and I'll be able to go home and see your baby girl and not be mad.*

*I'm in rehab right now, and that's my promise to myself. Someday, I'll be able to do that. I think that's when I'll know that I've found peace.*

*I really loved you,*
*Mackey*

Trav had to breathe slow and easy through that one. It was about as honest as a breakup letter got. It was a pure, unfiltered glimpse into Mackey James Sanders's heart, and it was battered and bloody and still a little broken.

But healing.

Trav felt selfish, hoping there was enough of it left for him. Selfish, childish, all sorts of terrible things, because he wished he had a letter too.

He turned the page, though, and was still a little startled to see his own eyes looking back at him.

Underneath the sketch was the song.

*I'm here*
*You thought you'd drive us crazy*
*All rules and lists and things to do*
*But that wasn't the kind of crazy*
*That I got about you.*
*You looked at us and saw a mess*
*And put us back in order.*
*You looked at me and saw a mess*
*And instead of making me all pretty*
*You told me how to fix it.*
*You looked at me and saw me*
*And you saw I was still good.*
*And just that moment I thought*
*That I was born to scream and disappear*

*I realized that I'm still here.*
*So here we are in places freshly cleaned*
*Made neat with folded clothes*
*A roof a yard a picket fence*
*And privacy we've never known.*
*I'm scrubbing up my heart and soul*
*And getting rid of what's mostly black*
*Because I know when I look at you*
*You'll look at me right back.*
*Because that time when I was gonna try*
*To disappear*
*Has come and gone and gone away*
*When you see me*
*I'm still here.*

Trav's throat was thick, and he touched his fingers to the deep grooves etched on the paper by the ballpoint pen Mackey used. It was all so precise, he thought. No strike-throughs, no scratched-out places. Every word, both in the letters and the lyrics, had been chosen long before it was ever written down. Edited, yes, but edited in Mackey's head. Trav wondered if there were rough drafts on napkins, program paper, brochures, and if the cheap notebooks only saw the purest things Mackey wrote down.

Or maybe just this one.

Trav wasn't sure.

He closed his eyes tight, because it didn't matter. "That's my song?" he asked, voice shaking.

"Yeah," Mackey said. "Is it okay that I wrote that?"

"It's in your heart, Mackey. I'm not going to say it's wrong."

"But what do you think about it?"

Trav reached out and touched the letters again. His finger was shaking.

"It's beautiful," he said, his voice thick. God. This kid. This man. Trav could hardly speak. "The things in your heart, Mackey. They're beautiful." He was undone. All Mackey's words about being friends, and this was about the most poetic thing Trav had ever seen. It wasn't platonic. It was the song of lovers who hadn't touched.

"Thanks, Trav," Mackey whispered. Trav realized Mackey was crying, soundlessly, helplessly, and that this day with the chocolate cake and the catalogs and the family was probably a titanic undertaking for him.

"Are you going to send those to your family?" Trav asked, his chest suddenly aching. *Oh please, Mackey. Please come out to your family so this part of who you are can stop causing you so much pain.*

"Yeah," Mackey said. "Next week. Will you…." Trav heard him swallow. "Will you be there for my brothers when they get them?"

"I'll be there for you too," Trav promised.

Blake brought everybody back right then, and Mackey couldn't seem to stop crying. He hugged everyone distractedly, not saying a lot, barely able to wipe his face on his shoulder. Trav walked him back to Dr. Cambridge, worried, sad, and hopeful all at once.

"It's okay," Cambridge reassured them, looking at Mackey with that exasperated combination of pride and sadness and pain that Trav knew from his own heart. "If you're doing this right, it's going to be like an open wound for a while. Don't worry, Mackey. Let's go back to your room and lie down for a while, and we'll have a talk."

"Bye, Trav," Mackey said, and Trav folded him up, held him so damned tight he wasn't sure if Mackey could breathe. But Mackey hugged him back, his arms wiry, strong, and reassuring.

"You'll get better," Trav whispered. "You'll have to. I need to hear you sing that song."

Mackey popped back from his hug and grinned. "That's right!" he said, seeming to snap out of the tears for a minute. "You don't have the music in your head like I do. That's a deal!"

Cambridge led Mackey away, the battered spiral notebook still clutched in his hand. Trav walked back to the group thoughtfully.

Next week, he thought, was going to be *very* interesting.

ON THE way home, the brothers were… well, thoughtful as well.

"What're we doin' next?" Kell asked, like he always did.

Trav grimaced. He couldn't imagine Gerry had given this group that much guidance—he was pretty sure that had been Mackey. It was one of the reasons he'd started their running regimen. In a way he'd made the house into a rehab facility—they were all rehabilitating from being on the road and having nothing to do but hang out in hotel rooms and get high.

"How about you guys pick out some bunk beds and bedding for Mackey? We never did get to that, and we need to order it before next week if it's going to get here on time."

"Can we order some for Blake too?"

Trav sighed. Hell—that was his *own* prejudice against Blake, who'd been Mackey's self-professed dealer. "Yes, of course. If you guys text, you can ask him what he wants."

Kell smiled, and Trav thought that he really wasn't a bad young man once you got past the redneck. And the urge to protect Mackey, which had gone so horribly awry.

And like he was justifying Trav's faith, he suddenly asked a really perceptive question. "Blake said they're getting along okay now—do you think that will last outside of rehab?"

Trav picked absently at his cast. The guys had all signed it—which was actually sort of cool—but mostly it felt like a fiberglass brick on his arm. It would be off a little after Mackey got back—he could only be grateful. "I think it will have to," he said carefully. "I think your brother didn't take losing your old guitarist well at all. Learning how to deal with change is something he's got to do if he doesn't want to start using again."

Kell hmmed. "It's just...." He sighed. "You gotta see. There wasn't any grown-ups. Mom was working and it was just... us. All of us. Wasn't much, but it was comfort. Grant left and...."

"No comfort," Trav said bleakly. "Yeah, I figured that out, you know?"

Kell reached forward and smacked him on the thigh. "Well, good thing we've got you—you're like the dad he never had."

He was, by chance, sitting between Stevie and Jefferson in the back of the limo. He actually *saw* them exchange glances before they fell apart, laughing silently, one on each shoulder.

"I can't *believe* this," he muttered while Kell said, "What? What? Guys, what'd I say that was so goddamned funny?"

As one, the twins recovered themselves, but it was Shelia who spoke.

"You're not very bright," she said, wrinkling her little freckled nose. "I mean, you've always been real nice to me, and it's great you haven't given me shit for being with the guys, but seriously, Kell. Read a book."

Kell scowled and glared at them all—and then lowered his sunglasses over his eyes and leaned back. Even Trav could see the disguised hurt.

He turned and looked at Jefferson and said just loud enough for Jefferson to hear, "Give it a rest. Mackey will tell him when he's ready."

Jefferson straightened and rolled his eyes. "God. Finally. If that's what's eating him alive—"

Trav thought of the song—*his* song—and the cry from the invisible boy who slept in forgotten corners and lived to make people love him or hate him or anything so long as they didn't forget his name.

"It's not," he said, knowing it was true. "It takes more than one break and a bad tube of glue to make your brother."

Jefferson started to crack up again. "Damn, that was almost poetry. You and Mackey—"

Trav shook his head, just that much, and Jefferson stopped talking, which was a good thing.

Trav didn't even want to hear it spoken aloud.

TWO DAYS later they got back from their run and scattered for their showers. They had a public appearance scheduled later that afternoon, a benefit they wouldn't be playing at, but they would be signing autographs, and Trav's entire day was focused on not pissing off Kell enough that he would actually *say* where the two missing members of his band were. Trav's phone buzzed in the charger as he came out of his bathroom (a luxury, that, a bathroom all to himself) and was drying his hair.

Terry's name flashed across the caller ID, and for a moment he was tempted not to answer.

"Terry?" God, he wished he was the type to hang up.

"You got *hurt*?" Terry's voice pitched shrilly, and Trav grimaced.

"I'm sorry, they were supposed to send my bills and stuff here. I guess that hasn't gone through yet."

"What did you do?"

Trav half laughed. "I hit a wall."

"*In a car?*" To his credit, Terry sounded worried for him, but Trav was too embarrassed to summon much sympathy.

"No, not in a car. With my fist. It was stupid, and childish, and I regretted it before I did it."

Terry's laugh was mostly disbelief. "Jesus, Trav—next time just hit the person!"

"I did," Trav snapped. "And that didn't make me feel any better."

Terry's low whistle seemed to stop time. "You *hit* someone?"

"I pulled the punch," Trav argued weakly. "I mean, he said I pulled the punch."

"You walk in with me with another man in the shower and I don't even get a raised voice!" The hurt was unmistakable. "What did this guy do to make you hit him?"

"Took Kurt Cobain's name in vain?" Trav hedged, and in the puzzlement that followed, he heard the boys, excited, downstairs.

"Hey, Trav—Mackey sent us letters! Did you know about this?" That was Stevie, calling up the stairs, and just the fact that he was calling for Trav's opinion on something was reason for Trav to go down.

"I've got to go," he said apologetically. "I'm sorry to worry you. B—"

"Trav?"

"Yeah?"

"I hope it works out."

The guys were getting *really* excited, and Trav didn't have time for this. "What works out?"

"This guy you love enough to get pissed over."

Oh hell. "I gotta go *now*," he snapped, and hung up the phone. In record time he'd barreled down the stairs in slacks and a polo shirt and loafers—no socks—half-afraid of what he'd find when he got there.

Kell sat on the cold tile floor of the kitchen with his arms around his knees, a lot like Mackey had sat next to Trav on the hospital bed, except Kell had a crumpled piece of paper in his hand.

Jefferson and Stevie were right next to each other, Stevie resting his chin on Jefferson's shoulder as he read their letter, both of them smiling a little while Shelia rested her chin on Jefferson's knee.

And Trav's letter was sitting clear as day on the counter that separated the kitchen from the entryway.

"The letters came," Trav said, wondering when they were going to get a call from Mrs. Sanders. "Good. It's about time."

Kell looked up through red-rimmed eyes. "You knew? You knew what this said?"

Trav sighed and hauled his creaky old man's body to the kitchen, where he sagged against the island and slid down to join Kell on the floor. "Yeah," he said, when they were eye level. "I proofread them—he didn't want to piss anybody off."

Kell swallowed and leaned his cheek against his knees. "I was supposed to keep him safe," he said, looking lost. "I was supposed to—that was my job. Enos Cheever about ended him—he was just a little kid and his face was all bloody, and I hammered that fucker. Made him back off. And I thought, 'This is what I am. I'm supposed to keep 'em safe.' Kept Jefferson and Stevie out of Stevie's house, 'cause—" He looked up to where the twins sat on the couch, and Stevie shrugged, like whatever Kell was saying, it wasn't going to bother him. "Because," he finished with dignity. "But... but that whole time I was killing him inside, and now I've got... I've got nothing. Who am I supposed to be for him?"

Trav sighed. For the umpteenth time since he'd walked into that crappy hotel room in Burbank, he wished he was a hugger. *My mother should have gotten this job.* Wasn't the first time he'd had that thought either. "I don't know, Kell. Who are you supposed to be for *you*?"

Kell looked at him like he'd started barking and scratching behind his ear with his back foot. "I'm me," he muttered. "What am I supposed to be? We all know without Mackey I'd still be in Tyson, married to the first girl I knocked up and running cars for Grant's old man." He gave an irritated shrug. "Fact is, Mackey could have ditched us at any time. We're just lucky we ride his fucking coattails."

Man. He'd wanted so badly to hate Kell, but that just wasn't going to stand up, was it? "So you kept your brother alive and he gave you an opportunity. What are you going to do with it?"

Kell glared at him. "I just told you—I'm not the kind of guy who gets opportunities. I got no fucking idea."

Trav glared back. "Kell, this floor is making my ass hurt and you're pissing me off. I get it. You're more a doer than a thinker. There's all sorts of shit you can *do* when you're not playing for Mackey. You work out three hours a day. Great. Do you want to take some personal training courses, some nutrition classes, make that happen? You like cars—fucking awesome. Buy a car and restore it. It's called a hobby, dumbshit. Fucking get one. Your brother still looks up to you. Did you not notice that he was afraid of losing you? Well, be a better person and you won't feel like such an asshole!"

Kell curled his upper lip and sucked air through his teeth. "You know, you sound a lot like Mackey when you're riled. You're gay. Maybe you two should hook up."

Trav pretended not to hear the riot that exploded from Stevie and Jefferson's corner of the living room. He pushed himself up off the ground and extended his good hand to Kell. "Glad to have your blessing," he muttered, but when Kell turned his attention to Jefferson and Stevie, he was relieved.

"Hey, guys—what'd Mackey say to *you*?"

Stevie looked over his shoulder and grinned, and for just a minute, he looked like any other young man in love. "He said congratulations," Stevie said, shining with absolute joy. "He said he was happy that we were happy. He said we were all okay."

Kell squinted at them. "And this was important to you?" he asked, not like he was being shitty but like he was trying to understand.

"Sure it is," Trav said, realizing it as he said it. "It's why there's all the fuss about legalizing gay marriage. When you're happy, you want the world to acknowledge that your happiness is valid."

"That's a lot of big words," Kell said, looking at him levelly. A month ago Trav might have missed the faint quirk to his lip.

"Don't be a fucker," Trav said amicably, and Kell burst out laughing.

"Yeah, yeah—Mackey's right. Congratulations, the three of you, on whatever the hell you are. Man, you're better adjusted than the rest of us fucktards, that's for sure."

There was general laughter, and Trav's pocket buzzed insistently. He knew who it was.

*They get them?* Mackey asked, and Trav could imagine him lying on his back and texting, hands shaking, that fuck-off-and-love-me expression on his face because he didn't want anyone to know this was important.

*They're fine. They still love you. Kell's going to get a hobby, and I just saw Stevie's teeth.*

*He has teeth?*

*See—it's going to be okay.*

There was a pause, and even Trav's hands started sweating.

*Anything from my mom?*

*I don't think she has my number.* He pushed Send and then thought to ask, *Maybe if you give it to me I can call and check. Wouldn't she ask you?*

*I haven't called her in a year,* Mackey confessed. *I begged Gerry to schedule us a concert last year during Christmas so she didn't have to see me be a waste of skin.*

*What's Cambridge say about that?* Because Jesus—a year?

*He says to wait to see what she says about the letter, dumbass! Why do you think I'm freaking out?*

Trav looked away from the phone and up at Mackey's brothers for a minute. "Hey, guys, anyone hear from—"

Kell reached into his pocket at that exact time. "Hey, look, it's my mom!"

"God bless the USPS," Trav muttered.

A confused moment of Kell talking to his mom and Trav calming Mackey down via text followed. Finally, after Trav's impassioned all caps-message of *LET ME TALK TO HER AND CALM THE FUCK DOWN,* he turned to Kell, who was holding the phone and backing up like he could somehow get away from the voice on the other end.

"Mom, I swear, it wasn't like that. We didn't set out to fuck him, I mean get him hooked—it was just everywhere. I was—Mom, I was looking out—no, I swear, I never called him that to his face. *He just told me,* Mom! I swear! I had no id—"

Trav grabbed the phone from him and spoke crisply.

"Ms. Sanders? Yeah. I'm Trav Ford, the band's manager. I'm the one who dragged your son to rehab." *Three goddamned times.* But he kept that part to himself.

"Oh," she said. His first thought was that she seemed sort of soft-spoken to have raised four boys. "You're not the guy they signed on with."

"I work for the same company, ma'am. Their first manager passed away a couple of months ago." Trav looked around the room—at Kell, who was having his late-adolescent epiphany without his other guitar player, and at Stevie, Jefferson, and Shelia, who gathered together in their own private tribe. "It was rough on everybody, but Mackey especially."

She sighed sadly, but her words were surprisingly perceptive. "Mackey's sensitive," she said, "but he's also his own worst enemy. I imagine this whole last year has been something of an adjustment."

Trav wanted to laugh bitterly, but he didn't. He was just so relieved not to hear any judgment, just so happy that Mackey's hopes for his mother's love were founded in truth. "Ma'am, I think you have that about right. Did you want to come up and see him? I could get you a plane and have you here in time for Sunday's visiting hours."

He heard the quiet catch of breath. "Could you?" she asked. "When the older boys were in school, it was all about keeping them fed, you know? And I wasn't there—because, you know—"

"Food, clothes, rent," Trav said. When he'd been a kid, those things were words. When Mackey was a kid, that stuff was not guaranteed. Ever.

"Yeah," she said, conceding. "But this last year, Cheever's been in special school, and I visit for dinner and volunteer, and it hits me, how much I've missed. How much I wanted to see but couldn't." Her voice wobbled a little, broke, but came back swinging. "I should at least be there for this, you think?"

God. These people were going to undo him. "I think Mackey would really like that," he said. "Do you have an e-mail, ma'am? I can send you—"

"Not really," she interrupted, and he blinked. "I mean, I didn't have one before the boys bought the house, and I just didn't seem to need one now. The phone was enough, you know? But the boys never call anyway."

Trav glared at Kell, who shrugged uncomfortably and said, "Yeah, I know that look. Kell fucked up again."

Trav hit Mute. "Damned straight. I've got some chores for *you* guys in the next few days." Then he hit it again. "Ms. Sanders, if you can text me your name and birthday and that of your youngest son, I can have two plane tickets waiting for you at the kiosk of Sac Metro. All you'll have to do is put in your ATM card and the kiosk will walk you through."

"Okay," she said, sounding a little overwhelmed. "But you don't need to get one for Cheever. He's had me to himself for a year. He can stay at the boarding school over the weekend—I can come down and see my boys."

Oh Lord. Trav closed his eyes and thought of how desperately these kids had needed parenting over the past year. And how badly he did *not* want to be Mackey Sanders's daddy. "I think that would be an *awesome* idea. Would you like me to send a car?"

"I can drive myself," she said proudly. "The boys got me a real nice SUV for Christmas. Grant Adams delivered it last year on Christmas day."

Trav took a deep breath. Of course he had. Jesus, this town sounded like a speck of wormshit on a soiled map, but it sure did seem to be eating up *Trav's* life, and he hadn't even visited. "Well, good, ma'am." He grimaced. During the conversation, the shrill, staccato "brrring!" of text messages received on his own phone had punctuated his every sentence. "You text me that information and I'll arrange your travel. Kell's going to give you my number if you need it, okay?"

"Yes, sir—thank you so much."

Trav's voice softened. "Any time, ma'am. You call me *any* time. I'm their manager, and my job is to make the things happen in their life that make it easier for them to do their jobs. Making sure you get to visit is part of that."

"I didn't know," she murmured, her voice wobbling.

Trav let a lot of rage out on his next breath. "Neither did they. Your kids had a lot to learn, Ms. Sanders. I think they're finally getting the hang of things."

He handed the phone back to Kell and picked up his own. He ignored all of the freaking-out crap Mackey had sent—stuff like *Talk to me, asshole!* and *Rot in hell if you're not going to text me back!*—and punched in his own beef with the world.

*You didn't call your mother for a year?*

Silence. Then, when Trav was about to text again: *She was always so busy. We never wanted to bother her when shit got real. She knew when I got into fights, but if I could keep a lid on it, she didn't know about the assholes and the way Kell and Grant stepped in. She didn't know about Stevie's dad. We just didn't tell her shit, so she could keep functioning. Got to be a habit.*

Trav groaned and scrubbed his face with his hands. *Should I worry about Stevie and Jefferson?* he asked.

Mackey's next text reassured him. *Man, you're asking the junkie fuckup in rehab. Ask them—Jefferson will tell you the truth. Might make you work for it, but he'll tell you. So what about my mom?*

*She's coming on Sunday. She really loves you.*

Silence.

Silence.

Silence.

*Thanks, Trav. I'm grateful.*

That wasn't good enough. Trav wandered out of the living room and up the stairs, hitting Mackey's phone number on the way.

"You're calling again? Really? Doesn't that defeat the purpose of the whole texting thing?" The words sounded sharp, but Trav heard Mackey's voice, choked and full, and he sighed.

"I needed to hear how you sounded."

"I sound like a big oozy hole. People pour in 'how you doing' and I pour out tears and bullshit. Am I putting a cap on the whole rehab experience for you?"

"You know, the worse it hurts, the less likely you are to need to go back."

"That's really fucking profound, Trav. Can I quote you when they build me my own goddamned suite?"

"Well, when they do, they'd better make sure I have a room in it, because I'm telling you right now, if we have to do this again, *I'm* going to need some fucking Valium."

Mackey laughed, and it stuttered out after a moment. "Would you really?"

"Take a Valium? Probably not. Why?"

"I mean, do this with me again?"

Trav froze. "Are you going to need it again?" he hedged, and then waited through another silence on the line.

"God, I hope not. But if I did…? Never mind." Mackey started to backpedal, and Trav couldn't let him.

"Yes." He took a deep breath and made sure he meant it. "I mean, I can't promise unlimited get-out-of-jail-free cards, Mackey. No one can. But right now? I'd do this again, because I've got hope."

Mackey's voice thickened up again, and the next noise over the phone was not subtle and it was not hidden. "I am such a weenie," Mackey apologized, but even Trav could hear that something in him had broken again but that maybe Mackey was learning how to fix these things.

"Baby," Trav said, hating himself, "don't cry. Man, I know you need to, I know it's healthy, but… but your mom is coming. We'll be here. Your brother still loves you. And hell, I think you made Jefferson and Stevie's *year*."

He heard the weak chuffle on the other end that indicated he'd made Mackey laugh through his tears, and he felt better.

"See? It'll be okay. You keep thinking you'll get out of rehab and you'll have to do it all again, and do it alone. But I'm here this time, and it'll be better. I mean, it'll be *hard,* but it won't be like the last time you had to run the band and be a rock star and have all this shit inside you that hurt. You'll have less shit, for one thing. But we're here to help for the other. Okay?"

The sobbing on the other end of the line got worse. "Trav, man, I'm losing it here for a minute," Mackey managed. "I'll get back on the line when I'm not a fucking pussy."

He hung up then, and Trav let him.

# Getting Better

MACKEY HATED crying. He hated crying and he hated rehab and he hated crying in rehab.

But he had to admit, every time he cried, it got easier to stop.

He was lying on his back, wiping his face with his umpteenth tissue, when someone knocked on his doorframe. Shit. That was Blake—they'd been going to practice today.

"Come in," he said, proud that he sounded mostly normal.

Blake sauntered in, guitar in hand, and Mackey nodded in approval. "Here, let me get mine. Sorry—got a phone call—"

"Are you okay?" Blake asked bluntly. One of the side effects of the place, Mackey guessed. Everybody felt entitled to ask that and expect an honest answer. Well, fuck. It wasn't like Mackey didn't need to talk about this anyway.

"Sit down," he muttered.

Blake did—on the bed, because that was where they played—and Mackey looked at him carefully. He'd known the guy for a year, but until he'd heard him talk in group, he hadn't really known anything about him. Dad in another state, a mom who expected him to haul his weight or move out, and a guitar. Not a pretty story—and Blake wasn't really a pretty guy. His face was sort of thin and weaselly, and his teeth buckled in the front. He still had acne scars. But he'd been shoved into rehab, same as Mackey, and he was working with the same sort of sincerity.

And whether he got along with Mackey or not, he still showed up to practice when they had time, and he tried harder and harder every session.

And he obviously loved music. He could talk about Pink Floyd and Led Zeppelin longer than Mackey, actually, and he seriously worshipped AC/DC.

They could bond, Mackey thought, his heart hurting a little. Mackey just had to give him a chance.

"See," Mackey said before clearing his throat a couple of times, "the thing is, I had to send my family letters, so they're all going to know, and there might be a press conference and shit—"

"You're leaving the band?" Blake asked, sounding panicked and hurt.

"No, genius, I'm *gay*!"

Blake actually laughed, and then, realizing Mackey was serious, he stopped. "Wait. I mean, you thought we didn't know that?"

Mackey rolled his eyes. "Well, it was a real goddamned surprise to Kell, I can tell you that!"

"Oh." Blake sobered and sucked air through his teeth. "He... he kept saying 'Only bi when high,' you know? It was... I mean, it sounded funny, and we figured it was...." Blake sort of sought Mackey's gaze, like he'd done something wrong and couldn't apologize for it.

Mackey took pity on him. "Yeah, well, if I'm only bi when I'm high, I'm never getting laid after rehab, so I think I maybe want to cut that bullshit out."

Blake looked away. "Well, it's not like I never glazed a donut when I was trying to make rent. Not that I want *that* spread around—it's not usually my thing unless, you know, food and shelter's on the line. You told your brother?"

Mackey nodded, feeling a pang of sympathy. Well hello and hallelujah—let the bonding shit happen. "Yeah, I told my brother—and no, I won't spread that around. That's between you and me. But I sent Kell a letter. Made the words small. But I think he got it. And I'm telling *you* so you can talk to him about it like it's a thing and not a joke, but there's something else I'm telling you that's not a joke, so you need to listen."

Oh God. Was he really going to say this? He closed his eyes and thought about all the times he'd ripped Blake a new one because he just wasn't fucking enough.

Wasn't fucking Grant.

Mackey looked down at his fingers as they played with the guitar strings, and he kept his vision there, mesmerized by his own fingers, which knew what he was playing when he had no idea. The notes from an old Gordon Lightfoot tune materialized, light and melancholy and tragic.

"See, the thing is, before we came down to LA, I'd had one guy. One boyfriend. My whole life. And he was the guy who had your job."

Blake made that teeth-sucking sound again, and Mackey couldn't make himself look up. "I'm sorry. I'm so sorry. Kell didn't know—still doesn't, if you want to keep that to yourself. And I still think you fuckin' slack when you shouldn't. But you gotta know... some of that shit wasn't you. Some of that was that you weren't who I needed, and that's not your fault."

Mackey swallowed into the silence. He had to look up. He owed Blake that much.

"I'm sorry," he said, and then grimaced and swore to himself. Blake's weasel-thin face had crumpled and blotched. His eyes were bright, shiny red. "And I'm really fucking sorry that I made you cry."

Blake had put his guitar down and pulled his knees up to his chin, sobbing into them. Mackey grabbed the box of Kleenex behind him and shoved it into his hand.

"Fuck. God. I'm so fucking sorry. Man, I never should have told you. You didn't have to know. I'm sorry I treated you like shit—you seemed to be doing okay with Kell, and I didn't think it even fucking bothered you, which just made me more pissed, and—"

Blake nodded and took the Kleenex. Mackey just gaped at him, feeling stupid, until he remembered himself, fetal on the damned floor of the shrink's office, and the one thing he seemed to need more than anything.

"Aw fuck," he muttered. "Blake, would you like a fucking hug?"

"God yes," Blake mumbled through the snot and the sobs, and Mackey found himself perched on the edge of the bed, guitars forgotten, as he comforted a guy he'd thought he couldn't stand.

# Breaking the Habit

TRAV'S TEXT was appropriately sympathetic. *Forty-five minutes?*

*Did I just say?*

*Well that's special. That's what you get for treating the guy like shit for over a year.*

*You're a peach, you know that?*

*Hey, it's not my fault you BROKE your lead guitarist.*

He stared at the text for a minute, and stared and stared, thinking about it, the words resonating around in his head like a song.

He started texting like mad, hitting the End key at the end of every line, texting a lyric for the first time in his life.

*If I break you can I fix you*
*Using bandages and tape*
*Kleenex and soft words*
*Is that all that it will take?*
*If I fix you is it worth it to*
*Touch the ragged ends*
*Of your shattered expectations*
*Of a man who's not your friend?*
*If I break you will I miss you,*
*Should your pieces disappear?*
*After all I have been with you*
*For a shitty, painful year.*
*Can I break you into fragments*
*That I paste and glue again*
*Or will you gather your arrangements*
*Cause breaking's too much pain?*
*Does it help to say "I'm sorry"?*
*That I didn't mean to make you cry?*
*Does it help if I am truthful*
*And tell you truly why?*
*So if I break you, should I fix you,*
*Will that be a bitter end?*
*Or maybe just not break you*
*Just shake hands with my good friend.*

Mackey finished, breathless, and looked at what he'd written. Trav had tried, here and there, to get a text in edgewise, but finally he'd just stopped in the middle and said *Tell me when you're done.*

He read the texts again and again, hearing the music curling up from his stomach, and even though it wasn't about lost love, and even though he didn't hear any screaming in the middle like with his other songs from rehab....

He liked it.

*That's good,* Trav texted. *I like that a lot.*

*Well, should I call it "Apology to Blake"?*

*Either that or "Grant You Bastard."*

Mackey narrowed his eyes and thought. Well, yeah. Maybe the song *could* be written from Grant to him—but he wasn't writing songs about or for Grant anymore. That was part of his rehab, he'd decided.

*How about "The I'm Sorry Song."*

The pause told him Trav was probably thinking about it.

*Yeah, fine.*

*Your enthusiasm will end me. I can feel it. It's destroying my psyche with daisies, rainbows, and bunny burps.*

*Yes, Mackey, it's a WONDERFUL song. I'm mad at you for not being madder at Grant.*

Mackey stared at the text, surprised.

*It's nice to know I'm not the only spoiled child in this relationship,* he texted, feeling a little bit superior.

Silence, silence, silence....

*He broke you.*

*You fixed me. Doesn't that mean you win?*

*I didn't fix you. YOU fixed you. I just kept booting you in the ass until you made that work.*

*Or clocking me in the jaw.* He laughed. God, that had been awesome.

*Go to bed, Mackey.*

*After I write the song down.*

*Yeah, fine. Do that. It's a good one.*

*Wait until you hear the riff.*

SO ALL in all, Mackey was doing pretty good. Even the meeting with his mother didn't suck too badly.

For one thing, she was dressed pretty. Shelia must have taken her around to the fancy boutique shops, because she was wearing a little column skirt that went right to her knees and a matching tank top/jacket thing. Her hair was done up nice, in one of those chignon doo-dads, and she had earrings that matched her outfit.

Just seeing her made him smile.

"You look real nice," he said, grinning, as she and the others walked uncertainly into the big visiting room.

She ran up to him and hugged him, wrapping her tiny arms around his waist like wire. She was the one person besides Shelia who was shorter than he was—but not by much.

"You look tired," she said, and he smiled gamely.

"Tired, but I'm not in tears. Hey, Trav'll tell you that's an improvement."

Heather Sanders looked over her shoulder at the guy Mackey was starting to dream about. "He's the one who told Shelia and the boys to take me shopping." She grinned, suddenly twenty years old, and held her arms over her head as she pirouetted.

Kell was at her side in a minute, wrapping his big arm around her shoulders and kissing her cheek. "You look good, Mom. Shelia and the twins did you up nice."

Mom looked over at Shelia and smiled tentatively, and was greeted by a real stunner from Shelia. Mackey figured that maybe the little threesome would do just fine.

And that was it. The lot of them looked at each other awkwardly for a minute, and for the life of him, Mackey couldn't think of a damned thing to say.

Until Blake walked by, looking wistfully into the visiting room.

"*Blake!*" Mackey called desperately, grabbing the guy practically by his collar. "Man, come here and meet our mom. Give her an hour and she'll be your mom too."

Trav sidled over to him while Blake and Kell were doing the back-pounding hug thing and murmured, "I saw that," looking at Mackey grimly.

"What am I supposed to say?" Mackey grumped. "Hi, Mom, I'm a fuckup, love me anyway?"

Trav pinched the bridge of his nose. "Okay. Start with that."

Mackey didn't look away from him. Short auburn hair, sepia eyes, lantern jaw, chiseled chin, broken nose—and lean lips that would look better swollen with kissing, and cheeks that would probably leave stubble burn on Mackey's neck. "It's like when we're texting, I think of you and I *think* I know what you look like, but I *see* you, and you're even better. How does that happen?"

Trav's mouth quirked up at the corners. "Same way I think you look good with your hair grown out so it's almost all brown and big shadows under your eyes. It's that whole tenderness thing kicking in—happens when people like each other."

Mackey grunted. "That's lame," he said, not really meaning it but not having anything else to add. "It's *just* like coke. You use it so you want it so you don't have the feeling of it going away. I see you so I want to see you so I don't have the feeling of you...."

Trav slid his hand, warm and comforting, to the back of his neck. "Not going away," Trav murmured near his ear. "Can't promise we're going to be lovers, but I'm not going away."

Mackey turned his head and looked longingly at Trav's straight-up brown eyes. "That's mean," he said after a minute. "Not being lovers. That's not the good way for this to end. Just being friends is—"

"Is probably what you need right now," Trav said patiently, and Mackey was going to get mad at him, but damn. He just looked so good.

Narrowing his eyes in resolution, Mackey turned so they were facing each other instead of side by side. While everyone else was engaged, he took a step into Trav's personal space, liking the heat of his broad chest and way his cheeks and chin were absolutely clean of strawberry-colored stubble.

Very deliberately he reached out his calloused index finger and traced the curve of Trav's upper lip, and then his lower lip. He was in midcurve when Trav's whole lower lip plumped up, grew softer, and Mackey stroked it carefully and grinned with extreme impudence.

"If we were touching below the waist, would I feel your 'friendship'?" Mackey asked, not giving an inch.

Trav scowled and took a step back. "If you grope me in the waiting room, you're going to feel the same friendship that got you here," he growled.

Mackey took a step right into his space. "You're still wearing the cast, smarty-pants. You feel so bad about that whole thing, there's no way you'd hit me again."

"Mackey," his mom said, looking over at the two of them meaningfully, "the boys are taking Shelia to the dining room. They're going to get some ice cream—what flavor do you want them to bring back?"

Mackey grinned. "Chocolate/strawberry," he said, because the machine swirled them both together. "What flavor do you want, Trav?"

Trav looked suitably grim for ice cream. "I'll go get you an extra helping," he said meaningfully.

Mackey sighed, resigning himself to a conversation with his mother.

Feeling vaguely haunted by all those times he'd gotten in trouble at school, Mackey walked his mom to one of the tables in a corner of the room, in the sun.

"He seems nice," his mom said as they sat down and the others disappeared around the corner.

"He's a hardass," Mackey said, meaning it, "but in a good way. Keeps us from losing our shit, you know?"

"Yeah, well, he was stressing about a press conference right before we left—had a couple of nasty arguments about it yesterday. You may want to get him to let his ugly bugs out of his panties and tell you what all the fighting's about."

Mackey hmmed. "Yeah, he texted me yesterday. Wants to know when Blake and I are ready for this. I told him Blake's a pro, same as me. We can do one from rehab, get the brouhaha all over with before we leave."

"What brouhaha?" his mom asked, and for a disconcerting moment, he felt older than she was.

"It's a big deal when public people go to rehab," he said, echoing something Gerry had said a long time ago. "So we're going to have to talk, and I'll probably do the big 'Yeah, I'm gay, so what' thing. It'll be fun! Like the fucking ballet, right?" Gerry had made them go to one of those when they'd played New York—something about a swan. Mackey remembered doing blow off of some guy's dick in the bathroom and, really? Not much else.

Mackey's mom searched his face and then covered his hand with her own. "Mackey?"

"Yeah?"

"Bullshit."

"Bullshit what?"

"Bullshit that's what I'm here to talk about. I've seen your press releases. I even collect all your magazine articles. I've kept the card from every bouquet of flowers you boys have sent me. But I haven't had a real conversation with you in over a year, and now you're in rehab, and you look like hell. Tell me something real, baby." Her mouth pinched tight, and her eyes grew overbig. He remembered that expression from the times she'd come to pick him up for fighting, from the times he'd gotten in trouble for cutting school. She hadn't known he was getting bullied at school, and she sure hadn't known he was sneaking off to see Grant, but she'd known *something*.

Mackey blinked slowly and lowered his head to the table, pressing her hand to his cheek. "It's okay, right?" he said helplessly.

"Is what okay?" she asked, lowering her chin to balance on her free hand. For a moment he could close his eyes and pretend they were on the bed, watching television, and he was fourteen and confused and frightened, but everything was all right.

"I'm gay."

"So you said," she said, and he opened his eyes to see the gentle smile on her face. "I probably sort of knew, Mackey."

"Yeah?"

"That night after prom, I gave you crap about the hickeys on your neck. You didn't say anything, and I kept expecting a girlfriend—but nothing. No girl. Ever. You'd have hickeys or love bites, but you never went on a date. You never talked about a girl. I'm sure the boys had girls throwing themselves up on the stage once you all started performing—but not once were you late because you got lucky."

Mackey grimaced in spite of himself. His mom wasn't stupid.

"Or not with a girl," she said softly. Then, painfully, like she knew the answer already. "Grant Adams, right?"

"Yeah," Mackey whispered, and he realized he'd been hoping for this as much as dreading it. Mom knew who Grant was to him. Mom knew that his brothers were all he had and that losing Grant….

"Is that when you started using? When he got married?"

Mackey smiled bitterly. "That and the money," he confessed. "We ain't never had money before, Mom. And suddenly I was in charge of keeping it."

She stroked his cheek. "Honey—you couldn't have told me?"

"Told you what?"

She sighed. "Yeah. Yeah, I get it. But now—have you told me all of it?"

God. But he had to. Two weeks—he'd been here for two weeks, and every time he'd spoken the truth, he'd gotten a little lighter, a little better. So he closed his eyes and let her touch his cheek and told her about the men. And then, before he could stop himself, he told her about the treating Blake like hell, and finally, Charleston Klum and the rape.

*She* was crying by the time he was done, but Mackey? He just kept his eyes closed and pretended he was fourteen. He'd fall asleep and his mom would stroke his hair, and just knowing someone out there loved him would make it better.

"Baby," she whispered, and he opened his eyes because he had to look at what he'd done. If nothing else, Blake had taught him that.

"Mom—I'm sorry."

"Don't be sorry," she said on a shaking breath. "Not about the gay, not about the rape. That shit's hard. Growing up in our town?" She laughed bitterly. "Honey, I am the *last* person to complain about a person's sexual history. But about the... the attack...." She just cried harder.

"Mom...," he said helplessly.

"The papers said 'assault,'" she hiccupped, and he took her hand and kissed the back of it.

"I haven't... I don't remember it," he said honestly, stroking his mother's hand. "I... so much other shit. Doc thinks it'll pop up one day—suddenly I'll be talking about ice cream and what's gonna come out is 'I was raped.' So, you know. Be careful when we're talking about ice cream, okay?"

She sputtered laugh-tears into her shoulder. "Will do," she choked. "So you're going to keep it a secret?"

Mackey sighed. He'd been coming to grips with grown-up things for a while now; this one was no exception. "Mom, I'm barely hanging on about this other shit, okay? Don't let the drug-addicted man-whore in rehab fool you—I'm *really* a disaster." She laughed some more, and he clung to that, because he still loved making his mother happy. "I can't do it in public. In private it'll be hard enough."

She nodded, trying so hard to keep it together. "And the gay? You said you were coming out on TV."

"Yeah." He paused. "Is that going to be a problem for you?"

Her response was gratifyingly quick. "Oh, honey, I've given up giving a fuck what people say. Cheever might not like it—especially when it hits the press—but you let me deal with him, okay? I still love you. I wish to hell I'd been here for you, but I don't see why that would change when you're all grown up." She completely broke then, no words, her head sinking into her arms, and Mackey had nothing to do but get up and hug her while she cried. While he was there, he realized that she was really, really tiny, because Mackey had been nothing but short his entire life, and she tucked into his hug like a little kid.

Trav and the others must have seen them, he thought later, because by the time his mom wiped her eyes on the aloe Kleenex that haunted every damned corner of this nice hotel for the chemically dependent, he had two giant paper bowls of ice cream—and it wasn't melted at all. Since they'd been talking for over an hour, Mackey could only eat his ice cream gratefully and say thank you.

Finally, finally, Trav rounded everybody up. Hugs all around, of course, and his mom's promise to text him often. Trav stopped and squeezed his shoulder, and Mackey said, "Screw that bullshit!" and launched himself into Trav's arms, seeking a real fucking hug.

Yeah, Trav faked not knowing how to give one at first, but after a moment, Mackey felt it. He wrapped his arms around Mackey's shoulder, and Mackey buried his face in Trav's navy polo shirt, smelling aftershave and sweat and even strawberry ice cream, because he'd dripped on the front pocket. Mackey didn't care. He stayed there, letting that warmth and that smell seep into him.

"I want more of these," he insisted, his voice muffled against Trav's pectoral.

"Yeah, fine," Trav said breathlessly. He pulled back and grimaced at Mackey. "You need to finish the program first," he cautioned.

Mackey managed to pull a blazing smile from his toes. "Man, fucking try and stop me. I'm not doing this again. It's gonna be a slide down a snow hill on a sled after this, you feel me?"

To his delight, Trav tightened his arms. "Like I've got a fucking choice," Trav muttered, and finally let him go.

The band walked down the nice concrete walkway to the limo, and Mackey's pocket buzzed. It was his mother.

*Trav seems nice. You two an item?*

*We're a hope.*

*I'll hope for you too.*

Mackey smiled and pocketed the phone, then looked up to where Blake was standing.

"Your mom's real nice," Blake said wistfully.

Mackey managed a smile with only a little twist at the ends. "Yeah, well, she liked you. Welcome to the family."

"You mean she doesn't wish I was the almighty Grant Adams?" Blake asked, but without too much bitterness.

Mackey had gotten good at telling the truth in the last two weeks. "Nope," he said as they turned back to the facility. "In fact, she never did take a shine to Grant."

"No?"

Mackey shook his head, remembering his mom's veiled warnings, her inarticulate fears. "She was never sure how, but she always sort of knew he was gonna break our hearts."

"Hot damn!" Blake said, a smile lighting up his thin, scruffy face. "For once I am not second-best!"

Mackey sighed inwardly. Well, he was never going to be Mackey's best friend. But he *was* Kell's, now that Grant had bowed out of the band. "Man, if you practice the bridge of that new song a little more, you might even tie with Kell. That asshole never practices when I don't ride him. Let's go fix that up."

Blake's smile turned gentle, like he knew Mackey was talking bullshit just to make him feel better, and Mackey shook his head and stomped off. But he knew his friend would follow him, and he knew they'd play music, and for now, that was plenty.

# Sweet Emotion

TRAV WATCHED the interview with the guys when it aired on *E!*, and wondered if he'd ever been prouder of another person.

Mackey had asked that Trav not see him awful—and he'd apparently hired a stylist to come in and cut and dye his hair to make sure. He'd put some makeup on and hidden the shadows of his eyes, and he didn't look quite so thin, quite so pale, and he was wearing his concert clothes—a red-and-yellow-striped jacket and a salmon-colored shirt with a lot of froth at the collar over jeans that almost showed his scrotum.

God, he was sexy, cocking his hips in the sunshine, front of the center, waiting for Blake to finish talking.

"Yeah, well, you go from the streets when you're lucky to eat to being surrounded by *everything*, you're going to lose your head, you know?" Blake smiled, and he managed to look both shy and sure with the same smirk. Trav had to hand it to him: he'd grown up too in the last month. He was even wearing a sports coat over his jeans. Kell had brought him one—Blake's request, but probably Mackey's suggestion, just like the clothes Trav had fished from Mackey's closet.

"How about you, Mackey?"

Travis had handpicked the reporters, and he'd gone with a bevy of women and men in their thirties—older, wiser, not pushy. The woman asking this question was in her forties but dapper and fit. Mackey smiled at her with the same kindness he'd used on his mother.

"How 'bout me what?" he asked, smirking.

After a spattering of laughter, the reporter nodded. "What do you think brought you here?"

Mackey smiled grimly directly at the cameras. "Well, a bunch of stuff, really, and some of it's private. But part of it was I'd had a breakup before we came down to LA, and it was something I didn't really get over."

*Good, Mackey. Make 'em come to you.*

"Is that why we never see you with any women, Mackey?"

Yup—sweet middle-aged woman asking that question, she made it sound like a joke, nothing invasive, nothing earth-shattering.

"Well, the reason you don't see me with any women is that I'm gay," Mackey said casually, and then he winked at the camera, like he and the audience could ignore the fact that all of the reporters had just lost their fucking minds.

"Mackey!" cried one woman, a little taller, a little louder than the others. "Do you think your sexual orientation had anything to do with your drug addiction?"

Mackey grimaced like this was the world's dumbest question. "Sweetheart, it's not the gay that made me want to use drugs, it was the fear of how you people react. You all promise to behave, I promise to lay off the hard stuff."

And like that, the atmosphere went from charged like a feeding frenzy to gentle laughter. Yup, he'd made them promise to behave—they had to play nice or they'd look bad.

"What was it that prompted you to come out?" called another reporter, and Mackey and Blake made eye contact while Blake nodded enthusiastically.

"Well," Mackey drawled, "I could have said I was only bi when I was high, but if I was gonna stay sober after rehab, that would mean I never got laid again."

This time the laughter was louder, and Mackey nodded, touching Blake's shoulder. Off-screen, Trav had been giving everyone the wrap-it-up signal, and they'd moved back into the center and out of the limelight.

"Did we dance well enough, Mr. Music Box Man?" Mackey asked dryly as they cleared the foyer.

Trav had no choice but to nod. "You did great, guys. Do you want a banana, or would you settle for a ride home in three days?"

"*God*, I want to go home," Blake burst out, and Mackey seconded it.

"You weren't shitting about the gym, right?" Mackey'd asked, and Trav had to smile, thinking back on it. Apparently working out was part of their daily regimen. When Trav had put Kell in charge of setting up a gym in the second garage, Mackey and Blake had about wagged their tails and lolled their tongues in gratitude. Well, good. In Trav's experience, hard-worked bodies were bodies that kept out of trouble.

He'd said good-bye and come home, to where Kell was recording the press conference on *E!*. After watching it with the gang, he felt a little thrill of warmth in the pit of his stomach.

"They look good," Kell said avidly, and Jefferson and Stevie concurred.

"I hope we've practiced enough," Stevie said, sounding worried. "Man, he kept sending us songs and shit—if we don't hit the studio sounding prime, he's gonna lose his fucking nut."

"Yeah, well, I'm sort of missing the studio," Jefferson admitted, throwing himself back on the couch. "I miss *the band*. This is the longest we ain't played since Mackey gathered us in a circle in our living room, you know?"

Trav couldn't keep his curiosity contained. "Mackey formed the band? How old were you?"

Kell closed his eyes like he was setting the date up in his head. "Yeah, it was a couple of months after Cheever's dad left. Mom went on a religion kick for a year—she was cleaning the organ player's house anyway. So she had us go learn guitar and piano while she was working."

Trav nodded, seeing the scene clearly behind his eyes as Kell talked. Mackey in the middle, ordering all the older kids around, the older kids desperate for a diversion, and the song about fighting just spilling out of Mackey's agile brain.

"God," Trav said when Kell was done, "he's really something, your brother. You know that?"

Kell squinted at him. "Yeah, but straight guys don't usually say that about other guys."

"I'm sayin'," Jefferson agreed.

Shelia stated the obvious. "Well, it's a good thing Mackey's not straight," she said. "Next time Trav can say it to *him*!"

Trav's face went hot. "I'm gonna go start dinner," he muttered.

"Don't worry, Mr. Ford," Shelia chimed in. "Astrid put stuff in a Crock-Pot for us tonight. I'll put the buns in the oven in an hour. We're good."

Trav sighed. "Then I've got work to do in my room."

Anything, anything, but think of three days and Mackey walking through the door, and what the hell they were going to do with themselves then.


TRAV'S BROTHER, Heywood, had two kids. Trav remembered asking once, "What's it like? You go to the hospital with your wife and come home with a whole other person?"

Heywood, who grew his carrot-red hair to his shoulders and did the same wispy beard thing Blake did, smiled shyly. "It's the weirdest thing—it's like you spend *months* getting the place ready for the baby, right? Stacking the clothes, buying the dump truck of shit that goes with this little person, studying baby, taking baby classes, just preparing to change your life for the frickin' baby. So we get the baby home, Nina goes into the bedroom to sleep, and it's just him and me, right? He's asleep. He's gonna sleep for the next three hours. So there I am, a clean house, nothing to do but take care of the baby. Would you believe I watched football? Hadn't caught a game in weeks, but I saw the whole damned thing before Ian woke up and needed to be fed. It's not always like that—most of it's not like that—but changing your life is really weird. Nothing's the same with kids except us. We're still the same people. It's all you got."

That was Mackey's first couple of days in the house.

He arrived and looked around in appreciation. "All this?" he asked quietly. Blake was loud—he toured the outside with the swimming pool and the downstairs with the gym, whooping and hollering the whole time.

Mackey just looked around with big gray eyes, and Trav wondered what was going on behind them.

"Yeah, Mackey. I had control of your finances for a bit—you can look at the numbers, but with all of you here, you still have plenty to manage."

Mackey smiled faintly. "Would you believe I didn't even think about that?" he asked, full of self-deprecation. "I'm just so damned excited we have a house."

Trav smiled back the same way, because Mackey was being *damned* quiet, and he didn't want to scare him. "Would you like to see your room? I ended up ordering the furniture myself, but—"

"Thank you," Mackey said, tilting his head. "I'd love to see it."

Trav had taken pains with Mackey's room. The biggest window faced the backyard, so when the drapes were open, you could see the pool and the fanciful flowered frieze that surrounded the backyard for privacy. Trav had picked the drapes, simple and bright blue against the white of the room. The furniture was a warm wood, and the bunk bed wasn't the simple military cot style—no. The bottom bunk was a queen-sized bed, and the top bunk arched over the head of the bottom one. Both beds were made up, one with red and the other with green—bright, simple colors for Mackey. The desk set matched the bed set, and Trav had included a music stand, a full keyboard setup, and a rack on the wall for Mackey's guitars.

Mackey animated when he took in the music corner. "Hey-hey! *That's* what I'm talking about." He did a slow pan of the room, which included a stack of framed concert posters Trav had gathered for him but hadn't put up. "You didn't want to choose for me?" he asked.

Trav shrugged. "I felt bad enough ordering the furniture without your input."

Mackey grimaced. "Sorry about that—I kept planning, but I sort of had my head up in my own ass—"

"In other places," Trav finished for him, and they both stopped awkwardly.

Mackey laughed weakly and rubbed his mouth. "It's like you know all my secrets, and I don't even know my own room," he said after a long, pregnant pause.

Trav nodded, figuring. He'd dreamed about seeing Mackey jumping up and down in excitement like a puppy, because Trav had seen glimpses of the playful Mackey even under his worst moments. But Mackey lived up enough to other people's fantasies when he was on stage. It was Trav's job to let him be himself.

"Trav?"

"Yeah?"

"Can I have, like, a fucking hug or something? I really just want to take a nap and hear the quiet, but I'm feeling so lo—"

Trav didn't let him finish.

Ah, God, how good he felt, how real, in the circle of Trav's arms. Trav crushed that slight, sturdy body against his own, and when Mackey went pliant against him, Trav had a sudden, disturbing impression of what making love would be like. All of Mackey's lightning in a velvet bottle. Trav shivered for a minute and tried to keep his prurient interests to himself.

But it was no use. Mackey knew his secrets too.

"Are you as fucking horny as I am?" Mackey asked, muffled against Trav's chest.

"God, yes."

"It was like jerking off was an art form in rehab, you know that, right?"

Trav's skin sang with Mackey so close. He shivered, clenched Mackey tighter. "We can't," he muttered. "Not when you just got out—"

"I know," Mackey said, surprising him. "Not... I gotta not be addicted to you too."

Trav groaned. "God, Mackey, I'll move out if you—"

"No!" Mackey looked up at him. "No. 'Cause someday, I'll be okay in my own skin, okay? 'Cause we got to go record this album and start this tour, and you and me are gonna be together, and I gotta think that you and me are gonna be together. Just not...." He rested his cheek against Trav's chest.

"Not just this moment," Trav finished, and Mackey made sort of a purring sound in his chest.

"No."

But soon. Trav could feel it. Either he'd have to leave, let this thing between them die, or it was going to happen soon. Trav, famed for his self-control, was hard and aching from a simple hug, and the touch of Mackey's skin against his, the warmth of his body, made Trav shake.

Soon.


MACKEY SETTLED in a day at a time. That first day, he spent a lot of his time in his room, knocking around, hanging posters, putting his ass print on the bed (Mackey's words), and getting on the phone and ordering three big ficus trees to put in the sunny spot under his window.

"I really want a dog," he told Trav, "but we're going on tour, what? Right after Christmas? I may have to settle for a ferret or something. Those things can travel with you."

Trav wasn't surprised. It was a standard rehab technique: the guy who got high because he didn't give a crap about himself would possibly stay sober if he had to feed a fish or a cat or a dog—or a ferret.

Or a ficus.

(Blake's choice was fish—Trav sort of liked the fish tank. It was peaceful, it was decorative, and guppies didn't have the mortality rate that ficus trees did. Trav privately asked Astrid to double check the ficus trees when she could to make sure Mackey wasn't watering them to death. He also started researching purse dogs, because dogs he knew, but ferrets were right out of his ken.)

So Mackey slept a lot in the first few days, and within a week, they were back in the studio.

Where Trav got to see Mackey shine.

For one thing, they all knew he'd been writing like a lunatic in rehab. They got to the studio planning to do all of the stuff they'd been practicing *before* rehab as well as the songs he'd sent from the place. And *then* Mackey pulled out five different notebooks—some of them obviously with pages ripped out—and passed them around.

"I wrote forty-fucking-five songs in rehab," he said grimly. "Instrumentals and fuckin' all. You guys gotta play this shit, and we can only record fifteen. Take a look at what I've got, decide on the ones that make you curious, and we'll go from there."

"Are we keeping the songs we were working on before?" Stevie asked, not complaining, just making sure.

"I figure half of 'em," Mackey said. "There's some good work there, some hard hooks, but not all of it was my best work. This here—this is my best work. I figure we pick the very best shit so the CD sells like a motherfucker, and we work on the rest of it on the road. There'll be bootleg YouTube shit out the yang, and we'll have another CD in a year."

Trav tried not to gape. God, *he* was supposed to be the manager here, and for a minute, he thought about charging into the studio, grabbing Mackey by the sleeve, and pulling him out with an "Uhm, excuse the fuck out of me, but...."

And then he saw that Grayson was nodding.

"Good idea," Grayson said. "If you guys are out of the country and want to record, let me know. You going to Europe?"

"Sixteen stops," Trav confirmed, because he'd made those bookings himself.

"Ireland?" Grayson said hopefully. "I've always wanted to visit."

Trav had to laugh. Well, it was pretty much the middle of the tour. "Dublin, then," he muttered. "I'll start making contacts for studio time."

And Trav's little ego tantrum was effectively erased by the *stunning* competence and creative brilliance that was McKay James Sanders when he was clean, sober, and on a fucking roll.

"The I'm Sorry Song" got a unanimous vote. So did the song called "Fiddlefuckin' Around," another one called "Window," and "Words in a Glowing Box." So did Trav's song, "Fixing."

"I like the words one," Kell said hesitantly when that decision was being made. "But Mackey, it's... it's a love song. Aren't people gonna, you know, freak? 'Cause they know you're singing to Tr—a guy?"

Mackey stared at his older brother and grimaced.

Trav tried really hard to ignore the look of disbelief from Grayson.

"Man, did you know 'Wish You Were Here' was written for Syd Barrett, the guy in Pink Floyd who burnt out before they got big?"

Kell blinked. "No."

"Did you know Nina Simone did 'Don't Let Me Be Misunderstood' before Eric Burdon?"

Again that slow blink. "No."

"Did you know Melissa Etheridge recorded 'Tuesday Morning' as a tribute to one of the guys on that airplane that crashed who was gay?"

Kell grimaced. "No."

"So you know what people are gonna think of when they hear that song?"

"What?"

"Their own fuckin' problems, that's what. They're gonna hear that song and they're gonna think of their own fuckin' world and how perfect that song fits the person *they're* in love with, so just don't worry about the gay thing. We don't make a gay thing about it and the world will just shut the hell up."

"Yeah, yeah, okay. It's *your* heart up there on the fuckin' stage, Mackey, don't blow a gasket."

Mackey grunted and proceeded to other business.

Grayson kept staring at Trav.

"What?" Trav snapped after a minute.

"Is he really in love with you?"

Trav grunted. "There hasn't even been a kiss. He could have written it to a guy he saw on television for all we know."

But that grizzled, unwavering stare didn't quit. "Are *you* in love with *him*?"

Trav rubbed at his eyes. "This band is making me crazy," he said, each word distinct.

Gray let out a chuckle and turned back to see how the band was getting on, then refocused on Trav. "That's a yes," he said softly. "You guys done anything about it yet?"

Trav sighed. He and Terry—they'd met, courted, made love and moved in together, and split up, and pretty much the only people who'd known or cared had been the people they were having dinner with. If Mackey's song went big, Trav and Mackey's little flirtation/fixation would be part of music history forever.

"No," Trav said and went back to watching Mackey grab each of his band members by the heartstring he'd wrapped firmly around his fist. "Not. Yet."

RECORDING WENT well. Trav had never seen guys pick up songs, rehearse them, and lay down the tracks so fast. He started to realize that even high, Mackey's work ethic had kept his band on its toes, and sober? They were not backing down.

As October wound down to November, Trav was *stunned* to see that they would actually have their CD out on time.

"Holy crap!" Heath snorted inelegantly over the phone. "I am not paying you enough!"

"I didn't do much," Trav said, meaning it. "Once you get those kids some structure, they can take care of themselves."

And structure they had. Wake up, go running, go to the studio, come home, plan dinner, and, oddly enough, watch television as a family.

That last one sort of blew Trav's mind. None of the kids—not Blake, not Stevie, not any of the Sanders kids—had known family gathering time. What started out as Jefferson and Stevie leaning against each other on the couch watching *The Voice* while Shelia went to town in the kitchen had become a strategic planning of DVR capacity and when the gang would watch what where. Together. *That* blew Trav's mind. They had personal appearances, dates at dance clubs, trips to the beach—but getting home in time for television had become a priority. Trav had actually heard Blake—*Blake*—tell a girl that he had to get home early from the club or he'd miss out on *The Bachelor*, and he and Kell had been taking bets on which girl would get the rose.

Mackey was the sci-fi/fantasy king, and he'd pick *Arrow* or *Teen Wolf* over any of the reality shows any day.

And he made sure Trav watched with him. In fact, infuriatingly, he made sure they were sitting next to each other when they watched. Trav had gotten used to scheduling two hours a night with his back shoved against the corner of the couch and Mackey leaning against his chest, under his arms.

Simple human contact. No sex. No kisses. Just *Mackey* lying against him. Smoothing his hand unconsciously on Trav's stomach. Tapping out absent rhythms on the top of Trav's thigh. Making little noises when interesting things happened in the story. *Smelling* like high-end patchouli and like musk and like *Mackey*.

Trav found that more and more, he had to go down to the gym and pound on the punching bag after television time. The good news was he hadn't lost any of his fighting trim since moving in with the Sanders boys.

The bad news was that he went to bed every night thinking about Mackey curled up in a little ball in the corner of that brand-new bunk bed, and missed the days when he slept on Trav's floor.

Except Trav didn't want him sleeping on the floor anymore.

One night as the album wound to a close, Trav trotted up the stairs after a hard workout. They'd been watching *Hawaii 5-0*, which Trav thought was about the world's dumbest show, but the interaction between the two leads was a hard smack in the face, because it was *just* like him and Mackey.

And Mackey hadn't sat still the entire time. He'd squirmed and wiggled and grunted until Trav had smacked him playfully on the top of the head. "Mackey, you are driving me batshit. Sit still or go to bed."

"Like a little kid?" Mackey asked, but he didn't sound particularly wounded.

"Exactly like a little kid! What is this, kindergarten? Jesus, Mackey, wrap your arms around your knees and keep yourself from vibrating like a wind-up toy, could you please?"

Mackey grunted, but he held still, and they finished the program in peace. When it was over, Trav excused himself to go work out. When he came back up, Mackey was nowhere to be seen and everyone else was watching *Dracula*.

Trav walked past Mackey's room, feeling sort of bad about keeping family time short. He was going to stop and tap on the door when he heard a… noise.

A grunt. A breathy moan.

Oh hell, face it, the unmistakable sound of a hand beating flesh as quick as humanly possible.

Trav's knees went a little weak, and he leaned against the entryway with a thump. In the bedroom he heard a muffled groan—climax, orgasm, come.

Trav's cock lit up like a solar flare. His entire groin—his thighs, his asshole, his taint, his stomach—throbbed harshly with the ache of arousal.

He was leaning, head against the wall, shuddering, too undone even to move, when the door flew open.

Mackey stood there wearing plain gray sweats and a white T-shirt, faded thin and hanging to his thighs. Both of them were stained around his crotch, and he held a white towel in one hand.

The look he leveled at Trav was saturated with sexual heat and not friendly at all.

"You got anything to say to me?" he demanded.

Trav shook his head weakly. "No, Mackey," he said, feeling helpless and exposed, like he was the one standing onstage with his boner extended for the whole world to see. "I'm… I'm sorry. I heard a noise and… I didn't mean to mess up your… private time." God. Could he sound any more like a spastic teenager?

And like most things that made Mackey laugh, Trav didn't see this one coming.

"Yeah, well"—Mackey smirked—"don't mind interrupting my private time. I see you so good in my head, it's like you were actually there, helping make the mess instead of messing me up."

"I'm… nungh…." Fuck.

Mackey's smirk grew wider. "Yeah, Trav. You know what you were doing to me? It's too bad you missed it. I was on my knees, and you know, I ain't paid attention to a cock in a long time. I used to *love* having one in my mouth. I used to swallow that thing down, bury my nose in the pubes, and swallow, fondling the nuts too. I loved that. I loved it when I could get my finger all wet with spit and tease up the crease and just plug that thing right in the as—"

"Stop it!" Trav commanded.

Mackey's smirk didn't fade. "Sound good?" he asked, moving closer. Trav could smell the come on him, could smell his sweat and whatever he used as aftershave that already turned Trav on.

"God," Trav begged. "Mackey... fuck...."

"You let me know if that sounds good," Mackey whispered, close enough to lean his head forward. Trav didn't leave him hanging. He leaned his head forward too, until they met in the middle. "'Cause you say the word, Travis, and I'll be on my knees—"

"I'm already there," Trav rasped. "I'm on my knees, begging you, give it just a little more time."

"When? Dammit, tell me when! I want a sign, an end game, a *something* to let me know this is real and not just a stupid carrot on the string at the end of rehab. You wouldn't fuck me just to be a carrot on a string—I trust that, Trav. But the pit of my stomach, the root of my cock—they don't got no promises, you hear me?"

Trav nodded dumbly, realizing he'd been out-mind-fucked by someone he kept trying to think of as a kid. "Date," he said, grateful for an answer and feeling a little stupid. "We gotta go on dates. Make it real. In public. Holding hands. Like it's real. More than one. Can you deal, Mackey? Can you deal with a guy you gotta date and look in the eye the next day?"

Mackey sighed, and the smell of come and sweat got stronger for a minute. He rubbed his lips against Trav's.

"More'n one?" he asked, like he was making sure.

"Real dates, Mackey. Three at least."

Mackey chuckled low and evil. "Can I go down on you on the second date?"

"*No!*" Trav snapped, jerking back.

That fuck-off-and-love-me grin never faltered. "Then we'd better make it some kiss," he purred. He brought his hand up and rubbed Trav's lower lip with his thumb.

"Taste it," he demanded. "Dream of me."

With that he turned back to his room and the attached bathroom. Trav watched him go, licking his lips unconsciously, and then tried not to curl up in the hallway and come in his jeans when he realized the bitter-salt he was tasting.

He made it to his room instead, slammed the door behind him, shoved his hand into his jeans like a teenager, and squeezed his cock just hard enough to hurt—which made him come.

Then he sank to the floor, breath rasping in his chest, and leaned his forehead against his knees.

Dates. That was it. They were going to date. He was going to date a kid just over half his age, and if he was lucky, that kid wouldn't chew him up and spit him out before they actually got to make love.

A part of him was laughing viciously, like Terry would laugh if he ever found out, but a part of him was terrified. Mackey had him enraptured, shredded, dependent on a recovering addict for all smiles, all tears, all joy.

What would happen if Mackey couldn't keep those promises to stay clean and sober, not to drive himself beyond exhaustion, not to yearn for Grant Adams?

*Oh, fuck it, Trav—rehab won't fix you if Mackey breaks you. There won't be enough of you left for Mackey Sanders to snort.*

*Fuck.*

He willed himself to get up and change into a clean pair of sweats, wash his hands, and go to work at his desk. He would do this eventually, but not at first. At first he had to stay curled on the floor, seeing all of the possible ways this could go wrong and Travis Ford would never find himself again.

For the very first time, he felt with all of his heart why Mackey had taken that first pill, that first bump, that first shot of juice.

Because this? This promise of pain? This was one of the fucking scariest things Trav had ever felt.

He should be as strong as Mackey.

# I Wish That I Could See You Again

IT WAS unaccountably nerve-racking, going on that first date. For one thing, Mackey did not have a *clue* what to wear. He finally had to ask for advice from the one person in the household who could actually dress but who *wasn't* Travis Ford.

Shelia was thrilled.

"Something sexy," she said, poring over the computer catalogue with him, "but not… you know. Not your concert stuff, where you look like sex on legs."

Mackey grinned at her. "I *am* sex on legs," he crowed, but she didn't follow him down the bantering lane, and he was disappointed.

"Here," she said, thoroughly engrossed in the shopping aspect. "These jeans, right here. The black ones that come right to your hips—"

"Not the low-waisters?" Mackey had waxed again and everything.

"I thought we weren't doing strangers in the green room anymore," she asked, but without judgment or even sarcasm. She was just trying to make sure.

Mackey smiled at her, and it occurred to him that she was a sweet kid, and he liked her, but they weren't ever going to be best friends. "No," he replied, perfectly sincere. "No strangers in green rooms. Just a trip to the movie theater. It's not even a premiere. Then dinner. Then a walk on the beach." Mackey held up the Post-It Note, which, true to form, had the date, Saturday, and the time—leave the house at six—and the itinerary. "See? Schedule and everything."

Trav had probably been aware of the irony.

Shelia just nodded.

"Okay. Good. Then we know what we need. A jacket—nothing too fancy, something sort of classic…. Here. Black, like the jeans, with that white seaming so it's trendy? Yeah, you see."

"And if we order this now, it'll get here in time?" he asked.

Shelia nodded. "It will if you pay the extra shipping. It'll probably get here tomorrow—I think the distributor is in LA. I used to work for them."

Now that *did* surprise him. "So you worked retail before you… uhm, met the twins?"

"Oh yeah. You probably don't remember, but the last time you played the Coliseum in Oakland, there was a radio contest to go backstage. It was one of those festival things—you guys were in the middle, which meant you did like six or seven songs—and there were a bunch of us just eating off the cart. You disappeared, but Stevie and Jefferson came over to talk. I'd gotten fired to show up that day, you know? And we stayed up all night talking, and they asked me to go to Portland for the next concert, and eventually I just resigned my lease to my roommate and stayed."

Mackey couldn't even laugh at that. "Just followed the music, huh?"

Shelia smiled, so completely at peace with her life, Mackey sort of envied her. "Yup. Just lucked out that Jefferson and Stevie were part of it. And that they didn't make me choose, because I couldn't."

"Are you kidding?" Mackey snorted. "They've been looking for someone who could love them both for their entire lives."

She had magnificently wide green eyes, and she turned them on Mackey and blinked slowly. "You and your mom are maybe the only two people in the world who get that. Who totally accept it. That they're not gay and we're not perverts, we're just in love." Her smile didn't even twist. "Your brothers really love you. I'm so glad you're going to be okay."

Mackey turned away, uncomfortable. "Well, happy is happy," he muttered. "Can I get the bright blue shirt? The one like a November sky?"

"Oh my God," she murmured. "That's why you write songs, isn't it?"

Ack! "Can I?" he insisted. "Because I don't believe you when you say it's going to show up before the damned date."

"Yeah, sure, but I think the emerald green would be better since you're all blond again."

Mackey looked at both the colors side by side. Yeah. He could see her point. "Green is fine. Shoes? Socks?"

"Yup—here's the website right here. I still don't know why you didn't want to go shopping—there's boutiques just down the...." Shelia looked outside the window and sighed. "Yeah. Still there. It was nice of them to give you a break right after rehab, wasn't it?"

Sure enough, the small cadre of paparazzi who had started camping out on the sidewalk in front of the driveway was still there. Soccer chairs, Starbucks, long-range cameras. Mackey had asked if he could stand on the roof and beat off in public just to give them something to do. Trav said he'd move back in with his old boyfriend if Mackey did that; apparently the fucker had cheated. Mackey figured that was a serious threat right there.

"Yeah, well, it wouldn't have been a big deal if someone hadn't gotten the bright idea of going to get a quote from my little brother." God. Fucking Cheever. They'd warned Mom, and she'd warned Cheever, but the fucking school had let the reporters in anyway, and there was Mackey's pain-in-the-ass little brother, living off their dime, saying, "Just because he's a rock star don't mean that's right that he does that. I ain't gay like my brother."

Jesus.

"You could take the car," Shelia said. Everybody *but* Mackey, Trav, and Blake had gone out the night before. Some new nightclub—Kell wanted to scout it out to see if they played any good music. They all came back early to report the music was trance bullshit, and that was that. But Kell hadn't been able to drive the sweet little Mercedes he'd just bought, because they'd needed the security guy who was authorized to run those people over behind the wheel—or at least that was what Mackey hoped.

"Well, that's how we go to work, sweetheart," Mackey said, trying not to be bitchy. "And that's probably how we'll go out on this damned date. But right now? I don't need that shit. I just spent four goddamned weeks learning how to live a simpler life—how in the hell am I going to do that if I can't make the damned choice between catalog shopping and going somewhere the girl will offer to blow me if I make commission?"

"Do they do that?" Shelia asked curiously. "I barely get soda water."

"Kell and Blake used to go shopping *just* to get BJs," Mackey confirmed sourly. "Man, once I got my fucking jeans, I was *done*."

"Well, punch in your credit card right here and you can buy your fucking jeans and be done," Shelia said. He got the feeling that she was laughing at him just like he sort of thought she was stupid. Well, that was only fair.

"Thanks, Shelia," he said, meaning it. "You were a real help today."

She kissed his cheek. "Just have a good date, Mackey." And then she danced away.

"Your mouth to God's ears," he muttered. For just a stupid trip to the movies followed by dinner and a walk somewhere that didn't suck, this was starting to really scare the shit out of him.

HE FIDGETED in the driveway as the car pulled up, trying not to fiddle with his hair. He'd just gotten it layer cut, so it was a little too short to fit comfortably back in the ponytail, and he resisted the urge to drag his fingers through it.

Trav was late. Trav was late and he lived in the same goddamned house.

*Get your ass down here*, Mackey typed irritably.

*OMW.*

"Fuck that," Mackey grumbled, turning around and getting ready to stomp into the house. "On your way? You'd better be fucking on your way. Get me all dressed up and sweating through my pits at the end of fucking October, and you're on your fucking— oh." Mackey scowled at him. "Hey, Trav."

Trav twisted his mouth in that way that told Mackey he wasn't fooled at all. "Getting impatient?"

"You're ten minutes late. We can't leave for our run more than thirty seconds late or you are up our asses like an ugly bug. I dress up for a date for the first time in my *life*, and you are fucking *late*?"

Trav grimaced. "I was confirming our reservations and they put me on hold. I got pissed, I canceled the reservation and got a line on some place not quite so exclusive but hopefully pretty good. How's that?"

Mackey squinted at him. "You didn't pull any Hollywood douche bag crap about 'Do you know who I work for?' Because if you did, this relationship is over."

"You worried that I was dropping your name, Mackey? Well, don't."

Mackey grunted. "Well, good."

"I dropped Heath's—got me right in."

"You're fucking hilarious. Are you ready?"

The car was idling, and the driver, who, to Mackey's shame, Mackey didn't even know, was standing out by the door, ready to let them in. Mackey started hustling toward it when Trav stopped him with a hand on his shoulder.

"What?" Mackey couldn't quite meet his eyes.

"You know why people date, Mackey?"

"To get laid?" Because *duh*!

Trav growled and moved in closer. His heat was breath-stopping. "To get to know each other when we're at our best. You said you wanted me to see you not awful. This here's your chance."

Oh, fuck *him*. "Awesome," Mackey muttered. "And now if I *am* awful when I'm not trying to be, I'm *screwed*."

"Which is why there's more than one date."

Mackey eyed him dubiously. "God. This is exhausting. I'm starting to see why people marry their high school sweethearts. Who wants to audition their lead guitarists more than once or twice a year?"

Trav winked. "Well, just think. These dates could be the last audition you ever hold."

"Yeah," Mackey muttered. "Like I'll ever do *this* again. If this fails, I'm gonna be jerking my own chain for the rest of my life."

"Well, I hope I'm a better option than celibacy," Trav muttered. "Get in the car, Mackey, we've got a date to endure."

Not an auspicious beginning, no, but they managed to banter all the way to the movie. The movie was, thank God, something with lots of explosions and hot guys and someone with *magnificent* pecs wielding a bow and an arrow. Mackey could deal with a movie like that—some great scenes between the two leads, some poetry in the story, and a lot of adrenaline and cheering. And no real intimacy, and no chance to hold hands, especially because Mackey was downing the small bathtub of soda and giant popcorn that was half the reason to go to the movies when you could just wait for the whole thing to come out on DVD anyway.

But the other half was the giant picture and how that made you feel when you got to be immersed in the story, which meant Mackey couldn't stop talking on the way out of the movie theater. "Okay, so you know the scene where the motorcycle is in the air, and you know it's not going to make it, but the guy is the hero and you *know* he's not going to go out in a fiery ball of death? See, *that's* what a musical riff is like, the hard-core ones like 'Ramble On' or 'Limelight,' because they *shouldn't* come back together—it's all massive music destruction, a, whatyacallit, cacaw… no… *cacophony*, right? But I *love* it when that happens, because then it just goes, like, *kablooey*"—he made big, vague gestures with his hands to indicate "kablooey"—"and then"—he laced his fingers together in a cohesive unit—"it meshes. The guy lands the motorcycle, the chord comes together to a perfect B-flat, and it's like the universe *glows*. Because in that moment, everything is frickin' perfect, then the guy recovers the motorcycle, the song progresses to the finale, and that heartbeat, that moment where everything is perfect, has gotta be over." He took a breath, because that was a lot to say, and looked up at Trav to see if he was following along.

"Anyway," he finished. "That's why I love action adventure movies."

Trav's lantern-jawed face was inscrutable for a minute, and then his lean mouth sort of went soft like he'd just been kissed, even though no one had touched him.

"That's why I love, uhm, action adventure movies too," he said, but he sounded humble and not at all military and shit, and Mackey squinted at him, suddenly embarrassed.

"What'd I do wrong?" he asked helplessly as they made their way to the curb. The car hadn't arrived yet, but he knew Trav had texted for it as soon as the movie had ended.

"Nothing," Trav said, looking at him with that soft mouth and shiny eyes. "You did everything right. Don't worry about it, okay?"

The car pulled up and Trav opened the door and gestured for Mackey to proceed. Mackey slid into the back, still puzzled. "But Trav…."

Trav slid in and shut the door, leaned over, grasped Mackey's chin, and pulled him into a short, sweet kiss—soft lips, the brush of tongue, the whuff of breath on each other's face—and then he pulled back.

Mackey gazed at him, lips parted, and tried to get a handle on what just happened. One minute there were motorcycles, and the next—

"Don't worry about it," Trav said gruffly. "It's just that I've finally seen you not awful. You're stunning. Don't ever worry about it again."

The moment stretched, and Trav extended his arm. Mackey tucked himself against his shoulder and relaxed. He could do this. This was just like watching television at home. He'd gotten used to that, used to the guys hanging out, talking bullshit nonsense, bitching about which clubs to go to and which movies they wanted to see. He and Blake had decided not to club for a while—not until the clean-and-sober thing was really locked in stone—because they could get into so much trouble at one of those places. But that didn't mean Mackey didn't miss the live music, and that was what occurred to him now.

"I bet we would dance real good," he mused. "I mean, I'd love to go out dancing with you somewhere. Not to get high," he hastened to add. "Just to… you know…."

"Music," Trav said dryly.

"Yeah. Music. It's what drives the fuckin' world."

Trav tightened his arm around his shoulder and nuzzled his temple. Normally the nuzzling thing didn't turn Mackey's key, but he suddenly found it hard to breathe, and his skin tightened everywhere. He turned his face to Trav's and stole a quick kiss; then Trav stole another one, a little longer, a little wetter, but still slow.

Mackey closed his eyes, lost himself. Slow kisses, not going anywhere because Travis wasn't going to bang him in the back of the town car and that was that, but sweet. Kind. Lingering. He was getting hard, and if they kissed a little deeper, it would be urgent, but for maybe the first time in his life, Mackey recognized that he didn't *have* to. Trav had told him straight up, no sex on the table today. Just them, like a couple. Like in real life.

Mackey pulled away abruptly.

"What? Wait. I'm sorry," Travis said dazedly. His eyes were glazed and his mouth was swollen and slick, and Mackey took a moment to gloat. *He'd* done that, and it felt *magnificent*.

"Relax, Chief," Mackey said dryly, rubbing that swollen lower lip with his thumb.

Trav closed his eyes, grunting a little, and that was reassuring. It wasn't just Mackey getting all hot and bothered. Good.

"Why'd we stop?" Trav asked, sounding put out.

"What's a happy couple look like?" Mackey asked, totally intense. "We're dating—that's real. I mean, you saw me through *rehab*, and we're waiting, 'cause it's important. What are we trying to *be* that's so important?"

Travis tilted his head to the side, thinking, and some of that sleepy, gonna-have-me-some-long-slow-sex satisfaction slipped away. "Uhm, I don't know," Trav said, clearly buying time. "My parents, maybe? My brother and his wife? I want what they have."

Mackey nodded, totally sober. "Awesome. What do they have?"

Trav considered him seriously, which Mackey appreciated. "Right after I got out of the service, during break from school, I got to see my brother's wedding."

"Nice," Mackey said, wondering if Stevie, Jefferson, and Shelia ever wanted a ceremony. Or maybe Kell or Blake. "Was it one of those big church dos? Lots of flowers and fluffy dresses?"

"No." Trav absently ran his hand down Mackey's arm. "Small. Parents' backyard. They're both doctors—they were going to Uganda to work with Doctors Without Borders for two months after the wedding, and then they both had positions waiting for them when they were done."

Mackey gaped. "That is just way too fucking altruistic for me," he said, feeling flea-speck small. "I mean... holy *fuck*, what is the fucking karma backlog on that? Can they just walk up to people on the street, smack them in the face, and say, 'I am *still* a better person than you'?"

Trav laughed, his chest shaking under Mackey's head. "Uhm, no. I think part of the rules of karmic backlog is that you don't get to gloat over how good you are. But yeah. They're nice people. And they don't gloat. They just like their life simple. So they had a small wedding in my parents' backyard. Heywood's wife's family paid for the catering and a housekeeping service so my mom and dad didn't have to do anything, and they had someone officiate, and they made up their own vows on the spot."

Mackey felt a supreme mental dislocation at that. "They just... I mean, they didn't have a blueprint?"

Trav grimaced, but he did it gently. "What are you asking, Mackey?"

"How do they know how to make it work? You go to rehab, they give you tools, visualization, asking for help, meditation, physical activity, all this shit, and it's... it's *rules*. What rules do you follow to make this work?"

Trav narrowed his eyes, again, thinking, but slightly exasperated. "I think we start by not getting heavy on the first date, but since we just blew that to hell...." He sighed, and some of the exasperation slipped away. "We don't lie to each other. We respect each other's feelings. We do what we can to make each other happy. We spend time with each other. We keep our own opinions and trust that the other person can deal. We—"

Mackey held up his hand. "No, no, those are good. I can deal with those. Those are rules—I can follow those."

Trav looked at him disbelievingly, and Mackey scowled.

"No! I *can* follow rules!" he protested. "Swear! I just have to know there's a good reason for 'em. Or, you know"—he smirked—"something's got to be in it for me."

"So what's in it for you, that you follow these rules?" Trav asked, still dubious.

Mackey snorted. Honest to God snorted. "God, you're stupid. Flat-out stupid. *You* are! Jesus!"

Trav's mouth fell open, and the car arrived at the restaurant at that moment.

Mackey was overjoyed. "Look! Steak! Awesome, Trav—you pick the best shit!"

"Yeah," Trav said, but he sounded a little stunned. "I'm a genius. Okay, let the driver get the door."

Mackey turned to him with a curled lip. "What's the hell's the matter with you?"

"That's about the most romantic thing *anybody* has ever said to me, do you know that?"

Mackey rolled his eyes, mostly to hide how very pleased he was, and slid out of the car, Trav hard on his heels. "*You* haven't hung out with enough rock stars. We pull *that* shit out of our—"

Trav stopped him with a hand on his shoulder. "Don't make it small," he said, his voice low and urgent. "It was important. Like a gift."

Mackey was going to shoot off at the mouth again, but then he remembered that he'd meant it: he'd follow the rules because there was something in it for him.

He looked at Trav sideways. "*You* talk poetry. That's *damned* impressive."

To his surprise, Trav's face grew a little ruddier as they neared the restaurant entrance. "Yeah, well, artists are a weakness of mine," he confessed.

Which was a good and bad segue, because it meant they spent most of their meal talking about his ex-boyfriends. That could have been horrible, except Mackey, who hadn't really been able to fathom what Trav saw in him in the first place, suddenly understood.

Trav really liked guys with poetry. The boy on the sidewalk, Terry the pretty guy Trav had made cry, a computer animator, a voice actor—all of them were artists in one way or another.

Mackey was fascinated.

"Why?" he asked, his chin in his palm as he watched Trav devour most of a T-bone steak. Mackey himself had ordered the London broil, like he'd had with Doc Cambridge, because it was smaller and he liked the sauce. "You got all that big-dick hard-ass bullshit from the military—why you got a thing for artists?"

Trav smiled—and it wasn't an expression Mackey had seen on his face before. For one thing, he looked a little embarrassed and more than a little bit shy.

"It's something I can't do," Trav confessed after chewing thoughtfully and swallowing. "It's… I mean, it's beautiful. Painting, poetry, acting, music—it *moves* people, emotionally. And I've never been that sentimental, you know? I never kept souvenirs from the places I've been, from the guys I've dated. But when I'm with someone with all that in his heart… it feels like it rubs off a little. Like they give me some of that power, some of that emotion." He looked away, his shyness intensifying, which delighted Mackey no end.

"Stupid, right?" he said, and the face he turned to Mackey wasn't the hardass or even the sincere friend.

He looked vulnerable and honest, and Mackey realized with a sort of twist in his stomach that this was real for Trav too.

"No," Mackey said, petting his hand as it sat on the table. There were lots of people in the restaurant, most of them het, but some of them two boys or two girls. For a moment he reveled in the power of not being a dirty secret, but he had other things to do. "No, man. It's not stupid. We write songs so ten or a hundred or a thousand people can say, 'Yeah! I know exactly how that feels.' The person who can do that for you... that's some serious magic. I mean, to me, it's just...." He closed his eyes and found his words. "This *thing* inside me, and I need to let it out or it will just keep screaming. It's all in my head, and it doesn't feel public until I stand up on the stage and give it to people. But to the people, it feels like I said those things *just for them.* And maybe it's not that you're sentimental. Maybe it's just that you don't have the words or the music or the pictures that you can share with people—but that doesn't mean you don't want to connect. It just means you need an artist who can make it happen."

He opened his eyes to check Trav's expression and make sure what he said made sense. Trav's eyes were wide and shiny and luminous, and his smile was half-formed and wistful. "You know people pretty well, McKay, you know that?"

Mackey grimaced.

"What?"

"People do that," he said, shrugging. "It's like my real name is a secret spell to the real me. Weird."

Trav laughed, and Mackey didn't blame him for sounding bitter. "Yeah, well, if I'd known it was a magic spell, I would have used it a lot earlier."

"Travis," Mackey said. "Travis Ford. Like the truck but not."

He watched in satisfaction as Trav closed his eyes and let his full name wash over him like a touch.

"See?" Mackey challenged. "It's not so much fun when someone can do it to you."

"Have you ever thought that it's not the name but who's saying it?"

Mackey twisted his mouth and looked at his empty plate. "Dessert?"

"Yeah. Absolutely."

Dessert it was, and then the promised walk on the beach. Mackey was about talked out by then, so he held Trav's hand and just walked, smelling salt and sun, even though the sun was long gone.

And then they made the two-hour drive back to North Hollywood, Mackey dozing a little in Trav's arms.

"No sex?" Mackey confirmed as they pulled into the driveway.

"Not this time," Trav rumbled in his ear.

"'S'okay. It was a real good date. What're we gonna do for the next one?"

"You tell me," Trav laughed. "It's a two-way street."

"You got more practice," Mackey said earnestly. "You pick the next one, I'll figure out something good for the third."

"Yeah, baby. It's a deal."

It sounded like a good idea. Mackey should have known by now that ideas didn't always come out like you hoped.


NOT ALL days off could be dates. Mackey and Trav both had administrative work the next day, but Mackey finished his shit early—most of it was sign this and agree to that, and since Trav told him to do it, Mackey trusted it. Trav had told Mackey about his breakup, and even when Trav was breaking up with someone like an asshole, he was still straight.

Hell, it wouldn't have mattered if he'd been crooked. Mackey had signed everything Gerry had given him too. He was just lucky that even when poor Gerry was as fucked-up as Mackey, he'd had the band's best interest at heart.

So Mackey was done. He'd gone running in the morning with the herd, and he'd snacked on salty shit and played video games and he'd even settled down with a book. Everyone else was out and about—Blake and Kell were checking out a new arcade, and normally Mackey would have eaten that shit up, but not today.

Of all things, he wanted to *talk* today, to someone *not* Trav, so he could talk *about* Trav. And he couldn't talk to his brothers, because his brothers might have been totally behind him, and not spazzing out with the press, and a big happy family unit, but Mackey wasn't going to test that by talking about his big gay crush. That would just be pushing his luck, right?

He needed a friend.

Hell, Mackey's entire life, friends had been thin on the ground.

The only friend he could ever remember having was Tony, and Tony had declined to come with them and roadie when they first moved to LA. His mom was half-sick and half-crazy, and Tony had passed up on college to stay home and take care of her. His mother's health had been one of the things that made him stick with Outbreak Monkey after graduation—they had been his one escape.

Of course, shortly after the move, Mackey had disappeared down the rabbit hole, and Mackey had sort of lost touch—not that he'd confided a lot in Tony anyway. It had just been nice at the time to know someone who didn't hate him for being gay, that was all.

But that didn't mean....

Mackey pulled out his phone as he sprawled on the couch and listened to the silence of Trav doing paperwork upstairs. Hey there—Tony was still in his phone! Well, it had been less than two years—why not?

His first try got a discontinued signal, but Mackey had Tony's home phone, and he tried that one.

A young woman answered—probably Tony's sister, who was a few years older and had left town.

"Yeah, is, uhm, Tony there?" God. Social awkwardness. Could you beat it after a yearlong absence from someone's life?

"Tony?"

"Yeah, is this his sister? This is, uhm, Mackey Sanders—it's been a while, but—"

"Tony, uhm, passed away."

The words sounded hesitant and a little hostile.

"Passed away? He was like twenty. I mean, I know I been gone a while, but Jesus, I got *busy*—what do you mean passed away?"

"My mother got worse, and... he was here alone with her, I guess. He... well, he killed himself—"

"*How*?" Mackey's heart thundered in his ears, and he realized he was unconsciously digging in his pocket for the little prescription bottle that he hadn't lived without for over a year.

"Does it matter how?" she asked bitterly. "You got to go away and be a big rock star—yeah, don't think I don't recognize the name, Mackey fucking Sanders! You *left*— did you think he'd just be *waiting* for you, *pining* for you when you got back?"

"I asked him to come with me," Mackey snapped, because he remembered it, remembered Tony's first look of excitement when Mackey brought it up. Mackey had almost read his mind then: the thrill of leaving home, of not being the only out gay guy in Tyson, the sheer stinking joy of going somewhere else *besides* the place they grew up.

Then Tony's pretty, latte-complected face went slack with self-imposed misery. *I can't, man. My mother. She needs me.*

"The hell you did!" the sister shrieked. Mackey didn't even know her name. "Why wouldn't he—"

"I *asked* him!" Mackey shouted, because he had, and because Mackey may have dropped a lot of fucking balls, but dammit, he hadn't dropped Tony. Not on purpose. "I asked him—and he didn't, because *you* were out of town and *he* was all she had. Man, I'm a lot of fucking bad things, but I tried to get him out, do you understand me?"

"He was playing your fucking CD when he hung himself, do you know that?" she asked.

"I didn't even know he was gone!" Mackey said. "If you thought it was my goddamned fault, couldn't you have called me and told me he was gone? It would have been a fucking plus to come to his fucking funeral, you bloodless whore—you ever think of *that*?"

She started to cry. He heard her big rollicking sobs, and he screamed and chucked his phone across the room. It hit a glass on the kitchen counter, which fell to the ground with a crash and a tinkle, and Mackey stalked across the room to clean it up. He was throwing glass in the trash, blood dripping from three separate cuts on his hands, when he heard Trav on the stairs.

"Mackey—are you okay?"

Mackey looked at his shaking hands, the blood, felt the knot of pain rediscovered at the pit below his heart, and realized that no, he was not okay.

"I need some fucking Xanax," he snapped, throwing the last piece of glass in. Oh God. He did. But he wasn't getting any. He wasn't getting any Xanax, because he didn't have that crutch, did he?

"You need some—Jesus, Mackey, your hands!"

Mackey reached blindly for the paper towels and roughly scraped off the blood.

"I need some coke," he muttered, although the Xanax would have been better. He turned blindly and ran past Trav, because he *knew* what to do to make this go away, and it wasn't Xanax and it wasn't coke, and it wasn't vodka, although none of that shit was in the house anymore, was it?

He blew up the stairs and into his room. His running clothes were still on the hamper because he hadn't straightened up, and he stripped in record time, ignoring Trav, who was standing in the doorway, helpless, staring, and unsure.

*Physical activity creates natural endorphins—and it provides structure as well as tiring you out, all of which help you with rehabilitation.*

*So Doc, you're saying I'll be too tired to get high? That was part of the reason I got high in the first place.*

*Well, if you get some real goddamned sleep, Mackey, the PT won't send you screaming for coke.*

Okay, fine. Fucking PT. That was their fucking cure-all, wasn't it? Go running, beat up the fucking bag downstairs, maybe lift some fucking weights—*go running.*

Mackey laced up his running shoes, ignoring the open cuts on his fingers. Trav had bought him some nice running clothes, but his red microfiber shirt and white shorts were crusted with salt from that morning. He threw them on and wiped his bleeding fingers on them anyway before he blew past Trav again.

"You're *running* for Xanax?" Trav asked, sounding a little panicked. He was pounding down the stairs behind Mackey, but Mackey couldn't focus on him right now. Not getting high—*that* was a priority, right? *That* was what Mackey was supposed to focus on.

"That would be a dumb fucking way to buy drugs," Mackey muttered, jamming a Mickey Mouse baseball hat over his bright hair. "Running for drugs—new fucking sport."

And with that he sprinted for the back door like Satan was on his heels with a mirror full of coke and a Xanax-vodka chaser.

# Running On Empty

*THIS*, TRAV thought, watching Mackey bounce off the hallway walls on his way down the stairs, *this is why addicts are hard to live with.* You never knew what was going to set an addict off—hadn't Cambridge warned him of that? That veiled, subtle disapproval literally dripping off his tongue? You *never* knew what was going to set an addict off. You never knew whether being a lover instead of a friend made it better or worse. So many things could go wrong if you were too close to someone.

*He's going out the door without you!*

That thought galvanized Trav—he stopped debating whether Mackey's shrink was right and hauled ass up the stairs for his own running clothes. And the other things Mackey had forgotten—a cell phone and a wallet—because God knew where they were going to end up.

The group of big, high-priced homes in this neighborhood shared a trail that ran between fences for a good two blocks before finding its way to the parkland on the edge of the canyon. From there it rambled, sometimes intersecting city streets in good neighborhoods, sometimes in crappy ones, mostly just sticking to the edge of the canyon, sometimes venturing down a little in twisty paths, but not often.

As he ran out the door, it occurred to Trav that the canyon was a little bit dangerous to a guy who was wiping blood on his pants.

The thought spurred him on, and he caught up with Mackey in the first mile.

"How'd you—" Pant. "—elude the press?" Trav asked, cursing because dammit, he'd been all cooled down and relaxed right up until he'd heard the glass crash off the counter.

"I look homeless," Mackey muttered. "Nobody knew it was me."

Trav grunted and tried to catch his breath, because it was probably true. The crowd had thinned in the past week, and although the band usually needed a limo and a security guard to block the path for their group run, this had taken everybody by surprise—including Trav and probably Mackey.

Who wasn't even running like he usually did. God, Mackey was usually a pain in the ass on a run—he slowed, stopped, talked until he got a stitch in the side, rambled all over the path—but not today. Today he narrowed his eyes, hitched his shoulders, and settled into a ground-eating gait that could probably win marathons if he ever settled down to do this shit for real.

Trav took a deep breath and tried to forget that he'd been up early that morning, pounding the hell out of the bag so he didn't have to remember the feel of Mackey's body against his, didn't have to remember he'd made promises to support Mackey's rehab by not just taking him to bed and keeping him there.

Didn't have to fight the disappointment that a date with him seemed to have triggered Mackey right back into relapse.

Pound, pound, pound. Mackey's rhythm was impeccable. One mile. Two.

"Jesus, Mackey," Trav asked, his wind back by now. "What crawled up your ass and taught you how to run?"

"Tony," Mackey muttered.

"Who in the fuck is Tony?" Jesus. Grant? Tony? Just what Trav needed. Another fucking ghost from Mackey's past.

"Friend," Mackey grunted and then increased his pace, tried to pull ahead, probably so he didn't have to answer.

Trav had longer legs and more stamina. He drew even and left off the questions. Down the dusty path to the canyon overlook, up the dusty path to the side of the road, listening to Mackey grunt in exertion as their steps got shorter, harder, more powerful. Even Trav was out of breath for the next two miles, but then, straightaway, they were even, maybe ten miles out, and Trav was glad he'd brought his cell phone.

"You thinking about maybe turning around?" he asked, because usually they did three miles and Mackey called it quits.

"No," Mackey replied shortly. He was clenching his bottle of water, probably until it hurt, but he hadn't drunk yet.

"How long?"

"Till I'm done!" Mackey snarled, and put on another burst of speed.

Trav pulled even with him and took a look. Mackey was blowing hard, his face pale, sweat pouring down in the middle on a mild seventy-degree day. They were up over the canyon by now, running on the shoulder of an overlook, and Trav thought maybe it was time to call bullshit.

"When you gonna be done?" he asked, still running. "When's it gonna be enough?"

"*Till I'm done!*" Mackey shouted, turning around. He tripped, went down on his ass, bounced up again, and screamed it again. "*Till I'm done! I'm not done! I need to get this shit out, Trav. I need to run till it's gone! 'Cause I don't want it in me anymore!*" He turned again, hopping because he'd probably rolled his ankle, and Trav grabbed his arm, ducking when Mackey whirled around swinging.

"You wanna spar, Mackey?" Trav baited, dancing backward. "You wanna spar? Then let's spar! Here on the goddamned road. We're ten miles out, you know that? You wanna fucking run back? I mean, I can do it. But that's about a fucking marathon right there—your legs aren't like rubber bands yet? Because maybe you wanna stop trying to run and stop trying to fight and maybe tell me what in the fuck happened!"

Mackey paused for a minute, struggled, his face twisting until he looked like he was going to cry.

He turned and rushed the guardrail instead.

Trav wasn't sure if he planned to go over, tumble down the canyon through the brush until he rolled off an outcropping and died, or if he planned to do what he did anyway, as Trav grabbed him around the middle just when he slammed against the corrugated tin.

He screamed.

Loud, primal, something Trav would expect from a microphone, screaming, rending his throat, the echoes of his pain ripping down the scrub-covered hills, bouncing along the suburban valley below.

Again and again, until Trav shouted too. "Stop, Mackey, stop! Stop, dammit, breathe, baby, breathe!"

Mackey's next scream broke, his next scream crushed, disintegrated into dust at his feet, and Trav held on tight as Mackey gulped in air and let out a rubble of sobs.

"Breathe, baby, breathe," Trav murmured. "Breathe."

"God, Trav," Mackey mumbled, and he turned in Trav's arms, crying helplessly.

Trav held him, thinking only, *Thank God. Thank God. He'll take me and not the drugs. Me and not the horrible fall. Thank God.*

MACKEY CALMED eventually, pulled away and wiped his face on his shoulder, then laughed weakly.

"Jesus," he muttered. "My legs hurt. And we gotta walk back."

Trav held on to his shoulder, leaned forward, and kissed his sweaty forehead. "Nope. I'm earning my keep today. I brought my cell phone." He pulled it out and asked for their driver to meet them as they walked back. "We'll be the ones looking like ass and smelling worse. Bring towels and a fuckton of water and chocolate milk," he ordered, very aware of Mackey cracking up in front of him.

"What?" he asked innocently.

Mackey shook his head. His running hat was soaked through, and tendrils of hair snaked out from under it, plastered to his cheek. Trav risked everything and pushed some of that back behind Mackey's ears. Mackey looked away, out into the hazy valley, and sighed.

"Someday," he said ruminatively, "you're going to get tired of bailing my ass out, you know that, right?"

"Hasn't happened yet," Trav answered promptly. "You going to tell me what just happened? I was in the middle of a conference with Heath and fucking Japan—it would be great if I could lie to them convincingly about a burglar, you know?"

Mackey smiled faintly. "Would you? Lie about a burglar?"

Trav hated lying. They both knew it. "If it would keep you from another run like this one, yeah."

A brief nod. Mackey sighed. "Let's start back," he said, voice only a little wrecked from all that screaming. Well, Trav had seen the concert footage—the primal scream was Mackey's bread and butter.

They turned around and started the long trudge back. Silently Mackey opened the water bottle and took out half in a gulp. Then he handed it to Trav, who did the same thing. Trav crumpled the bottle and held it, and they walked on.

"Thanks for following me," Mackey said after about two hundred yards. "That was nice."

"I was worried."

"Well, that was probably wise."

Trav sighed but didn't press. Mackey just might surprise him and talk on his own.

Three hundred yards. Four. A train of cars came by, going fast enough to make walking on the scant shoulder a little scary.

"Fuckers gonna kill us," Mackey mumbled. They kept walking until they came to another turnout, where they both walked to the guardrail and made themselves comfortable, waiting for the car.

"Tony was a friend," Mackey said, and Trav was grateful, but not surprised. He'd hoped that Mackey had started healing. Maybe Mackey had healed enough to talk.

"Was?"

"He was our roadie—only out kid at our high school." Mackey laughed without humor. "Kell tried to be horrible to him, but me and Grant—"

"Wouldn't let him."

"Yeah—and then he started helping with our roadie shit, and Kell backed off. Just liked the music," Mackey murmured. "Our first fan. Heard me practice, guessed about me and Grant. I guess he had a crush on me, but I was straight with him. Told him the truth, let him tag along when we did out of town gigs."

"Why didn't he come with you?" Because obviously he hadn't. The kids had apparently stepped out of their own lives with only the shitty hand-me-down clothes on their backs.

"I asked," Mackey said, sounding wounded. "I asked. But his mom was sick and his sister was away at school. And we left, and I... dropped out of my head and dropped out of life, and he was all alone."

"What happened?" But by now Trav sort of knew.

"I wanted to talk to him," Mackey said plaintively. "I was... I was happy. I'd had a *date*, and you know? Neither of us had one of those. I thought I'd call, share. Tell him to get the fuck out of Tyson so he could have one too."

"What—"

"He hung himself," Mackey said abruptly. "Listening to my fucking CD. Fucking Jesus."

Their sweat had cooled by now, but they were both sticky, smelly, and sore. Trav moved to the side a little and grabbed Mackey's hand anyway. Mackey squeezed, and Trav nuzzled his temple.

"That's horrible, McKay. I'm sorry you lost your friend. But it's not your fault."

Mackey grunted and leaned into him. "Why's shit gotta be so awful, Trav?"

It was a child's question, one that adults could never answer.

"So we know the good stuff when we see it."

Mackey nodded, and they stayed there, just stayed there and breathed, until the car drove up the hill.


MACKEY DIDN'T say much on the way back—just sat and gazed out the window—but Trav didn't blame him. Probably arranging stuff in his own head. They got back and showered—thank God—and Trav got out and dressed in sweats and a soft T-shirt. His running clothes had chafed the holy fuck out of his thighs and nipples, and he figured Mackey's had probably done the same.

That was when he remembered the cuts on Mackey's hand.

The minute he heard the shower turn off in Mackey's bathroom, he was there at the doorway with the first-aid kit in his hand and a no-nonsense knock.

"Trav?" Mackey opened the door with a towel wrapped around his waist and dripping hair. "I thought no—"

"No sex," Travis sighed, almost flattered that that was the first place Mackey's mind went. "I get it—"

"Not that I don't *want* sex," Mackey hastened to add. "I mean, like—dayum—but you said. It's like rules. No sex until... I don't know." His shoulders slumped in sudden exhaustion. "Sometime," he finished disconsolately.

Trav wanted to appreciate his trim little body—the muscles popping out along his abdomen and arms, the pebbled pink nipples against his tanned skin—but his nipples were, in fact, red, and he had marks on his neck where his collar had rubbed too. The slices on his hand—between his thumb and forefinger on both hands and across the palm of his right—were the most troubling, though.

"Sometime," Trav promised, swallowing. "But let me doctor your boo-boos first. Let's stop everything from hurting, okay?"

"Sometimes it feels good when it hurts," Mackey said. He tried to make a joke of it, but his eyes were bright and shiny and his face was a peaked little triangle against the blue of the towels.

"Sit down on the bed," Trav ordered. Mackey did, without any fight at all. Well, it had been a long run. Trav pulled the numbing antibiotic out, and the big bandages first. "The hand," he instructed. Mackey's meekness when he held it out almost frightened him. "I know sometimes it feels good when it hurts," Trav said, his voice pitching gently. Mackey looked so defeated—this was not the good kind of hurt. "But I think you've been hurt enough." Trav applied the ointment on the cut on his palm, and then the big Band-Aid.

"I ain't a nice person," Mackey said. He used "ain't" primarily when his self-hatred was the harshest.

Trav smoothed the Band-Aid with careful fingers. "Not always," he admitted, working on the cut between his thumb and forefinger. He was going to use gauze and tape on this one—it would need to bend. "What did you do now?"

"I...." Mackey sighed. "I just got so mad. Nobody told me. Kid hung himself listening to my CD, you think someone would have called and told me. I mean, I was a fucking mess, but... God. He was a friend. And his sister was yelling at me about how it was all my fault and...."

Trav finished doctoring the right hand, held it up to his lips, and kissed the knuckles. "All better," he said softly. "What'd you say to her?"

He'd started on the cut on the left hand—a particularly nasty one that would probably hurt Mackey like a motherfucker when he was playing—before Mackey answered.

"I called her a bloodless whore," he mumbled.

Trav laughed. "Wow, McKay—tell me how you really feel."

"I was stupid," Mackey snapped. "I thought we covered this!"

Trav squatted down so they were eye level and held a finger to Mackey's lips. They were cold. The two of them had gulped water and chocolate milk in the back of the car, but it was pretty clear Mackey needed some real food. And a blanket. And a snuggle on the couch.

"Don't you have something in your affirmations about forgiving yourself, McKay?"

"My whole first name again? Jes—"

"Answer the question."

"Yes," Mackey sighed, some of the tension going out of him. "I am supposed to forgive myself for being human and try to make it right."

"You weren't responsible for Tony," Trav said, because Mackey wasn't up to saying it himself right now. "You may want to call the young lady back and apologize—but only if you think it will make *her* feel better, and not just you."

Mackey grunted like he wasn't sure. "Maybe a letter," he said after a minute. "Or a song."

Trav gave up any pretense of distance and sat on the bed next to him, wrapping his arm around Mackey's shoulders and pulling him into the warmth of his chest.

"You write good songs," he said, probably needlessly. "God, Mackey, you're so cold. I'm going to give you some ointment for the chafing, okay?"

"You don't want to put that on yourself?" Mackey's voice was sly.

Trav kissed his blond head and wondered what it was about soap and Mackey that just undid him. All his chafed places were tingling, and his groin and thighs were thinking heavy, aching, sexy thoughts when they should have been thinking carbs and sleep.

"You have no idea how much," Trav whispered. "But I want to make you dinner and hold you, okay? You ran for that guardrail and my heart stopped. I don't want to have the kind of sex that hurts with you. I want to have the kind of sex that makes you feel *outstanding*, do you hear me, McKay?"

Mackey sighed and pulled away. "It's a sweet idea," he said, his voice bleak. "I'll try to hope it happens."

Trav closed his eyes and sighed too. This was Mackey. One step forward, two steps back. He knew that. He knew that through three trips to rehab. He knew that when Mackey first walked into this house looking unnerved and skittish as an alley cat, his packed suitcase next to him. You had to love those cats for who they were. If you tried to love them for house cats, you got stripes torn from your hand.

"I'll go downstairs and get us some dinner," Trav said. "The others will be back soon. Do you want me to tell them?"

Mackey closed his eyes. "Crap. Yeah. They'll want to know." He opened his eyes and squared his face determinedly. "I should tell them," he said. "I'm the one—"

"Please," Trav said, something in him wavering, crumbling. Later he'd realize how big a thing this was, but right now it was a simple act of kindness. "Please, Mackey. You didn't do anything wrong. Let me do this for you. Goop up your owies and come downstairs. Let me protect you. It's my job—let me do it."

Mackey narrowed his eyes. "I'm pretty sure your job is to book us gigs—"

"As your lover, Mackey. Not as your manager. Let me do this as the guy who wants to get in your pants."

Mackey's jaw dropped in surprise, and Trav took his opportunity to exit. It was as close to an "okay" as he was going to get.

He got downstairs just as the rest of the household arrived with Thai takeout, for which Trav was supremely grateful. He and Shelia set everything out on the counter, and he gathered the guys together.

"Uhm, guys from Tyson? Mackey got some bad news today—you all remember a guy named Tony?"

Kell said, "Oh. Oh no."

"What?" Jefferson and Stevie said, predictably in stereo.

"You knew?" Trav gaped. "You didn't think of telling Mackey?"

"He was... I mean, we were in Japan! We were in Japan, and there was fucking drugs everywhere, and Mackey wasn't letting up on the fucking rehearsing unless he was getting high! And it was sad, but Grant didn't text me until the funeral—what the hell was Mackey going to do then?"

Trav held up both hands and blew out a breath. "God. Okay. God. Man, just a word to the wise, Kellogg, but if your brother is ever too damned high to tell him someone's *dead*, maybe you grab him by the *hair* and haul him to rehab, you think?"

"Yeah, whatever," Kell said, crossing his arms in front of his chest. He looked like he was going to cry, and Trav tried hard to remember that the reason he was doing this was that he was supposedly more mature than Mackey.

"I'm sorry," Trav said on a breath. "Mackey didn't take it well. If you guys want to be especially nice to him, say something nice about Tony—and *don't* tell him you didn't tell him back in Japan."

"How?" Stevie and Jefferson asked. They were holding hands, not like lovers but like little kids, and Trav wondered for the fifty-eleventh time if Mackey was pulling attention that these two desperately needed.

"He killed himself," Kell said, saving Trav from the hard words. They all looked at him and he shrugged, looking away. "I'm only a little stupid, guys. Mackey was walking a fine line—even I could see it. Grant texted me and I told him not to tell Mackey. I just.... Tony was a sweet kid. I wasn't always nice to him, but he was a sweet guy, and he didn't deserve to be all alone. But I'll be honest. If we hadn't gotten the hell out of Tyson, I might have done it first. I don't even have his baggage, or Mackey's, or—" Kell looked at his brothers holding hands like kids, and looked away. "I'm glad that if one of us was gonna stay, it was Grant. He's got a life there. He'll be okay."

Trav looked away and by sheer accident met Jefferson's red-rimmed eyes. They were both thinking the same thing, it was clear: Grant was probably not as okay as Kell thought.

As far as Trav knew, it was the first time he'd had a nice thought about Grant Adams, and it left him with a sort of queasy feeling in his stomach. Abruptly he decided that taking care of the band was probably going to have to be where his circle of sympathy ended.

"Whether he is or not, maybe if we could go a little easy on your brother tonight—let him pick the damned show, fetch him orange juice like it is your goddamned mission in life, whatever, I would be supremely grateful. Are we all on that train?"

"Choo-choo!" Stevie and Jefferson said. Their hands were still clasped, but they both pulled the imaginary steam-release valve with their free hands.

Trav decided that those creepy kids from *The Shining* had *nothing* on Stevie and Jefferson when they decided to be the same goddamned person.

But in a way, that helped things go better too. Shelia served the Thai food, and Mackey came down to a full plate of Thai, some orange juice, and a new episode of *Real Detectives* pulled up from HBO Go. Outbreak Monkey, band of lost boys, spent the night in, and by the end of the night, with Mackey limp and melted against him, Trav had cause to be grateful.

Look what they had become.

Kell had even gone and made milkshakes for everyone—Mackey got extra chocolate ice cream—and Mackey's shy smile at his older brother let them all know he wasn't fooled.

But he wasn't a dick about it either.

Still, he went to bed early, and Trav was tired enough from the run and the emotion to follow him. Downstairs he heard the others settling down for what sounded like another hour of television, and that was fine too. Sometimes it was harder to fall asleep when you thought yours was the only waking heartbeat in the big, lonely house.

But that didn't mean Trav didn't spend a few sleepless moments wondering how Mackey would sleep this night or wishing they were in a place where Mackey could just stay with him, sleep in his arms, be comforted.

The thought of Mackey in his arms made him hard, and he fell asleep aching and wanting and not comforted at all.

"TRAV?" MACKEY'S voice shook, and the soft glow of the hall light outlined his slight, wiry body in the doorway of Trav's room.

"Mwha?" Trav yanked himself out of a pleasant half sleep where he'd been imagining Mackey warm in his arms.

"I…. God. I know the stuff about rehab. How you're supposed to wait."

"Mackey?" Trav couldn't focus—his entire body was caught between the waking and the dream.

"That's why we're not together right now, isn't it?" Mackey whispered.

Trav grunted, sitting up. "Yeah," he murmured. "I can't be your new drug—that's what it's about."

"*You* would be the world's shittiest Valium," Mackey grumbled. "Man, I can't fall asleep thinking about you right here. Can't we just skip this part?"

"The abstinence part?" Ugh! Trav wanted to say no, they couldn't just skip this part, because it was important. But he ached to hold Mackey, to show him what sex could be like clean and sober and cared for and….

Could he even say it?

"I'm not saying I'll go out and use if you say no," Mackey said hastily. "I wouldn't do that to you, because that's not what it's about."

Trav sat up straighter. "Mackey, come in. Sit down." He yawned and tried to take stock of Mackey's mental state in the faint light from the hallway. "Tell me what it *is* all about."

Mackey turned and shut the door, which didn't help at all, but by the time Travis felt his weight depress the bed, he had a pretty good bead on Mackey's expression:

Longing.

"Mackey?" he said uncertainly.

"I'm trying to do it all right, Trav," Mackey begged, meeting Trav's eyes bleakly in the dark. "I'm trying to follow all the steps and check all the boxes. But my heart hurts and my skin aches, and God, I just want to be touched. I'm sorry I can't raise the plant and then the dog and wait a year and… I just…. Can you touch me and then look at me tomorrow, and it will be okay?"

Trav was all awake now. "Mackey," he said gruffly, reaching out to cup Mackey's cheek. Right up until he felt the stubble rasping on his palm, he was going to say no. "We're not hiding," he said instead. "You can't sneak back into your room and pretend we didn't do this."

"I wouldn't—"

"You could," Trav said, his chest aching. "But it would…." He hated to admit this. "Secrecy would hurt me, Mackey. I gave up too much to be a dirty little secret. You will sleep in this room, and you'll mention your boyfriend at press conferences, and we'll be a thing. And then if we break up, we can still be manager and band guy, because everyone will know. Do you understand?"

Mackey shook his head. "No—I mean yes. Not all of it, but some. I get that this is real. That it's not just an after-rehab thing, or convenient 'cause we're in the same house. I get that you want to tell people like my mom or your parents. That it's not dirty and it's not anybody's business but our own but it's not secret either. We're not a reality show— the fuckers outside the house don't get to film us. We got enough bullshit to deal with besides them. Is that what you mean?"

Throughout the long speech, Mackey kept his cheek against Trav's hand, laced Trav's fingers with his own, trapping them there, in this still moment in the dark.

"I didn't leave the military so I could be just a rock song, Mackey," Trav said, feeling the ache, the hole in his chest, that the thought caused.

"It's real," Mackey said, leaning close enough that Trav could feel his body heat through the comforter. "You want us to be a real thing. Not a one-time comfort thing. Not a thing after rehab thing. I get it, Trav. If you can help me when I screw up, I can try not to."

Trav felt Mackey's breath on his face and closed his eyes in the dark. How much honesty could Mackey take? How much could Trav stand not to give?

"I love you, McKay. I love you so much it would kill me not to try."

Mackey's breath caught, and his gray eyes lit up the darkness. "That's a big magic word," he said softly. Hurt resonated from every syllable.

"Someday maybe you'll say it to me."

Those careful months with Terry were forgotten, the responsible adult plan for Mackey cast out the window. Trav's hands shook on Mackey's cheeks, and he slid them back through Mackey's hair. The clean strands caught at his fingers, and he did it again, clenching his hands, holding Mackey still, lightning in a bottle, before he crushed Mackey's mouth to his for a kiss.

Blood rushed his skin in a torrent, a conflagration of need leveling him. He groaned softly, pressed Mackey back into the mattress, and took over. Soft, warm, wet, urgent— Mackey opened his mouth and let Trav in again and again, fingers squeezing, digging into Trav's biceps, the muscles in his back, his sides.

Trav was shaking, every kiss harder to pull away from, every touch on Mackey's small body harder and more insistent.

"More skin," Mackey gasped, shoving at Trav's T-shirt and sweats.

"Pushy little shit," Trav muttered, stripping as fast as he could.

"You know me." Mackey kicked off his own sweats and skinned out of his own shirt. "You know me. You know I'm pushy and selfish and mean."

He paused, naked in the ambient light from Trav's window, and Trav stood up, naked himself.

Mackey stretched out on Trav's sheets almost defiantly, one knee drawn up, his cock larger than Trav had expected now that it was hard and extended up over his thigh.

"You're a good person," Trav whispered reverently. He put one knee on the bed and bent to kiss the inside of Mackey's leg. "You're brilliant and hardworking and kind. You have the best intentions in the world." He took a mouthful of the soft skin of Mackey's thigh, and Mackey pressed himself into the bed, arching his hips up, hoping for more.

"Intentions don't mean shit," Mackey muttered. "I meant to do it all right, to wait for the plant and the dog and the… ah…."

Trav moved around his swollen cock and balls, going for a nibbling kiss on his lower belly instead. "You're an artist," Trav murmured against his abdomen. "Reality is fluid."

Mackey's giggle had a strained, painful sound to it, and Trav moved up to the delicate pink nipple against his fair skin. He outlined it with a pointed tongue, and Mackey's little cry told him the teasing was doing its job.

"You're fulla shit," he breathed. "But God, you touch me nice."

Trav glided his hand down Mackey's ribs, rubbing softly on his tender stomach, tracing the outline of his cock as it rested on his thigh.

Mackey grunted some more and Trav took pity on him, grasping him, erect and urgent, and stroking, hard and slow.

"Ah…." Mackey arched up into his palm and then sighed, sounding lost and a little frightened. Trav took his mouth again and Mackey devoured him, thrust his tongue inside, swept Trav's palate, tasted, possessed. Trav let him. *Damn*, Trav wanted this, had barely dared dream of it, yearned for the time Mackey Sanders would be old enough, whole enough, *well* enough, to possess like this, like a man, an equal, a partner.

Mackey had all but admitted he was claiming some of that adulthood on faith, but after the months of rehab, of rebuilding, of clinging to hope, Trav needed that faith.

A spurt of precome in Trav's palm made him let go, almost weeping.

"You're *stopping*?" Mackey demanded.

Trav grunted, reaching for his end table. Lubricant—every boy needed it, especially when he was spending nights next to the person he wanted most, their bodies divided by moral constructs and thin walls.

"I'm taking you," Trav muttered. "No half measures. We've seen each other's HIV status, Mackey—you got any qualms about no condoms?"

Mackey made a sudden sound, and Trav looked up into his eyes, suddenly young and vulnerable, all Trav could see in the shadowed room.

"I've… only done it that way with…," he muttered. "We did it once without condoms, 'cause he used them with his girlfriend. But yeah. I want it to be all of you." Mackey paused and reached out, taking Trav's face in his hands. "All of you," he whispered, a sort of wondering smile on his face. "All of you. I can have all of you."

He pulled Trav down into a kiss, a soul-searing lightning strike of flesh and passion, and Trav wanted to cry.

*You have all of me. How can you have all of me? I'm breaking rules for you, McKay, and I'll give you more of me than that.*

And still the lightning went on, raising the hairs on the back of Trav's neck with the electricity, the anticipation of what Mackey was demanding. Trav fumbled with the lubricant bottle, squeezed a dollop into his hand, and eased his fingers between Mackey's cheeks so he could find Mackey's delicate, scarred entrance. God, he seemed to hit everything in between, didn't he? He grazed Mackey's balls, his base, his taint on his way down, and Mackey spread his legs wide, propped up both knees, and ripped through the kiss like he was trying to rip through Trav's soul by way of teeth, mouth, and tongue.

Trav massaged his rim gently, and Mackey moved his hands down, spreading his asscheeks and pulling back long enough to make a demand.

"Ain't my first time," he muttered. "Need it *now.*"

"Mackey, slow?" Mackey might not remember, but Trav remembered the blood, the violation, Mackey's torn body.

"Mackey *fast*!" came the impatient reply, because apparently Mackey didn't connect the dots there.

"But—" God, who wanted to bring that up now?

"Now!" Mackey insisted, and Trav thrust two fingers in, his own impatience showing.

"Ah.…" Some of Mackey's urgency faded, and his hands fell back against the bed. He spread himself before Trav like an offering, and as Trav moved his fingers, stretching, he was suddenly conscious of what he was doing in this bed with a scalpel's touch of power.

Mackey, who gave nothing to nobody, was giving him *power.*

All Trav had to do was take it.

Trav thrust fingers, invaded, caressed. He spared a moment to push on Mackey's prostate, see how sensitive it was, and while Mackey jumped a little, it was clear that his real joy was the stretch.

"More," he begged, eyes closed, and Trav built the pressure inside him a little more, and a little more. "Ah…. God, Trav, please. I need it… need *you!*"

Trav greased himself up quickly, almost cursing Mackey's youth and impatience. He wanted to feel Mackey's hands on him, have Mackey explore, find his places too.

But right now, not as much as he needed inside Mackey.

He paused for a moment, his erection poised right at the gate, and Mackey opened his eyes.

"I'll do for you, Trav," he promised. "I'll make it real."

Trav closed his eyes, helpless. Mackey's best try. It was all he could hope for. Slowly, slowly, he thrust inside.

Mackey sighed, pushing out against Trav's invasion, conversely swallowing him whole.

Trav moaned and dropped his head to Mackey's shoulder, getting his bearings, trying not to just rut and come as Mackey closed around him with a grip of iron.

"So tight," he whispered, shaking, almost embarrassed by his lack of control. He'd done this before—couldn't remember *not* topping, actually, although he'd bottomed once or twice. But Mackey's heat was destroying him, taking out his controls, and it didn't help that Mackey's eyes were closed, his face slack with abandon.

He was just *giving* himself to Trav, and Trav had the sudden notion that he hadn't earned this yet.

But he couldn't fix that now. Mackey was taking him on faith too, and Trav needed to give a little back by taking care of Mackey's needs. Trav started to move, gentle thrusts forward, gentle pulls back, and forward, and back, until Mackey wrapped his legs around Trav's hips and urged him on.

Mackey's stomach knotted tautly with muscle as he clenched and jacked his hips up so Trav could pound into him.

"Ah, God, yes!" Mackey muttered. "Needed this. Needed *you.*"

Trav closed his eyes against Mackey's fierceness, needing his own space, the basic selfishness of sex, to keep him from losing it, from rutting and claiming and howling like an animal.

He'd promised tenderness.

That thought slowed him down.

"Sh," he whispered, dropping a kiss on Mackey's forehead. "Sh. It's okay. I'll take care of you."

"Faster?" Mackey begged, but his voice quavered.

"More," Trav whispered back, moving strong and sure. Not faster. Not frenzied.

Mackey sighed and clenched, and Trav had to laugh helplessly as a wave of need, of almost-orgasm, washed over him. Mackey knew how to fight dirty.

"More," Trav whispered again. He wasn't going to be quick and forgettable. He wasn't going to be a teenaged grope in the dark. They were men. Men made things right.

Slow. Slow. Dropping kisses on his closed eyes. Clenching Mackey's hip to pull him tighter. Nuzzling his temple to calm him. Swallowing his moans of need.

"Augh! More!" Mackey demanded when Trav's skin tingled icily, frozen with want. Trav shook hard with need and closed his eyes as his body took over.

"*Yes!*" Mackey hissed, triumph sounding in every sibilance. He dug his fingers into Trav's biceps hard enough to hurt, but Trav liked it, liked the strength, the closeted violence. Mackey wasn't weak. He wasn't a toy. He was small and strong and he could survive anything. Sweetness in bed included.

"Yes!" Trav whispered back. "C'mon, Mackey, help me out."

He pulled back for the better angle, relieved when Mackey fumbled for his own cock to give himself a hand.

"*Nungh!* God, *Trav!*"

Trav had no words. He needed. He took. It was the sum of who he was, and every breath, every frenzied smack of flesh, his on Mackey's, Mackey's on himself, made the need more and powerful and painful.

He *needed*!

His hips rocketed without his permission, and he wrapped his hands around Mackey's shoulders, the better to contain him to make sure he stayed *right there* where Trav could fuck him, could keep him, could possess him inside and out.

"Augh!" The come-sound tore from Mackey's throat, and Trav felt it spurting on their stomachs, hitting his chest as Mackey tilted his head back and ripped out that sound again.

His final clench around Trav's cock did it, and Trav closed his eyes, the brutal onslaught of climax tumbling him in its wake.

Oh hell, he'd wanted slower, softer, sweeter—

"*Now!*" he hissed, then convulsed, so buried inside Mackey he lost himself, lost the core of who he was, all of him taken in by McKay James Sanders, never to return.

He couldn't stop shaking, didn't want to pull out. Mackey's body was furnace hot, pulling at him even when he was spent, and Trav fell to his elbows, burying his face in the hollow of Mackey's neck and shoulder.

To his surprise, Mackey stroked his hair with come-sticky fingers. "Sh," he whispered. "Sh. S'okay, Trav. S'okay. We're gonna be okay."

Trav sob-laughed for a moment, still shaking. "Promise?" he asked, feeling pathetic, a thirty-five-year-old child in the arms of a man barely old enough to drink.

"Hope," Mackey reassured him, nuzzling his ear.

Hope had brought Mackey to his room, had brought Travis to Mackey's life.

"Strong enough," Trav murmured, and he let Mackey's body bear his weight and trusted that maybe he wouldn't hurt Mackey Sanders like the rest of the world. And that if he did, even by accident, Mackey could take it.


HE GOT up eventually, came back with a washcloth, and wiped them both down. He was especially careful around Mackey's backside, and Mackey grunted, then looked away.

"What?" Trav asked, and Mackey shrugged.

"Lotta strangers got the key to that room," he said, clearly embarrassed.

"I am shocked," Trav said dryly. "Shocked and appalled by anonymous rock star sex. I shall turn in my orgasm card now, never to go backdoor again."

Mackey smirked at him irritably. "Now who's being a snarky little shit?" he asked.

Trav smiled, feeling slow and mellow. He'd been keyed up for so long. "Scoot over, Mackey. I want some covers too."

"Wait—let me get my underwear. My balls get in the way if I sleep naked."

Oh geez. Of all the things. Trav started to giggle. "Are you saying you don't want to get your balls in a twist?"

Mackey glared at him, but his lips were quirked up and it had no real heat. "Well, since *you* seem to have yours in a twist enough for both of us, I'm thinking one of us has to keep hanging low." He'd wiggled out of bed, and Trav rolled into his place, not even grimacing at the wet spot. When he was situated, he turned sideways, extending one arm over his head and waiting for Mackey to snuggle in next to him.

Mackey fished his tighty-whities out of his sweats and wiggled in, then looked at Trav warily. "You meant it—I'm staying the night."

Trav swallowed. "You promised," he said, unnerved at how easily this man made him feel about twelve years old.

"What if I get up to write?" Mackey asked, holding very still.

Trav remembered those times in the hotel room, Mackey up, tuning his guitar, playing softly, making notations in the cheap notebooks Trav now bought in gross.

"Come in here," Trav said, his throat dry. "I can sleep through anything but shelling and antiaircraft fire."

"Okay, then." Mackey slid in next to him and mirrored his position, arm over his head, eyes wide in the dark.

Trav put his hand out just so he could flatten his palm against Mackey's chest and feel the air move it in and out. "What are you thinking?" Trav asked softly.

"You said the big scary word, and I'm a coward."

Trav closed his eyes. "It's real," he said. "Let's go with real for now."

Mackey's kiss surprised him, and he opened his eyes.

"I do, you know. Love you. That's real."

Trav felt the smile before he knew it was going to happen. "Then turn around and let me spoon you, McKay. Can we do that?"

"Yes, Travis Ford, we can do that."

Warm, warm and still, trusting, limp as a sleeping puppy. He filled up Trav's arms like nobody had in his life, gave himself more wholly than any other lover Trav had known.

Sure, Trav was borrowing him against a time when he felt whole and complete inside. But Trav was certain Mackey would claim himself whenever he was ready.

# The Difficult Kind

MACKEY'S STOMACH muscles flexed under the sting of the needle. "'Kay," he told the muscular woman with the black-and-purple hair and heavy eye makeup, "I'mma roll my ass here a little and let out some tension. You ready?"

"Go," she said, and the electric buzz of the needle paused while he took a deep breath and adjusted his position. His cock tightened in his jeans, and he tried really hard not to be embarrassed.

The nice woman behind the needle got *that* out of the way. "Don't worry 'bout the package," she said, her voice carrying over the death metal echoing through the parlor. "Happens to some guys—especially this area."

Mackey looked down at the waistband of his jeans and grimaced. The waistband was at his standard jean fit, so odds were good none of his other pairs would rub on this thing in the next ten days.

"Well, it's tender," he muttered, and then the needle returned. Once again he grabbed the bar at the head of the backless couch he was stretched out on and tried hard to get back into that Zen place in his head where the pain didn't matter.

It was hard when dumbshits kept trying to talk to him.

"Trav's gonna be pissed," Blake said dubiously.

Kell looked at him, puzzled. "Why's Trav gonna be pissed?"

Blake and Mackey met eyes and Mackey grimaced. "He can't possibly be that—"

Kell wrinkled his nose. "Yeah, I know you're banging each other, Mackey, I'm not that stupid. I ran into you both when you were pushing your dresser and music stand into his room, okay?"

Mackey suddenly grinned at him. "So what you *really* wanna say is that Trav's got no reason to be pissed one way or the other, right?"

Kell nodded, an "of course!" expression on his face. "Man, it's not his fuckin' skin. He'll like the tat or not like it. He don't own you."

"*Thank* you!" Mackey hissed. He appreciated the sentiment, but there, right where his happy trail would be if he hadn't just gotten waxed—that there was *sensitive*.

Blake grunted and shook his head. "Okay, I'll admit it. It's been a while since I had a steady girl, but you know? People want a fuckin' say. I mean, did you even tell him about this before he left?"

Mackey scowled and concentrated for a minute. He had, he figured, another hour, maybe two, to go. And he had to be honest in the middle of it.

"No," he grunted after some deep breathing. "There was no discussion of the tat. In fact, the only discussion was about how I wasn't gonna go do no fucking chemicals when he was gone for four days. This is day three. He's meeting us in Oakland day after tomorrow. I figure I'll get this fuckin' thing on my stomach and surprise him."

Kell laughed a little. "Surprise the fuck out of the fans too, huh?"

Mackey grinned. That was part of the reason he was doing it. Trav had gotten a late invitation for the band to play at one of those holiday festival sort of concerts for the week after Thanksgiving. The concert was in Oakland, and the band was high up on the rotation, so Trav figured they could practice some of their numbers for their tour. They tended not to do too many light effects, which was good because so far Mackey hated all their damned light engineers and loathed a good many of their crew. Yeah, he was pretty sure that was backlash from Tony, so he kept it to himself, but seriously. How hard was it to come up with a light effect that hadn't been done to death? But it didn't matter, because they had the people they had, and all he wanted to do was play the damned music.

And that was what they were doing. Two tracks from their breakout album, *It's Not Catching*, and then six from the CD in postproduction, *Goin' Viral*. Trying to pump up interest for their full-length tour, which Trav was planning to launch in February. According to Trav, it wasn't that hard. *It's Not Catching* had sold multiplatinum, which Mackey had always thought sounded really cool, even though he had no idea what it meant besides they had money now.

And Mackey finally had a head clear enough to know what he wanted to ink on his body.

"That's a great tat," Blake said, eyeing Mackey's stomach appreciatively. "I think we should all get one."

Mackey grimaced. "You already got a dragon there!" It was a nice piece too, with scales that practically glittered.

"Well, not the same place," Blake laughed. "I got some room on my shoulder here, right?" Blake didn't wax, and his chest hair was creeping up, but it looked sort of raw and cool, so Mackey didn't criticize. Blake pulled the neck of his T-shirt down, and sure enough, he had room for the black-and-white version of the screaming monkey from their first album cover, bursting out of stylized, fractal pieces of a shattered mirror to fit. The band's name was reflected in the pieces, and done in red and black, and it was haunting and fun at the same time.

"I ain't got my stomach done yet," Kell said ruminatively. "You know, I might not regret this one—that'd be nice." Kell had gotten some godawful artwork inflicted on his body in the last year. Mackey's favorite was the pinup girl on her stomach with two left feet dangling over her ass. The thing that killed Mackey was that the tattoo artist had made it up to Kell with *another free tattoo*. That one was a Celtic knot that, swear to fucking Christ, was tangled. Mackey had been pretty high, but he vaguely remembered telling Kell in all seriousness that they could put out a hit on that guy and no one would ever know.

"So you guys want—" He winced, because apparently that close to the inside of his belly button was a mite bit sensitive. "—to get matching tattoos?" Wasn't *that* Sweet Valley High?

"Yeah," Blake said, nodding. He made deliberate eye contact with Mackey. "It'll be a celebration, right? I mean, forty-five days out of rehab, right?"

Mackey nodded soberly back. He hadn't wanted to say anything because he didn't want the others to worry, but that had been what drove him out of the house, searching for a thing, a thing, *anything* to do, to escape the restlessness, the craving for something in his head.

It had been hard watching Trav leave without him. They'd only *just* moved Mackey's shit into his room, and although nobody had even acknowledged that they were doing the thing, Mackey had been somehow comforted by the idea that everybody knew they were doing the thing.

Waking up with Trav, even for a week, had been.... It had made his stomach jumpy. It was like, he'd be running or playing his guitar or even watching television when he was actually *touching Trav*, and it would hit him. He'd remember what it felt like to wake up next to Trav's warm body, or the feel of Trav's hand rubbing circles on his back or his stomach, which he did when they were both almost asleep.

It made him want to cry, but in a good way.

And then Trav just walked into the room one day when Mackey was practicing and said, "Mackey, can I get into the closet there? I need my suitcase."

"Where in the *fuck* are you going?"

Trav laughed, probably because he didn't hear the panic in Mackey's voice, and said, "I've got to run to England the day after tomorrow—apparently one of your venues just got shut down. We need to find another place or cancel the gig—they need me there. This dogging each other over the phone bullshit is *not* happening."

Mackey's heart was thundering practically too hard for him to hear his own voice. Not leaving. Not really. Business trip. Gerry had needed to take them. Happened all the fucking time. Trav had even gone to New York when Mackey was in rehab—Mackey just hadn't really registered it because, well, rehab, when the whole world had been about Mackey and other people didn't need to bother him with their relocation bullshit as long as they were available on the little glowing box.

"Yeah," he said, being as natural as possible. "Whatever. Let me know when you're going—I'll take the car with you to the airport."

Trav smiled, looking adorably shy for such a hardass. "Yeah? You'd, uhm, see me off?"

Mackey blinked and shrugged. "Yeah. Why not? I mean, you may be all 'It's no big deal' and shit, but my people, until last year, we didn't do planes. Still a big deal."

Trav nodded, that tiny half smile still on his face, and then, in a way that was still wonderful, walked up behind Mackey and bent down to nuzzle his ear. "Will we get to have goodbye sex?" he asked softly.

Mackey giggled like a high school kid. "Can we have hello sex and howyadoin' sex and all the sex in between?"

Trav's low groan did things to him—sweet things in his stomach. They had made love three nights running, and Mackey's body was starting to thrum, satiated, replete, like a fully powered amp. It was like his skin felt more during sex than it used to—and not just because of being off drugs. He tried to remember those moments with Grant, the two of them touching roughly, quickly, in secret and dark corners, and all he could remember was wanting more, trying to pull more from the air like a sponge pulling rain from overhanging clouds.

With Trav, he always had enough, even when he wanted more.

And now that that was going away, even for a week, Mackey was trying not to be needy, trying not to be greedy, but the truth?

The minute Trav got out of the car with his luggage, Mackey had felt it. A low-grade gnawing in the pit of his stomach, a restless flutter, a terrible need.

Trav had texted him as the car pulled back into the driveway, and Mackey stroked the face of the phone with his fingertip.

*Boarding now. Text you when I get there. Scary word.*

*Scary word back.*

And that was it. It was just Mackey knocking around the house like a rubber ball, trying not to think about the thing he used to do to pass the time.

So the first day, he went running by himself, and then came back and worked the bag downstairs. He sort of loved that—fighting without hurting anybody—but he had to be careful. No breaking his fingers or anything—had to keep in shape, right? They had a concert when Trav got back.

But that first day, he wore himself out before he rehearsed with the guys. It was pretty smart of Trav to get a house with studio space—that sure did make shit easier on them when they wanted to rehearse. They didn't need to record there, and they didn't set it up with tiles or acoustics or anything, but they had a place where Mackey could practice his showmanship, and they didn't have to risk the paparazzi to get there. (Mackey wondered if maybe Trav could just pay those fuckers off. The ones who hung on doggedly after the whole "coming out" thing had faded seemed more in love with Mackey and the twins than anything else. Maybe some money and some willing head would just make them go the fuck away.)

But Mackey could, in good conscience, only do so much in the home studio. The guys wanted to go out and do shit—Christmas shopping, surfing, whatever—and Mackey couldn't make them hang out with him and practice ad infinitum (or he could, but he was trying to recover from his workaholism as well), and he couldn't hide from the outside world, paparazzi and all.

So on day two, after the still-functioning family run, he made some forays into malls, bought his mom some stuff for Christmas, and started buying for the other guys, but every trip to every store just built up that hunger. He didn't understand shopping, didn't understand prices, and was still so damned overwhelmed, sometimes, that they weren't all wearing hand-me-downs and Walmart that buying high-end shit seemed like some sort of sacrilege.

By day three, he was climbing the fucking walls.

He tried to run, tried to practice, and was having serious thoughts about taking the car out and asking the driver to take him to a strip—anywhere he could find himself a score.

He had, in fact, put the guitar away and had stood up to grab the house phone to do *just that* when Trav texted.

*How you doing?*

Mackey closed his eyes. This was where he said he was fine, right? No big deal. Didn't need Trav for recovery.

*Jonesing.*

He couldn't believe he'd typed it.

Couldn't believe it even more when the phone rang in his hands.

"Where are you?"

"At home. Don't worry—no shit here."

"Good. Did you try to get out?"

"Man, shopping makes me sick. I'm thinking I need to start heading up a charity or something—maybe get my degree. I'm losing my mind here without you."

"Well, the degree sounds like a good idea. Maybe after the next tour. Or maybe computer classes. We'll see. In the meantime, think about it, Mackey. What's something you always wanted for yourself but you haven't had time to do? You got time now—*your* time. What have you left out? Hang gliding? A boat trip? You just got to stay clean until we meet in Oakland, baby. That's three days. What do you got?"

And Mackey had remembered wanting ink, and how the guys had gone and gotten some but he hadn't thought of anything that he wanted to define him for permanent.

And then he realized what *did* define him, right here and now, and decided to go with that.

"I got an idea, Trav. Thanks."

"Are you going to clue me in?"

Mackey closed his eyes and thought of Trav seeing the tat for the first time, touching it gently with his big, surprisingly smooth hands.

"No," he said with an evil sprinkling of laughter. "Gonna let you see for yourself."

And then he called his driver, 'cause those guys knew everything, and asked him for some recs.

The whole band wanted to go—everyone except Shelia, who stayed by the pool with a book and the sunshine, even in December.

Mackey brought their first CD, cover art and all, and the idea that the guys were going to follow him into this like they'd followed him into the band? After the whole rehab thing and the gay thing?

That made him really fucking proud.

And Blake's reminder?

Even better. "Yeah," he said, looking at Blake as the needle continued to ravage his skin. "Forty-five days sober. We'll have to think of something *real* good for a year, right?"

Suddenly Blake's chin started to quiver. "You think we'll make it a year?" he asked.

Mackey let go of the rail over his head to grab Blake's hand. "Man, I made it through today. I made it through today. I told someone I was hurting and I'm here doing this instead of out scoring a buy. I can make it through today, we can make it through a year."

Blake grabbed his hand tighter, and Mackey caught his breath as the needle hit another hot spot.

"Thanks, Mackey," Blake said quietly. "I'm gonna go talk to the next artist."

Mackey squeezed his hand hard and then let him go, losing himself in the Zen of pain control once more.

Okay. Today was a tattoo. Tomorrow he and Blake would start looking at online classes.

The next day they'd pack their gear and their clothes.

The day after, they'd leave for Oakland and check out the venue. And then, finally, Mackey would be performing in front of a real audience again.

Today was a tattoo. The thought got him through.

Trav texted him that night, as he was lying in front of the television with the others, sort of limp and sweated out from the pain.

*You made it through, right?*

*Yeah. Sorry. Didn't mean to worry you.*

*Thank you for worrying me. I mean that. Asking for help is good, McKay.*

*Shut up.*

*Truth.*

*I hate asking for help.*

*My folks texted. Reminded me that I bought tickets months ago to go back east for Christmas. You told your mom you were going to Tyson. No Christmas together.*

Mackey grunted. In a roundabout way he'd known this, but looking at it now, while his skin still ached from the tattoo and he remembered how close he'd been to running out of the house to score, it seemed like a bad fucking idea.

*Fucking epic*, he texted back.

*You could come with me?*

Mackey closed his eyes and breathed.

*Appreciate it*, he texted. *But you don't need to be bringing a junkie home to mom and dad. Gimme a year. If I'm clean in a year, I'll meet the fam.*

The phone rang, and he grunted and pushed himself off the couch to have this conversation in the next room. "You know, I don't know why you even bother texting if you're going to do this every time."

"That's stupid."

"You're the one who keeps calling."

"The year thing. That's stupid. That's like… like hoping you'll fail."

"I thought it was my reward if I succeed."

Trav's frustrated grunt carried loud and clear. "Do you know what time it is here?"

"Four a.m.," Mackey said promptly. "What in the hell are you doing on the phone to me at fucking ass-crack-o-dawn?"

"I miss you."

Mackey sucked in a hard breath. "Yeah, well, I miss you too! That doesn't explain four—"

"I knew this was when you'd be watching television, so I set my alarm to talk. I'll go back to sleep in a few." And that was when Mackey heard the sort of smoky undertones of a man who'd just woken up and was talking in the dark.

"So you woke up early just to talk to me? That's sort of swe—"

"I'm not like this," Trav snapped. Oh yes, there was a man without coffee.

"Not like what? Fucking grumpy? 'Cause I beg to dif—"

"I'm not this thoughtful, dumbshit. Terry and I broke up because he was begging me to be there, and I kept telling him to grow up and be a man."

Mackey's bowels froze a little. Yeah, he knew that Trav. That was the Trav who'd yelled at him until he went to rehab. It wasn't the Trav who'd been his texting buddy when he was there. It certainly wasn't the guy he'd been living with for the past month. But it was the Trav he'd first met.

"Well, I'm not always a nice guy either," Mackey said truthfully, trying to keep that level of freeze from creeping up to his lungs. "I pretty much bitched Blake into addiction—"

"He was heading that way anyway—"

"And I deserted Tony—"

"You offered. You can't save every—"

"And I think the tech crew is gonna fuckin' kill me, but I might rip out their throats first."

"Yeah, well, I don't know what the hell to tell you about that."

"How hard is it to set the amps where we put the line in Sharpie and coil the mic wires so they don't get tangled when I run around the fucking stage? I mean, where in the hell do they get these people? Flunkies-R-Us?"

"Not anymore, Mackey. Flunkies-R-Us quit on your scrawny ass. Heath had to negotiate with another labor union to get you guys covered in Oakland. But you're missing the point. The point is, I'm not a nice guy. I'm not a supporter. Or I wasn't, until…."

Suddenly Trav's voice sank, grew uncomfortable, and Mackey cocked his head, liking the way the silence was as expressive as the words.

"Until what?" he prompted, hungry for the end of that sentence.

"Until you. In rehab. That third time." Mackey heard the long exhale of something painful. "I just… I couldn't think of you alone in there, Mackey. I… couldn't think of you alone, period. It was like, suddenly I got what Terry had been trying to tell me, about how being with someone keeps the scary monsters away. I'd never seen the monsters, honestly. But you were alone in rehab, and I just… all I could do was imagine them around you. And I needed to keep them away."

Mackey closed his eyes, let the image wash over him. Mackey huddled in the dark, Trav standing in front of him with a knight's sword, keeping the scary monsters away.

"You do a good job of that," Mackey said, feeling better than he had all day. Maybe that would be his next tattoo—a child huddling in a corner, surrounded by monsters.

Or maybe Trav in shiny armor.

"Not so much when I'm not there," Trav sighed. "Maybe, maybe if we're going to do this, you need to come with me on some of these."

Mackey smiled a little. "Maybe that's a good idea," he said, thinking about the wonder of that. Just going with Trav because they didn't like being apart. Did people do that? Well, they were on the phone together—people must.

"But not for Christmas."

"Trav, do you really want them meeting me now? I mean… I'm a fucking mess. I'm… I don't want to get anyone's hopes up, you get me? It's bad enough you're hoping for me, and I don't want to let you down. And Mom thinks it's all better. I went to rehab, so it's obviously just going to all be okay. But… but you know it's not always. You know it's one frickin' day at a time. But you and Blake—you're like the only ones who get it." He remembered Blake's clammy hand in his. "Blake's coming with us to Tyson, by the way. And Shelia too. 'Cause I know you like making our travel arrangements too." Mackey hadn't actually *asked* Blake to go to Tyson with them, but he just now had decided it had to happen. He'd tell Blake when he let Trav go back to bed.

"Okay, Mackey. I got it. And I get that you're a little afraid of my parents—"

"That's not what I said!" Mackey shot back, feeling surly.

"It's the truth," Trav said shortly.

Mackey's turn to sigh. Of course it was. That was why he was being surly. "See?" he said, feeling weak and sad. "That's why I'm a mess. You can't take me home to Mom and Dad right now, and your sister the teacher and that saintly brother/doctor/husband/kid thing. God. His wife probably glows and talks to angels. And in the middle of that you're gonna bring *me*? I can't even guarantee I won't act out just so I don't have to live up to that shit, you feel me?"

He was babbling, almost tearful, but suddenly the thought of meeting Trav's parents made him feel small. He'd had to practically rip off his skin to stay sober today—he was nobody to take home to Mommy.

"Sh… I get it, Mackey," Trav soothed. "I get it. Don't worry. I'm not taking it personally." Of course he was, but Mackey was too ragged to interrupt. "And I get that you need me. I swear, I may not have gotten it before—I made the arrangements, booked the ticket, and didn't even ask you. It didn't occur to me until you drove away that I probably just ripped apart your world, you know?"

Mackey leaned against the smooth painted wall of the hallway. He saw a flaw in the paint, a tiny one, and started to pick at it with a thumbnail.

"This conversation hurts," he acknowledged. "Maybe we should keep bantering on text from now on."

Trav grunted. "Tempting. You have no idea. But maybe we have the painful conversations until they don't hurt anymore." He sounded tired.

"Go back to sleep, Trav. You did your good deed. You called me for real, heard my voice. I'm hurting a little, but I'm okay. I love you." It got easier to say.

"I love you too. Text me before you go to bed."

"'Kay. I'll say something dirty." Mackey laughed softly, thinking about sexting in the middle of the night with his fist on his cock. "Real dirty. Dirty enough to—"

"I'll use my imagination," Trav interrupted dryly.

"You do that." It was probably better that way. Mackey was actually not great at dirty talk. When he and Trav were alone and naked, they didn't need words and their bodies made the music. "I'll just think of you."

"Night."

"Night."

Mackey hung up and, for a minute, thought about going up the darkened hallway to his room. But he wasn't tired, and he didn't want to be alone.

He wandered back into the living room instead. The twins and Shelia were on the floor-pillows, Kell was taking up the whole love seat, and Blake was in Mackey's spot on the couch. Mackey—careful of the tattoo Blake had on the upper quadrant of his chest—sat down on him, chuckling a little at his startled "oolf" as he set his feet up on the coffee table.

"Dammit, Mackey!" Blake struggled to sit up, and Mackey let himself be rolled to the other end of the couch, laughing in relief. He could play. God, when was the last time he played?

"Serves you right," he said smugly. "Next time don't take my spot." He sat down on the far end of the couch this time and waved Blake to the opposite end. "Here. You and me can share."

Blake grunted and laughed too, sitting down like Mackey indicated. They were watching *Sleepy Hollow*, one of Mackey's favorite shows—thank God not into reruns yet.

"Blake, you're coming upstate with us during Christmas, right?" Mackey said it casually, not even looking at him. Blake liked to follow. If Mackey didn't make a big deal out of it, Blake just might follow them there.

"Yeah, uhm, I guess."

"Good. Trav'll make the arrangements. I sorta like us all together—we don't need to be scattering to the four winds just yet."

"Hey!"

Mackey looked up and was embarrassed by the naked gratitude in Blake's eyes.

"Thanks, Mackey."

Mackey shrugged and turned his attention back to the screen. "No worries—can we back it up a little? I got no idea what that thing on the screen really is."

Blake aimed the remote at the television, and Kell squatted down by Mackey, leaning over the end of the couch.

"Thanks, little brother," he said quietly. "I think he really needed that."

Mackey shrugged. "We gotta make it work with each other," he said, thinking about Trav. "I could always stand to be nicer."

Kell ruffled his hair in acknowledgment and left Mackey to watch his show in peace.

TRAV'S FLIGHT got held up, and Mackey was *not* in a good mood as he did the sound check in the stadium. In his head he knew Trav would be there in time for the performance, and Debra had overseen the equipment and getting them all on the damned plane, but in his heart he knew that he was going to perform for the first time since Gerry'd been there, and that he was used to his Xanax and pot before the performance and his vodka afterward.

He'd been counting on Trav instead.

Oh, and his tattoo itched like a motherfucker.

Blake had seen him trying hard not to scratch the still raw ink when they were on the plane, and offered him a little tube of painkilling ointment to go on it.

Mackey hadn't even bothered to go to the bathroom to put it on, just lifted his shirt and greased that shit up right there in his seat, blessing Blake's name the whole time.

"Looks sort of cool," he said, liking the glossiness. "I should do this before I go up on stage. We can all show them off."

Stevie and Jefferson had gotten theirs on opposite biceps (which were getting bigger on both of them with the gym in the downstairs and all), and Kell had gotten his on his stomach. Shelia had offered to get hers on her ass, which was really sweet, but Mackey told her that was up to her. Maybe she wanted to get something with just Stevie and Jefferson, right? She'd looked sad, and said she felt like she was little sister to the whole band, and Mackey felt like shit.

"Okay, then, darlin'—but maybe more a tramp stamp than an ass pass, okay? That way everyone can see it. Your ass is sort of members-only, right?"

She grinned and kissed his cheek, and he felt a little better. Okay. Only an asshole sometimes. Maybe he could make it through Oakland without Trav after all.

So even Shelia had a tattoo she could grease up. That would be cool—not subtle, really, but then, The Red Hot Chili Peppers wearing tube socks on their penises hadn't been subtle. *Memorable*, yes, but subtle? Not so much.

So the family tattoo thing was nice, and so was Blake's offer of ointment, but even with the numbing on his stomach, Mackey was still a raging red-hot bitch monster when they arrived at the stadium, and the sound check was getting on one snarled nerve at a time.

"Okay, y'all," he snapped at the roadie getting under his feet and trying to coil the microphone cord, "I get that the equipment should be different. You keep telling me I shouldn't have cords on my mics. But that's not the equipment we got right now, and we gotta make do with what's here. Anybody got any idea how I'm supposed to deal with you guys running under my feet like monkeys for the whole fucking set?"

"How about you move right and we move to your left?" said a rather timid voice.

Mackey glared over the heads at all the borrowed trouble Tailpipe Productions had apparently hired for this gig.

It was a girl. A *pretty* girl, not that she was trying to be. She had a strawberry-brown braid down to her waist, with lots of curls frizzing out of it and little sweaty ringlets around a heart-shaped face. Unlike Shelia, she wasn't twig thin—no. She wasn't fat either, just not willowy. Sturdy and soft, round in the right places. In a way, sort of a girl version of Trav, right down to the redheaded brown of her eyes.

She was wearing black jeans and a black T-shirt like the other roadies, but they were all looking at her like she'd sprouted breasts.

Probably because she was the only girl.

"I move right and you all move to my left," he said, at first ready to rip her a new one. And then it hit him. "That's fuckin' *genius*, darlin'—no fuckin' lie. You all hear that? If I'm going left, I will *expect* you on my right. If I'm going right, I will *expect* you on my left. None of this dodging around the back or ducking under the front bullshit. I will *expect* you there and leave you the fuck alone to do your jobs. Now I'll bitch at Trav to get us some new equipment, but right now, this is a fair solution. You all with me?"

He saw some numb nods and some resentful looks at the girl, but Mackey was satisfied. Emergency choreography at its best, right up until he tripped on the tall skinny guy with the blond hair for the six thousandth time.

With a snarl, he hurled his *broken* microphone stand off the stage. "What in the actual *fuck* are you doing here?" he hollered, the clatter of the mic stand punctuating the ring of his voice. "Where's the girl? She knows what she's doing, get her the fuck up here!"

"She's not certified—" the guy whined.

Mackey almost smacked his subservient little face. "I could give a *damn* if she's certified. Give her a fucking field promotion, but get her ass up here before I *kick* your ass down! Oh! And I will write an actual check and double it for the first person who can get me a mic stand that *actually fucking stands*!"

"Well if you'd quit throwing them off the stage, they wouldn't break," said the girl, clambering up on the stage with more nerves than grace.

Mackey was about to rip her head off, and then he realized what she'd just done had been sort of why he called her up in the first place.

"This is true," he said, conceding the point. "But that one had it coming."

"I'll try to scrounge up one that'll behave," she said earnestly, and some of the tension that had been squeezing Mackey's head since they'd arrived relaxed a little.

"I'll take that as a personal favor," he grudged. "What's your name, sweetheart?"

"Briony," she muttered, wrapping the cords around at the foot of the stage while she talked.

"Briony, you are my personal tech for the evening, you got that? If anyone needs to say something to me, they say it through you. You are, hands down, the one person not in the band that is not pissing me off right now, and if you could do that for me, I may let the rest of humanity live."

She got to her feet and dusted off her knees, grimacing. "You're sort of an asshole, has anyone told you that?"

Oh God. Mackey *loved* this girl. "Yeah," he said, nodding and smiling. "But the folks I love best don't give a fuck."

"You don't treat me like I'm stupid, I might not give a fuck either," she said, smiling back a little, like she was amused to find herself talking to him like this.

"I can do that. Anything else?"

She wrinkled her nose. "Stop putting the mics in your mouth. That primal scream thing you do sounds real fucking spiffy on your CD, but we don't got the equipment for it here. I mean, I know they *make* equipment that'll take that, but this shit is gonna short out, zap your brain through your skull, and fucking kill you!" She nodded earnestly with that, and he almost wept.

He'd been waiting for this kid his entire fucking life.

"Heard and understood," he said, staring. "*Debra*! Did you hear that?"

"Yeah, Mackey," she said, bustling up to the stage. Trav hadn't seen their touring equipment yet, the amps and such they needed to project in a large venue—this was supposed to be a trial run, and Mackey wondered sadly if this hadn't been one of the things Gerry had let slide.

"You make sure Trav gets a list of shit goin' on here. I wasn't in a great place the last time we had this shit out—looks like a lot of it is sort of fucked-up. I'm gonna run through the playlist with the guys and the light effects with…." Mackey looked around for Lester and Keith, the two guys Gerry had hired to do effects. Again, Mackey knew their names, they warned him when something cool was coming up, and that was about it, and while Mackey had a whole list of shit he'd wanted to change and work up in the month after Christmas and before the tour, right now they were just running through the songs in public. Maybe. "Where in the fuck are my light and sound engineers?"

He looked at Briony like maybe she had the answer, and from the way she blushed and looked away, maybe she *did* have the answer but just didn't want to tell *Mackey*.

"They're either fucking each other or doing blow," he said flatly. They'd been a little twitchy, but then, people got twitchy around Mackey when he was trying to set up a show. He had no idea why.

"Or getting blown and doing fuck," Briony said with a grimace. "But yeah. You started ranting and they took off."

Mackey took ten deep breaths, closed his eyes, and pictured his room. Not Trav's room, where all the sex and magic happened, but his room, where he'd been sleeping since Trav had been gone. When he was alone, he curled up in the dark space between the beds, crumpled into a little ball, where all he could feel was the peace and the music in his own head. He took ten deep breaths in that space, then ten more, and when he opened his eyes, Briony and Debra were looking at him patiently, and he thought maybe he could take homicide off the table for today.

"Here's what we're gonna do," he said with exaggerated patience. "We're gonna bump ourselves up in the rotation. The guys before us have pretty spiffy lights and sound. Right now we couldn't find our asses with both hands and a forklift in that department— we don't want to let the audience down. We're going to do the first number absolutely bare. All the lights—*all the fucking lights*—and we're gonna come ripping out of the fuckin' gate with 'Tattoo' and destroy them, does everybody got me?"

He looked around to the band, who were hanging on to his every word and trying not to look lost. It had been a while for them too, he realized, and they missed Trav as well. Gerry hadn't made it to every performance—or even half of them—but Trav had been so good about easing all the fucking details, they hadn't even missed him until he was gone.

"Good. And then after that we're going dark and romantic—Briony, do you know the light and the sound board?"

"Not that well, boss," she said apologetically, and he loved her even more for not trying to fake it.

"Then give me a couple of names of guys who can't fuck up a wet dream—"

"What about Keith and Lester?" she asked, making sure.

"They are no longer on the fucking payroll," he said grimly. "They weren't that fucking good in the first place. Holy shit—all that time we spent sitting on our hands this last month, thinking this shit would be here when we came back to it. It is time to get our thumbs out of our fucking asses and act like we get paid."

"Righteous, Mackey," Kell muttered, and he heard some more murmurs of assent from his guys. Okay. They'd sold a fucktonna CDs on their last tour—they could either skate on their asses, using the old CDs for sleds, or they could fucking bring it. And while Mackey knew they were going to bring it musically, until this moment *right here*, he had not realized how much more to bringing it there was. Trav was good at helping them be their best, but Trav did not have the tattoo and he hadn't come up from nothing. Mackey could love Trav for all he was worth, but the fact was, this band, these guys, they were a whole different entity, and the people who bought those CDs could either be their fans or their fuckers.

It was Mackey's job to make sure they were fans, and that they stayed with him and the guys as long as they put out.

"'Kay, Briony—go pick your light and sound board guys. Debra, you start making a list of shit me and Trav hafta fix. Guys, we've got five minutes to go through the new playlist—and then make it the fuck so. Are we ready, all?"

"Fucking ready, Mackey!" That was in tandem—Mackey spared a minute to grin at them, suddenly so grateful for his brothers he could cry.

"Ready, pit crew?"

"Give me five, dickhead!" Briony yelped as she scrambled down from the stage toward the big-eyed group of roadies praying to be promoted.

"Awesome—let's fucking get this road on the show!"

And with that he turned to his guys and started to fix what was wrong, adrenaline thundering through his veins as he looked at the clock. They had an hour and a half before the next band came in to claim this space. Fucking spiffy.

For the first time since Trav left, Mackey wasn't thinking about Xanax, coke, or vodka. Good to know there was a cure.

# For Your Love

THE TEXTS hit his pocket the minute the plane landed. One minute he was leaning back in his seat, closing his eyes while they began their descent and imagining what Mackey would look like stretched out in bed, thighs held up and spread wide while Travis swiped long, hard, and deep with his tongue. He was remembering the sounds Mackey made when Travis was inside him and imagining what sounds he'd make when he was pleasured slowly, like a love song, in that easy, dreamy, playful way a good rim job gave you. Mackey had just gotten to that rare moment when he relaxed, sighed, and begged sweetly because he trusted Trav wouldn't deny him, when the plane touched down.

But work awaited, and Trav hit the On switch on his phone and straightened up in his seat, buttoning his coat. He took one breath, and then two, and then....

His phone exploded into so much chaos, Trav couldn't believe it had been just sitting there in the airwaves, waiting to attack him.

He texted frenetically while he grabbed his suitcase and his laptop, and barely looked up as he walked down the aisle like the other sheep. Up the ramp, down the ramp, and around the maze of SFO, he navigated the clusterfuck that a simple festival performance had become.

*Goddammit, Heath—you told me our tech crew was sound!*

He had to. He'd taken Heath at his word and had poured his time into publicity, CD production, setting the schedule—and into getting his band to a place where they could perform. So, yeah, he'd spent his free time sleeping with Mackey Sanders, but he truthfully hadn't done much of that.

*I'm sorry! I'm sorry! Debra's been reaming my ass all fucking day.*

*I asked you one goddamned thing. I asked you if we could bring the band to Oakland and do a simple light show. You said yeah, no problem. Crew was in place from last year.*

*It was.* Even in the text, Trav could hear the abject apology. *I just didn't know how bad it had gotten. I'm sorry, Trav. I take the hit for this one. You've done wonders, and I dropped the ball.*

Trav stopped right there in the middle of the airport and counted to ten. Then he closed his eyes and pictured Mackey, in those rare moments when he let his guard down, playing the guitar softly in the middle of the night, the lamplight passing through his blond eyelashes, illuminating his gray eyes. He counted to ten again and resumed walking.

*Do you know how hard he's worked?* he asked, because someone had to.

*I know.*

*Really? How hard THEY ALL worked? They kicked that CD out for you in record time.*

*They did.*

*He wrote songs in rehab, dumped half the first album and revamped the whole thing. He did it because he promised us—you, me, the fans. And we drop him in Oakland without a tech crew?*

*Man, Trav—I'm sorry. I don't know what else to tell you. I fucking dropped the ball.*

Trav was going to do it. He was going to twist the knife in, pull it out, add some salt, and twist it again, but Mackey's text got in first.

*Don't sweat it, Superman. Deb says you're having kittens. We don't need any fucking kittens—I can barely keep the plant alive.*

Trav took a breath and then another. *Heath's ready to blow us both in total apology. You sure you don't want to milk that?*

*Straight guys give shitty head. Get your ass to the Coliseum—we're on early.*

*EARLY?*

*My idea, hotshot. Now put the phone down and get your ass to the driver. Deb says she sent a guy to get your luggage and cab it back. She also says to stop yelling at her. You asshole. You made the poor woman cry.*

Trav grabbed his laptop and carry-on tighter and trotted down the stairs. Sure enough, the driver was waiting by the doorway, and Trav walked straight past baggage claim, hoping the suits in his garment bag would find their way home.

He slid his ass into the town car and nodded urgently to the driver, then went back to his text. *Tell her that if you and the guys make it through this, I'll send her flowers and brush her cat.*

*I'm not telling her jack. Get your ass over here and stop being a prick. At least when I rip people up, I back it up by firing their asses. Jesus, fucking amateur.*

Trav laughed—he couldn't help it. *Shut up and warm up. Aren't you in the waiting room?*

*No. I'm in the dressing room, hiding from the massive fucking clouds of pot smoke. The whole band is with me. Sobriety sucks fucking ass in the social department, you know that?*

*I'll totally rim you as a reward,* Trav texted, remembering that sweet, dirty fantasy he'd been having.

*DID I MENTION I'M IN THE GREENROOM WITH THE GUYS? Jesus—Kell read that over my shoulder. He's gagging in the bathroom. Way to kill the mood, Trav.*

Trav stared at the text in absolute horror.

*I'll see you when I get there,* he texted lamely, then groaned and threw his head back against the seat.

"Everything all right, Mr. Ford?"

Trav looked at Walter, the driver, and grimaced. Walter was a white man in middle age, nondescript, very discreet, and as reliable a person as he'd ever met.

"Dating a rock star has its drawbacks," he said after a minute. This guy had taken them to their first date, after all.

"Yeah, but I understand they fuck like gods," Walter said pragmatically, and Trav stared at him, wondering when his own teeny brain was going to explode.

WALTER TOOK him to the VIP entrance and handed him his pass, which was great, because it meant he could charge through the myriad tunnels and back ways until he got up to the stage entrance. His guys were there, standing back to let the other band come through the loading bay, with lots of high-fives and "Great set!" praise as they went. It had never hit Trav before, but his guys, for all their flaws, were gentlemen that way. Even Blake and Kell, for all the girls they'd had, hadn't ever disrespected them—just gone through a lot of them. These were good boys, he realized, an absurd lump in his throat.

He hated to let them down.

The Coliseum lights went down, indicating that the band had ten minutes to set up, and Mackey looked behind him and caught sight of Trav.

"You're here!" he said, his eyes widening. He'd gone to town with the guyliner and mascara, and his customary lacy shirt was nipple-piercing pink and cut right under his pecs. He didn't have a coat over it like he usually did, so his entire midriff was exposed, as well as the narrow line of his back.

But as he turned, Trav wasn't looking at his back.

"Nice ink," he said through a dry mouth. And oh *damn*, he wasn't being sarcastic in the least. That screaming monkey tattoo, the guyliner, the layered white-blond hair—Mackey was there, the living embodiment of every trashy punk artist fantasy Trav had ever entertained. The added bonus was that Trav knew the real boy underneath, and he was three times as beautiful as the image—the image that was currently charging at him full tilt.

"*You're here!*" Mackey crowed, leaping into Trav's arms without hesitation or doubt. Mackey's mouth descended hard, crushing, invasive, and proprietary. Trav cupped his hands under Mackey's ass as Mackey wrapped his legs around Trav's waist, and then just hung on for dear life.

Mackey was going to ravish him, unrepentantly pull all of Trav into his body, and leave him drained, a brittle husk, in the clutter of the backstage loading bay. Hot, Mackey's mouth was hot, and his touch was hard and possessive, rubbing Trav's neck and the shoulders he could reach with his hands. With a growl of impatience, he hopped down and glared. Trav's brain was still shorted out from that kiss, and he rubbed the back of his hand over his wet, bruised mouth and stared back, totally without words.

"Take off your jacket," Mackey demanded, and Trav let it slip from his shoulders. Without another word, Mackey reached up to his collar and undid the first button. Then he grabbed both sides of the shirt and yanked, ripping all the buttons off the front.

Trav was too shocked to do more than say his name. "Mackey?"

"Take that off," Mackey ordered, moving his hands to the neck of that frothy, lacy thing he'd apparently cut off right under his pits. He wriggled out of that while the rest of the band started calling his name, and then held his hand out imperiously for Trav's plain old white button-down. "Take off for a fucking week, leave us in the middle of the lurch." Mackey yanked Trav's shirt out of his hand and slid it over his shoulders. He gave a bare, sensual wiggle and smiled evilly into Trav's eyes. "And then run in here like I wasn't shitting my pants. The only thing I ever fucking wanted from you was to see me look good, and here we are, *in my house*, and you barely fucking get here in time to see me play. You're lucky I don't take your pants too."

Trav was still breathing hard as Mackey stalked off to prep his equipment. He was tying the ends of Trav's shirt together over his tattoo as he went.

Debra came up next to Trav, blowing out a breath in relief. "Man, if you'd seen the way he tore up the tech crew, you'd know you got off easy."

Trav looked at her and shook his head. "There is no getting off easy with Mackey," he said sincerely, and wondered what else the night had in store.

"We'd better get to the side if we want to watch," Debra said knowingly. "They're not going to kill the house lights for the first number."

Trav was getting tired of staring at people and catching flies, but he couldn't think of anything else to do. "They're doing what?" he asked, wanting water, a shower, and a chance to beat off and get rid of his hard-on, not necessarily in that order.

Deb shrugged. "Hey, I think they can pull it off. Have you seen your guy in action?"

"In videos, yes," Trav admitted.

Debra tucked a bit of silver-gray hair behind her ear. "I think he's gonna shock the hell out of us both," she admitted.

Trav shook his head, slid his jacket on over his cotton undershirt, and followed her to the back bay, where they could watch the band from the side of the stage without being seen.

The stage was set up, and even from there, Trav could see the equipment inadequacies Deb had talked about. *Heath, you got off easy*, he thought, but his phone was dead, so he kept the thought to himself.

It felt like seconds. In a heartbeat, every light in the fucking Coliseum was up, including the blinding ones in the ceiling that revealed every pore in the face of the person next to you. He heard some murmurs of confusion—SOP for most festivals was that the lights went low between performances, and then a few lights came up on the stage when the band was ready to go.

But not this time. The lights went high, the audience stopped and looked at the stage for a cue, and Mackey stepped forward.

"Yo!" he called without preliminaries. "You ready for Outbreak Monkey? Are you ready to *scream*?"

A heartbeat of stunned silence followed, and then a pulse of the crowd screaming as the band launched, full throttle, into "Tattoo"—and the audience lost their fucking minds.

"Oh my God," Trav breathed, his whole body thrumming, high, sexed, with the music that came up from the soles of his shoes. Mackey was up there dancing, singing, flirting with his bandmates, flirting with the crowd, and the full, undivided, slavering attention of twenty thousand people quivered in the palm of his hand, and he song-fucked them for all they were worth.

He gave back what he got and brought them higher, higher, surging emotionally until they lost themselves in the electrically charged ecstatic surf of screaming metal climax.

Trav got hard again just looking at him.

The song thundered to its finale, leaving Trav reeling, trying to stay upright in the dark after seeing his lover bring off an audience of thousands. And Mackey wasn't through with him yet.

The crowd roared and the band bowed, and the lights went dim just that fast, with a spotlight left on every band member, with only a few glowing spots on the floor so the tech crew could move.

Mackey took the microphone. "You guys sound pumped," he said, that fuck-off-and-love-me smile sexing the crowd. When the roar faded, he pulled the mic from the stand and swaggered around the stage, skillfully dodging the techs winding the cables at his feet. "I'm pumped to be here tonight," he said, and then he waggled his eyebrows and did suggestive things to the mic. "Not as pumped as I was to get out of rehab…."

The crowd's approval reached some new decibel levels, and he grinned at them, got their attention, and moved on with his story.

"Yeah… seriously. At rehab, there wasn't nothin' to do, all day, and all night"—his voice rose and fell rhythmically—"but stroke"—he grinned—"my self-esteem." A sprinkle of laughter followed. "But see—I was already good at stroking my, erm, self-esteem." He squatted on the edge of the stage conspiratorially. "See, my mom… she had *four* boys. Four. And three of us were all teenagers at once. Man, poor woman." He stood up and shook his head in sympathy. "She made us all wash our own sheets. I'm sure you can guess why."

Kell spoke up, and Trav wasn't sure if it was preplanned or not. "Aw, Mackey!"

Mackey looked at the crowd and nodded, eyebrows raised suggestively. "Oh yeah," he said to the audience's unspoken question. "And see, Mama wasn't no fool. There we were, raising hell one day, our little brother running around in circles, and there, knocking at our door, was the sex police."

The crowd caught its breath at the absurdity.

"Well, you know, church people."

Titters and giggles—oh, naughty Mackey.

"And they had the *balls* to hand my mother—*my* mother—a pamphlet on, get this, 'The Perils of Masturbation.'"

The crowd's gasped cackle was like a gift.

"And my mother…." Mackey stood up and put one hand on his hip, thrusting his flat abdomen out a little and showing off his newly inked glossy tattoo. "My mother, she said, 'Do you assholes *know* how many kids I'd have if I followed your rules?'"

The laughter began.

"And I've got teenaged boys—*three* of them! We don't got no money! Jacking off's the only thing they can do that's free and legal! Jesus H. Christ, do *you* want to raise their babies if they're out making the whole town pregnant? It's probably better just to *brrrrrrreeeeakkkk* the sheets into the washing machine and get on with my life!"

The crowd was laughing hard by now, and Mackey grinned, pleased as Peter Pan to have the lost boys riding his wake.

"So there you go, folks. Sound life advice from my mom."

Trav saw his glance at Stevie, who started the drum count, low and urgent. Jefferson nodded and picked up the low sex-throb of bass, and Blake and Kell started lacing the air with silver sound.

"It's free, it's legal, and it involves no controlled substances… are you with me?"

Low muttering replied.

Mackey started to arch his hips and grunt, not so much as suggesting as simulating. "Are you *with* me?"

The next reply was a gorgeous swell of sound.

"Oh, guys, my boyfriend done been gone a fuckin' week. *Are you with me?*"

*Yeeeeeeeaaaaaaaaahhhhhhhhhh....*

"'Cause it's *free!*"

"Free!" chanted the band.

"Legal!"

"Legal!"

"And you can't say no! No! No! No! Don't take away our...."

"*Masturbation!*"

The crowd practically rioted as the crackle of the opening chords clanged across the stage.

Trav had possibly never been so turned-on in his whole life. His sweet little fantasy of rimming Mackey as he opened himself up willingly was replaced by a harder, dirtier fantasy of Mackey with a dildo and a fist, fucking himself until he screamed.

He was in the back, screaming along with the crowd as the band spanked that monkey and made it their fucking own. Even Debra banged her head through the end of the lyrics, and the song only got hotter after that.

Toward the end of the song, when the band was riffing, Mackey did something truly terrifying—something Trav knew he did but hadn't really counted on seeing in person.

Carefully, using the hands from the crowd, he stepped across the walkway from the stage to the rail holding the crowd back. He held his hand out for his mic and a pretty red-haired girl handed it to him right on cue. Over the sound of his band jamming, he said, "Are you ready? Are you ready? Did I stroke you enough? Are you ready to *stroke me back!*"

The crowd roared, and Mackey spread his arms and flew.

They caught him, hundreds of hands raised to pass him forward and backward as he screamed the refrain, trusting that they wouldn't let him down. As the song wound down, he gestured back to the rail and was standing again in time for the final chorus, and Trav remembered to breathe. Mackey was covered in sweat, his makeup was running down his face, and he grinned at them, demonic as a rabid child, and they screamed in bloodlust back.

And then they launched into the next song, and he did it again.

By the time they hit "The I'm Sorry Song," which had sort of a poppy, hooky edge that closed down the set nicely, Mackey and the band were sopping, the equipment was starting to short out, and the crowd was exhausted. Trav didn't even have to look at the lineup to know that the next three bands had been outclassed and outplayed by a group of guys with shitty amps, a crumbling sound board, and a light board that had died in the middle of the set in a shower of sparks.

And a microphone stand that gave up the ghost about the same time, pissing Mackey off so much that he grinned at the crowd and kicked it off the stage, just like a misbehaving cat.

Trav couldn't even blame him. And the crowd?

Apparently ate that shit up with a spoon.

The final chord sizzled through the air, and the crowd screamed raw freedom until the sound was palpable, inescapable, a real live entity like a tentacle monster, wrapping around every body in the place.

The band ran off the stage in a spatter of sweat and cheering from the band and tech crew ready to take their place, and Trav closed his eyes, letting some of the tension that had ridden him for the past two hours wash out.

"Are you sleeping?" Mackey called, and Trav opened his eyes, shook his head, and grinned.

"Recovering," he said, and Mackey started trotting across the backstage bay. Trav got himself ready, because Mackey wasn't going to stop, any fool could see it. It was Trav's job to catch him—always had been.

"Recovering?" Mackey bitched, launching himself in the air and landing in Trav's arms, wrapping his legs around his hips.

"Oolf!" But he really didn't weigh anything, and Trav closed his eyes and convulsed his arms around the solidness he did feel.

"Recovering?" Mackey nagged. "You ain't even begun...."

Trav took his mouth this time, tasting salt and lactic acid, but Trav didn't care. Dirty, sweaty, salty, Mackey James Sanders, and Trav couldn't taste him enough. The equipment and the roadies and the band and even the screaming of the crowd all disappeared, lost in the clash of teeth and tongue, the bitterness of Mackey's running makeup, the hot, moist feel of Mackey body under Trav's palms.

Mackey groaned in his arms and pressed forward, as erect and probably as hard and aching as Trav was, and Trav had the presence of mind to pull back. They were *not* having sex here in the loading bay of the Coliseum—

"Greenroom," Mackey moaned into Trav's mouth. He shoved Trav's chest and hopped down, then grabbed Trav's hand and hauled him past the band who were busy clapping each other on the back, past the other bands getting high in the waiting area, through a maze of hallways, and to the dressing rooms behind the stage. Without pausing, he spotted the room he needed, dragged Trav in, and shut and locked the door.

The face he turned to Trav was grim and triumphant, and Trav didn't have a chance to do anything but stare at him, stunned, as Mackey closed in, reached up, and pulled Trav down for another kiss.

Mackey moved to his jaw, bit hard, pulled on his earlobe, and Trav tried hard to be in control of the situation.

"I'm not—" Oh God, Mackey just shoved his hand down the front of Trav's slacks and grabbed and squeezed. "I won't—" Mackey used his other hand to lift Trav's T-shirt up under his jacket, clamped his mouth over Trav's nipple, and pulled, biting delicately as he did it.

Trav whimpered.

"I won't fuck you here," he growled.

Mackey pulled up from his nipple and grinned. "But I'll blow you, and that's all I want."

There was a pillow on one of the folding chairs by the makeup counter, and Mackey reached for it and threw it on the ground. He shoved Trav's pants down, underwear too, and took little bites of skin and suckles of Trav's sweat as he sank to his knees at Trav's feet.

Trav heard some rustling and looked down to see that Mackey had shoved his own skintight, cock-cinching jeans down and he was mostly naked himself as he looked at Trav's cock, bobbing at a ninety-degree angle and slapping him lightly on the face.

Mackey grinned, all evil, taking it in his hand and slapping his cheeks and his chin a little harder. "You beat off this week?" he asked.

Trav whimpered. "In the dark," he admitted hoarsely. "When we texted."

Mackey smiled, pure, sweet gratitude, then opened his mouth and took Trav deep into his mouth.

Trav's cock swelled, aching, and Trav flailed, looking for something, anything to hold on to. He managed to find purchase on the counter to his left, and he let his hand take his weight while Mackey was trying to suck his balls through his cock like golf balls through a straw.

He was rough, his hand hard, his mouth tight and brutal, and every so often Trav felt the dangerous brush of teeth, but that just made it better. Trav's whole body crackled, zinged, swelled with need. He stood, chilled and hungry, in the center of the brightly lit greenroom, and caught the image of all the mirrors, every one showing Mackey sucking Trav off with a fierceness Trav hadn't known existed.

He had to close his eyes or he'd fall to his knees and break his promise, spread Mackey's thighs and take his ass right there, lube or no lube, fucking him rudely on the greenroom floor.

As it was, closing his eyes just made him aware of Mackey's sweaty palm cupping his balls, his rough fingers sliding back and groping at Trav's pucker. Oh... oh God... so quick the surge of come in his balls hurt, his taint and ass ached, and Trav wanted more, more, even when his vision washed black and a scream of sudden orgasm ripped at his throat.

"Ah…. *God, Mackey!*" Trav knotted his fingers in Mackey's sweaty hair, dragging Mackey closer until he gagged, some of Trav's come spilling from his lips and trickling down Trav's thighs. Trav eased his grip on Mackey's head and concentrated on his ragged breathing. He gasped slightly when Mackey licked the crease of his thigh and over his balls, cleaning him up, and then even more when Mackey started tonguing his shin, and his calf, and the inside of his knee.

"Mackey!" Trav half laughed, half groaned. His cock was getting hard again, and he was afraid that if he backed up, he'd trip over his own pants.

"Cleaning you up," Mackey replied smartly, that evil grin growing lazy and dirty with repletion. "You think you're the only one who came? I just sang an entire *song* about fapping—you think I'm not gonna take advantage?"

Trav tried not to giggle and offered Mackey a hand. "Get up here," he ordered. "My pants'll hide it, and I need to kiss you."

"Mm…." Mackey got lightly to his feet and kissed Trav eagerly, but not desperately. Trav tasted his own come and his balls tingled all over again. With a sigh, Trav pushed him back and bent down to get his pants.

"I can't believe we just did that," he said, pulling his pants up and tucking his T-shirt in. "I didn't even do this shit in high school."

Mackey rolled his eyes. "Man, until last week, I thought this was the only kind of sex there was." He started worming into his own jeans, which looked a hell of a lot harder; they were a hell of a lot tighter, and all sweaty to boot. Trav backed up and let him struggle, because the alternative was taking Mackey out to greet the band completely naked, and it was going to be hard enough just knowing that the whole world would guess what they'd been doing.

"Why'd we just do that?" Trav asked when it looked like Mackey might be victorious over public nudity.

Mackey ignored their cooling sweat and threw himself into Trav's arms. "You came," he said happily. "I mean, you came just now, but first you got here. You promised and you did—"

"Mackey, I totally fucked up. I left the equipment and shit up to Heath, and I know he's my boss, but it was a mistake, and—"

"Shut up," Mackey murmured without heat. "You're here. You got no idea, but that counts. You're here."

He turned his shining face to Trav then, and Trav pushed his hair back from his sweaty, makeup-smeared cheeks. Underneath all that, he could see Mackey, the real Mackey, with the luminous gray eyes and the freckles across his nose, and that surprising sweetness when it looked like he and the world might not be at odds after all.

God, Mackey Sanders was blindingly, terrifyingly, scorchingly beautiful, and Trav couldn't believe that even for this moment, Mackey was all his.


THEY HAD to move, and the next hour as they took care of their gear and grabbed cars for the hotel was an agony of embarrassment for Trav. He felt like he had "I just got a closet blow job" painted over his face in come, and he wanted to shower, preferably with Mackey either in the shower with him or waiting, clean and happy, for when he got out.

He had things to do first. He had to oversee the worst of the equipment (which he ordered donated to the local YMCA) and the official firing of the two guys Mackey wouldn't let touch the shitty equipment. He also, apparently, had to adopt a techie Mackey had fallen platonically in love with. Mackey spent the entire trip back in the car talking about Briony this and Briony that, and how they had to get her to LA and let her stay in the guest room and set her up as a journeyman so she could be their tech master before they left for Europe.

Trav simply nodded, texting Heath and Debra as Mackey spoke, making sure they got it done, but after they got to the hotel and Mackey stumped off, an irritated tornado, he turned to the band.

"What in the holy blue fuck?" he asked, completely bemused.

Kell shrugged. "I don't know. It was like… like she stood up, told him the truth, and he said, 'You! You are the one! Come here and work with me!' Fuckin' weird."

Shelia blew out a breath. "You guys are stupid," she pronounced. "I'm going to go take a shower, and you all try and figure out what kindergarten meant to you."

Trav watched her go, feeling thick. "I'm an idiot," he muttered.

Jefferson and Stevie low-fived. "Mackey made a friend," Jefferson said with satisfaction, and they followed Shelia with a solid dependability Trav admired. It occurred to him that with the exception of the fact that there were two guys and one girl in that relationship, it was the quietest, most solid dynamic he'd ever encountered. They were practically boring.

Kell and Blake nodded, and Blake looked sincerely happy. "Yeah," Blake said seriously. "It's like, all that shit he has to explain to us, she got right away." He looked embarrassed. "I mean, we all know he's really smart, and we're...."

"Not," Kell said grimly. "We're not. It's why he just gets in the middle and leads us. The only one who could ever match him was Grant." Something melancholy crossed Kell's stolid workingman's face. "I think Mackey might have missed Grant as much as I did for that."

Trav swallowed, and Blake looked away. "Grant was pretty smart?" he asked wistfully.

Kell sighed. "Yeah. Left me behind most of the time. I can't believe he's not climbing the walls in Tyson." He grinned then, tiredly, because the adrenaline of the concert was probably wearing off, and since the two of them weren't going to party or find girls, they were probably looking at a quiet night with the television and some video games to come down. Kell shrugged. "Well, I guess it's his fault he's not out here in the world, yanno?" His smile at Blake, the friend he'd been shoring up since rehab, whom he'd given up his own partying for in order to provide moral support, was blinding. "I mean, me and Blake do okay, right?"

Blake's smile was shy, like a schoolboy's when asked to play with the cool kids. "Yeah. And we're gonna do better than okay when I'm grinding you into the ground in *Titanfall*, right?"

"You wish." Kell nodded at Trav then, and the two of them wandered away, leaving Trav to follow a few paces behind.

They didn't get a suite this go round—it was only one night in Oakland before they took an early flight back to the house, so everybody doubled up except Debra, who, Trav assumed, was still explaining to this Briony girl how she'd become Mackey's pet techie, probably for life.

Trav was too tired to care at this point. When he let himself into the hotel room, Mackey was wrapped in a robe, towel-drying his hair and talking on the phone to the front desk. Trav's stomach growled and he caught Mackey's eye and held up two fingers. "Double," he mouthed, and Mackey winked and nodded.

Trav's soiled clothes hit the tiled floor before he even remembered that he might not have any clean clothes in the morning, and as he stepped under the hot water, he found himself wondering if they'd let him on the next plane wearing a robe.

He scrubbed hard, glad for the moment that Mackey wasn't there. He needed the time alone in his own skin, the heat and the ocean roar in his ears his only companions.

God, so many things about this night he couldn't believe.

He couldn't believe he'd allowed Heath to take over a detail like the equipment. But so much of the past month had been desperately trying *not* to leave Mackey alone, and he'd needed to take Heath's word for it for that to happen. He couldn't believe he'd flown nonstop to get to Oakland just to let Mackey see he could be a stand-up guy. And he couldn't believe he'd let Mackey haul him into a greenroom and give him the blowjob of his life.

Especially that last one.

Get up in the morning, go running, have breakfast, work, have lunch, do some light exercise to keep your mind up, make calls, do work, maybe have a snack, enjoy leisure time, sleep, repeat. He liked the order of things: it had worked in the military, and he'd made it work in his real life.

But not with Mackey. With Mackey, doing what you were supposed to do, behaving logically, just didn't fly. With Mackey there needed to be a better reason than logic. He *liked* sleeping in a corner or on the floor. If he was going to sleep on a bed, he needed a better reason than "you're supposed to." Truth was, he could be just as demanding as Trav sometimes—but never just because the world expected a certain thing. He required the best in the name of his craft being its best.

Mackey had a way of turning things upside down, like making the corner between the bed and the wall home and making a dress shirt sluttier than nothing at all.

And Trav, for all he liked order, didn't feel like his life was really in order unless Mackey was in the next room.

On that thought, he turned off the water and toweled himself dry, feeling strangely at peace. Of all things, knowing Mackey held Trav's equilibrium in his callused hands evened Trav out. There wasn't a force in the world that could change Mackey unless Mackey let it happen. Yeah, Trav had taken him early, borrowed him against the time when he'd be completely healthy, whole inside himself, but Trav couldn't make that happen any quicker if he kept turning Mackey away. All he'd do was maybe lose Mackey by not having any faith.

He couldn't bear that thought, not at all.

When he got out of the shower, Mackey was lying on the bed on his stomach, watching Nick at Nite, eating a hamburger. His robe was rucked up past the bottom of his ass, his thighs spread wide enough for Trav to see everything, including his balls, but Mackey didn't seem to care. He was laughing at a kids' cartoon and licking ketchup from his fingers when Trav walked into the room and slid a grateful hand along the back of his thigh.

And stopped and grimaced at the black marks surfacing on his pale skin.

"Jesus, kid, did that happen when you were crowd surfing?"

Mackey turned to him and grinned. "Yeah—ain't they somethin'? I got a doozy on my hip and my ribs and my shoulder too. It was madness out there tonight!"

Trav grunted and resisted the urge to flop him over on his back so he could check every bruise and make sure it wasn't worse.

"You *do* that? On purpose?" he asked, trying—failing—to keep the creak of panic out of his voice.

Mackey threw a look of disgust over his shoulder, still munching on his burger. "*You* have three scars on your side that look like a knife fight, a thing on your left arm that looks like you lost *all* the fuckin' skin, one through that same shoulder that looks like a bullet, and one through your thigh that looks the same. And I think you took grenade shrapnel on your back at some point. You think I didn't notice that bullshit, Trav? You took your shit defending our fucking country—which, since I haven't said it, makes me think you're pretty damned heroic, you know that? But do I complain about the state of *your* body?"

Trav's mouth went dry. He reached over Mackey to the tray and grabbed a glass of milk, then gulped half of it down at once. When he was done, he bumped Mackey's elbow with his hip and settled down on the bed. He was close enough to palm Mackey's backside and the backs of his thighs, which he rubbed lightly so he didn't press the bruises, enjoying the coarse, silky hair under his hand and the softness of Mackey's skin underneath.

"You noticed all of that," he acknowledged humbly.

Mackey rolled his eyes and took another bite of his hamburger. "I'm not stupid," he mumbled. "And I'm only a little self-involved."

Trav closed his eyes and ran his hand over the round of Mackey's ass again. Yeah, it had muscles in it, but just relaxed here, it was almost as much softness as Travis could stand. "I don't think about the scars," he said softly.

"You should." Mackey wiped his hands down and then his face. He started to move, probably to put the tray over on the table, but Trav took it for him. There was another hamburger on the table, complete with fries and another glass of milk and even a slice of apple pie, but food wasn't as urgent as it had been before the shower. Trav set the tray down and sat next to Mackey again.

Mackey wriggled over on his back and let the robe fall on either side of him. God, he was just as Trav had imagined him over the past week: pale and stringy with muscle, sweet and needy. The bruises and tattoo were different, but then Trav had learned to live with different since he'd walked in on the Sanders boys.

He bent down reverently and kissed Mackey's hip bone, oh so careful of the darkening skin that covered it.

"I don't think about the scars because they're part of me now," he said, meeting Mackey's wide gray eyes in the soft light from the lamp. "I worry about you getting hurt by stuff that you do to yourself when maybe that's not part of you anymore." He punctuated that kiss with another one to the edge of the tattoo. The tat had ointment on it, newly applied, and Trav traced the edge of it with a delicate finger.

"I'll always be a little bit edgy," Mackey said soberly, closing his eyes when Trav replaced his finger with his tongue.

"And I'll always worry," Trav whispered, resigning himself to that as his fate.

"You think I won't, Captain America?" Mackey laughed softly.

Trav licked the crease of his thigh and the laugh turned to a gasp. "What do you have to worry about?" he asked, nuzzling between Mackey's balls and his cock. Ah, the juicy bits.

"You," Mackey said, grunting a little when Trav pointed his tongue and started a delicate line over Mackey's left sac. The skin puckered under his touch, and he kept licking, up, up, along Mackey's abdomen, skating the tattoo. Up, up, along Mackey's ribs, licking softly along the big, blotching bruise.

"I'm right here," Trav whispered before licking his nipple.

Mackey wiggled a lot, arching off the bed as he gasped. Trav put a hand on his thigh and pushed gently until he was back on the bed, kneading Trav's neck, his back, his shoulders as Trav tortured that nipple with love.

"I'mma come just from that," Mackey confessed. "I'mma come and it'll be over and...."

"No," Trav mumbled, moving to the other nipple. "You're going to come—" Lick. "—and I'm going to swallow it—" Suck. "—I'll lick it off your chest if I have to—" Play with the end, nibbling a little. "—and then I'm going to rim you until you beg." Suckle, oh, God, Mackey's skin tasted so good! Trav rippled his hips, grinding against the bed, hard, needy, wanting Mackey so bad his skin hurt.

"Any other plans?" Mackey gasped.

Trav pulled back and looked him square in the eye. "Fuck you until you scream," he said, needing it, needing to see Mackey sprawled out, flailing, screaming because what was racking his body was too huge to be contained.

"Never happen," Mackey panted, trying hard to knot his fingers in Trav's short hair.

"Not gonna fuck you?" Trav had to laugh and then bite Mackey's earlobe. No earrings for his boy—Trav wondered how long that would last.

"Too busy talking," Mackey muttered. "Got your dirty talk groove o—*ah ah ah*—"

Trav bit his neck hard and propelled down, engulfing Mackey's cock in his mouth, shoving his head down to take it in all the way to the root. Mackey flailed, clenching one hand in Trav's robe, dragging it down, baring Trav's body to the air. Trav didn't move, only swallowed and bobbed as Mackey spurted precome, aroused quickly in the way only the young could be.

Trav almost wanted to beg him not to come. His mouth stretched, filled, and he felt Mackey inside him, salty, clean, and so magnificent Trav felt a craving to bottom, to have Mackey inside him everywhere. Maybe, he thought hazily, filling one hand with Mackey's hard, swollen balls and pinching Mackey's wet nipple with the other. Someday. When he didn't need to hold him, didn't need to keep him, quite this much.

Mackey's breath came quickly, little sex grunts filling the air between every in and out, and when Trav slid his palm between Mackey's thighs, putting even pressure along his taint and the bottom of his crease, he keened, obviously close and needy.

*C'mon, baby, come, and I can start for real.*

Mackey's hips pumped unexpectedly and Trav almost couldn't hold him. It was hard—he gagged a minute—but then Mackey's grunts changed to that low, blooming moan that came from a deep, quaking climax, and Trav swallowed, taking him all in, wanting more, while Mackey convulsed in his mouth.

Like that, Mackey went limp, and Trav was left shaking and not anywhere near done. He sat up, letting Mackey's cock flop limply on his stomach and sliding his robe down his arms and off.

Mackey was still dazed, gulping for breath, when Trav shoved his thighs up and parted his asscheeks. He didn't tease, because Mackey was too far gone to feel teasing, but instead dove in, licking, probing, holding Mackey's thighs hard because otherwise he was in danger of getting kicked.

"Trav," Mackey moaned, his voice drugged and slurred. "Trav... I wanna... I'm not sure what I wanna.... God... that thing you're doing... it's... ah, *fuck*, I wanna...."

The rambling was good—it meant Trav was doing his job—but it wasn't enough. Trav sucked on two fingers, getting them good and wet, before shouldering one thigh and holding the other with his other hand. Then he brought both fingers into play, massaging Mackey's wet rim, teasing now, because Mackey was sensitized and losing his mind.

Mackey gave up on words. All he managed were grunts, needy, and groans, thready. Trav taunted, never fully penetrating, just stretching, making him ready while Trav shook with craving.

His whole body cranked tight, quaking, *screaming* for Mackey, but he needed to wait… needed to wait…. Mackey needed to beg so Trav knew it was him, just him, not the crowd, not the old lover, just Trav, and for this time, skin to skin, Mackey was his in earnest and not on loan.

"*Augh!*" Mackey screamed. "Trav, *fuckin' please!*"

"Lube," Trav gasped, because he figured Mackey would have some, being naked and clean and ready when Trav got out of the shower. Mackey flailed some more, grunting when he thrust the bottle at him. Trav caught it, lacing their fingers briefly before standing up and greasing himself.

Mackey gazed up at him, thighs falling open loosely, cock erect again, his hands fisting in the covers. The bruises were coming up, big dark blotches against his hip, his ribs, his shoulder, and smaller ones all over in the shape of jabbing fingers. Trav felt primal, angry, that Mackey had had other people's hands on him. *Mine*, he thought, half in despair.

"Pull your nipples," Trav ordered.

Mackey nodded, mouth slack, before complying. His fingers were rough, rough and hard, and Trav took his cue from that. He grabbed Mackey's thighs and hauled him to the edge of the bed, then positioned himself. He pushed in just enough to know he was on target, and then Mackey pushed against him, inarticulate and greedy.

Trav shoved his way inside and watched Mackey's whole body come off the bed.

His scream grated, rough, wanting, and Trav would die if he didn't hear it again. He didn't go easy—he pumped hard and fast and viciously, the slap of his thighs against Mackey's ass resounding loudly in the room.

For a moment, that was all that existed—Trav's tortured grunts, Mackey's wordless begging—and then Trav adjusted his position, pushing up, pegging Mackey's gland, and Mackey's shout almost shattered the windows.

He beat at the bed next to him and clenched and convulsed so hard around Trav's cock that for a minute Trav couldn't move.

"Grab your cock, McKay," Trav rasped. "Squeeze it, beat it, jerk it, *fucking grab it and get off!*"

Mackey was as rough with himself as Trav was with him, and a new smacking sound filled the room.

"*Fuckin' Trav!*" Time stopped and Mackey's entire body bowed painfully off the bed. His legs shot out straight and his toes curled, and Trav spread his thighs with force and shoved inside one more time.

The room turned black and every muscle from his cock to his taint to his own empty asshole clenched painfully as he poured himself into Mackey Sanders, and Mackey's groan could probably be heard across the hall.

Trav fell forward, Mackey's hot come sliding on his stomach, and buried his face in Mackey's shoulder, panting and sweating but not wanting another shower, not yet.

For a moment that was the only sound in the room, but Trav had to move. He did. He pulled out, pulled away, and licked his way down Mackey's stomach, licking away the white and clear puddles across his abs, ignoring the lingering taste and texture of the ointment and distantly hoping it wouldn't make him sick. He was addicted—the sweet and salty taste, Mackey's sweaty skin, and he kept licking down the crease of Mackey's thigh, then spreading Mackey again and tasting himself as his spend ran down Mackey's crease. And again. Cleaning Mackey's dilated body, then taking Mackey's cock into his mouth one more time, even as it shrank, flaccid and exhausted, against his pubic mound.

Mackey started moving his hands purposefully in his sweaty hair. "Pleased with yourself?" he rasped.

When Trav looked up, his face glazed and dripping, his shoulders still heaving with hard work, he smiled. "I fucking missed you so bad," he said, raw and stripped and wishing he could feel ashamed.

Mackey moved his hand quietly on his cheek. "Backatcha," he said. "C'mere, kiss me, share some of that."

Trav did, falling into Mackey's warm open mouth and pulling his lithe, small body into his arms.

The kiss ended, and Mackey laid his sweaty head on Trav's shoulder. "I really like the taste of come," he confessed. "I missed that."

Trav smiled a little. Mackey would say that, would admit to it. Trav had to say he missed Mackey, but Mackey would notice the taste of come.

"McKay," Trav murmured, just to say his name. "McKay, you've killed me."

"Fine. Take me with you," Mackey said, and that was how they fell asleep, heads down on the end of the bed, Trav's feet dangling off toward the head.

THE NEXT morning was a sprint to the airport, but since they'd been awakened by a knock on the door and Trav's baggage, at least Trav had fresh clothes.

Mackey put on sweats and a hooded sweatshirt, and with his face clean of makeup and his earbuds traveling from the pocket of the hoodie, he looked like any other kid getting on a plane.

Trav was functioning on one cylinder out of six—he was the first to admit it. At one in the morning, he'd awakened and pulled Mackey around so they could sleep with their heads on the pillows. Mackey had backed right up to him, naked, slick and sloppy, and Trav had taken him again, quietly, as they lay on their sides. Their climaxes were small, pained, and their sleep afterward was coma deep.

So on the way to the airport, he sat and nursed his coffee, blinking hard and trying to wake up. He didn't even catch the conversation until it yanked him into it.

"What do you mean he didn't notice our tats?" Kell asked indignantly, and Mackey's response was typically dry—and self-involved.

"He was sorta focused on mine, Kell. You can show off your body after I've had him."

Kell grunted and then said what apparently everybody in the band was thinking. "Jesus, Mackey, speaking of—the whole damned floor heard you getting laid last night. Do you have to be so fucking loud?"

Trav's eyes almost popped out of his head, but Mackey didn't even blush. Instead he rolled his eyes and said, "Remember Houston last year, Kell? I do not remember much about Texas, or even last year, but I remember Houston." His voice rose two octaves, and he did a passable imitation of a girl in the throes of passion. "Do me, big daddy, and then lick my ass!"

The rest of the car broke into raucous laughter, Shelia included, and Mackey shook his head. "Sweartagod, Kell, you left the door open and everything." He shuddered. "That there is the closest to seeing a girl's cooter I ever hope to come. So you don't get to give me no shit about how much noise I make. Unless you can tell me what I was doing when, you *still* know less about my sex life than I know about yours."

Jefferson laughed. "That's not entirely true, Mackey. At least *we* know the name of the person in there with you!"

More laughter, and Trav pursed his lips and gave a reluctant smile. Yeah, well, if he couldn't take ribbing about sex, he wasn't much of a group member, was he?

Still, two hours later, when he and Mackey were seated together and the plane had just taken off, Mackey leaned over and said, very quietly, "Does it bother you? That they know—and know everything?"

Trav looked at him, big gray eyes, swollen lips, and remembered for the thousandth time how much Trav knew and Mackey didn't. "Are you kidding?" he asked, taking a page from Mackey's book. "My brother and I used to keep track of how often we jerked off. It was like a contest. I mean, I didn't tell him *who* I was jerking off to until we were out of high school, but no. I grew up in a family just like yours. Sometimes they're too close and sometimes they're not close enough. That's family of all sorts, you think?"

Mackey smiled a little and rested his head on Trav's shoulder. "I think my family ain't making up for you not being there during Christmas," he said honestly, and Trav grimaced and dropped a kiss in his hair.

"I could still take you—"

"And I'd still be a rock star junkie," Mackey said decisively. "A year, Trav. If I can manage to not break your heart in a year, I'll be good enough to take home to Mom."

Well, it was a timeline. Trav had a year to see that Mackey paid up in full so Trav didn't have him on loan anymore. God—he'd come so far already. Trav could only hope.

# Slipping Away (NIN Lives!)

SHOPPING FOR Mom, shopping for Cheever, shopping for the guys, shopping—ugh!—for Trav. Mackey was about done with shopping by the time December 19 rolled around.

God. Too many people to buy shit for—and not *just* the shit, the *perfect* shit. Something for Blake, something for Shelia. And to make matters worse, Trav had commissioned all new equipment from the big guy in the suit, so Mackey couldn't even go back to his standby and get music equipment. It had to be *original* shit.

He *asked* Stevie and Jefferson about Shelia, and she got a ticket to a spa day. He sort of liked the idea of that—sitting around and getting your toes rubbed and your hair primped and your eyebrows waxed and shit. He would have gotten one for Jefferson and Stevie, but they both said they were straight and didn't do shit like that. Mackey privately thought that straight men would probably *love* shit like that if they didn't think it would make them look gay, and that only made them dumber than gay men on a whole *bunch* of different levels, but in the interest of keeping family peace, he kept that opinion to himself.

Finally he decided on fancy suits for all the guys, so they could go out to cool places in Europe and not look like rock star trash, and a collection of high-end psychedelic ties for Trav, because right now he wore burgundy and blue and that was about fuckin' it. Even the fancy suits had some edge—Mackey had been looking at a lot of fashion web sites, and he was getting good at spotting edge. Trav had to update or lose the tie entirely, and Mackey was betting that last one wouldn't happen until the moon turned to blood and Trav ate cooter.

For his mom, he and the guys went in and got a computer, and a tech guy to come and install it, and a tablet so she could carry that shit around with her. For Cheever, they got video games, and he hoped that was about all the little shit wanted from them, because they were *not* happy about the paparazzi who had barely stopped dogging their steps, and they blamed the little fucker. If he thought he got a free pass because faggots were not fashionable up in his neck of the woods, he was sorely mistaken—he was attending that damned school on their dime. Even Stevie had voiced his supreme displeasure.

Mackey got Briony furniture for their spare room, which was no longer spare, and a quickie apprenticeship with a light and sound guy who would be touring with them. Mackey wanted her with them on the tour, so he also got her some outfits she could wear when hanging out with the band, which he put in the closet and she would see after Christmas, when she'd fly out to stay.

He didn't exactly wrap these gifts—more bought them and set them up and told her not to worry about a goddamned thing over text. And by the way, he appreciated the hell out of texting with her. She was funny and she got him, much like Trav, but unlike with Trav, there were no heavy emotional undertones and definitely no sex. He didn't particularly care that he'd sort of taken over the poor girl's life and made her his techie and shanghaied her away from family and her original plans of being an animation artist.

He should have grabbed Tony by the back of the neck and *hauled* him with Outbreak Monkey when they'd come to LA, but he hadn't, and look where respecting someone's space got him. She didn't have a boyfriend, she didn't have a job or a career yet, and he was going to make her have one so she could hang out with him. One person in a thousand got Mackey, and he knew it, and she was fucking stuck with the consequences.

So there. That took about two weeks. Mackey was exhausted. But the worst part about having that done was thinking about where all that shit was going after they shipped it upstate.

Mackey realized now that he was clean and sober and sort of owned, body and soul, by someone who didn't mind holding hands with him in public or telling his folks, that he didn't particularly want to go home.

He hadn't wanted to go home the year before, but that had been in sort of a hazy way, cushioned by chemicals. After all, who wanted to go home when they didn't know what and who they did the night before, and were pretty sure they weren't going to get through the next night without doing the same thing with a different name?

But now that he could think—and had been forced to think honestly—he didn't want to be anywhere near Tyson, California, not even the little town of Hepzibah next door, because he didn't want to run into Grant.

He had to stop and think about this.

Did he not want to run into Grant because it would hurt? Because he was still in love with him? Because he thought seeing Grant would fuck things up with Trav?

He conceded one and three, but he was pretty sure two was off the table.

What he felt for Trav was so much... bigger. More important. *Saner* than what he'd felt for Grant. Trav didn't want a quick fuck in a greenroom. Trav wanted a *long* fuck in the hotel room and the cuddle after in the plane, and a nice night watching television and waking up next to Mackey and kissing him on the cheek before breakfast.

For Trav, these sort of seemed to be standard things for two men who loved... liked... lived with each other.

For Mackey, those things held magic, each and every day.

Mackey wouldn't go back to being Grant's backdoor man for all the music in the world. Just the thought of it made his hands shake and made him remember the taste of vodka.

But the thought of seeing him and dealing with all of that—the letting go, the saying good-bye, the end of Grant in his heart as something big—that hurt. That made his hands shake too.

No, Mackey was ready to move on with Trav, and in a year or so, he might be ready to deal with Grant the way Trav had dealt with his ex—coldly and cleanly and with the clinical precision of the doctor who'd removed Trav's splint the week after Mackey got home from rehab—but not now.

And the thing was, going with Kell and the guys, there was no way they wouldn't see Grant. Kell had been talking the past couple of weeks about getting everyone back together and Grant meeting Blake, and maybe they could all jam together, and....

The thought of playing with Grant onstage again made Mackey feel like throwing up. He was *just* getting used to the idea that wouldn't ever happen again. He couldn't do it. He couldn't do it and he didn't want to.

But he'd told Trav he wouldn't go back east either.

So he pondered.

He pondered when he was shopping, with or without his brothers. He pondered when he was on conference calls with Artie B., the master technician Heath had hired personally to help them get their light show together, and Briony, who was dry and sarcastic even when she was a little overwhelmed.

He pondered it late at night as Trav lay at his back, broad shoulders reassuring and protective.

He'd told Trav he would get there eventually. He'd *promised* Trav that he'd be whole and well and able to give all of himself to the two of them, and Trav had taken him on faith.

He didn't want to let Trav down.

But he wasn't ready to see Grant either.

So he did what he'd done on the road the last year: He allowed inertia to take over, made the plans, packed the bags, sent the gifts. He allowed inertia to close his eyes the night before they were supposed to leave and to make him touch Trav in the dark with shaking hands, torn between wanting to unburden his heart and begging Trav to stay and being the grown-up and going back to Tyson and facing all that Grant bullshit without him.

He allowed inertia to silence him in the end, to accept Trav's good-bye kiss at the airport as they split for their different gates. He allowed it to turn his eyes away, to gather in himself, a child in the shadowed closeness of the corner of the bunk bed, torn between wishing he could disappear and screaming so the world could see him.

But as he and his brothers were standing in line for the plane, he had his first panic attack since Gerry had first given him Xanax. His stomach clenched, his hands shook, and he could barely breathe.

Oh God.

There *was* no Xanax. There *was* no vodka. *These things no longer existed in his world.*

He closed his eyes. Thought: *I'm gonna throw up.* Opened his eyes and turned to Jefferson, who was looking at him with concern.

"I'll be back in time to board," he murmured, then picked up his guitar and his carry-on and ran for the bathroom.

When *that* was over with, he walked out of the bathroom, looked to the right, where his brothers were getting their tickets scanned, and then took an abrupt left.

Just like that, the shaking eased up and his vision stopped dancing. That persistent trickle of sweat that had started down his asscrack pretty much from the time Trav had kissed his forehead and wished him safe travels suddenly dried up, and he trotted back through the airport to the exit, where he walked out to ground transport and flagged a cab.

It wasn't until he was safely in the back of the cab, heading for home, that he dared to text, *Don't worry about me, Jeffie—I just couldn't do it this time. Call me when you land—no chemicals in sight, I swear.*

He finished the text and leaned against the window, breathing free air for what felt like the first time since they'd left the hotel in Oakland. His phone started to blow up almost immediately after that, and the first name he saw on the top was Trav.

Well, tough. Trav should be in the air in a few, and he didn't have to worry about Mackey for the next two weeks. Mackey would be just fine.

AN HOUR later, in the shower, he had to concede that no, he wouldn't be just fine. The minute his foot had fallen in the empty house, he found himself wondering if Kell had something stashed in his bedroom that he wouldn't use in front of Mackey and Blake. Probably not, because the only reason Kell used in the first place was to impress Blake, which was why sending Blake to rehab had worked so outstandingly well.

But Mackey leaned his head against the shower wall and rinsed off the stink of fear sweat, and tried to visualize himself turning on his phone and dialing Dr. Cambridge's office. Spending Christmas in rehab as an outpatient wasn't ideal, but it was better than the alternative.

Because he'd promised. He'd *promised* Trav he'd come through. Trav had let Mackey into his bed on the promise that he was an improving work in progress. Mackey couldn't destroy all that because he was lonely.

Or he could, but he really hoped he was strong enough not to.

He got out of the shower and barely dried off. His phone. Cambridge's number. Then the car service. He had it all in his head. He was going to do this, and he was going to do it by himself, because he couldn't stand being the only heartbeat in this big house, and everything hurt, and—

"Trav?"

Was sitting on their bed, loafers kicked off, leaning against the headboard, auburn hair mussed from careless fingers, eyes closed, the fine lines at the corners of his eyes deepened by lack of sleep and worry. His carry-on sat next to the dresser, his jacket hung over his desk chair, and he held his phone loosely in his lap.

At Mackey's voice, he opened his eyes and swallowed. "Do we have to call Dr. Cambridge?" he asked quietly.

Mackey felt tears starting at his eyes. "No," he answered through a rough throat. "But it was a near thing."

Trav swung his legs around the edge of the bed and held out his arms. Mackey, for all that he was dripping wet, stepped into the V between his legs and let him wrap his arms around Mackey's waist and bury his face in his middle.

"Why didn't you tell me?" Trav whispered.

"Because you took me on faith." Mackey ran his fingers through that awesome brown-red hair. It would curl if he let it grow longer, but as it was, it felt thick and healthy between Mackey's fingers. "I asked you to take me, promising that someday I'd be fully functional, and you did. And… and I wanted to live up to that so bad." His voice was breaking, and God, he hadn't cried since rehab. He *so* didn't want to do this shit again.

"Yeah," Trav said, looking up at him. "I took you on faith. You haven't betrayed it yet. You could have *told* me—"

"What?" Mackey asked, feeling bitter and angry, mostly at himself. "That I'm not ready? That the guy who broke me is still there and I'm not strong enough to see him right now? Not by myself, anyway," Mackey admitted, "and that's the only way it should be."

"Why?" Trav demanded, and to Mackey's horror, his eyes were getting shiny too. "Why would you think that? Why wouldn't you ask—"

Oh, this was worse than Mackey had ever imagined.

"Because you didn't ask for this," he said, kissing Trav's forehead gently, trying to give him something, anything, to make up for the two weeks with family he'd just given up, for the trouble, for the worry. "You signed on to manage a band, not to deal with me or my bullshit, and meeting Grant Adams should be the last fucking thing on your ros—"

"Stop," Trav begged softly. "Yeah. I signed on for a rock band. And I got you and your brothers. And I got this big fucking glass monstrosity of a house that is starting to feel more like a home than I felt at Terry's after two years. It's different than I planned, but… God, Mackey, I think you're worth it. Don't you think you're worth it?"

Mackey found he was shaking his head. "No," he rasped. "No, I'm not. I'm not worth it, Trav, but I can't make you go back. I'm gonna hold on as long as you'll have me. And Jesus, I'm so, so glad you're here…." He took a breath, but it was more of a sob, and then he just stopped talking and held on while Trav held him, shaking, trying so hard to get it together when both of them were flying apart.

Trav kissed his stomach then, and Mackey sucked in a breath. The next kiss landed on his ribs, and then under his belly button, and then Trav worked his way up along Mackey's sternum. It wasn't just the pressure or the softness of his lips that undid Mackey, it was that his face was wet, and his hands were shaking, and when he reached up to palm the back of Mackey's head, Mackey saw everything he'd ever wanted from a lover written right there in Trav's eyes.

"I'll meet you halfway," Trav said softly. "I know this isn't over. I know someday this thing with Grant is going to be faced. But I'll take you on the hope that someday all of you will be mine, home-free, if you promise me you'll be honest with me right up until the reckoning, do you understand?"

Mackey nodded, searching for words. "Yeah," he said, closing his eyes. "Someday, I swear I'll be strong enough, Trav. Someday, for you and me, it won't even be a thing."

"I told you before, Mackey. I'll take you on faith."

His sepia brown eyes were fathomless, wide, trusting. Mackey didn't think he'd ever felt faith without pressure, hope without need.

"Deal," Mackey whispered.

The kiss wasn't hard or greedy. It went long and soft, gentle, shaking hands, delicate breaths. Trav pulled Mackey on top of him and then rolled, and spent a year mapping Mackey's face with trembling lips. A decade working his way down Mackey's vulnerable, exposed throat. A century placing delicate caresses down his shoulders and his chest.

Mackey had nothing, no return strategy for him, just the need to feel Trav's hands on his skin, his lips, his kisses, and to bask in the massive heat he put off—protective heat, the gorgeous, glorifying heat of safe haven.

Trav's clothes came off and he covered Mackey with his body, bulkier, a little hairier, but solid, substantial. Trav was something Mackey could cling to when he was needy, could batter with his hands when he was overwhelmed, could wrap his limbs around and merge with and know Trav could take it. Trav could take anything Mackey could give.

Trav greased and at Mackey's entrance felt like part of that, and he needed Trav inside him, like breath. They became one, and Mackey could breathe. Trav was a part of him, and Mackey had strength. Trav moved, and Mackey's body became light and Trav's body became sound and together they were the thing Mackey worshipped most.

Music.

Every thrust was a crash of cymbals and the thud of bass. Trav's hand on his cock was the lead guitar. Trav's voice in his ear, urging him on, saying filthy, pornographic things, was the lyrics, throbbing in rhythm, throbbing in time with Mackey's cock.

Climax was a roaring, gentle thing from the pit of his stomach. Trav's body in his arms should have grounded him, but instead they flew, flew together, and Trav's groan against Mackey's shoulder, the hot spurt of his come in Mackey's ass, that was the crescendo, the soaring of the heavens against his face, the ocean roaring of the wind in his ears.

They floated to earth, feathers, light and hollowed out, drifting together, chilled and sweating on their bed.

The first thing Mackey said when they were people again and not sound and light took even him by surprise.

"I'm sorry you didn't see your family, Trav."

Trav rolled to his side and nuzzled Mackey's ear. "Next time, tell me you can't do it. We can make plans for staying in town."

Ah God. That was his Trav. Practical to the bone. Mackey wouldn't have loved him so much if he wasn't.


THEY STAYED in and ordered takeout, and Trav called up Astrid and asked her if she could find a replacement to come over for the next two weeks.

Chinese food on the couch hadn't been quite what Mackey had in mind for his Christmas break, but Trav was there, and they got all of the foil-wrapped chicken to themselves when Kell and Blake usually hogged it, so Mackey called it a win.

Trav called his mother and told her not to meet the plane. Mackey sat in the room for that, since he was partially responsible. She didn't sound mad, Mackey thought, sort of relieved. Good. Trav didn't have that to worry about.

Mackey texted Kell about whether or not he should call. Kell texted don't bother, they'd talk in the morning, but next time to just fricking tell everybody before he freaked them out at the airport like that.

Mackey called him. Just called him.

"What in the fuck?"

Mackey sort of liked how puzzled he sounded. Good strategy, Trav!

"I'm sorry," he said sincerely. "Man, too many bad memories. I wasn't gonna make it, not and stay clean. Maybe next year."

"You got a problem with saying that, little brother?"

Mackey swallowed and closed his eyes. "You don't like weakness," he said, and as he said it, his throat swelled and he knew how much it was true, what Kell thought of him.

"I don't like shit hurting my family," Kell said firmly. "If it's going to hurt, tell me about it, okay? Man, we were gonna fucking lose you, do you know that? I didn't know that until… God. Fucking everything. But I look at it now and I see how close we were to not having you. And how much we need you. So… so just tell us, okay?"

Mackey smiled a little, finding it easier to breathe. "Next time. I promise. Thanks, Kell."

Kell hung up, probably before he could say something "gay" like "I love you," but Mackey didn't care. His brothers loved him. He knew that now. He shouldn't forget it again.

He and Trav fell asleep early, exhausted emotionally, and it wasn't until Mackey heard the rhythm of Trav's breathing next to his ear that he realized he hadn't picked up his guitar all day.

But that he could, and it would be all right.

It was something of a revelation, that, and it helped him understand the nature of his addictions in a whole new way, but for that moment, he could only be grateful. Trav wasn't going anywhere. The music wasn't going anywhere. Mackey could breathe in that rhythm, and he could sleep.

They were still in their underwear the next morning, stumbling around the kitchen making coffee and oatmeal, when the door burst open and Mackey's family rushed in, his mom in the front and his little brother bringing up the reluctant rear.

In the midst of exclamations and hugs and Mackey's complete bewilderment, he caught Trav's eyes.

Rhythm, music, and home. He wasn't in the perfect place yet, but he had the things in his heart to make it that way. Mackey could keep breathing. It was going to be okay.

# Going to California

LATER, AFTER the band had left for the tour and survived, Trav would be more than grateful for Mackey's family on Christmas morning. Of course at that particular moment, he was a little disappointed. He'd thought he'd have Mackey to himself for a couple of stress-free weeks. That desire fizzled and died after one look at Mackey's face. The stunned knowledge that his family hadn't left him, they were *right there*, and that this new life he and Trav were forging wasn't ephemeral, practically lit him up inside. Trav and Mackey were real and their house would be full of people without the ever-present strain of poverty and barely hidden taint of despair.

The two weeks weren't perfect. Mackey's little brother was a complete punk-ass dick, for one. He said "fag" four times in the first five minutes after walking into their kitchen. Trav, after one look at Heather Sanders's miserable, helpless frustration, took the little asshole by the collar, threw him outside, and slammed the door behind him. He was standing in their driveway in his boxers, but he didn't give a shit.

"Cheever, how old are you?"

"Thirteen, fagg—"

Trav grabbed him by the throat, which might have worried him if it had been Mackey, but it wasn't, so his control was perfectly, icily in place. "I am thirty-five. I defended my country, put myself through college, and built a career in a land of sharks. What you say about me does not mean a spot of seagull shit, do you understand me?"

Cheever nodded, his brown eyes huge in his pale, freckled face. He had a reddish mane of curly hair that tumbled over his vulpine features, and he probably got a lot of attention at school as a good-looking kid.

Trav had known him for a nanosecond and wished his mother had put him up for adoption.

"But when you use that word around your brother, when you talk to the press, when you throw that small-town bullshit around like you own being a bigoted asshole, you remember something for me, will you?"

Again, that terrified nod.

"Your other brothers? They just drove all night to be with Mackey because he *means* something to them. His talent and drive got the record contract and bought your nice pretty house and your school fees and the car you think you're going to get and those kick-ass shoes on your feet. And he didn't have any of that shit growing up, so it doesn't mean anything to him. But you're enough of a squirrel shit that it means something to *you*, and I love your brother. You piss me off too much, and I'll make sure that money he's just forking over to you and your mom doesn't find its way into your pockets ever. Do you hear me?"

Cheever squeaked—and now he looked like he wanted to cry. Great. Trav had bullied a middle school student. He was so proud he could puke.

"You keep that ugly word and your ugly bullshit to yourself, little man. If I hear you using it around your brother, I'm going to ship you home via Greyhound bus, and that is the truth."

He removed his hand from Cheever's neck and glared until Cheever looked away. "Are we clear, Cheever Sanders?"

"Yessir," Cheever mumbled.

It didn't feel like enough. The thought of Mackey, ragged from drugs and grief, killing himself to support his family, rose like bile in Trav's throat. "Did Mackey ever do anything for you?"

"Used to take me to the library and the park when he watched me," Cheever said promptly. And then he *really* looked like he wanted to cry.

"Yeah, dumbass, it's the same guy. You ratted that same guy out to the press, and you just walked into his house and tried to destroy the happiest I've seen him in months. Don't talk to me. You started off on the wrong foot and I don't have another one to spare for you. But if you talk to your brother, you'd better fucking respect him, do you hear me?"

Cheever's lower lip wobbled. "Yessir. The guys at school say—"

"Did you hear me say I don't care? Tell one of your brothers—but until you show me you can be kind to the one I love most, don't fucking tell me."

It was sixty-five degrees outside, and Trav was getting chilly in his underwear. He walked into the house and slammed the door in Cheever's face.

Cheever came back inside eventually—after having himself a good poor-is-me cry. When the brothers took him to Disneyland and Six Flags and Legoland and the San Diego Zoo, he mellowed out and rode the roller coasters with Mackey and ate junk food until he threw up in the bushes. (Trav hadn't seen the appeal of that, even when he *was* thirteen, but the kids from Tyson seemed to think it was high fucking comedy. God. Kids. Trav was pretty sure he and Mackey weren't the adopting kind, and he was so damned grateful his mother would be ashamed.)

Mackey and his mother never asked Trav what he said to Cheever, but the night before Heather and Cheever were set to drive home, Mackey gave Trav a watery smile and an especially amazing blowjob. Trav figured that dealing with Cheever was as close to being a good father as he'd ever come, and that Mackey was grateful and happy for what he could manage.

He could live with that.

And, of course, after Christmas, he had to live with the chaos of getting ready to go on the road. The band started putting in twelve-hour days working on the light show, the choreography, the sound mixing. Trav watched Mackey and Blake carefully—if there was ever a time they'd want to use stimulants, this was it.

But they went tirelessly, it seemed, fueled by high-protein vitamin-B-supplemented milkshakes and Chicken in a Biskit crackers, and Trav stopped searching the boys for red eyes, red noses, and dilated pupils. He gave himself permission to relax and figured that he knew them well enough by now—at ease or under pressure—to know when the bad shit came out.

Mackey and Briony were apparently an insta-love couple, and Trav could only be grateful. On Mackey's restless days, when the band was practiced out and Trav was busy trying not to fuck up like he had in Oakland, Mackey would grab Briony by the back of the collar and haul her to the movies or a concert or a celebrity appearance or even to a miniature golf course, and they would snark at each other and laugh at stupid kid jokes that left Trav feeling helplessly old.

At first Trav thought he'd be jealous, but one afternoon he came down from his office to refill his water bottle and heard them talking. They were sitting on the couch in the living room, playing *Halo*, their chatter punctuated by comments on the game.

"He still working?" Briony asked, like Mackey would know who "he" was.

"Yeah. Doesn't want Oakland to happen again—*die, motherfucker, die!*"

"Yanno, until I worked with Artie, I—get him, Mackey! Jesus, you're slow. Reboot. I'm killing this round. The game's no fun."

"Until you worked with Artie what? Okay, are we the same guys again? My character sucked ass."

"You have to build him up. You don't build him up, he's going to fail. I tell you that all the time, and you just—"

"Do we have a point? Here—reboot. Are you happy?"

"Yes. I'm happy. And see, when I started hauling equipment, it was for this little midlevel band right out of San Diego. My friend Janelle needed help, and she was the only girl, and she was tired of guys grabbing her tits—"

"Gross—"

"Sayin'. But anyway, they didn't know what the hell they were doing. It was like, they couldn't figure out why their shit wasn't working, and I stepped up and said, 'Guys, meet extension cord, extension cord, meet outlet. See? They fit together and have electric sex!'"

"Sweet!" Mackey crowed. "Run, dammit, stop talking and make him run, you're gonna—how'd you do that?"

"Built up my character. Told you. Anyway, so I figured that *nobody* knew what the fuck they were doing. And then we started doing festivals and I realized that *everybody* had a better setup than we did, and that's where I was when you met me. I'm just saying—your setup was still better and more organized than most of 'em I've seen. I've seen some *great* bands look like shit because of crappy equip—*fuck yeah! Woot!* Your turn, Mackey. Kill the fucker."

"And I'm dead." Trav heard the sound of the remote hitting the couch. "Here, I need to get up anyway. Let's listen to that riff from 'Tattoo' again—I think we can do something really cool with strobe lights and shit, you think?"

"Yeah, definitely. Music room?"

"Yeah."

They got up and wandered away, but Trav had to smile. It wasn't like Mackey had found a soul mate in the wrong body. He'd found a *sister*—and that made all the difference.

Trav's resentment faded and he filled up his water bottle. He figured his fierce albeit small circle of protection had just extended to Briony. (Who hated shopping and disdained all girl things but seemed to adore Shelia. Trav loved Briony, but he had a hard time figuring her out when she wasn't talking to Mackey. She was just one more dynamic presence in a house already bursting with them, truthfully, and he was glad Blake and Kell hadn't brought any more women into the mix.)

By the time they all packed up their shit and hopped a jet plane for Europe, Trav was on solid ground again. Mackey had a person to talk to so Trav could do his job, and Trav had a good enough feel for the whole gang of them that, with Debra and Walter onboard to round out the entourage and hired security on site, he trusted. He trusted Mackey would stay sober or warn him if things went wrong, he trusted the band would get along and keep making music, and he trusted that the girls wouldn't rock the boat and make bad shit happen.

And for the most part, his trust was well placed.

In Dublin, when the crowd got too unruly in a soccer stadium, the trust they'd built helped them grab Briony from the ground and run for the exits, where they hid in the dark until the mob cleared. In Amsterdam, when Mackey and Blake got separated from the main group on a bicycle tour, it helped him not make them pee in a cup when they got back. In spite of his own experience that the red-light district was really a very mild, lovely place in the daytime, the rumors of decadence alone made him leery. Apparently Blake thought so too, because he called his sponsor when they got back to the hotel, which made Trav proud of him and just that much more secure.

In Germany, when Blake missed a light cue and fucked up an entire song on stage, Trav trusted that Mackey would get over it, see that *all* the guys were done in, and call a break for the week they had between stops.

When Mackey did exactly that—and with more grace than Trav expected—Trav trusted the band to find their own diversions while he took Mackey to Greece for a three-day stay in an island hotel, the kind with the private swimming pool and the room that overlooked the ocean and the sitting room that was partly a spa and that opened up to the amazing view.

He and Mackey made love all night long and saw the sunrise sitting in that spa, Mackey leaning into Trav's arms. The moment was so perfectly at peace with the world that for the first time in his life ever, Trav knew what it was to tear up from happiness and nothing else.

Trav learned to trust that Mackey was whole and well, and whatever was coming down the pike, they would be okay enough to face it together.

Sometimes the universe really could not bear for that sort of trust to exist without fucking with it.

THEY HIT America last and worked their way from New York to Chicago to Houston to the Pacific Northwest. They were in Seattle, in a little pub-slash-bar, when the call came.

The pub-slash-bar hadn't been part of the stop, really, but they were taking a tour bus as they made their way from Seattle to Portland to Oakland and then LA. The bus broke down and they ended up staying in Seattle and canceling one of their dates in Portland, and, well, here they were. The place offered good barbecue and okay music, but the bartender was a fan of the band's—and Mackey's in particular, which made Trav growly until the guy cheerfully told them all he had a boyfriend. Mackey grinned and offered to sing for their supper, and the guy asked for an hour to call everybody he knew.

The crowd was *huge*. Briony ran the soundboard on her own, as she'd been doing since Germany, and they put on an hour and a half of toned-down set that, to Trav's ear, really showcased what they'd learned in the past six months of touring together when they actually liked each other. Mackey wrapped up with the song he'd written Trav in rehab, which he'd been working on during the tour, and Trav held that moment when Mackey looked out over the crowd and winked at him close to his heart.

Early on, in England, Mackey had flirted hard with the crowd, coming on to men and women from a tiny stage that had been close enough for him to get groped almost constantly. When Mackey came off the stage, sweaty and aroused, Trav had hidden his exasperation really poorly.

But Mackey wasn't stupid. "Look, Trav, I promise, I won't make a fool of you. Whatever happens with us, I won't do you like that in public, okay?"

And like their relationship, based on the hope that Mackey was working toward wellness every day, Trav had to take his word on it. So far Mackey hadn't let him down.

So hearing his song—small, intimate like this, played solo by Mackey himself as a quiet closer—that meant something. Afterward, though, as the band all drank soda and Briony and her band of monkeys (as she called the roadies) helped put the equipment to rights, he had a moment of wondering when the shoe was going to drop—the shoe Mackey had been carrying since he'd run out of the airport, sure that he couldn't go back home.

It was like the thought invited trouble.

Kell's phone actually rang, and his sort of squinty eyes grew wide, like the news automatically had to be bad. (It cracked Trav up how much a phone call interfered with everybody's sense of the universe. He figured they should call Mackey's generation the Texting Generation, because actual personal contact was so alien to them all.) He nodded soberly to the band and excused himself outside, saying, "It's Mom."

He was out there for a long time.

When he came back, he blinked red eyes at everyone and spoke with the choked voice of someone who didn't have a good grip on the world.

"Trav, we're done with this next week, right? I mean, the whole tour, done next Saturday."

Trav nodded. "There's sort of a party planned at Heath's office on Sunday, but yeah. We end up back at home. Why?"

Kell grimaced. "Can we skip the party? And...." He looked at Mackey unhappily. "And maybe all of us go back to Tyson for a few weeks? Mackey, I know you're mad at him, but we got to get over that. Mom said there's not much time to get over it, and—"

Without even looking at him, Mackey snuck his hand into Trav's and squeezed.

Trav made himself ask the hard question, because Cheever had left on good terms, and this could only be about one person. "Kell, what's wrong with Grant?"

Kell met Trav's eyes like a man. "Mom says he's dying, Trav. He's bald and skinny, and his lips are chapped, and.... Mom asked him, and he said the doc said maybe two months. Probably less. She said he looked like he wanted it to be less."

Trav heard Mackey's little moan and closed his eyes.

"I'll tell Heath to cancel the party," Trav said calmly. "We can be on the plane to Sacramento two hours after the show."

OH, SURE, he *sounded* like he had it all together in the bar—or, rather, he didn't say anything at all—but that night, in the *truly* shitty Hotel Seattle America, Mackey and Trav had the biggest screaming match of their relationship.

It started before they even closed the door.

"We're *what*?" Mackey rounded on him furiously. "You didn't even fucking ask me if I wanted to go, Trav. Last year I couldn't even get on the fucking plane!"

"Well, it's this year, Mackey—are you telling me nothing's changed?"

Mackey glared at him, hauling at the hem of his sopping hooded sweatshirt. The rain had started after Briony had stashed the equipment, and the short walk back to the hotel had drenched them all.

"Of course shit's changed," he said when the shirt was in a puddle at his feet. "We're like... we've been living like... like a couple. Every night together. It's awesome. I ain't—haven't—felt this safe in my life. But you want to go put all of that at risk? Just because...." He trailed off and swallowed, glaring around the room and kicking the sweatshirt like *that* was what was stopping his throat from working around the big bad word.

Trav ground his teeth, feeling older than Mackey for the first time since Christmas, when he'd gotten the text from Jefferson. He almost hadn't had time to grab his carry-on before running the hell off the damned plane. He'd never be able to fly American Airlines again.

"Because he's *dying*, Mackey. I need you to say that word for me. Can you say the word?"

"I don't need to say the word—"

"Oh yes you do, you need to say the fucking word. You need to say the fucking sentence. That guy may have fucked with your heart when you were a kid, but he was your whole world and he's dying."

"We don't need to dwell on that shit, goddammit—"

"That shit is the whole point," Trav insisted. "The point is this guy meant something to you—and not just *something*, he was your fucking *everything*. I know it was a thousand years ago, but even *I* remember my first crush, and it broke my fucking heart. You only get that kind of pain once, and you... it was your whole world. I *watched* the aftermath, remember? If you think it was bad holding this inside because he broke up with you—"

"We weren't even going out!" Mackey retorted, wounded, backing up against the hotel wall like he could escape. "It was just a fuck in a car or a grope in a backroom or—"

"*Bullshit!*" Trav yelled, seeing red. "You were a goddamned child bride, McKay! You were *claimed* at fourteen—if he hadn't called it off, you would have toured together joined at the cock and the ass. You think I don't know that?"

"But it's not the same," Mackey yelled back almost tearfully. "What he and me did, what you and I have, it's not the same. I don't want to give up you and me for me and him—how can you ask me—"

Trav's lower lip wobbled. "I'm not asking you to go back to him, baby. I'm asking you to say good-bye to him. Yeah, if life was fair, you could've waited another five years, and you would have been fine with that. But life's not fair, and he's *dying*—and I've yet to hear you say that, by the way. You have to say good-bye to him. If you don't, you'll never be square inside."

"You think seeing him again is gonna make me square inside?" Mackey snarled, so vicious that Trav actually flinched. "You think we're ever gonna have a chance to talk? You watch—it'll be the same old bullshit. I'll be there, watching him die, and my insides will be screaming *Grant Adams Fucked Mackey Sanders More Than He Ever Fucked His Wife* and he'll just nod and smile and shine the whole world on."

"Well then you can say good-bye to that too," Trav snapped. "You can go see him, and be with me, and he can die knowing what he missed out on. Does that make you any happier?"

"That's fuckin' *mean*," Mackey said, horrified, and Trav knew it was and didn't give a ripe shit.

"Yeah, but you think I don't need to see it happen too?" Trav shot back, feeling like a heel for the first time since Terry. "You were *killing* yourself over the guy—and I picked up the pieces. If you can't go back to say good-bye for *you* or for *him*, do it for me!"

"Why?" Mackey demanded. "Why? What've I ever done to make you think I need that? Have I ever cheated, Trav? Have I ever even *looked* at another guy?"

"I'm not talking about cheating, Mackey. Goddammit, have you never heard of closure?"

"Maybe I'm not strong enough for closure!" Mackey shouted.

Trav sucked in a gasp of air and froze, his mouth open. Oh. That was the problem. Mackey had just seemed so damned *capable* this past year—Trav had forgotten that he'd never known his own strength.

"Maybe I'm not strong enough, you ever thought of that? Because I love you, and I wouldn't have him if he was served ass-up on a silver platter, but maybe I go in there and see him all sick and shit, and my insides, they'll just open up and I'll die too! I spent a long time being a big oozy fuckin' hole, Trav—maybe I don't want to do that again! Maybe I only get once to heal from something like that, you think?"

Trav thought he'd learned a lot about compassion in the past year, but apparently he hadn't learned enough, because this was the time to show mercy, and instead he found himself twisting the knife.

"Well, you better toughen up, Mackey. I need to know you're strong enough to face this, because I'm older than you and I'm not getting any fucking younger. And if I don't drop dead because you give me a heart attack, I could die in a car wreck or a plane wreck or we could break up because you want kids and I don't or *something* bad could happen, and I am not going to be all right until I know you can fucking *deal*!"

Mackey blanched, practically green, and Trav realized he'd gone too far. "You take that back," he hissed. "You take that *back*, or I will go out right now and open a vein and dump in a bag of fucking meth—"

"*Shut up!*" Trav's eyes would be red with broken blood vessels the next morning from the force of that scream. In two steps he had Mackey pinned up against the back wall. "Drugs aren't the answer and screaming at me isn't the answer—you've got one thing you can do here, dammit, and you need to fucking own up!"

"What am I supposed to do?" Mackey shouted. "What am I supposed to do? Go back to my hometown and fuck Grant Adams for old time's sake, proving to you once and for all that all guys are gonna cheat on you and break your fucking heart?"

"*No!*" Trav choked, fighting against shaking Mackey against the wall. "You're supposed to say good-bye so I don't ever have to worry about this guy in your heart again!"

"Why, because he'll be…." Mackey's face twisted.

Trav wanted to laugh. *Near miss, little man. Near miss with the huge, furry, fanged word.*

"No, not because he'll be dead," Trav said, softening his grip on Mackey's shoulders. He would have bruises the next day, and Trav would have to forgive himself for those too. "Because you can admit that you loved him when he was alive."

Mackey shook his head. "How can that still hurt?" he asked, impossibly young. "How can it still hurt? What do I have to do to make it not hurt?"

"Let it hurt," Trav said, putting his wide-palmed hand on the side of Mackey's head and pulling him into his chest. "Then let him go."

"I don't want to hurt you," Mackey whispered. "I don't want to hurt him, but I really don't want to hurt you."

"You will," Trav said, knowing in his gut that it would happen. Yeah, it was one thing to tell Mackey to go open up a vein, but Trav was pretty sure there'd be plenty of blood on the ground to spare. "You'll hurt us both, but, well, backatcha."

Mackey looked away. "I…." He took a deep breath and broke away from Trav's arms. "I need a fucking walk," he said and bolted out of the hotel room, past Blake, Briony, and Kell, who were all standing near the semiopen window and had been, it looked like, long enough for Kell to have heard too much.

"Mackey!" Kell called, but Blake stopped him with a hand on the arm.

"He's right," Trav muttered. "Let him go."

Briony nodded at Trav and took off after him, and Trav blessed the girl. Mackey had people—maybe even the right people for the right pain.

"But it's raining, Trav," Kell said helplessly. "It's raining, and they're just in T-shirts."

Trav roared in frustration and pressed the heels of his hands to his eyes. "You wanted something?" he asked, because he didn't want to look at Mackey's brother after the bomb exploded. He'd heard. Kell's eyes were glassy and he kept licking his lips nervously—Trav did not doubt that he'd heard everything.

"How come nobody told me?" Kell asked simply, looking at Trav and then Blake. Blake looked away, and Kell whimpered. "Nobody? Blake, you knew?"

"He told me in rehab," Blake admitted grudgingly. "It was... he said it so I'd know that all that time he was giving me shit, it wasn't my fault."

Kell's mouth opened and closed and opened again. "Grant and my little brother?" he asked when he obviously knew. "Why... how long?"

Trav wished Mackey was there. He did. But Kell had maybe earned the right to know. "Mackey said he was fourteen."

Kell let out a little moan. "Oh fuck. Oh fuck. This makes *so* much sense. Jesus... fucking Jesus. That trip to San Francisco—Grant kept trying to tell me. God, he... I don't know, kept hedging with Sam—for *years*—and God. He must have thought I was a fucking idiot!"

"He didn't want to hurt you," Trav said, sounding flat and wooden even to his own ears. He remembered dully when he thought Kell had it all coming. All the pain of self-realization, all of the horrible guilt of treating other people like shit—Trav would have wished it solidly on Kell's shoulders.

But not now.

Kell and even Grant had fought for Mackey when nobody else in the world had, and no matter how bad they'd fucked up, Trav couldn't hate Kell enough for the hurt that was probably welling up like blood in his stomach. In fact, he sort of loved the guy.

"Now you're just being nice," Kell said bitterly. "He didn't want me to cut him off. I was his best friend, and he didn't want me to stop being his best friend. And... and...."

All of the pain of the past year, and this was the first time any of them had ever seen Kell cry. He dashed his cheeks with his hand. "All that bullshit Mackey went through—nobody told me? I was to blame—"

"No," Blake and Trav said in tandem, looking at each other through old, self-aware eyes.

"Mackey made his own disaster," Blake said with passion.

"Easy to say," Kell snapped, wiping his cheeks again. "Just because I didn't have a computer until I was twenty-five doesn't mean I don't use it now. You think I didn't look that shit up when Mackey came out? You think I didn't read all the articles and shit about how hard we make it on people, how they'd rather use drugs and hurt themselves than not be loved?"

Kell was shaking, and without warning, Blake launched himself at his friend with a full ten-points-for-the-fist-bump on the back style hug. Kell let him, trembling in Blake's arms, and Blake sighed.

"Trav?"

"Yeah?"

"Would it be awful if I asked you to take him out and get him drunk? He's not an addict—he stopped without even being asked. But he needs something... something...."

Trav sighed. "Something. Yeah. Blake, you wanna wait here for Mackey and Briony? Text me when they get back, okay? I think Kell needs a fucking drink."

Blake nodded. "Can I watch your TV?"

Trav wanted to laugh. Kids. All of them. "Mackey's tablet is in his carry-on—you guys play games on it, right?"

"Yeah—and I even know which icons to ignore." Blake shuddered. "Gay porn is for gay men and straight women, I'm not telling you something you don't know."

Trav laughed. He had to. "Thanks, Blake. C'mon." He slung his arm over Kell's shoulders and steered him toward the bar. "Blake?" Trav said over his shoulder before they walked out from under the hotel overhang and into the pouring rain. "Text Jefferson—have them come down too. I don't want any of you alone."

The look on Blake's face—God, it was grateful. Trav steered Kell to the bar they'd left not half an hour ago, thinking that addictions and comfort were a very, very tricky business.

"DO YOU know how hard it is?" Kell asked soggily. "Being his brother? He's like, all bright... like the song. Like everything is a song to him. There's shooting stars, and there's Mackey, and the stars are trying to catch him. And the rest of us... we're... I mean, he's so *smart*. He just got in the middle of the living room and said, 'You, you're gonna play lead,' and I did. Man, I didn't even know what lead guitar *did*, and he made me practice, and now I wouldn't change it...."

Trav took a deep breath and patted Kell on the back. He thought about offering up another beer but then figured Kell would have enough to throw up as it was. No wonder the boy never got drunk—this was just embarrassing.

In a way.

In another way, Trav thought as he nursed his own beer bitterly, Kell sort of hit the nail on the head. Mackey was a shooting star. The kind of guy Trav had *always* gone for. Whether it had been his painful half-realized crush on the soccer forward who played the lead in the sixth-grade school play or the blistering first affair with the guy who played saxophone on the corner by the library and the drugstore the summer before he went into the service, Trav had loved the shooting stars, the talented, the magnetic. He'd never been able to *understand* what drove them, but he loved it just the same. It hadn't been until Mackey that he'd seen his same obsessive need for order mirrored in Mackey's creative drive, and still—Mackey was the shooting star. Trav just cleared the cosmic debris from his path.

"It's hard," he said, feeling melancholy with two beers. "It's hard loving people that bright, that shiny, that they make everyone else in the world look dim."

Kell nodded. "Grant was like that," he said ruminatively. "Grant did what you did, real smart, but.... God. He was only happy when he was on the stage with me and Mackey, playing the guitar. He was good. So good." Kell sighed into his beer. "So, so good...."

Trav pulled out his wallet and set his card on the table, nodding at the night-shift bartender. The place had cooled down after the band's set, and no one seemed to recognize the lead guitarist of Outbreak Monkey working some shit out with his brother's boyfriend.

"It's not your fault you didn't know," Trav said, wondering if Kell would remember in the morning.

"It is," Kell said, proving, once again, that people underestimated him a lot. "I told them they couldn't be who they were. I told them they had to hide. So they did. Grant hid until he disappeared. Mackey tried, but—" Kell laughed fondly and drunkenly, rubbing his hand over his growing buzz cut in thought. "Mackey was always torn, you know? He thought he was no one, but he didn't wanna be." Kell rubbed his head again. "Why's my little brother so much more interesting than I am?"

Trav wished for the zillionth time that he was a hugger. "You remember that Joe Walsh song?" he asked, smiling a little. "Ordinary Average Guy?"

Kell laughed. "Yeah. Boring life. Picking up dog doo, hoping it's hard. I remember. Is that my fate, Trav? Wife, kids, dog shit?"

"Happiness," Trav said softly, thinking about his parents and his brother and meaning it. "It's going to be easier for you, Kell. Mackey'll keep you fed, keep you in a job, and you will help him make music history. But when it's time to find that wife to follow you around and have babies, it's gonna be easy." He sighed and shut his eyes. "That fight that Mackey and I had? There's gonna be none of that shit for you. No breaking your fist on walls, no sixty-eleven trips to rehab. Just falling in love and having babies and doing your job with all your heart. It's gonna be a good life."

Kell nodded with big eyes, like he was clinging to Trav's words with all the strength in his big, rough hands. "Yeah?"

Trav nodded and smiled. "Yeah, man. You're gonna have a good life."

"Not spectacular," Kell said, and then looked Trav in the eyes with startling sobriety. "Is it worth it?" he asked. "The trade-off? The spectacular for the ordinary? Is it worth it?"

Trav sighed and closed his eyes. "Ask me when we bury your friend, Kellogg. I might know then."

The tabletop they were sitting at was overvarnished, tacky with too much spilled booze, riddled with stickers and stamps, which was apparently this place's idea of kitsch. Kell worried one of the stamps with his thumbnail and looked around the little dive with the surprisingly tasty barbecue.

"This is a good place," he said after a minute. "Someday I want to come back to this place and remember the shit you said to me. It's important shit."

Trav ran his finger idly around the rim of his empty beer mug. "I'm not going anywhere," he said, laughing a little. "I promised your brother I'd be here, whether or not we were a thing. You can ask me any day, and I'll tell you this important shit."

Kell nodded and drained the last two inches of his glass. The bartender came over and took Trav's card, and they met eyes, both of them aware that the sobering time had come.

"What I'm going through with Grant, it's gonna hurt," he said. "The guy was our brother for most of our lives."

Trav grimaced. "Understood."

"But what you and Mackey are gonna go through?" Kellogg sighed and stood up. "I get why my brother became an addict," he said after a minute. "I mean I do *now*. But I'm telling you, there's not enough beer in the world, Trav. And I don't got no other remedies, yanno?"

Trav took his card back and signed for the tip, nodding at the bartender with finality. He and Kell were still in their shirtsleeves, and it was still pissing rain, and Blake hadn't texted them yet, which meant Mackey and Briony were still out in it.

"You don't have to," Trav said after a minute. "If me and Mackey can't work it out on our own, it wasn't meant to be."

"Now that's just bullshit," Kell muttered. "There's meant to be and not meant to be and there's just being put under the pressure cooker until you explode."

Trav smiled at him. "Kell?"

"Yeah?"

"Don't let anyone tell you you're stupid. Ever. And if they insist on it, let them talk to me and I'll take them out."

Kell's answering smile was a little sad, but sound. They turned and walked out of the bar more than friends—brothers.

Trav thought about Heywood and wondered bitterly if he'd ever really known what that meant. His brother was working in the ER right now while his wife minded the kids. He knew this because Heywood texted him when he was bored. When they'd been in Europe, Trav had texted him random pictures: *Mackey in Rome—the cats loved him. The guys on the Eiffel Tower—they didn't see it last time.*

Suddenly Trav had a terrible, terrible yearning that Heywood meet Mackey and the guys. His brother had been a little shit when they were kids, but it didn't seem fair, somehow, that they should grow up and be such separate people. The Sanders boys—plus Stevie and, from the sound of it, Grant—might have been dysfunctional and claustrophobic, but at least they had had each other.

Halfway back in the rain, Trav's pocket buzzed. It was Blake—Mackey and Briony had come back. They were having a Doritos party in Trav's room.

*OMW*

Trav raised his face to the rain and closed his eyes, letting the relief wash over him.

*Thank you, God. Thank you for letting him be okay. Thank you for bringing him back to me. Please, let him stay.*

They walked back into the room to find Blake, Jefferson, and Stevie playing each other on their DS3s while Shelia, Mackey, and Briony cheered them on. Mackey's hair still dripped down his back and into his eyes, but he was wearing dry sweats, and when Trav walked in, Mackey grabbed two pairs of sweats and T-shirts for Trav and Kell.

Trav took them gratefully and passed Kell his. Both of them looked uneasily at the girls, who rolled their eyes and waved their hands and turned back to the games. It felt cowardly to go to the bathroom after that, Trav reflected, smiling grimly to himself. Propriety was a weird thing.

They changed and hung their clothes up in the tiny mildewed bathroom and towel-dried their hair. When they were done, Trav sat on the bed and Mackey sat in his lap, just like when they were at home and the guys were playing something on the big screen. They started rooting for their favorite characters and listening to Briony's acid commentary, passing the tiny bags of Doritos Blake had apparently gotten from the vending machine when Mackey had shown up hungry even though they'd already eaten.

Nobody mentioned the tour, nobody mentioned Grant, nobody mentioned the terrible, rip-roaring fight that had torn through the little hotel like a touched-down tornado.

And nobody went back to their beds either. Mackey slept between Briony and Trav in one queen-size bed; Jefferson, Stevie and Shelia took the other. Kell and Blake took the floor, using the fluffy blankets Trav had bought them in Albuquerque because the nights dropped surprisingly cold and the bus just didn't seem warm enough.

The room was close and humid between the rain and the too-many bodies, but nobody wanted to split up just yet.

The last person who had left was dying.

When gentle breathing and soft snores echoed in the tiny room with the peeling paint and the bald carpet coming up from the moldings, Mackey rolled over in Trav's arms and nuzzled his chest.

"You awake?" he whispered.

Trav opened one eye. "We're not doing that right now," he said, sure that they were clear on this one thing.

"Yeah, I gotcha. I just wanted to say...." Mackey sighed so deeply Trav's arms rose and fell with his chest. "I wanted to say I don't know if I'm sorry—I can't think of anything I said that was meant to be mean or shitty, so I'm not sure I can be sorry for it."

Trav felt a smile tilting at the corners of his mouth. If Mackey Sanders loved you, it meant he didn't hold back a goddamned thing. Trav could deal with that.

"Understood," Trav murmured.

"I didn't finish. I just want to say that I don't want you hurt. Shit's gonna happen, and you're going to get hurt, but I never meant to do it." Again, that big sigh. "I don't know if that's worth anything, but it's all I got."

Trav dropped a kiss in his knotted, water-ratted hair. "Intentions should count," he said after a minute. Mackey's hair smelled animal and real, and he wished for a moment that they were alone. But they'd get lots of time to be alone and not a whole lot of time to be the lot of them, the band, where anyone else could understand. "I promise to try to remember that."

"We got weak sauce for promises," Mackey muttered in disgust, and it was Trav's turn to sigh. Somewhere in the hotel, someone was having one hell of a bachelor/fishing party, and Trav could only hope they woke up feeling like dogs shit in their mouths. God, they were making a vicious racket—it echoed in the brightness beyond the tattered blackout curtains. Trav was one version of "Freebird" away from going outside and kicking righteous fucking ass.

"Then maybe we should be making different promises," Trav said after a moment.

"You write the music, I'll do the lyrics," Mackey mumbled. Then, slightly more awake: "If one of those bozos wakes up dead tomorrow, will we be asked to testify, or can we still get the hell out of Dodge?"

Trav grunted. "I am a better manager than that. If one of those bozos wakes up dead, we were never here."

Mackey laughed softly. "You were a scary motherfucker in the Army, weren't you?"

Trav closed his eyes, remembered sweat, grit, terrified men, and that certain amount of fear and loathing that prisoners emanated when they were around an apex predator. "Nothing but the scariest motherfucker for you, Mackey. Swear."

"Good," Mackey said seriously. When Trav opened his eyes, he saw Mackey regarding him soberly. "'Cause the whole fucking world knows I'm dating my manager, and all of Tyson is going to be running around trying to prove they're bigger and scarier than you so they can feel good about themselves for not being gay."

"Charming," Trav grunted. "Can't wait."

"And Briony and Shelia shouldn't go anywhere alone either—"

"Briony isn't going anywhere," Briony mumbled. "Briony is sick, and the two assholes talking next to her are driving her to homicide."

Mackey rolled in Trav's arms and felt her forehead. "Aw, man—Trav, she's burning up—"

"I can take a cold tab," Briony grunted. "Just shut up, for sweet fuck's sake."

Mackey sighed and Trav nuzzled his neck. And put buying cold and flu medication on his mental list of things to do in six hours, when the whole puppy-pile mess of them got up, finished the tour, and went to meet their past.

# My Hometown (Bowling for Soup version)

THEY LEFT LA like Trav promised, hardly two hours after they took their final bow on the tour. By the time the little plane Trav had chartered touched down on the tiny landing strip outside of Hepzibah, Briony had a fever of 103 and a graveyard cough.

Mackey's first priority once they landed was getting her to the hospital so she could get some antibiotics and fluids.

Trav rode with them and sent Debra in the other rental he'd had waiting to take the others to Mackey's mother's house, which, she assured them, could hold the whole lot of them, Briony as well.

Apparently they'd wrought better than they knew when they'd bought that house.

Mackey's first glimpse of it was dozing in Trav's arms, Briony curled against him as much as a girl who was over five eight could curl. Her fever was down, she'd had fluids for six hours, and now she was just exhausted.

She also wanted her mother, but she'd tried to hide that fact from Mackey and Trav. But the fifth time she checked her phone to get a random text from her mom, like she got most days, Mackey and Trav met eyes and Trav started texting Briony's mom too. He wasn't sure he could get the woman up there, but he could certainly try.

But in the meantime, Mackey's first glance at his mother's home was through bleary eyes, and it looked, well, a lot like the big houses in LA. Two stories, with wings on either side, it was white stucco, which would hopefully keep the inside cooler during the area's broiling summers. Mackey remembered something about passive solar, and he figured that was why there were no windows on one side of the house.

"Who lives in this neighborhood?" Mackey asked fuzzily.

Trav recited, as though from memory, "Two wealthy retired starlets, two Olympic skiers who skate down the hill trails as practice, a guy who made his fortune selling used cars and then retired here, and the mother of a rock band whose boys take care of her. You want any more details?"

"Yeah," Mackey muttered. "Whose SUV is that in the driveway?" He knew his mother had a little Kia Sportage and figured that was in the garage. The Navigator Trav had rented was sitting outside, so Mackey knew Debra had gotten everyone home the night before. The slightly battered midsized SUV looked a lot like….

Mackey closed his eyes and opened them again.

"That's Grant," he said, his whole face going cold from the shock. "That's his car."

But the guy in the driver's seat, leaning back and closing his eyes like he was in pain, didn't look at all like Grant Adams.

"His timing is *awesome*," Trav said with a sort of wonder. "Oh my God, I can finally see you two as a couple!"

Mackey glared at him and then laughed sourly. "Yeah, well, we had years to work at it." Walter pulled to a stop in front of the house, and Mackey turned to a pale, dozing

Briony. "Sweetheart?" he murmured, touching her face. God, she'd been such a trouper, downing cold medicine and drinking orange juice pretty much from their two-hour walk in the rain on. She hadn't said anything, just walked, shivering, like him in a T-shirt, because apparently they really were two peas in a pod. "Sweetheart, we're here."

She squinted at him. "Are you calling me pet names? I may throw up."

If anything, Mackey shivered harder. She'd done that too, when they'd gotten off the plane. "God save us. No, I just want you to know we're here, and if you can walk—"

"I'll carry her," Trav said, hip-checking Mackey to the side. "You've got things to do. Walter, could you get the door?"

"Trav…," Mackey said, feeling pathetic. But seriously—weak, suffering girl or whole and healthy (for once!) Mackey Sanders, who had never needed anyone to take care of him ever? Who was going to get taken into the house and coddled?

"I'll be out as soon as she's settled," Trav said softly, and Mackey looked up to where the gaunt, chalk-white old man in the bandana tilted his head back against the seat, exhaling what looked to be a cloud of marijuana smoke into the September morning air.

"Take your time," he said, meaning it. However this came out, Grant wasn't ready for a fight, that was for damned sure.

Mackey waited for a moment as Trav, Briony, and Walter made the procession into the house. The gaunt, hairless man in Grant's car sat up and watched them, then looked around the yard.

Mackey met his eyes, and the breath froze in his chest. He'd never smoked crack, because he'd never been offered it, but for a minute he wondered if that was what it felt like. If that was true, it sucked, because it was an excruciating, acidic rush that burned every nerve ending around his heart with pain. He couldn't believe crack was addictive if it felt like this, and he couldn't believe people ever made up after a divorce.

He'd never inhale again.

The only thing that kept him walking was that Grant's eyes were the same color. The flesh around them was almost translucent, blue with fatigue, but that beautiful, leonine golden hazel color—that was all Grant.

His thin lips twisted, and he looked away. "You're not even going to tell me I look like shit, McKay?"

Mackey kept walking up to the window, fighting the urge to sob and run his hand over the bald scalp he knew lay under the blue bandana as he drew near. "You shoulda seen me the first time I went into rehab," Mackey said, trying hard for fuck-off-and-love-me. "You look like a rock star compared to that."

Grant smiled shakily. "You always look like a rock star," he said, his eyes so full of adoration that Mackey couldn't hardly keep his mad in his chest.

"Well, I have to," Mackey said with a wink. "Haven't you heard? I am!"

Grant laughed dryly and leaned his head back and took another hit, staring out his front window at Mackey's mother's house, which Mackey hadn't even seen the inside of.

"Do you know what your mother did?" Grant asked, completely bemused. "Your mother, who didn't even talk to my parents when we all practically lived in that tiny apartment together—do you know what she did?"

Mackey blinked and leaned up against the door. "I got no idea," he said truthfully. "She's surprised the hell out of me this year. I'd say it's potluck there."

Grant turned a sweet smile to him and put the roach in the ashtray. "She drove to my parents' house, knocked on the door, and asked to talk to me."

"You're not at your own home?" Mackey asked, confused.

Grant closed his eyes and shook his head. "I got sick, I couldn't work, couldn't help much with the baby—it was easier. Your mom must have heard that round town. So my mom tries to get all 'I got money' on your mom, right? You never met my mother— there's a reason for that. But my mom's on her high horse and riding higher, and my wife comes in and she's going on about how I don't hang out with the Sanders boys no more, and your mom looks me dead in the eyes and says, 'Grant, my boys are coming home to see you. They'll be here in two weeks. You are welcome in my home any time, and yes, Mackey told me everything.' And then she ignored my mom and Sam and turned around and walked away."

Mackey closed his eyes and chuckled. "My mom—God. She will surprise you."

Grant made a grunt of affirmation and Mackey felt the weight of his stare until he opened his own eyes. "You told her everything?" he asked, a simple longing in his voice.

Mackey swallowed. "Yeah. Everybody in that house knows everything, Grant. Jefferson, Stevie, Blake, Shelia, Briony—"

"Kell?" Grant's voice throbbed, and Mackey thought about how scared he'd been these last two days for Briony. Best friends would do that to you.

"Yeah," Mackey said, nodding. "Kell. He might *not* have known, but Trav and I had a big screaming match about coming here, and he heard it all."

"Trav didn't want you here?" Grant asked, like he would have understood.

"I was afraid to come," Mackey said. His eyes burned and his throat was swollen, and damn, damn, damn, there were no drugs, *no drugs*, that would help make this better.

"Of me?" Grant smirked, and even though his face was a gaunt blob of dough on a stick, his dimples still popped.

"You left me once and it almost killed me," Mackey admitted, his chest feeling like raw meat. "I mean… if rehab hadn't took, I wouldn't be standing here right now, and that's the truth. And now you're leaving me again, and if Trav can't stay with me through this, I'm not gonna make it." His voice cracked, but he pulled it back in. He was stronger than this, dammit.

Grant closed his eyes and nodded. "Well, you tell Trav that it's enough you guys came. You tell him to stick around. I don't want any more of your soul than you already gave me, Mackey. I don't deserve more. I just want my brothers back before I go."

"Well then get the fuck out of the car, man," Mackey said, pulling himself together by spit and shoestrings. "They're probably all at the kitchen table, letting my mom feed 'em. It's been a long fucking time since dinner."

Grant nodded and opened the door. The stench of pot that had lingered as Mackey stood there rolled out of the car, and Grant looked embarrassed. "It's legal now," he said with a wink. "I can't drive for an hour, but don't worry. It's all legal."

Mackey rolled his eyes. "Oh sure. *Now* it's legal. When I realized how many years of prison time I shot up my nose, I almost crapped my pants!"

Grant grunted and shut the door with an effort. His belt flapped halfway around his waist because he'd pulled it to the last notch in an effort to keep his skinny jeans on his hips, and Mackey had a glimpse of pale, countable ribs as he slid out of the car. Jesus, this cancer bullshit wasn't for the weak.

"Coke, Mackey? I'd say it's tacky, but at least you got your teeth. Them's rock star drugs right there."

Mackey stuck out an arm. Grant took it unashamedly, his fingers gripping weakly through Mackey's thin hoodie, and Mackey felt a sudden pang through his chest. Grant wasn't going to be mobile for long. Another couple of weeks, maybe three, and Grant wouldn't be walking creakily through his mother's door to have breakfast. They'd be trying to push Grant's mother aside so they could visit him by his bed.

"I tried heroin," Mackey admitted. "Made me queasy, so I tried it more than once. Good dreams, but it makes the space-time continuum *really* fuckin' hazy."

"Does it make time stretch out longer?" Grant asked. "'Cause as shitty as I feel, I ain't been this happy since... since...."

Mackey found the courage to give him this. "Since I wrote you your song," he said, and Grant paused. Mackey turned his head to the side and saw that Grant's eyes were closed, and a little smile tilted his once full mouth.

"You probably hate me," Grant said, his eyes still closed. "You're probably trying really hard not to yell and scream and just rip me up with your tongue. Well, maybe you can do that if you stay for a little while. You'll forget I'm sick, and you'll just get out how pissed you are, and I'll be okay with that. But right now I don't care, McKay. You gave me my song, and it's on your CD, and that gets to be me and you, going into other people's homes and making them fall in love. You can go ahead and hate me because we've got that, and it's all good."

*But I got Trav's song too! His song's what I feel in my blood right now. I don't feel "River Shadows," I don't want "River Shadows," I don't* remember *what that song felt like inside of me, I don't I don't I don't I don't....*

And maybe Mackey would have forgotten that Grant was sick and said all that to him right there on his mother's lawn, and maybe not. It didn't matter, because Trav opened the door and, seeing them making their way across the pathway, he hopped down to Grant's other side and let Grant take his arm too.

If Trav could make that effort, then Mackey could put aside the bitterness and acid and bring Grant home.

"Grant, this is my boyfriend, Trav Ford—Trav, this is Grant Adams."

Trav hmmed noncommittally as he helped Grant up the stairs.

"Pleastameetya, Mr. Ford—"

"I could have put off the honor, actually," Trav muttered. "Jesus, you had to be dying of cancer?"

"Well, I wanted to be dying of something rare and exotic, but the missionaries in Africa got that shit and I got cancer," Grant replied.

Mackey could tell by the startled look Trav sent him that Trav probably approved.

"Well, I'll be sure to remember that when it's my turn to go," Trav said shortly. "I'll have to fly that plane upside down through the shark tank all by myself."

"I'm going out fighting aliens, myself," Mackey said soberly just to see them smile. "I'm going to take out a zillion of them, save the planet. People'll be writing my name in lights for *years.*"

Trav opened the door and led them both in while Grant replied, "Oh, leave it to you to find a way to go out that'll leave you famous. No just lying down and taking a dirt nap for you!"

Mackey wrinkled his nose and looked to his left. The kitchen—the freakin' huge white-tiled kitchen—held pretty much everybody who needed to be there. Like Mackey thought, everyone was still up, cycling in from the showers after their run—all they were missing was Debra and Kell.

They all looked up in surprise to see Grant leaning on Mackey and Trav, and Mackey did his damnedest to keep the moment normal.

"As *if*," he said in response to Grant's comment. "Seriously—Stevie, Jeff, if you guys got to choose how you went out, how'd you go out?"

Jefferson and Stevie looked at each other—partly to make sure of their answer, Mackey knew, but also partly to recover from seeing Grant looking like he did.

They got up in tandem and came over to hug Grant. "Together," they said as they stood, and Grant laughed like the answer somehow comforted him.

"Good to see yous" echoed about the entryway, and Mackey stood back and let the twins flow around Grant and surge him toward the table. They introduced him to Blake, who stepped forward hesitantly and offered his hand. He looked over the crowd and met Mackey's eyes as he did so, and Mackey nodded. Blake had been through enough—no reason for him to feel bad about meeting the first guy who played his axe.

Grant sat at the table with some help. Mackey's mom, looking stylish in leggings and a running jacket with her hair up in a little twist, offered him some orange juice.

Grant closed his eyes. "You got any apple juice, Ms. Sanders? OJ's a little acidic for my stomach."

Heather Sanders nodded. "Sure do, Grant. I bought some special. Thank you for coming."

Grant looked around at the table and smiled slightly. "Thank you for asking me over. I feel bad, though. Mackey and Trav don't look like they got any sleep at all."

"Yeah, Mackey," Blake said, taking the glass of juice from Mackey's mom and handing it over to Grant. "How's Briony?"

"She'll be fine," Trav said for him. He came up behind Mackey and put a possessive hand on the small of his back. Well, he was entitled, Mackey guessed. "Mostly she just needs to sleep and take the fever meds and not go running the sound board in the middle of a germ storm—or go walking in the rain."

"Way to go, Mackey," Stevie chastised. "You finally find a friend and you almost kill her by taking her walking in the rain."

"Wasn't like that," Mackey retorted without heat. He and Briony had taken some shit for this over the past week. Everybody knew why they'd gone, everybody knew he felt bad, but it was going to get chopped up and dragged over until the hash wasn't tasty anymore. "And I tried to send her home last week, but she was gonna see the damned tour out—let's all forget that while you try to make me feel like shit."

"Is she comfortable?" Mom asked.

Mackey looked at Trav to answer.

"She's sleeping. I don't know if your house can take one more person, Heather, but I've offered her mom a ticket to come take care of her. I'm not sure she'll take it—she's got younger kids at home—but I hope that's okay."

Mom closed her eyes like she was trying to do math. She opened them and looked uncomfortable. "Are, uhm, Debra and Walter staying here?" she asked delicately.

Trav shook his head. "I think we can book them at a hotel. Will that help?"

"It'll help me," Walter mumbled from the sofa down in the front room.

Mackey looked down from the entryway and grinned. "You getting sleepy there, Walter? You go ahead and take mine and Trav's room, and we'll visit Grant."

"If it's okay with you, Mackey, when Debra gets out of the shower, we'll go get a hotel room in town." He grimaced apologetically. "It's a nice house and all, but seriously? I prefer a one-room apartment."

Mackey looked around himself at the vaulted ceilings, the expensive wool carpeting, and the ecru and eggshell walls. "Don't blame you," he said seriously. By the time they'd left the house in LA, the walls were different colors and the carpets were too. No big white house for the boys, but their mother, God love her, had earned some tranquility in her life. "This place is a little pastel for me. But soon as she gets out, you guys take off and get some rest." His head hurt and his eyes were swelling shut with exhaustion, but he wasn't ready to do the same thing.

Suddenly the number of times he would have to see Grant Adams and make sure they were square had diminished to practically none. Mackey didn't want to miss a nanosecond that would ensure Grant could leave this earth and leave Mackey with his heart whole and ready to go on.

"I don't know if anyone else wanted to shower, but the hot water's practically gone!" Kell came out from the hallway presumably leading to the bedroom, wearing only a pair of jeans and drying his hair. His stocky, muscular body had more than one tattoo, but the Outbreak Monkey on his stomach was the biggest. Mackey felt the sudden urge to grab a marker and sketch one on Grant, make him a part of the band again, make it like it was.

Behind Kell came Debra, in what looked like an emergency outfit of black yoga pants and a trim white T-shirt. Mackey wasn't sure he'd ever seen Trav's second dressed in anything but black and white. His tired brain tried to loop to Debra in evening wear, but it wasn't happening—hadn't, in fact, happened during the whole time in Europe. Wow. Mackey *was* an imperialist pig, wasn't he?

"Dammit," Mackey muttered, swaying a little on his feet. "I needed that shower."

"You need to sleep, Mackey," Trav muttered. "We both do."

"But—" Mackey gestured with his chin to where Kell had stopped abruptly. They could practically hear him swallow as he took in the scrawny form of the guy who used to be Grant Adams, sitting at his mother's kitchen table.

"Grant?" Kell's voice wobbled, and then he firmed it up as he walked into the kitchen. "Grant Adams, you sodomizing fuckhead, you couldn't keep your hands off my little brother?"

Grant heard his tone and not his words and rolled his eyes. "Kellogg Sanders, you oblivious sonuvabitch, you couldn't have let the elephant sleep in the fucking corner for another goddamned day?"

"You coulda fuckin' told me," Kell muttered, hauling Grant in for a hug that looked too strong for the brittle bone-man in his arms.

"No I couldna," Grant muttered back. "None of us were the same people then." They stayed like that, holding close, and Mackey realized that he hadn't hugged Grant yet either. He swayed on his feet again, and Trav grabbed him by the elbow.

"Go hug him and let's get to bed," Trav whispered roughly.

Mackey found himself steered up to the tableau, and Trav tapped Kell on the shoulder.

"We're about dead on our feet everyone. Grant, if you're not here when we get up, we're going to be playing tomorrow night in…. God, Mackey, what's it called?"

"The Nugget," Mackey muttered, because the last time they'd played the Nugget had been the last time they'd ended up in jail for fighting. The other guys had asked Trav to book the gig special, since Outbreak Monkey had cut its teeth at the Nugget long before even Kell and Grant were legal to drink.

"Yeah, whatever. We're playing there tomorrow night."

Mackey squinted at him. They were both tired and cranky, but he'd sounded a little short. Well, maybe he wasn't all okay with Mackey seeing his old boyfriend and getting the warm feels. Who could blame him?

Abruptly he wanted to go to bed. Not even so much to sleep but more to get away from what was happening in his chest as he put his hand on Grant's shoulder and leaned in for a hug.

"Night, Mackey," Grant said softly. "Get some sleep."

"See you tomorrow, right?" Mackey said, a bit of apprehension washing over him. He could feel Grant's shoulder blades through his sweatshirt, and the body in his arms felt light as dust.

"Yeah. I'll be at the Nugget if I have to get a cab."

Mackey pulled away, and it was on the tip of his tongue to ask Grant what that meant when his mom, God love her, intervened. "Someone will pick you up, Grant. Will Sam be coming?"

Grant looked at her gratefully. "That would be awesome, Ms. Sanders. And no. Sam, uhm…." The pause left leaden silence, and his chapped lips twisted in his bone-white face. "She's not particularly excited about the return of Outbreak Monkey. If you're, uhm, lucky, you might not have to see a whole lot of her until right before you leave."

Mackey could see the translation in his head, but not a soul was going to say it out loud. *My wife knows my old lover is here, and you won't see her until the funeral.*

Well, didn't that make things easy?

"I'll see you there," Mackey said quietly, and he pretended not to feel Grant's blatant kiss on the cheek in front of his family.

He stood and took three steps forward, then turned to his mom. "Where am I again?"

"Up the stairs, sweetheart, third door on the left. It's the one with the queen-size on the bottom and the bunk bed spanning the top."

Mackey had to think, which made his eyeballs hurt. "Isn't that the same setup we have at home?" he asked, turning to Trav in sort of a dream.

"Yeah, Mackey. I bet she's got Chicken in a Biskit crackers too." Trav sounded resigned. Hell.

"And soda," his mom verified. "Go to sleep, McKay. You can get boggled later."

Trav steered him up the stairs, and every stair felt like his body weighed three hundred pounds. They got to the room and Mackey was just going to fall on the bed, but Trav sighed and sat down, dragging Mackey to the V of his legs and hauling his sweatshirt over his head.

"How come you got all this energy?" Mackey asked irritably, pushing his hair out of his eyes as his sweatshirt hit the closed suitcase in the corner.

"I wasn't on stage less than twenty-four hours ago, screaming my guts out," Trav said. He sounded like Trav again, so Mackey dared to run his fingers through his hair, nuzzling his temple in one of those soft gestures they rarely made in public. Trav stopped untying his tennis shoe for a minute and relaxed into Mackey's stomach.

"Thank you," Mackey said, wanting to say this now, before he fell asleep and forgot.

"For what?"

"For keeping all the pissed inside."

"How do you know I'm pissed?" Trav asked, looking up into Mackey's eyes.

Mackey cupped his face in both hands and kissed his forehead. "You got a little wrinkle right there between the eyes," he lied.

Trav arched a skeptical eyebrow. "Do not," he said pleasantly.

Mackey sighed. "It's your voice," he said after a quiet moment. "I can hear it. When you talk to Grant, when you talk to me. I can't make your voice not do that. I… I don't know how to make myself feel a way to make your voice not do that." He closed his eyes tight, and to his horror, tears of tiredness slid out. "Oh God. Not this shit," he muttered. "This ain't rehab, and nothing bad's happened yet, and I'm not gonna be a big oozy hole anymore."

"Yeah you are," Trav muttered. "And so am I. C'mon, McKay, give me your foot so I can untie the other one."

"You know what I'm gonna miss? I'll tell you what I'm gonna miss!"

"Not hearing your real name?" Trav guessed, dragging down Mackey's jeans. Mackey stepped out of them and took his socks off by stepping on the toe of one and lifting his foot off. Trav didn't even give him shit about that stretching them out, which must have meant he was tired too.

"Damned straight." Mackey bent down and picked up his jeans and his socks and put them in the corner with his sweatshirt. They'd have to do laundry when they woke up, because Mackey wasn't sure he had more than one outfit and pair of clean underwear left.

"Get used to it," Trav said on a yawn. He'd stood up and was unbuckling his belt, and Mackey had no doubt his slacks and polo shirt would end up draped gracefully over the top bunk. Mackey didn't want to look around the little room—it looked way too much like the one Trav had furnished for him back at their home in LA, except with pink-striped wallpaper. Mackey didn't even want to think about what that meant.

"Why's that?" Mackey climbed into bed, and the touch of clean sheets made him shiver. "Get your ass over here," he demanded. "Don't want to sleep unless you're here."

"We all want a say." Trav *did* drape his clothes neatly over the bunk, but then he slid in next to Mackey, wearing only his boxer briefs.

"In me?" Mackey didn't much like the sound of that.

"We want to claim which part of you we've got. Me, Grant, your mom. We're all trying to say, 'I know him best. He's mine.'"

"That's a waste of time," Mackey grumbled. "Now put your arm over my chest and spoon me like a man."

Trav laughed a little against his hair. "Yeah, McKay, whatever you say."

Mackey was too tired to bicker with him. "Yours," he said, closing his eyes and snuggling back into Trav's welcome heat. "You know me best. I'm yours."

"I'll be expected to prove it," Trav said seriously.

"Well don't do it by being a caveman."

Mackey fell asleep to images of Trav wearing a *Flintstones* toga, taking it off, and folding it nicely over a bunk bed made of rocks.

And then he was out and he didn't dream at all.

# No More Sorrow

TRAV LOOKED around the Nugget and tried not to judge. It was no better and no worse than the bar in Seattle, and he'd enjoyed being there.

He did not enjoy being here.

For one thing, the friendly gay bartender with the fuzzy beard and warm smile was missing. In his place was a good ol' boy, around 350 pounds, with missing teeth. Trav highly doubted he put his mouth to good use.

He shook his head. *God*, he was being an insufferable ass—even in his own head.

Briony was still sick, so Trav and Mackey were setting up the sound equipment, ready to do a quick and dirty set. Mackey had talked to Briony enough, he knew how to work the laptop keyboard they'd set up for their smaller venues, and since he only picked up the guitar for a couple of songs, he was the best bet to fiddle with stuff if anything went wrong after sound check.

The guys were still setting up when Grant walked in, Walter at his heels. In the end, they hadn't wanted to leave Shelia and Briony alone, so Mackey had asked politely if they could use Walter's services so Grant could self-medicate at will. Trav fought the urge to say something snide—and he'd voted for medical marijuana. He believed in it. But thinking about these kids—*his* kids—running around this tiny town....

He was growling. To himself. But he'd *counted*. Between Tyson and Hepzibah, he'd seen two McDonald's, one Subway, five dive bars, eight churches, an appliance store that gouged people like crazy judging by the sale prices on the windows, a music store, a plant store, a car dealership—presumably Grant's father's—and, praise Jesus, a Walmart.

They'd driven by an apartment building, one of those old stucco ones built like a sardine box, divvied up into smaller saltine boxes. It was painted a noxious mustard yellow that showed every divot in the stucco—and there were a lot. As they drove by, one of the window screens fell off the second floor, and Mackey and Jefferson cackled.

"Was that our old apartment?"

"Oh my God!"

Stevie grunted. "Nope. 'Cause you can still see the sharpie where ours is."

"Yeah," Kell said as Trav tried to still his depression that people he'd known had actually *lived* there. "See? You can see where Cheever popped out the screen and started decorating the outside of Mom's room 'cause we wouldn't let him write on the walls."

"Jesus, I almost had a fuckin' heart attack," Mackey muttered. "Man, Grant and I were...." He stopped, and Trav glanced at him as a sheepish look broke across his face. "Conversing," he said with dignity, "and that kid woke up when we didn't know it—"

"*Conversing?*" Kell asked in outrage. "Oh my *God*—was *that* where he went once a week?"

Jefferson chortled from the farthest seat back. "Damned straight—do you know how *hard* Stevie and I had to work to keep you from ever going by the apartment so you wouldn't know?"

Kell and Mackey both groaned. "Fuck," Mackey muttered. "It's like a fucking sitcom episode—and it just *felt* so fucking important, you *know*?"

"Yeah," Kell said. He didn't look behind them as they passed the apartment and the cracked driveway with the oil spill and the weeds. "I remember... God, being so scared. I was *so* scared. Man, it was like, the whole town wanted to fuckin' kill us—probably only a couple of assholes, but it *felt* like the whole town. And I just... I remembered Mackey flyin' across the room, and... my brothers. We were all we had."

The SUV went quiet then, and Mackey turned around and grinned—Trav only got a part of it, but he could see it was fierce. "Yeah, but you taught me how to throw a punch, Kell. If it was even close to even, I took those fuckers down."

Trav could see Kell's grin in the rearview. "Yeah. You were a little scary on the preemptive strike, Mackey, but there's no denying you took them down."

Blake laughed and spoke up for practically the first time since they got on the plane. "You guys, there is *nothing* to fucking do here! Man, at least I grew up an *hour* from LA. You are practically an hour out from a pay toilet when you're in the center of town. Jesus, Mackey—no wonder you did drugs. You were just used to being bored shitless!"

Mackey chuckled. Trav couldn't decide if the bitterness was in Mackey's voice or Trav's ear. "Naw, man—I didn't start doing drugs 'cause I was bored. I did the *band* 'cause I was bored!"

Blake grunted. "Yeah, well, now that I know why you're so fucking driven, I'm looking forward to playing again. I can't go a day without the damned guitar now—it's like a whole new coke!"

The mood of the car lightened up again, which was just fucking *great*, because Trav wanted to hit something even worse.

His whole body was vibrating by the time they walked into the bar and got the evil-faggot once-over from the bartender—or at least that was what Trav assumed it was. While Mackey and the guys went to set up, Trav went to talk to the guy, and the impression didn't get any better.

"You sure they don't want the standard fee?" the guy asked, pulling up his upper lip. Okay—one of his front teeth wasn't so much missing as black. Awesome. "Them kids always needed money back in the old days. Man, their old manager, kid who used to be lead guitar? Threatened to have his dad call in my car loan if I didn't pay them the full fee."

Trav swallowed on some of his anger, because dammit, Grant wasn't the monster Trav wanted him to be. "These kids?" Trav said, and took a deep, even breath, "Have more in the bank right now than this entire fucking town is worth. They're doing this for their friend. If you try to pay them, I will take your cash and shove it up your—"

"Hey, Delmont," Mackey said cheerfully. "You giving Trav here shit?"

Delmont rolled his eyes. "He was throwing his weight around, yeah. I hear you went faggot on us, Mackey. That mean you don't fight no more?"

Mackey snorted. "As. If. You wanna see how fuckin' faggoty I got, you just go ahead and flash that word around some more. Hell, me'n Trav'll go neck in the corner just to get people to start shit."

Delmont's eyes got so wide Trav could see the red-shot white all around his beady brown iris. "You wouldn't do that to me, Mackey," he all but begged. "Man, I need the business—folks won't come in here, they think it's that kind of place!"

Mackey hiked his skinny jeans up in back and adjusted the lace at his collar. "You know in LA, being that kind of place'd make you rich, doncha?"

Trav's chest was tight with how much he *didn't* like hearing the good ol' boy slide back into Mackey's voice. But Trav could see why Mackey had earned such a reputation as a fighter—and why Kell had been such a badass. It all came down to survival, didn't it? Mackey could bait the guy now because he could walk away. When this place was your rent, that wasn't so easy.

"Yeah, well, apparently it gays you up too, so I don't wanna fuckin' go there. Seriously—he says you don't want the fee."

Mackey glowered at Trav. "Yeah, we want the fee. We're giving it to the local Goodwill—"

"Mackey!" Jesus, Trav didn't want to support those people!

"Well, gay or no gay, Trav, they put shirts on our backs, so we're giving them the fucking money." Mackey glared at Delmont. "And that *doesn't* mean you can screw us on the fuckin' fee. You fork it over full and clear, and we'll donate it same way."

"Feeling fuckin' full of yourself, Mackey?" Delmont sneered, and in a surge of hot, irritated men, Trav was surrounded by the rest of Outbreak Monkey.

"Jesus, Delmont, stop giving him shit," Kell ordered, obviously disgusted. "You're gonna make more fucking money tonight than you have in a month, 'cause Grant spread the fuckin' word. Now give the fucking money to charity and get off my brother's back!"

"This guy ain't your brother," Delmont muttered, looking sideways at Trav.

Trav was going to grab him by the throat with one hand and extract his eyeballs with his other. He had it planned. He would make it happen.

"No, idiot, he's my boyfriend and our manager. He's all legal and shit. Don't fuckin' mess with Trav—he'll rip your arms off and feed 'em to ya." Mackey smiled pleasantly with that, and then turned back to the guys. "You ready for a sound check yet? We had lunch back home and I'm not in the mood for fries and a beer."

The fact that he didn't mention he couldn't even *have* beer was telling. This man was not a friend, and they were not here for him.

The guys trotted onto the stage, and the crowd began to surge in. When they were ready to play for real, Grant walked in, people cutting him a wide berth like cancer was catching, but no one said anything to him—at least not that Trav could hear.

Trav had reserved a table in the corner, away from the speaker, a little off to the side, and Grant sank into the wooden seat gratefully. His eyes were red, and he looked a little out of it. But he also moved like he was in pain, and Trav was baffled for how to hold up any hostility for the guy, and that sucked. His hostility had been a shield for this past year, keeping Mackey innocent of his whole childhood, as much as Mackey had maintained he wasn't.

"Your guy didn't want to come in. He not a fan?" Grant asked under the crowd.

Trav shrugged. "He loves their music, but, you know. One concert, all concerts. Mostly he just likes to drive."

Grant smiled, his cheeks appling and dimples popping, and for a quick moment, Trav saw a handsome kid with a bit of mischief in him. He had to breathe hard through his nose, and still, a little bit of an answering smile popped out.

"You don't like me much, do you, Mr. Ford?" Grant asked, not fooled at all.

Trav grimaced. "I cleaned up your mess," he said bluntly. "I cleaned it up once, and it was ugly—you think it was only Mackey?"

Grant swallowed and looked at the guys lined up playing a bizarre game of "pick up the riff" that Trav had never understood but the guys—even Blake—seemed to get. For a moment Grant's eyes fastened hungrily on Mackey, who was in his element and happily oblivious to them both, and then his vision ranged the stage, lingering particularly on Kell and Blake.

When he turned back to Trav, his eyes were redder than they had been when he'd first walked in. "No, sir," Grant said simply. "I am aware I hurt them all."

Trav took a deep breath. "Awesome. What am I supposed to do with that?"

"My dad used to beat fags for fun, Mr. Ford," Grant said, his voice still even. "And my mom is from the south—old money, I guess. I think her granddaddy was Klan, which is not necessarily something I'm proud of, but I think she is. When I first fell in love with him...." Grant shook his head, and his remarkable eyes—bloodshot or not—grew dreamy. "I thought at first it was a fever, you know? And I figured if I just looked at him, I'd get my fill. But... but just knocking into him, wrestling, like you do, made everything hurt worse. So a kiss, I thought, to prove it wasn't madness. But the kiss made the madness worse. So a touch. More. And every time, it got worse. And by the time I knew—*knew*—that Sam was a nice girl and all, but that just wasn't where my heart was, I'd... I'd set up this lie. I was gonna be the good boy, the one who took my dad's business, the one who had the grandbabies, I was gonna toe the line."

A girl came over to take their orders. Trav took a beer, because Mackey and Blake weren't there and that was sort of a treat, and Grant took a Sprite, presumably to settle his stomach.

"So that's how you're going to *die*?" Trav asked, and the hell of it was, he wasn't even trying to be cruel. He'd left a career—completely changed his life—to avoid what Grant was talking about, and a little voice in his head whispered, *But you were older than he was when you saw that kid crouching in the street.*

"Nope," Grant said, all serenity. He watched Mackey adjust the feed for probably the last time. "Nope. When I die, I am going to be free."

Trav turned to him, lips parted, to ask what that meant, when Mackey set down the guitar and walked up to the microphone.

"Delmont, kill the fuckin' lights, will you?"

Everything went out but the spot on the small stage, and Mackey tossed his hair out of his eyes and grinned, then leaned back for a second so the whole world could get a load of the tattoo on his stomach.

The applause was half clapped hands and half catcalls, and Mackey narrowed his eyes and turned to the band. "Y'all, they seem to think this is a gay thing. You got anything to say to that?"

Trav closed his eyes, suddenly understanding why they'd needed to stop by Walmart for cheap T-shirts. Like it was choreographed, everyone on the stage not Mackey grabbed their shirts and ripped them off before chucking the fabric out into the crowd.

The hollers got a lot more enthusiastic—and less violent—and Mackey was onstage with his lace-collared middy and his skinny jeans while his brothers all grinned, pumped up and tatted up, shirtless on the stage.

Mackey grinned. "Now that don't seem fair at all, does it?" he drawled, moving his fingers to his buttons. "I mean, it's not like you all ain't seen us naked in the press for the past two years." That got a halfhearted laugh. "Hell, Cheever had the paparazzi camped out in front of our house for a *month*!"

That got a bigger laugh—and Trav pinched the bridge of his nose.

"Mr. Ford?" Grant inquired.

Trav just shook his head. "I now get why the press never bothered them," he said directly into Grant's ear.

Grant shot him one of those grins that brought up the vestiges of cancer-tattered beauty. "'Cause the whole world's been up their asses from the time their mama conceived Kell," Grant said with satisfaction.

And before Trav could say "A-fucking-men," Mackey was in full cry.

"So, y'all, we're Outbreak Monkey, and we used to live here. In fact"—he turned to the guys, grabbed the collar of his shirt, and ripped it off his body as he screamed—"it's been a long fuckin' time!"

Blake and Kell had been practicing that riff for a month—but this was the first time they had played the Zeppelin cover in front of a crowd. The unmistakable opening chords ripped through the tiny bar, flying like a dragon to plunder the suffocating cloud cover of bigotry that had blanketed Trav for two days and his boys for probably their entire lives.

For a full set—an hour and a half—Trav and Grant sat side by side and let the music do what Mackey always knew it would: take them away.

Trav cut his gaze in Grant's direction a couple of times. Grant was sitting with his face up to the amp and his eyes closed like a cat in a sun spot, just bathing in the sound and the band and Mackey's fearsome, fearless energy. About the only thing the band did as a concession to the small venue was turn the sound down from eleven and try really hard not to let Mackey fall off the stage. This was one crowd they knew wouldn't catch him, and Trav figured the guys had given enough of their blood already.

But Mackey's fierceness, Kell and Blake's rawness, Jefferson and Stevie's angry subversiveness, it was all there for the world to see, shining on their sweating bodies, spattering from their hair like heartblood on the stage.

At the end of the set, the crowd was rabid, *screeching*, frenzied, needing more. Mackey grinned at them, and Trav finally began to feel the roots of that smile under his feet.

"Yeah, I know you want more," he said, and the bar erupted into sound. "You all, you'd watch us play until we turned to dust, and then you'd call us pussies 'cause we didn't live forever."

The laughter had two edges this time—self-conscious and self-aware, realizing that he was telling the truth, and mean, ugly, and taking. Yeah, some of them knew he was telling the truth and figured that truth made them stronger.

"Well, I'm going to take the last two songs for two of the people here in the audience. One of them is one of our own, and this is his song."

Mackey grabbed the waiting guitar from Stevie, who had kept it behind him so it didn't get in the way. Jefferson threw him a towel, and he wiped down his chest before cradling the smaller Les Paul that he used on stage and rippling the first few distinctive notes to quiet the crowd.

Grant and Trav both grunted in pain, and "River Shadows" echoed through the darkness, taking Trav back to the time when this whole mess had first been spilled.

And Trav got it, there in the darkness. He didn't want to, but he got it. He saw the two lovers in his mind's eye, Grant and Mackey, deluded and desperate, hoping they could escape in each other, knowing it was impossible if they couldn't escape this town.

The song finished off, and Trav opened his eyes to the tacky tables and the splintered walls and the peanut shells on the floor, and saw Mackey in the spotlight where he belonged, the guitar cradled against him, bare body muscled and tight and shaking with emotion.

The last note faded, and he looked up, giving the crowd permission to applaud. They did, and even though Trav was listening, he didn't hear one murmur of disapproval, one suggestion that Mackey had written that for a boy they all knew.

The music suspended all of that. This was their anthem right here. These people knew that river, had probably made love in the shadows of the trees nearby. Everyone in this bar knew what it was like to love someone they shouldn't, knew that some things were doomed before they began.

In just that moment, Trav understood why Outbreak Monkey would come home.

And then Mackey started the next song, *Trav's* song, without preamble. The tune was a little rawer, a little less sentimental, but the hook was deeper. Trav had noted before, trying to be objective, that Mackey's instrumental for this one built, climbed, grew deeper. Unobtrusively Kell twanged some subtle power chords in the background, and Stevie punctuated with some soft brushes of the cymbal. Even Jefferson thrummed quietly into this song.

As those chords built, and the emotion with them, the audience started to mutter. For a moment Trav was hurt, even though it wasn't personal, really—not even the hatred.

This song was bigger somehow, not just the instrumentation, but the *feeling*. And a place this small, where secrets weren't ever secrets—that much real was uncomfortable in this bar.

Trav never in a million years would have predicted that a simple love song, gender neutral, could actually start a riot.

It was Delmont who voiced it, of course. He was standing right next to Trav—had, in fact, been leaning back against the bar between orders, listening the same as anyone else.

"Oh my *God*," he said loudly, "is this some fucking *faggot* song?"

Mackey let the song ride to its conclusion, and in the ensuing uncomfortable silence, he put the guitar down. "That there was a love song," he said unflappably. "If you people want to make a love song ugly, that there ain't nothing I can fix."

"Ain't no such thing as a love song between faggots," someone called out.

Mackey shook his head. "You know what? I think our walk down memory lane is over. You guys just got a fifty-dollar concert for a five-dollar cover. You piss on it if you want, but you can't say we didn't put out."

"Someone get the fucking lights!" Kell snarled. "I'm about done with you people anyway."

Trav stood up, suddenly aware of how vulnerable they were, no security, no ropes. It wasn't a big crowd by stadium standards, but it filled the room, and people were muttering ugly among themselves. Trav met Mackey's eyes and grimaced.

Mackey shrugged, not apologizing, because Mackey wouldn't. *It's our fucking song, Trav. If they want us to play, they're getting all of us.*

Trav didn't even hear the words. He could see them in Mackey's grimly pursed mouth and the way his gray eyes burned.

"You guys ready to pack up?" he asked, pitching his voice so people could hear him and associate him with the band. Of course he was the only one there in a collared shirt and slacks—odds were good they'd made him as soon as he'd walked in—but he wanted people to know his muscle was on their side.

"Oh my God—you're his fucking *boy*friend!" someone called out, and Trav….

Well, Trav lost his mind.

"Oh my *God*," he exaggerated, "someone in this dump can fucking *read the papers*!"

"You calling us ignorant, faggot?" Delmont growled, trying to impose his weight in Trav's space.

"I'm saying I'm brave enough to not keep shit a secret," he snapped, and behind him Mackey said, "Aw, fuck, *Trav*!" while Delmont grabbed Trav by the collar and started shaking him.

"You implying something about *me*?" Delmont shouted.

Trav jerked back, because his breath was foul and his dental work was even worse close up. "No, asshole! I'm saying—"

"He's saying that other song was about Mackey and me, and you all seemed to like it just fine!"

Grant had stood up, and he shook there, his face pale, his hands swollen as he gripped the back of his chair. Trav hated to look at him, naked and dying in the harsh house lights from the bar. The guys had asked him—they'd *asked* him if he wanted to duet with Mackey for "River Shadows," but he couldn't. His fingers were too stiff and unwieldy, and he wasn't sure he could hold the guitar for that long.

But he'd just come out in the middle of a mob scene, and Trav wasn't sure if he wanted to applaud or weep.

It was brave—really fucking brave—but it also might have just lit the fucking fuse.

"Oh my God!" Delmont turned his head and spat. "It's bad enough that kid is bringing faggots into my bar—he's gone and fucking gayed up the entire town!"

He still had Trav by the collar, and he was pretty tall. Trav couldn't clock him in the jaw, so he gave him two hard uppercuts to the gut instead.

Delmont dropped him and staggered back before bouncing off the bar and coming up with a roar.

Trav lowered into a boxer's crouch, prepared to stop him like you'd stop a runaway horse—with a sharp spar to the chest—when Mackey leapt off the stage like a shrieking eagle and landed on Delmont's back.

"Jefferson! Stevie! Get Grant out of here!" Trav bellowed, which was the last and only smart thing he did that night.

"THIS PLACE looks like the jail in *Dukes of Hazzard*," Trav said glumly for the thousandth time. His nose ached, his lower lip was split, and the smell of wet metal and piss wouldn't fucking leave him alone.

Mackey, sitting next to him on the cot with an ice bag over his eye, tagged him in the arm with his free hand.

"Ouch!" Trav muttered. "What was that for?"

"You've said it about sixty-eleven times, Trav. Is this the only fucking jail you've ever seen?"

"I was an MP, Mackey. Of course it's not." The pregnant pause seemed to accuse him, so he added, "It's the only jail I've ever seen the inside of" before leaning back tiredly.

Kell and Blake were leaning back-to-back and dozing, each with a mess of gauze and ice packs in their laps. Kell had a bruise the size of an egg peeking out of his growing hair. Jefferson and Stevie had no such macho postures—Stevie's head was in Jefferson's lap, and Jefferson was asleep on Stevie's hip, like little kids in the back of a car. Stevie had a splint around his middle three fingers, and Jefferson's jaw was swollen and his ear was split. They'd picked Grant up, sedan chair like, and hustled him out of the bar, and then come back just when shit got *really* interesting and before the cops showed up. Nobody had let them dress even though they had clothes in the SUV and the town car, so Trav was the only one in the town's single jail cell with a shirt on.

The fact that the shirt was torn and bloodied and would never be yellow again didn't change the fact that it was his.

Next to him, Mackey seemed unfazed by the fact that Travis Ford had never seen the inside of a cell he wasn't locking someone into. He seemed, in fact, absolutely gleeful.

"Look!" he said happily. "Over there—under the cot Kell and Blake are on—look!"

Trav squinted, and sure enough, someone had chipped through the industrial tan paint, revealing the red primer below. "Outbreak Monkey," Trav read, not surprised. "That's fucking adorable. This bringing back memories, McKay?"

Mackey leaned away from him and scowled. "You can get shitty all you want, Travis Ford, but it does not change the fact that this is not my fault."

Trav scowled back at him, stung. "I never said it was—"

"Oh, yes, you did. You can't even fucking look at me. Man, I played them two of our calmest songs to ease them down—I do that some nights, because you know how they get if they're too wound up at the end! But this time, no. It's our town, and it bit us in the ass—I did not know that would happen, okay?"

Mackey thrust his lower lip out and regarded Trav with a jagged sort of hurt, and Trav couldn't do anything but look away.

"This place is awful," Trav muttered.

Mackey leaned against him, apparently satisfied that they were square now. "It's a jail, Trav. It's not supposed to be a daisy field where you're purred to sleep by sunshiny kittens."

Trav fought and lost to the smile at the corners of his mouth. "Do they purr better when they're sunshiny?" he asked, feeling his foot on solid ground for just a moment.

"Mmmaybe," Mackey returned playfully.

Then the guard—who was looking at them all like they might start having ass sex right in the open cell—called out, "You faggots keep your hands to yourselves in there, you hear?" and all the good feelings went bye-bye.

"I'm not talking about the jail cell, Mackey," Trav said glumly.

Next to him, Mackey sighed and deflated, becoming five six, 120 on a good day, a kid in his twenties, with long bleached hair and smeared guyliner, and not a rock and roll icon. Not right now.

"I know you're not," he said simply. "Man, you think you're all a bad person because you got into one fight here as a grown-up? I've been fighting them assholes since I was five years old. Never fucking changes. They just get fatter and harder to beat."

Trav grunted, not wanting to touch his broken nose. Yeah, an on-site paramedic had looked it over and made sure it was set, but the truth was, Delmont hit like a sledgehammer. If Mackey hadn't been riding the guy's back and putting the stranglehold on him, he really might have killed somebody.

"Jesus," Trav muttered, not wanting to answer that, not wanting to *think* about that kind of pressure on the boys he'd come to really care for in the past year, "how long does it take for bail money and a lawyer to get here? I called Heath's assistant four hours ago!"

"Sorry," said an awfully familiar voice echoing down the corridor from the small office in front of the police station. "I *really* wanted to see this."

"Heath?" Trav all but whined. "Tell me you didn't!"

"Charter a plane to fly to a piss hole to bail out my dearest friend from jail after a bar fight? Why would I do that? Wait…."

Heath Fowler was wearing expensive jeans and a striped Eddie Bauer polo shirt in bright turquoise. He had a windbreaker on, because it was fall and a little bit chilly, and he fished his phone out of the pocket of his windbreaker and held it up.

"Everyone smile for the camera!" Heath said brightly, and six extended middle fingers shot up (well, Stevie's was part of the three-finger splint). Five of their owners didn't even bother to sit up and open their eyes.

Heath cackled and Trav closed his eyes against the flash.

"You're a fucking sadist and I hate you," Trav said with feeling.

"Are you kidding? This is a fucking Kodak moment!" Heath crowed, bouncing up and down on his two-hundred-dollar kicks. He fiddled with his phone for a minute. "Hello, Twitter!" He looked up to Trav's horrified expression. "Man, I could not get a straight answer from a *soul* as to what started that riot, by the way—and until I do, I'm telling you, I'm not paying any damages! What the hell happened?"

"You want to know what happened?" Kell said, jerking up to sit so quick that Trav felt Mackey startle. "What happened was my little brother played two love songs, and the first one was all good because that one was all about keeping shit a secret, and the second one—that one was all about fixing what's broken, and *that* one pissed them off."

Trav was aware that both he *and* Mackey were staring at Kell openmouthed.

Mackey recovered first. "That's real smart, Kell," he said with admiration. "You're dead on!"

Kell blushed. "I been reading your poetry books on Kindle," he said, nudging Blake so he'd sit up. "Man, it's worth skipping all your damned porn, you know that?"

"Well," Heath said, that edge of heartily enjoying himself not dulled in the least, "it's good to know you boys found something to do with your travel time." He fiddled with his phone again. "Outbreak Monkey jailed for playing love songs. *Awesome!*" He looked up. "And since it's not our fault these assholes don't know how to respond to a love song, I'm *not* paying damages." Heath pitched his voice for the guard on the other side. "But I *did* post bail, so let these guys out!"

The guard glared at Heath—he probably hadn't seen anything so city in his life, not in Tyson/Hepzibah.

"You sure—?" he started, but Heath waved a goldenrod form in front of him.

"I've got their release papers right here for you. They made bail. My lawyer will show up in court in"—Heath looked at the papers, squinting—"a month. You guys aren't going to be here for another month, are you? I mean, Trav didn't tell me what the family emergency was, but surely it's not going to last a month, right?"

Suddenly the air of levity that the little prison cell had managed crashed hard at their feet. Trav remembered Grant's swollen fingers, his wasted face, the way he was almost too weak to walk.

"No," Trav said, aware he was confirming the boys' deepest fears. "It's probably only going to be a couple of weeks or so."

No one said Heath was stupid. He waited until the guard slid the door open and the boys trooped out, Mackey and Trav last, before asking softly, "Who's sick?"

Mackey looked at them, eyes wide and betrayed, and Trav had to say it anyway. "Their first guitarist. He's got about three weeks, outside. Probably closer to two. We may fly home after that and then come back for the funeral, depending on when."

Mackey made a sound between a whimper and a grunt, and Trav, taking advantage of their last year together, reached out and grabbed his hand. He half expected Mackey to turn away, but he didn't. He came back to stand next to Trav instead.

Trav squeezed his hand and followed the guard outside to the waiting cars, the boys shivering, shirtless, in the predawn chill.

Trav's extra stuff was in the town car, he realized. Walter was driving the town car, and Debra was driving the SUV.

The town car could go straight to a hotel.

Trav could go straight to a hotel, shower, sleep alone, and not have Mackey's worry, his torn emotions, his perpetual fighting spirit, gnawing at Trav's skin. Just for a night. A week. A month.

A night. Trav could take a breather. Talk to Heath. Not have to deal with the boys from Tyson and their terrible baggage.

"Heath," Trav said, letting go of Mackey's hand, "here. I've got a change of clothes. I'll come to the hotel. I can talk to you there, okay? The guys are about done in."

"Trav?" Mackey said, his voice wobbling, and Trav turned to him, tried not to see the betrayal in his eyes.

"A night, Mackey," Trav said, and to his horror, his voice broke. "A night. Man, give me a night to put this shit together in my head."

"But Trav—"

Trav shook his head. "I have spent a *year* hating Grant Adams," he confessed rawly. "A *year* thinking every bad thing that happened to you, to your brothers—that it was all his damned fault. And I can't think that way anymore. Not and be there for you—for the guys. I can't think that way, and I can't *stop* myself from thinking that way, and I have got to get my head square, or I am going to be no goddamned good to you, do you understand me?"

Oh Jesus. And every moment of hating Grant and loving Mackey and having what he'd thought twisted into what he knew now—all of it torsioning in his head, his chest, his gut. All of that hurt spilled out now. In front of the whole band, in front of *Heath*, his oldest friend, in front of God, in the dimming sky of frosty stars, it was all there for the world to see, spilled on the ground.

Mackey scowled, that terrible defensive posture Trav remembered from their first few months—until the end of Christmas, actually—bowing his back and his shoulders, and suddenly he straightened.

"You do that," he snarled. "You take a day to get your head straight, Travis. And then you be fucking ready, because I am hauling you back by your military haircut. You *promised* me, and ain't *nobody* promised me before, and I'll hold you to that shit if it kills me!"

Mackey stood on his toes and hauled Travis down, mauled him in a bruising, sweaty, painful kiss that left Travis partially erect and almost in tears.

"I'll be back," Trav promised against Mackey's demanding mouth. "Just… just a night, Mackey. I'm begging you. A night to not have everything hurt."

Mackey pulled back, dragging his lower lip between his teeth. He let it go and turned his head and spit.

"Everything *does* fucking hurt," Mackey said, eyes narrowed. "It *always* fucking hurt until you came along. If you're not at my mother's house by checkout time, I will come and fucking get you."

And he turned and stalked away to the SUV, his brothers in his wake.

Travis watched him go and ran shaking hands through his hair.

Heath let out a low whistle between his teeth. "Brother," he said, looping an arm around Trav's sweat-soaked shoulders, "I have brought my second-best scotch. You want some?"

Trav conveniently forgot about that moment of getting Kell drunk in Seattle. "I just spent nine months on the road with recovering addicts," Trav said. "What do you think?"

"I think you've earned yourself a drink."

# Heart of Glass

MACKEY WOKE up in a strange bed, in a strange house, and Trav was not there. He took a moment to assess that fact. For the past year, hotel room or Trav's bedroom, Trav had been there. He'd done his best not to be gone for more than a couple of days at a time, and for those few trips, Mackey had slept in Briony's room, on the floor, wedged between the bed and the wall, where he was most comfortable.

But he wasn't there now, and his lip hurt and his eye ached, and he remembered this feeling, as well as the soreness in his shoulders and his ribs that came from one rip-roaring brawl.

And Trav was not there.

Mackey opened his eyes slowly, assimilated the pastel walls and hard, bright colors of the comforter on the bed, and closed his eyes again.

Trav hadn't come with them.

In his head, he knew it was too much to ask. Trav needed time. Needed space. Had *earned* Mackey's trust on the time and space issue, dammit!

But Mackey's head had never been the loudest voice in the instrument of Mackey. And Mackey's heart was butt-hurt.

God*dammit*, why hadn't Trav come home?

*Because, moron. Who looks at their boyfriend and says, "Hey, let's go watch the guy who broke me die. By the way, I may actually still love him, more like a brother, but I still love him, and you are now expected to love him too. Sorry about that. Just one more big fucking suitcase in the baggage I've been hauling around with me since the cradle. Hey, Trav, could you carry it for a minute? I gotta put on a performance here wherein I tell all the good ol' boys in my hometown that they're dumbasses and they suck. Oh, and while you're carrying my baggage, uhm, duck!"*

Okay. So, yeah.

Maybe *that* was why Trav hadn't come home.

Maybe he needed a drink—because he *could* drink and not make it an addiction—and maybe he needed a *friend*, because God knew Mackey had grabbed *his* friend and given her a job and hauled her by the scruff of the neck through Europe, Tokyo, and most of the US of A.

So, yes. Trav got a day off.

But that didn't mean Mackey didn't spend a minute, maybe two, lying in bed and closing his eyes, smelling Trav's pillow from two nights ago and wondering when the pain would well up like blood and he would reach for a bandage he could no longer use.

Right about the time he figured he should get up and call Trav and see what was up—instead of wallowing in what wasn't—he heard a scream from the bathroom, and then a shout, and then all hell broke loose downstairs.

Mackey pounded down the hall in his tighty-whities, glad he'd at least showered before falling into bed, and tried to make sense of the scene in front of him.

The whole world was there—all the guys in their underwear, Shelia in a pink floral baby doll, his mom in her upscale tracksuit….

And Briony, naked, with water dripping from her hair, wrapped in a shower curtain, shoving Cheever through the kitchen by a fistful of his red curly hair.

"Briony?" Mackey said, easy and slow, like you might talk to a beloved family dog who had suddenly bared his teeth and growled.

"That'll teach you to fuckin' *grab my boob* in the shower, you little shit!"

"Jesus, bitch, I was just copping a little feel! You'd think no one had grabbed a piece of that ass be—"

*Crack*!

Mackey had been on his way to do it—he'd vaulted the kitchen table the moment the kid said "bitch"—but Kell was standing closer and beat him to it.

"*Kell*!" Briony yelled, clutching the shower curtain tighter, and Mackey looked for Shelia.

"Honey," he murmured, "could you get her out of here and into some sweats?"

Shelia nodded. "Yeah—she borrowed my shampoo to take a shower. I didn't think to warn her that Cheever was here too." She looked away from Kell grabbing Cheever by the front of the T-shirt and shaking him, pursing her lips. "You *all* got beat the hell up, didn't you?"

Mackey grinned tiredly. "Even Trav. I think he was embarrassed. Kell—man, Kell, stop that. You're gonna crack his yolk inside his shell."

Kell dropped Cheever abruptly, and sure enough, the kid looked a little dazed.

"You little fucker!" Kell snarled, and then looked up at Briony, who, it appeared, was suddenly aware that she was surrounded by men, most of them straight. He was wearing a zip-up hoodie over his tighty-whities, and he yanked the zipper down and wrapped it around her shoulders. "Honey," he said, his voice dropping from vicious to tender just that fast, "you need to go get dressed. Curl up in bed. Someone'll bring you some tea—"

"Coffee?" Briony pleaded, because she was a little addicted.

"Tea," Kell said firmly. "Mom always said coffee made you sicker. You go get dressed and we'll take care of you, 'kay? Ignore our shitheaded little brother. He ain't even ours."

"*Kell*!" Mackey had almost forgotten his mom was there.

"No," Mackey said. For a moment, it was a little like he wasn't even talking. His lips had grown cold, and his fingers, his toes, his ankles, his knees. His hands were clammy and his cheeks blazing hot, and he couldn't see for the wash of red in his eyes.

Now that Kell wasn't about to kill Cheever and Briony was getting covered up and warm, it occurred to him what exactly had just happened in his mother's house.

"No," he said loudly, trying to remember whom he was talking to. "You can't defend him," he said, remembering a laughing face, a stranger's arm around his shoulder, the sick, helpless feeling that any control he might have had was just yanked out from under his feet. "There is no defense."

Mackey shook his head, a wave of dizziness swamping him. *Someday you'll be talking about ice cream....*

"There is no defense!" he screamed. "You don't take that from someone. You don't fucking *take that right from someone*! You think it's okay to grab an ass or a boob? God gave you that fucking right?"

"Mackey," Briony said, sounding stunned.

"Go get dressed," Mackey begged. "It's not right we should see you. You didn't ask for this. Man, you don't need to be out here, helpless, for the whole world to see."

Later he would figure that Shelia knew, and that the only way Shelia would know was if Jefferson and Stevie knew. Since he told Blake in rehab, that meant the only ones who didn't know were Kell and Briony, and he'd feel a little bad about that.

But right now, Shelia tugged Briony by the arm, and Briony left, pale, shaking, and looking behind her at Mackey, like she could help him through what was coming.

If he'd known what was coming, he would have drank himself to sleep.

"Mackey," Jefferson said as they disappeared, "that's not what this is about."

"Isn't it?" Mackey asked bitterly. "Isn't it? This asshole here"—and he swept his hand, including his little brother in the vast array of assholes he had known—"is just as bad as all of them we fought last night. It's like we left this fuckin' town and he *became* this fuckin' town, and became the guys who fucked us, and became Charleston fucking Klum—"

"Oh God. Mackey—"

"*I am so tired of these fuckers!*" he yelled. He was off his rocker—he *knew* he was off his rocker, *knew* it wasn't the same thing, *knew* Briony had taken care of herself when he hadn't been able to, but he couldn't seem to jump the track, couldn't swerve or leap or change grooves. He was just a massive nuclear train barreling down the track, hitting every goddamned barbed-wired brick wall in his fucking path!

"Mackey?" Cheever said, and to his credit, he began to cry. "Mackey, I didn't... I mean, she was pretty, and the guys at school say that girls like it—"

"The guys at school are *bullshit*!" he screamed, spitting as he did it. "Don't you get it? What's it fuckin' *take*, Cheever? We got you out of the town, we got you someplace nice—where we gotta put you to get you away from this? Do you know what it's like? Have you ever thought what it would be like, people just thinking they own you like that? Yeah, it's okay, she's a girl, I can grab her ass, grab her tit—she's a thing, I can own her. What if someone owned *you*? What if you were everybody's fuckin' meat? What if it was you, naked and unconscious in a fuckin' alleyway with your ass ripped open where anybody could fucking see—"

"*Mackey!*"

Jefferson lunged over his back, anchoring his arms to his sides, screaming in his ear.

"Mackey, you gotta shut up! You gotta fuckin' shut up. We can't trust him—he's not one of us, man. We can't tell him that shit—it's *yours*, it's *private*, wasn't no one supposed to know!"

"Oh hell, Jeff…." Stevie sounded, if anything, resigned, but it wasn't Stevie Mackey saw.

It was Kell, eyes wide on the three of them, then zeroing in on Mackey. "Oh hell. Is there any fucking thing this family *does* tell me about?"

"Oh, like I fucking knew until I couldn't sit down," Mackey said miserably. "God, Kell… I was so fucked-up back then—all I wanted was to fucking forget. And man, I thought I did." He closed his eyes tight, but he knew that when he opened them, his life would still be his life, and he couldn't make it different. "I thought I'd forgotten, because I had a year of being sober, and all that time with Trav, but last night… and fuckin' Grant… and—" Mackey turned to Cheever, naked and in tears. "—and this asshole, who thinks that he's got a right to shit he don't got no right to—man, *Briony*. You don't even *know* this girl. But she's our sister, and our friend, and she hauled her sick ass down the Pacific Coast to be here for us when we needed her, and *you* gotta treat her like shit. Man, I'm ashamed to call you my fuckin' brother."

Mackey sat down on the kitchen floor in his underwear.

His legs couldn't hold him no more. The sadness, the pain he'd been trying to parse out so he had some good for every bit of bad, was suddenly right there on his shoulders, and his legs couldn't hold him no more.

He leaned his head against his knees and closed his eyes. His breaths were shaking, ragged things, and he wasn't getting enough oxygen because he could see spots in front of his eyes, but he wasn't sobbing.

That was someone else.

Jefferson, Stevie, Blake, and Kell were wrapped around his back, shaking, and Mackey's mom was trying to comfort Cheever.

"C'mon, kid. You need to go to your room and pull yourself together."

"It's just like my whole life," Cheever whimpered, "they had the music and they had each other, and I was just the bratty little brother. Why's it gotta be like that, Mom? Why can't I be a brother too?"

"He didn't mean that," Mom said, but she sounded doubtful.

"Yeah, he did," Kell said from over Mackey's head. "If he didn't, I would. Cheever, it's not that you're younger than us—but man, all that shit you keep doing to 'fit in,' that's the shit that we fought against our whole lives. If you can't see that, see what you do to us every time you think the money *we* earned for you got you a pass, you're going to be less and less our brother and more and more a weight hanging from our neck. Man, you had *better* apologize to Briony, or I will take a belt to your ass, boy!"

"I'm sorry," Cheever whispered. "I'm sorry I grabbed your girl, Kell. I… she was just real pretty, and she was surprised, and…."

"And she's sorry she started the whole damned thing," Briony grumbled.

Mackey looked up from the lace of arms holding him tight and saw that she was wearing a pair of Kell's sweats and his T-shirt and the zip-up hoodie he'd been wearing over his underwear because he didn't have the sense God gave a goat.

"You shouldn't be sorry," Kell said, sounding almost deferential.

*When did that happen?* It was like everything in Mackey's life was free floating in his head right now.

"Briony?" he said, feeling suddenly lucid.

"Yeah?" She crouched down, looking at him through all those arms.

"I do *not* want coke or Xanax right now," he said because it was *the* most important thing in the world.

"What *do* you want?" Like it had never occurred to her that this would be a Xanax moment.

"I want Trav," he said, determination firming up his voice. "Guys, I love you, but I'm about to go kung fu on your asses, okay?"

The arms dropped and he hugged Kell first, hard. "I'm sorry we didn't tell you," he said by Kell's ear. "We had other shit that Mackey had to do at that exact moment."

"If you're going to refer to yourself in the third person, I'm disowning you," Kell muttered, and Mackey smiled. Kell had learned to banter this past year.

Blake was next—Blake, who hadn't said a word in the entire exchange. "God," Mackey said, and Blake grunted.

"Man, I like that you think I'm a brother and all, but next time I'll just take the extra gift at Christmas." Blake nodded enthusiastically at that, and Mackey wanted to kiss his thin, weasel-cheeked face, just because.

Stevie and Jefferson came next, and Mackey had to tell them he was grateful. "You guys kept that secret so good I didn't even know you knew," he said seriously.

They nodded together. "Well, we didn't expect you to lose it in the middle of a family crisis on the kitchen floor," Stevie said, and Jefferson nodded.

Mackey half laughed. "Guys—I love you, you're my brothers, but does anyone mind if I go drag Trav back here into this mess? Man, I'm just fucking lost without him."

"Yeah, okay," Briony murmured, grabbing his hand. "But let's get you dressed first, okay?"

Mackey shook his head. "Did the little bastard really grab your boob?" he asked as she guided him down the hallway.

"Swear to God. I heard him out in the bathroom taking a leak, and I looked out of the shower curtain, and his eyes got all big, and I realized, 'Holy crap! I'm flashing a fourteen-year-old,' and that was when he reached out and grabbed it."

Mackey sort of laughed, and then he got more to the point. "I'm sorry about that. Man, Trav tried to get your mom up here—you need to go back to bed, and you need someone taking care of you—"

"Shelia did just fine. I miss my mom, but don't worry, Mackey. It's like I told her when she called this morning, I *am* with my people, okay?"

"People who grab your boob." They were in Mackey's room by now, and he started rooting for his suitcase, which was on the floor by the corner. Briony crawled into his bed. He looked over his shoulder and saw that she'd brushed her hair wet and braided it, and he tsked. "Don't do that—have Shelia dry it. You'll get sicker that way. What were you thinking, taking a shower like that?"

"I didn't smell good," she mumbled, pulling the covers up to her shoulders. "And I may take the top bunk here. I'm too used to being on tour with you to not want to sleep in the same room with someone. Will you and Trav mind?"

Mackey took a deep breath and tried to put everything square in his head. He didn't need coke or Xanax—or, well, he was thinking about them, but that wasn't what he *really* wanted.

He wanted Trav. "If Trav comes back," he said quietly, "I think we can not have sex until you're better."

"Wait a second." She propped herself on her elbow. "No wonder you had a meltdown in your underwear. *If* he comes back?"

"He… did you miss the part with the fight?" Mackey asked, looking over his shoulder at her. Her face was pale, and she looked like her little adventure in the shower had capsized her, but she wasn't hacking up a lung anymore.

"No—I heard about the fight. Shelia and your mom were freaking out 'cause it took too long for you guys to get bailed out. Why *did* it take so long?"

Mackey laughed a little. "'Cause everybody's boss showed up so he could post a picture of Trav in jail on Twitter." Just thinking about it made him smile. "Trav was mortified. I mean, he's s'posed to be the grown-up, you know?"

"Is that why he went to the hotel?" she asked soberly. Well, she'd had to live with Trav too this year. Trav's freakish control issues weren't exactly a secret.

"Yeah, and the fact that Grant wasn't the devil and I'm a big fucking mess and he hates Tyson with the heat of a thousand suns—man, I think he just wanted some fucking scotch, right? And he can't even drink around me because he thinks it would be rude. Naw, he needed the night off." Mackey's voice dropped. "I mean, I hope that's all he needs. I'm…." He found a clean pair of jeans and a T-shirt and slid them on. Then, without fastening the jeans, he threw himself on the bed stomach first.

"I like bunk beds," he defended.

"I noticed." Her eyes were half-mast and her cheeks were getting red and flushed, but that sandpaper sarcasm was fully functioning.

"I like to disappear in the corner."

"Which is really hilarious, considering how you make your living."

"Thanks for not leaking that to the press, by the way."

She half laughed. "The best thing about being your entourage is that I'm some homely girl in boys' clothes that nobody gives a shit about. It's like I'm invisible to the press."

"What are you doing in my brother's clothes?" Mackey asked, because he was tired of talking about Trav and all the pressure Mackey put on him and all the reasons he might not come back.

"I dunno," she murmured. "Shelia went into his room special for them. He's big as a fuckin' house—I'm swimming in 'em. Now I know how Shelia feels, being all tiny and shit." Her cheeks were adorably freckled from this close, and Mackey stroked a finger across one.

"When I want Trav to know I want him, I wear his shirts," Mackey told her, and he saw that she was trying to pop her eyes open, but she was too tired and too sick to do it.

"Aw," she mumbled. "Who told?"

"Kell did," Mackey said, smiling a little. "When he saw you naked and pissed off. He put his shirt over your shoulders, and we all knew."

"Hate you all."

"Good. You'll fit right in."

"Fuck off."

"Get some rest." He kissed her cheek, stood up, and turned toward Trav's suitcase. They both needed laundry, so he started with a basket full of their clothes mixed together that he put in the washer.

Cheever was in the kitchen, nursing a hot chocolate and leaning against their mother. When Mackey walked past them, he met Cheever's red, teary eyes and sighed. He made it to the washer and dryer and did what he needed, his mind pleasantly blank for just long enough to do the mindless task.

When he came out of the laundry room, he walked up to the table and leaned on it with both hands. It was one of those sturdy carved-wood things—real wood, he thought with detachment, not laminate, which meant Heather Sanders had been looking at stuff for her dream house for a long time.

"You want us to be part of your life and we're there," Mackey said without preamble. "But for just a little while here, you gotta remember you're not the most important person on the planet. Man, we built our *lives* around you, Cheever Sanders. Kell gave part of his take-home to make sure you had clothes, Jefferson and Stevie bought your books, I watched you and took you to art shows and the library, and Grant brought you just random shit including the bicycle you rode to school in the fourth grade so you didn't have to be seen in the band van. We have *done* for you, and we'll do for you again, but we need you to do two things for us."

"What, Mackey?" His voice was clogged, but he wasn't being an obnoxious little shit, so Mackey hoped it was good.

"First of all, give us some space while we're here. The whole reason your house got filled with people you barely know is 'cause we're here to say good-bye to someone." He closed his eyes. "I know from experience this hurts. It's gonna hurt everyone. If you don't give us a fucking break with the brother-lemme-climb-your-body bullshit, we're gonna strangle you, and I know how to hide the corpse. And the second thing?"

"What?" Cheever asked, his eyes still wide and brown on Mackey's face.

"Stop selling out your brothers for whoever's got your ear. Don't talk about us to the press, don't posture in front of your friends. Man, I just sat in a jail cell with five guys who'd rather be in there with me than on the other side bailing us out. Even the guy who bailed us out wanted to be in that cell. If you want to be inside the stupid jail cell, the guy talking shit next to you needs to be the first guy to get dropped, you hear me? Not the girl in our home. Not the reporter with the blow or the car or the box of burgers or whatever. The guy talking shit needs to be the guy you go after, or we wouldn't go to jail with you, much less let you in."

Cheever was crying a little now, but it was a freeing sort of cry, so Mackey figured he could go put on one of Trav's shirts and call Debra.

He was ready to go tell Trav about emotional maturity and how they should all run out and get them some.

THEY'D BOUGHT a canvas beach bag in Greece, and Mackey put a pair of jeans and a T-shirt—yes, T-shirt—and a hooded sweatshirt in it for Trav. On impulse he put a pair of clean underwear and T-shirt in it for himself, then grabbed a sweatshirt, because the wind was sweeping cold and fierce, and slid into some loafers.

His mom took him to the hotel, at her own insistence, and he sighed. God. He just wanted to talk to Trav.

"Sorry, Mom," he said automatically as the silence descended in the car.

"Don't be. You *told* me it would come out some day all surprising."

"Well, surprise!" He made his voice bright and sarcastic, and she laughed a little too.

"Cheever's young," she said quietly. "He's young, and he'd do anything to impress his friends—and you guys are more parents than brothers."

Mackey grunted. "I think sometimes we should take him down to LA with us, but...." He shook his head. "There's a lot more to do there, but a *lot* more trouble to get into. It's like, here's probably better, but we can't—" He stopped himself. It sounded cruel.

"You can't raise him for me," she said, and yeah, she sounded hurt, but she also sounded like it was due. "I know. I mean...." Her shrug was tiny, and that much uncertainty made her look vulnerable. "It would be great if I didn't do this alone, but, well, choices and choices, right?"

"Mom, yeah, choices. Like who he's hanging out with at school, right? I mean, he made that choice, whoever they are."

Her sigh should have alerted him that this next part was going to piss him off. "Yeah," she said, "I have no idea."

"*Mom!*"

"Mom *what*, Mackey—it's not like I knew everything *you* were doing!"

"Well *yeah*, but it didn't surprise you who I was doing it *with*!"

"Yeah, but I didn't like him and you still did it!"

"But you knew. Dammit—you knew it was Grant and Stevie. You knew who their parents were, even if you didn't talk to 'em. You used to know Cheever's friends—remember Kevin? Whoever Cheever is dealing with now that makes him think this kind of thing is okay—you gotta know that and you gotta stop it! That's your job. Man, you've got a chance to spend some time with him—you can't just... give up on him because we're not here to help!"

His mom's voice wobbled when she spoke next. "Oh, Mackey—man, I tried. I did. I volunteered at his school and it just embarrassed the shit out of us both. I'm the only mom there without a fucking education, did you know that? Did it ever occur to you that I was not there enough to be the kind of parent Cheever needs? I don't even know how to start! I mean… you boys and me, I was the only lap you had to sit in. With Cheever, once you left, it was just him and me, and suddenly I had all this time, and he was away at school!"

"Well, take him back," Mackey snapped, disgruntled. "Make him room with you. Make him play video games. Do his hair—for *God's* sake do his fuckin' hair—but dammit. He's a nightmare. Don't let him slip away. Man, you thought visiting me in rehab sucked, think about visiting him in *jail*."

His mom started to laugh. It was choked and bitter, but still laughter—and Mackey realized what he'd just said.

"Yeah, yeah," he conceded. "But you never had to visit us there, not even before we had the boss with the bankroll."

"No," she agreed. "No. You've got good advice for a guy who claims he can't function without someone else."

Mackey grunted. "I can function—I always could. I'm just not happy without him. And you know what?"

"You deserve to be happy," his mom said, and a sort of warm, sunshiny caramel feeling filled his stomach then.

His mom pulled into the hotel parking lot, and he paused in the act of grabbing his beach bag and hopping out. "I love you, Mom," he said softly. "I'm sorry we're all so much trouble."

His mom wiped under her eyes like a man—using the palm of her hand. "I love you, Mackey. I'm sort of glad of the trouble sometimes, you know that? I missed you when you were all on tour. You called every week, and texted and e-mailed all those pictures—it was sweet, and I sort of lived for it, but…."

He heard her. The days they used to puppy pile on her bed to watch TV—a rare occurrence, but one he'd particularly loved—were a long way away.

"Maybe you and Cheever can come to LA after this," he said. "Get a house nearby. Leave this place in our rearview completely." He smiled a little. "Watch Kell and Briony make each other crazy."

His mom smiled brilliantly. "Oh, I like her, Mackey. It was real nice of you to go get a girl for your brother—he's going to owe you in Christmas gifts for the rest of your life."

Mackey grimaced. "Yeah, well, he tried to get me a guy instead, but it didn't work out. I gotta go get my own."

She grabbed his head and pushed a hard kiss into *his* cheek, and let him go.

He could not remember the last time he'd been so afraid of knocking on a door.

# You Really Got Me

HEATH STAYED until six in the morning, pouring scotch and talking about their days in the military and how easy it had been. There were good guys and bad guys, and he and Trav had been on the side of the angels. Now there were sharks in suits and desperate, drugged-out kids who killed brain cells faster than they could spend money.

Trav listened and agreed, and tried to keep his scotch intake reasonable and failed. Sometime before dawn, Heath regarded him steadily through a pause in the conversation and said, "What now?"

"You mean, with the band?" Trav said, just addled enough with alcohol to think that was what Heath meant.

"No, idiot. What now for you and Mackey?"

Trav frowned. He knew the panic he'd felt when he realized that he, Travis William Ford, had actually been *incarcerated* for losing his temper, but Heath's implication was that this moment, this separation was somehow permanent. That he was at a crossroads or something.

"Mackey needs me," he said, knowing it wasn't true. Mackey had his shit together now. Mackey was facing down one hell of a demon, and he knew the shape of this hell, and he was navigating it just fine.

"Well, there's needing and needing," Heath said, thinking about it. "My last girlfriend said she needed me. She needed my money and my connections so she could sleep with the right director. How do you want Mackey to need you?"

Like "need" was a magic movie word, the question looped two memories of Mackey behind his eyes. The first was the sobbing kid in the emergency room, strung out, one hit away from being a desperate junkie, so afraid of every thought, every real feeling inside, that he'd rather bait Trav into hitting him than actually say an honest truth.

The second memory was Greece, as Mackey rambled endlessly, spouting poetry and fairy tales and silly stories about his brothers.

"Mackey, God," Trav had finally chuckled sleepily. "It's a good moment. Why not let it sit in quiet?"

"'Cause I'm afraid you'll fall asleep on me," Mackey confessed, looking up from his childlike crouch in the water at Trav's feet. "And the sun's coming up, and I need you here with me when it does."

Trav wrapped his arms around Mackey's shoulders. "Look," he whispered. "See? You can see it getting pink in the east?"

Mackey turned to nuzzle his cheek. "Yeah. Wait'll it gets gold."

Trav jerked awake and looked at Heath muzzily. "The second way," he said, wanting the moment back. If he'd gone with Mackey, he could have held him right now. They could have gone outside this bleak little hotel room and watched the sun come up.

"What's the second way, brother?" Heath asked gently, and Trav started again.

"We *are* brothers," he said in wonder. "We are. You didn't need to give me a job, Heath. You know that, right? I would have stood with you anyway."

Heath cackled. "I gave you a job because you're *good*," he said seriously. "Man, I inherited Gerry—I *coveted* you. When I found out you were sleeping with Mackey Sanders, I about creamed my shorts. If you guys could make that last... man, I could have founded a music *legacy*. Wouldn't that be awesome?" Heath made a happy sound and closed his eyes. "Remember all those young men, those fucked-up young men we had in jail? The Army doesn't always make a man out of you, Trav. Sometimes it just teaches you how to hide the scared kid with more violence."

Trav shuddered, assailed by the same memories. "Amen."

"I love music. I fucking love it. If I could have a place where we foster music, let it grow... man, I would *love* to be that record company, you know? You and Mackey—you could be my cornerstone." Heath shook himself. "Not that I want all my managers sleeping with their lead singers—that's sort of an anomaly. But you know what I mean."

Trav smiled. God, for all his progression into the land of the heavy-jowled fat cat, Heath had such a pure heart in him. Trav never should have left Tailpipe for consulting work. How could he not want to work with Heath Fowler?

"Yeah, I know."

"But I don't want you to stay with him or him with you just because it would make *my* life better. How do you need him to need you?"

"He wrote 'Fixing' for me, did you know that?"

Heath rolled his eyes. "I sort of figured."

"Every time he sings it, he looks at me like he can't sing another note if I'm not in the audience, waiting for it to come out. *That's* how I want him to need me."

Heath rumbled in his throat. He was good with the rumble—it was damned near intimidating. "Just that song or the entire album?" he asked, like it was a serious question.

It *was* a serious question. "Just that song... well, a couple of them. But not all of them."

A radiant smile bloomed on Heath's broad face. "Then it's going to be okay. You can't be the whole album, Trav. You just can't. But you can be the best songs."

Heath left not long after, and Trav caught a few hours of sleep. He awoke suddenly, feeling grody and lost and needing Mackey more than he needed the ibuprofen Heath had left next to the bed with a bottle of water and a protein bar. He lay there for a few minutes, collecting himself, letting the ibuprofen kick in, and trying to remember how he ever got to sleep or woke up without Mackey.

Could he do it again?

What would it take for him not to want to wake up with Mackey next to him? For a moment a bleak film, a step-by-step instruction book of how to live without Mackey Sanders, looped in his head, and he saw every moment of leaving in intimate detail.

He gasped and shook his head. Whatever would cause him to leave Mackey hadn't happened yet. Odds were good it would *never* happen, and Trav had to believe in that. It was what got him out of bed and made him determined to get his shit together and get back to where he belonged.

He was about ready to step into the shower when Mackey practically beat his door down. Trav threw open the door to Mackey's furious face and a feeling that he'd missed quite a lot.

"You aren't out yet?" Mackey stalked in, his hair a tangle around his shoulders, his eyes shadowed and furious. He had a black eye, a split lip, and a bruise on his jaw that he'd probably forgotten about, and he was wearing his oldest T-shirt, one of the ones that had come from the Walmart down the street.

Trav almost fell on his knees right there just to have him, pissed and ranting, charge through his door.

"One night, Trav. You said one night. A chance to breathe. That's great. You've had your stupid night. Now get in the shower and we can go back to my mom's house. I'll even let you beat up my little brother for free."

Trav glowered. "And I was just thinking that you'd gotten so mature," he snapped, because, well, he had. He'd *just*, as he'd woken up with shards of glass exploding through his brain, come to the conclusion that Mackey and the band had probably grown up 100 percent in the past year. In fact, even if he and Mackey weren't lovers, they'd be just fine. His breath hitched and his chest ached and his eyes burned at the thought. God, *that* was what was sticking in his craw, wasn't it? Mackey would be just fine, and Trav would be like Mackey had been, a wreck, a disaster, unable to tie his own shoes.

"Yeah, you fucking wish." Mackey plowed through the open door and drove Trav backward, kicking the door shut as he went. "I'm a fucking grown-up—I could be President of Grown-ups of America—but you would still need to be at my side."

Mackey had a beach bag in his hands, which he dropped on the floor without even looking at it.

"Mackey," Trav said, taking a deep breath. "You and I—I mean, you're here, and Grant's here, and—"

Mackey shoved him in the chest *hard*, hard enough to send Trav onto the bed, where he sat down in surprise.

"You need to fucking listen," Mackey said, squatting down in front of him like he would talk to a child. "Do we have our listening ears on, Travis Ford? Really? Because I'm pretty sure *you* left them somewhere else when we got off the plane."

Trav glared. "Mackey, I have got a hangover and my mouth tastes like dog shit. Maybe you could let me take a shower and—"

"And what? Get drunk again tonight because you decided I don't need you anymore?"

Trav flinched back, stung. "That is *not* what happened last night—"

"Oh yes, it is—"

"Oh no, it's not—I got in a *bar* fight, Mackey. It's just like—"

"Just like when you nailed a smart-mouthed kid for scaring the shit out of you—what, Trav, you're too good for my life? Is that what it's like?"

"No," Trav snarled. "No—I'm not *strong* enough for your fuckin' life. I... man, Mackey, this is a whole other world here. And *everybody* loves Grant, and *everybody* wants to be there for him, and—"

"And you think we don't need you anymore?" Mackey laughed, his voice pitching hysterically. "Oh my *God*, Trav, you have *really* got to listen."

"To what—you tell me you don't love him? Because how can you say that? Anybody would love that boy—*anybody*. I can't even blame you—"

"Jesus fuck! You stubborn bastard—"

"I mean, he's going to pass away, and I'll be there to pick up the pieces and—"

"*Fucking shut up and listen!*" In one slick move, Mackey launched himself onto Trav, knocking him backward and lying on top of him, the rough denim of his jeans sanding the insides of Trav's thighs.

Trav made to move. He could do it—he was bigger, stronger. They both knew it too.

"Please," Mackey said simply, softly. "Please, Travis. You gotta hear what I'm saying here. I've seen you walk away from a crime scene. You don't get mad, you don't throw a fit—you just turn around and walk away and leave bloodied hearts behind you. I *saw* the wreckage you left of Terry. Man, I was a wreck and a misery, and I saw that man in tears. Quick and easy—Trav can't deal with the hard stuff, he decides he's too much of a grown-up, and he walks away. Well, you didn't walk away from me in rehab, and you agreed to take me on loan until I was whole, and then I'd be all yours. I'm whole, and I'm all yours. Are you really going to walk away from me now, without even listening?"

Trav closed his eyes, and some of the tension drained from his shoulders and his clenched stomach. He wasn't going anywhere. Mackey had him. Trav had promised him he could be equal when he could handle it. Trav owed him a say.

"I'm listening," he said, and in the weighted silence that followed, he heard every breath Mackey took, felt every movement of his body.

Wanted him.

"I had a full-on meltdown this morning. I woke up and you weren't there, and Cheever was grabbing Briony's boobs, and suddenly I was right back where I was after Charleston Klum had his way with me. The only thing missing was the torn-open ass."

Trav's face went cold, and he tightened his arms around Mackey's waist. "Oh, McKay—"

"Don't you use my full name like it didn't happen!" Mackey shouted, pushing himself up on his knees and standing up.

Trav sat up and Mackey poked at his shoulder.

"I said listen—now listen. Then shower. *Then* suck my dick, 'cause I'm telling you, we both need it."

"Listening," Trav said, bemused—and *aroused*, for sweet hell's sake. God, Mackey on a roll was something to be admired.

"So there I was in front of my family, just *losing my fucking nut*, and you know what? My brothers? They came through. My brothers came through. My best friend came through. So they are *all* lying on top of me, loving me, and I realize, hey! This is it. I am living my nightmares, but my family is here, and you know what? I didn't need nothing—no Xanax, no booze, no coke. I mean, I *want* 'em, sure. But I don't need 'em. You know what I need, Travis? The one lousy fucking thing that I need?"

Trav closed his eyes, dropped his head, and allowed a smile to hit the corners of his mouth. "I know I really need you to say it," he admitted, stripped and empty and knowing that even this might not get them through.

"I need you," Mackey said, dropping to his knees and resting his head on Trav's lap.

Trav stroked his hair restlessly, knowing it would be soft because all the bleach left it that way.

"You need Grant," Trav said, and he wanted to laugh, because it was childish and insecure and stupid, and his heart still felt it was true.

Mackey looked up and met his eyes. Trav's heart squeezed, thumped, squeezed again, and Trav had trouble taking his next fifty-dozen breaths. God, he was beautiful. Those big gray eyes, that turned-up nose. So beautiful. For the past year, he'd been Trav's—and Trav had known from the beginning that he was only on loan from his demons. But now his demons were barking at their door, and Mackey wanted to be more than on loan. He wanted to mortgage his soul. It was a bargain Trav very much wanted to make, but God, Mackey was right.

He was so afraid.

"Trav, man—I know your last guy cheated, but you've got to know something. I don't know what Grant is going to need. I don't know why he's so damned happy to have us here. But I swear to you, I could go down on my knees and blow him for old time's sake, for closure, for whatever the hell that comes up, and it would not have a *fucking thing* to do with how I feel about you. I *swore* I wouldn't make a fool of you. I was three months out of rehab, and every day was still a battle, but I promised. Have I gone back on that promise in any way?"

Trav closed his eyes. "No," he whispered, clenching Mackey's hair. He was wearing a towel—just a towel—and Mackey's head rested in his lap, his breath stirring the fine hairs along his thigh, and he offered such comfort.

And he was magnificent.

"I swear I won't," Mackey said earnestly. "I swear, Trav. Man, I want... I want it all with you. All I want with Grant is to give him some peace. You and me, we got *always*. Grant's got—what'd you say to Heath? Two weeks? Two weeks. And I'm going to need you for it, but... Trav, I'm going to need you *afterwards*. Can you be there for me? You ain't run yet. All the shit me and the guys have thrown at you, and you ain't run. Don't tell me this is what's gonna do it, Trav. Man, this *can't* be what does it. 'Cause this is where it all started, and we're about to leave it free and clear behind us. Can you hold on? I made it through rehab, dammit, I *know* you can hold on—"

Mackey squeezed his eyes shut, and his face blotched as he spoke. He trailed off because he couldn't talk anymore.

Trav couldn't leave him hang out there like that, alone and afraid.

"I can make it for you," he promised, framing Mackey's face in both hands and brushing the tears away with his thumbs. "I can make it for you, Mackey. I promise." It was the least he could do.

"Promise?" Mackey begged, sitting up so their faces were closer. "That's a promise. You don't go back on those—you never break a promise!"

God. He never did. This was a promise. This wasn't on loan and it wasn't temporary—this was *real*. Trav knew he might still lose a chunk of Mackey's soul to Grant Adams, but he needed to promise anyway.

"Promise," he said again. "I can make it for—"

Mackey's mouth was sweet on his, sweet and soft and greedy. Trav wanted to pull away and brush his teeth, wash his face at least—oh God, clean the sweat off his body— but sweet and soft turned into *need you now!* And Trav needed too.

He hauled Mackey up by the armpits and rolled, pushing Mackey into the bed and taking over, raking his stubbled chin down Mackey's jaw.

"You stink like booze and cigars," Mackey panted while Trav nuzzled his neck by his collarbone. "I think you need to shower before we do any more of this."

Trav had no answer to that. He rasped his face down to Mackey's chest, ripping the thin blue T-shirt clean off his body and dropping the front halves so he could rake his teeth down Mackey's skin and lave roughly on his tightened nipple. Mackey moaned and clutched at his head, and Trav nipped at his ribs, at the soft skin of his muscled stomach, and down.

Mackey wore his softest jeans, and the button came undone with a jerk of Trav's teeth on the denim. That quickly, Mackey was naked, and Trav planted nibbling kisses, small, savage nips that teased with an edge of pain.

"Suck your dick, isn't that right?" he rasped, punctuating the words by taking a shaved testicle delicately in his mouth and then releasing it. "You told me I owed you. I'm paying up."

"Fine," Mackey muttered on a challenge. "Fi—*uhng!*" Because Trav had taken his other ball and sucked on it gently. "You go ahead and suck my dick, and then we're going into the shower and I'm sucking yours. And then, if we got anything left, I'm fucking you up the ass, because we made promis—*augh!*—promises!"

Trav sucked him harder, took Mackey's soft-skinned cock down his throat as far as he could. Trav loved giving Mackey head more than any other lover he'd had, because Mackey didn't just lie back and take it. Mackey tugged on his hair and made sexy noises and said things like "Faster, faster, faster, *dammit!*" and he was just as responsive today as he had been their first time.

Trav couldn't get Mackey's cock far enough down his throat. He grasped the base hard, spit spilling over his fist, but he shoved down until the flared head caught in his throat, and then shoved harder past the gag reflex because he *needed*, needed to be filled with Mackey's cock.

"Omigod, Trav—I'm gonna come—just now. Stop. Don't wanna come yet—"

*Tough, Mackey. I need you inside me.* Trav swallowed again, a shot of precome spurting against his throat.

Trav's fist was swimming in spit and precome, and he let go of Mackey's cock, working his mouth lower, and shoving his hand between Mackey's thighs. He used his thumb to massage between Mackey's balls, stroked his slick middle finger down Mackey's crease, finding his pucker and soothing.

Mackey groaned, pounding the side of the bed in agitation. Too much too soon, Trav knew that, but he'd woken up alone too, woken up without Mackey. He'd rolled over and reached for where Mackey had lain for the better part of a year and had forced himself to imagine life without him.

He'd imagined walking away, finding an apartment with four white walls, managing the band from nearby but not living in the house anymore. He'd imagined watching Mackey perform from the sidelines, hiding when the band came off stage because he couldn't stand to see who Mackey would kiss when the set was over. He imagined the coldness of another lover's touch after the heat of what was filling his mouth, his hands, his nostrils, his skin, *right now*, and he needed.

With a groan, he pushed his finger in to the second knuckle as his lips brushed Mackey's bare skin.

"Trav, you *asshole*—!"

Come, hot, rank with musk, and bitter spilled down Trav's throat. Trav savored it, pulled back so it could hit his palate, hit his tongue, and he could milk Mackey until he was done spurting.

Their breaths sounded harsh and grating in the space of the hotel room.

Mackey sat up suddenly, scrabbling for purchase in Trav's hair. "Shower," he snarled, and Trav was at his mercy.

Trav went first while Mackey stopped to grab something from the beach bag, and for a moment, he had a reprieve. A second, a heartbeat alone in the bathroom while he stepped under the spray. Because Mackey wasn't going to give him any space. Trav promised and Mackey wouldn't let him go. Trav had been able to walk away from every relationship he'd ever had, but not this one. Suddenly the idea that he'd been Mackey Sanders's for over a year was ludicrous. That much bright, that much shining, that much fierce possession—turned on Travis Ford? It was laughable. Trav did stable. Trav was organized and….

Trav hadn't been that man since he and Mackey sang "Cocaine" together, when Mackey was more dead than alive.

He held his face up to the water, swishing some around his mouth, and spat. Mackey's taste lingered, and he was torn between wanting his toothbrush and wanting that proof that McKay James Sanders was his, soaking through his soul with his come.

Mackey stepped in behind him, a washcloth and hard hotel soap in his hand, and he started a rough scrub of Trav's body—his back, his ribs, his neck and chest. Trav tried to capture his hands when they were in front, but Mackey batted him away wordlessly. No softness. Trav got it. Mackey might not be mad anymore, but he wasn't in a sweet mood. He pulled at Trav's nipples, fingers slippery and irritated, and Trav leaned his head against the wall and groaned.

He'd been hard when they'd gotten into the shower. Now, with Mackey's hands on his skin, kneading his thighs, Trav's abdomen clenched so tightly with arousal that the muscles in his legs shook.

Mackey's hands disappeared, slid around to Trav's ass, and Mackey leaned forward to whisper in his ear. "Spread 'em, Trav. I'm gonna wash you."

Trav braced his hands on the wall and complied.

Torturous, rough, practical, *insane*—the washcloth left nothing secret, from the crease of his groin to the inside of his knees to his—*oh God*—now bright and squeaky clean cock, balls, and asshole. Trav's body parts got scrubbed, rinsed, scrubbed again, which felt worse than Mackey playing with him on purpose. Trav leaned his head against the wall, groaning.

"Mackey—"

"My turn," Mackey muttered. "You take care of us, you make us all into a family—someone's gotta take care of you sometimes, Trav. If this is gonna work, you gotta have faith that I can."

Mackey balanced one hand on the small of Trav's back while he reached outside the shower. He came back in with the bottle of waterproof lube they stashed in their luggage, and Trav closed his eyes and forced himself to relax.

"Your ass is trying to make shit into diamonds," Mackey snapped, flicking Trav's buttock with the tips of his fingers. "You either trust me or you don't!"

"It's not the same—*God!*" Mackey grabbed his cock and grasped hard, gliding long and slow, sliding the skin from the shaft over the head when he got there. His hand was slick with lube, and the pressure/pain was... *exquisite.*

"Yeah, it is," Mackey whispered over his shoulder, stroking, stroking, squeezing. He rubbed circles around Trav's backside with his other hand, and a particularly hard shiver rocked Trav, *forced* him to give up the control that kept him clenched.

Mackey rewarded his faith with a finger in his asshole, and Trav shuddered again, his muscles melting, sagging into that single lubricated, dominant finger penetrating him while Mackey kept stroking, stroking, stroking....

"I'm going to fall," he confessed thickly, his knees going weak.

"Bend over," Mackey said mercilessly. "Over the toilet, knees on the side of the tub. Grab a towel."

Awkward as hell, but Trav grabbed a towel and dropped it on the edge, just like Mackey said, Mackey's finger—*fingers, two!*—still in his body, his hand still stroking Trav's cock.

"Mackey," Trav rasped as he fumbled for the curtain. He stumbled, ripped the curtain off the rod, then found the towel with his knees by chance and rested his hands on the top of the toilet. The water spattered around them, and Mackey spared a moment from that insidious, hard-gripped stroke around his cock to turn it off.

Silence descended, punctuated by Mackey's harsh, muttering breaths behind him and Trav's own tortured breathing.

And someone was making little breathy, moaning sounds, grunts, tiny, giving mumbles of reluctant pleasure... was that... was it really....

Mackey kept finger-fucking him hard, harder, with two—four, oh God, four, it felt like a fist. Trav buried his face against the unyielding plastic toilet lid, slipping with the water dripping from his shoulders and hair, and heard those sounds echoing back at him through his crossed arms.

He was making them.

He was making those sounds as his lover took control of his body, stroking one end, penetrating the other. Trav was incoherent, begging, pleading, *screaming*—

"God, Mackey, fuck me... fuck me... *oh please, baby, fuck me!*"

Mackey's fingers disappeared and Trav gasped, missing him, invasive, larger than life, a pain he couldn't exist without.

And that quickly Mackey was inside of him, cock to ass, throwing his slight body, his stringy weight, against Trav's backside with the force of a runaway train.

Trav groaned, the sound bouncing around the tiny bathroom, becoming a roar, becoming timpani, becoming Trav's breathless need.

"Yes! God! Keep... need.... Mackey, fucking need... *oh please!*"

Mackey adjusted his angle, pushing up, probably standing on his toes, but he pegged Trav's gland hard enough that Trav saw stars and made a sound that should have shorted out the lights.

"*Yes!*"

Mackey let go of his cock, which seemed like madness, but it let him keep up that angle, keep driving into Trav hard. Trav closed his eyes tight enough to see explosions of red sparks with every thrust.

"Grab it, Trav," Mackey commanded. "I like it when you grab your cock!"

A year. They'd had a year, and they'd done almost everything they could think of—except for this. Mackey had seen Trav half-asleep as the sun came through their hotel window, palming himself into a sleepy orgasm, not sated, not even close, from the lovemaking the night before. He wasn't sated now, would never be sated after this, would always need Mackey, *crave* him, scream for the touch of Mackey inside him, the feel of Mackey's come saturating his skin.

Trav grabbed his cock with one hand and pillowed his face on the toilet seat, sprawled inelegantly like a rutting animal, begging to be fucked.

He closed his hand on his prick and it didn't matter. Mackey picked up speed and Trav hit his cockhead just so, and those fireworks stopped, Trav's breath stopped, everything in the goddamned world *stopped* as Mackey groaned, pumping frantically, shooting into Trav's body. Trav's body exploded, particles of light and air hurtling through the sterile white room to the clear sky outside.

Mackey collapsed across his back, panting against Trav's skin, still sheathed in Trav's ass.

Trav felt Mackey's come leaking out and half laughed. "We're going to need another shower."

"No," Mackey rasped. "I need to smell like you for a while."

The thought made Trav shiver—such a visceral, animal thing for a man who liked to think he had it all on his laptop.

"Okay," he whispered. He didn't have any other words. Like it or not, he'd just sold his soul to Mackey James for the price of a shower curtain and a bottle of lube.


THEY DRIED off in awkward silence, made it to the bed, and Trav extended his arm for Mackey to pillow his head on Trav's chest.

"God, I needed this last night," Mackey muttered.

Trav tightened his arm and held him tight. "I was overwhelmed," he confessed. "I—I can't keep you guys safe from this place. I mean, over a year, and my job has been to protect my boys, you know?"

Mackey grunted, rubbing his cheek against the damp skin and silky hair of Trav's chest. Almost absent-mindedly he licked Trav's nipple, and Trav arched his hips.

"Stop that," he ordered. "I'm sore."

Mackey stopped obediently, but throughout the rest of their conversation, he rubbed Trav's stomach, his ribs, his pecs, his neck. It was like he was feeding himself on Trav's skin, and Trav couldn't make him stop.

"You can't protect us from this," Mackey said after a moment of rolling his face on Trav's chest. "But we got things—not just drugs, Trav, just... like Jefferson and Stevie. They ain't been apart—hell, they probably go to the bathroom together. With Shelia there it's even tighter. Kell laid down the law with Cheever—he got to be the man of the house. Blake, he ain't said two words—he had his own small town. He knows to lie low and figure out the local customs if you don't want to find yourself getting beat the fuck up."

"And you?" Trav asked, letting a little of his worry out, a little of it rest on Mackey's shoulders.

Mackey grinned at him, showing his canines. "Were we or were we not arrested for being in a bar fight?"

Trav blinked. "You are *so* proud of yourself," he said, horrified.

"Oh yeah." Mackey nodded with complete satisfaction. "*That* was probably the best moment I've had in this piece of shit town."

Trav had to laugh. He was helpless to do anything else. "Thank you for making me a part of that," he said, irony dripping from every syllable.

Mackey nestled into him again, his naked body stretched out and rubbing all over Trav's. Trav was too sexed out to be horny, but it *did* make him sublimely happy to be touching Mackey again.

"My pleasure," Mackey said, purring, with no irony at all.

They dozed for an hour and then got up, dressed from the contents of Mackey's bag, and checked out.

"Where's Heath?" Mackey asked as Debra pulled the rental car around for them.

"Left around six," Trav said. "Never went to sleep—said he'd sleep on the plane."

"I like a man who can party like a rock star," Mackey said with a grin.

Trav rolled his eyes. "Since I live with them, I guess I'm not as impressed."

Mackey laughed as they slid into the car. By the time they got back to his mother's house, he was still chuckling. Trav didn't think it was that funny, but then, he really didn't always get Mackey's sense of humor.

That was okay. Apparently he got Mackey.

# Take Another Little Piece of My Heart

GRANT CALLED that evening and said he'd needed to rest the whole day, but he was glad they'd gotten out of jail. He thanked Trav personally, apparently because Trav had made sure he got out of there so he wouldn't get hurt.

His voice broke a lot, rasped, and he was probably stoned to the gills for pain. Mackey hadn't said anything to Trav or Kell, but he'd had dreams when they'd set up the gig at the Nugget. He'd wanted Grant up with them one last time. But Grant's fingers—they'd been so fine and strong and sure—were now swollen and clubbed and sore.

"Besides, Mackey," Grant said when Mackey suggested it, "I haven't played guitar in months. You guys play every day."

He'd been the best of them after Mackey.

Now he was telling them he would probably be down the next day—but the day after that, he wanted them out to his parents' house for a visit.

"To your *house*?" Kell said on the conference call, stunned. "Grant, we didn't go out to your house when we were kids!"

Grant made a humorless sound on the other side of the line. "I know. That was my folks. I sort of bypassed their consent here—which reminds me. Mackey, is Mr. Ford there?"

"Yeah, I'm here," Trav said, sounding surprised. "What do you need, Grant?"

"I'm going to be talking to the guys, showing them the place since they never saw it when we were kids. I need you to talk to my dad and my lawyer. There's stuff there I need you to make sure Mackey's going to get. Are you a lawyer?"

Trav grunted no. "A business major. But I can have a lawyer on standby so I can text him questions if you like."

"That would be great, Mr. Ford. My dad's gonna try to wiggle out of things—be ready for it. I was sort of counting on you helping me do right by Mackey and the guys."

"Yeah, Grant. I'll be ready."

Grant's relief was palpable, even over the phone in a conversation with all of them, huddled around Mackey's mom's kitchen table. "Thank you, Mr. Ford. It's good to know you'll be there."

The last thing Grant did before they signed off was ask Mackey to bring his guitar.

Mackey was so happy he almost started to dance right there. God, music. It had tied them together for most of their lives.

He needed to give Grant music.

THEY SPENT the next day at the music store. Mackey's old bosses were probably the only people in the town thrilled to have him, and Trav had brought a hundred free CDs to give away. The band signed free CDs and posters and smiled at high school students for two hours.

Mackey sort of loved it.

"Do you play?" He asked the same question to every kid who gave him something to sign, and he loved hearing the answers.

The answer that particularly tickled him came from the angular kid with dyed black hair and all the piercings, who said, "The steel guitar or the trombone?"

Mackey looked the kid over and saw him arching his spiked eyebrows suggestively.

Mackey laughed. "Well, I meant the guitar, but you know, that other thing is fun too!"

The kid laughed, blushing, and then shuffled uncomfortably, not meeting Mackey's eyes. "It meant a lot," he mumbled. "That you came out. Thank you."

Mackey scrabbled for something to say, but the kid had already snatched his free poster and run away. Mackey stared after him for a minute, a smile twitching at his lips.

"I wasn't the first one," he said softly. He turned to the person next to him humming "Holiday" in the back of his throat.

BRIONY SPENT that night in the bunk bed above them, which was fine—Mackey was too keyed up, wound tight by a cranked string from his groin to his throat.

"What's wrong with you?" Trav asked for the fifteenth time when Mackey tried to lodge himself between the perpendicular bottom bunk and the stairs to the top.

"I don't know," Mackey said shortly. "It's like... not like a date exactly, but like... like something big's going to happen, like Christmas or something, except bad. You know—you're the one who said he doesn't have long. It's like, no matter how I feel about him—love, hate, friendship, brotherhood, whatever—it's like... *bigger.* It's *louder* in my head!"

Trav let loose a sound between a sigh and a grunt. Then he rolled over, smashing Mackey between the railing and his big body, and draped his arm over Mackey, completely engulfing him in his heat, and his smell, and his pressure.

Mackey felt so much relief he had to check to make sure he hadn't wet his pants. "Ah, God, thanks, Trav," he murmured. "That's so much better."

"Can you even breathe?" Trav asked over his head.

"It's not air if it doesn't smell like you."

"Oh for Christ's sake," Briony muttered from above them. "Are you two done? I'll take my chances with Cheever—"

"No!" they both said in tandem, because Cheever had been lying low, but they didn't want to tempt fate.

"Briony?" Mackey said, his voice muffled from Trav's armpit. "Why aren't you sleeping with my brother yet?"

Briony's response was a long, wet cough. When she recovered, she said, "Because my inner sex goddess has not yet descended."

Mackey giggled and Briony did too—and Trav groaned.

"Children, I realize I'm getting no sex tonight, but do I have to separate you?"

"No," Briony begged, her voice piteous in the dark. "Please, Trav?"

Mackey tapped Trav on the shoulder, and Trav sighed. Trav wouldn't deny Briony anything, especially when she was sick and away from home.

"You wanted to be needed," Mackey mumbled, and he felt Trav's kiss on the top of the head.

"And I am," he said.

Mackey thought about the next day and shuddered. "You really are," he said fervently.

God. What would he say?

Everyone knew where Grant Adams lived. People whispered about it when they passed the long, curving driveway lined with decorative shrubs and framed with wrought iron. The suburb sported a couple of massive houses, hollowed out from the oak and manzanita that lined the hills. Landscapers reformed the earth, making things lush and green and trimmed, even in the summer, and even though most of the houses had an attached "farm" for horses and really expensive showpiece stock, what greeted visitors driving up was the grand multistory house—in this case faux brick—with gables and insets and bright black shale tiling the roof.

Grant's mom had come from the South, so they'd tried to make it look like Kentucky, which was funny because the terrain in this part of California was hilly and dry. Outside of this tiny little patch of perfect green, the landscape consisted of red dirt and brown grass—even behind the house itself—but driving up, it seemed like a whole other world.

When Mackey and his brothers were younger, they had never, not once, questioned that Grant would rather hang out in their two-bedroom apartment or, when Stevie's dad wasn't there, in Stevie's garage.

For one thing, it didn't feel quite real that *their friend* Grant, who traded his Lunchables for Kell's PB&J, would come from such a grand place. Yes, his clothes were better, but he got just as dirty as the Sanders boys when they played at school. Yes, when they started the band, his equipment was always new, but he worked just as hard as they did learning how to play it.

The fact that when he was sixteen he got to drive his mom's car was awesome—but he would have been their friend if he'd had to ride his bike.

He'd told Kell once—when Mackey could hear—that he'd threatened to ride his bike when his mom didn't give him a ride. He'd been desperate to escape.

So the house on the hill had never really seemed grand or real to Mackey—or any of his brothers. It had seemed more like a gate-keeping dragon, a brooding presence that allowed Grant to escape its grasp on occasion but that he had to elude if he wanted to play with his brothers. Yeah, sure, the Sanders kids were scrappy and their clothes were torn, they wore their shoes until the duct tape fell off, and sometimes they had PB with no J, but they didn't have to escape a dragon to play with their brothers.

After Grant's first kiss and his first admission that he'd be with Sam when he loved Mackey, that house had seemed even grander, even more imposing, even more of an obstacle to Grant ever coming out to play.

As the SUV glided up the recently paved road, Mackey had a sudden, absurd thought: The dragon was never going to let Grant out again. After all this time of Grant escaping in little pieces to play with his brothers, it was finally going to swallow him whole.

Briony and Shelia had stayed with Mackey's mom. Cheever had gone back to school that morning, so Mackey was glad for his mom, but he missed the two of them. They didn't talk much to each other, but they had bonded, being the only women in the group, and somehow Briony's sarcasm made moments like this easier to bear.

"What are you thinking?" Trav asked next to him. He had his arm slung over the back of the seat, which looked only natural because the lot of them were cramped, even in the big modified Tahoe, but Mackey knew he did it to give Mackey a place to hide.

"I'm thinking that even if this place is sunshine and fucking roses, I'm going to hate it like poison," Mackey said passionately, and his voice carried.

"God, me too," Kell muttered. "I swear, we see houses bigger than this every day, but somehow... I mean, he used to sneak out. I remember his mom used to call us because Grant had gone missing, and Mom would go driving toward his house and find him trying to find us. He always said he just wanted to play."

Kell's voice wobbled a little, and Mackey found his favorite refuge.

"Don't talk like that," he snarled, making everyone in the car jump. "Grant is still alive, and that place is just a fucking house. I brought his goddamned guitar—he says he can play if he sits down. We're gonna go play with our friend, and he's gonna meet Blake and talk about what a pain in the fucking ass Kell is. Stevie and Jefferson can talk about married life, and we're gonna see him hold his baby—that's what's happening today, do you all fucking hear me?"

There was a rather cowed response of "Yes, Mackey," and Mackey harrumphed in response.

"We will *not* get soft about this," he promised. "Not this visit. Maybe next one, yeah. But not this one. This one, we're just sayin' hi."

A stocky middle-aged man with gray curly hair, wearing a pricey leather cowboy hat, matching boots, and clean, unfaded Wranglers, waved Debra around the back of the perfectly sculpted yard to a hard-pan dirt spot behind the multicar garage.

"Damn," Trav said in surprise, and Mackey cackled.

"Wow—it's like a 50/50 ice cream bar! Wouldja look at that?"

The front of the house may have been all faux English garden, but the back of the house was dusty horse farm. There was a stable about a hundred yards off of the house and a practice ring behind that. Mackey marked four different pens—each one roughly half the size of a football field—with a galloping Arabian horse in each pen getting its panties in a bundle as the new car drove up.

"Horses!" Stevie and Jefferson piped up, excited.

"Grant hates 'em," Kell muttered, and Mackey nodded. He remembered that about Grant. His old man kept them, paid a live-in trainer, dragged the family to horse shows every weekend, and fawned over the creatures—but not Grant.

Grant had escaped them.

Mackey, who had always known *exactly* how small he was next to an animal that size, had never blamed him.

Right behind the house was a little shaded patio with chaise lounges and a picnic table complete with a big umbrella to keep off the sun. Even though the air was brisk and the wind edged with cold, the sun was still bright and hard.

The young wraith in sunglasses and a bandana, leaning back on a chaise lounge, turning his face up to the sun and smoking a joint through coughing fits, did not seem to mind either the cold or the brightness.

He just looked happy to be there, under the heartbreak blue sky.

He turned toward them when they walked up, though, sitting up painfully and lifting his arm to wave.

"You made it!" he said by way of greeting, although Mackey knew they were probably a little early.

None of the boys wanted to get there late.

"Yeah, well, when we heard it was a day getting high in the sun, we could hardly hold ourselves back," Mackey retorted.

Grant took a pull on his joint and raised his eyebrows. "Just 'cause you're jealous," he murmured. "Besides, I'm almost done, and then you all can come in and see the baby. You haven't met her yet."

Kell walked up and claimed brother-privilege by hugging him. Everyone followed suit like they hadn't just seen him two days before, but nobody said anything.

Unspoken things—stupid unspoken things: Grant Adams had a finite number of hugs left.

They talked excitedly while he finished up, giving him the details of the fight after he'd been hustled out.

"Yeah, you shoulda seen Mackey!" Stevie burbled. "Man, Trav just crouched low and caught Del like a charging horse—"

"Delmont, really?" Grant asked animatedly. He looked at Trav and nodded, adding a low whistle. "Man, that takes ball-balls—he's freakin' huge! There's rumors that man kills people with a swing of his fist!"

"He would have," Trav said, and Mackey wanted to weep when he didn't sound grudging or hostile or anything. "But Mackey jumped on his back and wrapped his arm around the guy's throat. Didn't quite put him down, but it did *slow* him down before the cops could Taser him." Everyone laughed, and Mackey brushed Trav's hand with a careful fingertip. God, he was trying. *Thank you, Trav, thank you thank you thank you.*

"Man, Mackey was always the fiercest, but he couldn't pick his fights for shit. He'd get *whaled* on by the biggest guys. Kell, how many times did we have to beat up little kids to keep him out of the shit?"

Kell groaned. "God, it was a nightmare. And Mackey, in like, the third grade—he's like that cartoon, right? The 'I'm a chicken hawk and I eat chicken!'—and then he'd walk up to the biggest, toughest guys and nail them in the jaw. It's like the whole school was lining up to dust his weenie little ass and Grant and I were taking guys out in hallways to keep them from jumping my little pain-in-the-ass brother!"

"Well, you suck," Mackey drawled, "'cause I know a bunch of them slipped through!"

"Well, dude…." Kell looked at Blake and shook his head. "He is *so* much less a pain in the ass now that he's come out. Man, I think if teachers knew that, they'd be asking *all* the scrappy kids at school if they were gay, just to get it out there and stop having to bandage up the poor Mormon kids who didn't see it coming!"

Blake grunted. "I'm sayin'." He looked at Grant and shook his head just like Kell had. "Man, he was insufferable. I was just not ever gonna be you. And then I found out why, and yanno, I didn't mind so much."

The group laughed like it was all a long time ago and it hadn't ever ripped Mackey into little pieces and stuffed him full of chemicals so he could get up and do it again.

But that was okay, because Grant laughed too and met Mackey's eyes in a moment of understanding for just the both of them.

He'd hurt too. Suddenly Mackey knew—they'd *both* been hurt. The only thing that had put the hurt to an end for Grant had been the end itself.

Mackey had been the lucky one.

"Oh!" Grant said excitedly. "There's my girl!"

Samantha had put on weight, but more than that, she'd put on *lines*, deep, deep, bitter ones in the sides of her mouth. She looked thirty-five instead of twenty-six, and she walked with the kind of aggression Mackey had seen in the women in town. The women Sam's age who had to buy their eight- or nine-year-olds recorders in the music store but who had to sacrifice their own shoes to do it—those women walked like Sam did. Like she'd given too damned much already and she was going to begrudge the whole fucking world until she got her some back.

"You said you wanted to see her," she said, her voice hard.

Grant smiled hopefully into her eyes. "Yeah we did. Here, let me hold her a minute."

She was barely a toddler—still tiny, less than a year and a half old. She was dressed in a little pink sweat suit, with her curly brown hair mercilessly scraped into two corkscrew pigtails on the top of her head.

"Daddy! Kisses!"

Grant took her, his arms visibly trembling a little with the weight. "Y'all, I want you to meet Katy. She's gonna be trouble, and she's my baby, so y'all need to watch out for her or I'm coming back to haunt you, you hear?"

"That's morbid," Sam said. "Grant, I wish you—"

"Sam," Grant said, looking at her beseechingly, "you haven't even said hi to the guys."

"Hi," she said resentfully. She didn't even look at Mackey. Her gaze lingered on Blake for a moment, and Grant introduced them. "You don't look gay," she said suspiciously.

Blake caught Mackey's eye and grimaced. "I'm not, mostly," he said. "I leave that to Trav and Mackey. They're good at it, so it's okay."

Mackey chuckled deliberately. "Well, I'm getting better with practice," he said with false modesty, and his brothers laughed.

"Well, I think it's disgusting," Sam said with venom. She reached out for the baby, and Grant angled his body protectively. "I don't want her out here with these people," she said, like she hadn't grown up with all of them.

"Well, that's not your choice anymore," Grant said levelly. "That's why the lawyer's here, and that's why Mackey brought Trav. She's a part of their lives, Sam, and she's gonna be after I'm gone."

"You're hateful," she hissed and then turned and stalked away, leaving the air frigid and toxic.

The baby snuggled into Grant's arms for a second and then struggled to be let up. "Damn," Grant said, setting her down. "Jeff, Stevie, could you guys chase after her? Blake, could you help? I gotta talk to these guys for a second."

They were walking after the little girl even before Grant finished speaking, and Grant breathed a sigh of relief. "She likes watching the horses work!" he called and then fell back coughing.

"You need to come inside." The voice was unfamiliar, and Mackey looked back toward the house. The man with the curly hair and the cowboy hat—Grant's dad—was walking from the front yard with a purposeful stride.

Grant kept coughing, shaking his head. He reached into his pocket, pulled out a handkerchief, and coughed into it. When he pulled it away, it was flecked with red, and Mackey closed his eyes.

"Dad, you need to take Mr. Ford inside and talk to the lawyer, okay?"

Mr. Adams narrowed his eyes. "Grant, you know your mother and I don't like this—"

"And I'm dying, and I hired my own lawyer, and he drew up the papers, and they're my last will and testament, and Mackey needs to know. Trav's going to be there to keep it all aboveboard." Grant might have been closer to dead than alive, but damn, he'd grown a backbone in the past two years. "I want this, Dad. I gave up everything, my whole life, for the things you expected me to be. But I want this—and for once, I'm going to get what I want."

"Fine!" Mr. Adams snapped. He glared at Mackey and Kell. "You boys should be proud of yourselves. Man, all the things my boy had, and the only thing he wanted was to be white-trash faggots like you."

Mackey was going to say something, but God. Grant looked so sick. He didn't have the heart.

Kell looked Grant's dad in the eye, though, and damned if Mackey's brother didn't say, "Our house is bigger than yours. And it's in LA, so the property values are higher. And more than a million people screamed my brother's name last year. If you'd been any less of a bastard, just think—your boy coulda married up."

Grant's dad actually took a stump-legged step toward Kell, but Trav left Mackey's side and stood in the way.

"Grant said I needed to talk to a lawyer? Why don't you show me the way."

It wasn't a question. Not really.

Mackey stood back and watched them go, missing Trav's warmth at his side already. He and Kell turned back to Grant, who smiled in relief.

"God, that's a load off my mind. I mean, I was going to do this anyway—I had the lawyer draw up the papers before your mom came by—but I'm just so glad I get to tell you."

"Tell us what?" Kell asked, squatting down.

Grant leaned forward and touched foreheads with Mackey's brother. "I have been sitting on this porch for an hour," he said, smiling. "Think you and Mackey could help me across the yard? Man, I hated this place for so long, but I sure would like to see more of it right now."

Kell nodded and stood. "C'mere, Mackey, get his other side."

He smelled like old pot and sickness—even a little like urine. Mackey guessed it was probably hard to get to the bathroom when everything hurt. As Mackey and Kell helped him stand up to walk across the yard, the scant weight on his shoulder felt hollow and insubstantial, like the bones of a dying bird.

But Grant kept talking like his body hadn't wasted away, and his life with it. "Yeah, Katy can't get enough of the horses. For a little while after we moved back, I was in remission. I used to get home from work and take her out for an hour, just walking around, talking to each horse and the chickens. At least one of us liked 'em. We'd ride the tractor and yell at the dogs. I miss doing that with her."

"She's going to miss you." Mackey was glad Kell could say it.

"Yeah, well, I like to think I'm not going to miss everybody. I'll be here."

Mackey'd thought about it—of course he'd thought about it. He'd been damned near suicidal—hell *yeah* he'd thought about the afterlife. "I like to think you'll be far away," he said apologetically. "Someplace green, like England. You'd like England. Man, the pubs are awesome. You can just walk in and drink a pint and if you root for the right team, you're everybody's best friend."

"So you want me to spend the afterlife in England?" Grant asked, but he was smiling, so Mackey knew he wasn't hurt.

"I want you to spend it somewhere you're happy," Mackey said sincerely. "Happy and free. All the beer you can drink, all the ass you can handle, and nothing but good fucking music unless you want a golden silence and a sunrise, you know?"

"Hmm." Grant's legs stilled for a moment. Mackey and Kell both turned to look at him, and his eyes were closed, and he was doing what he'd done on the porch—turning his face toward the sun. "That's a real nice afterlife you got planned for me," he said happily. "I'm down with that." He started moving again, toward the barn, so they followed, supporting as much of him as they could. "I do have to confess, there's really only one ass I'm interested in, but it's taken."

Mackey grunted. "Yeah, well, Trav's possessive."

"I appreciate that I got you on loan today," Grant said. "Kell, what do you think—is Trav good enough for your little brother?"

"More'n Mackey deserves," Kell grunted. "I swear, that man saved Mackey's life."

Grant halted again, this time in surprise. "What do you mean?" He searched Mackey's eyes, and Mackey realized that "rehab" had just been a word to him. A sorrow. Not the hard and true reality of "get clean or die."

"I was…." Mackey grimaced. "God. Grant, I was so fucked-up after you left me. And then our first manager died and…." He shook his head. It was like the only words he could find for that time were in songs. "Trav had to carry me to the ambulance to detox, you know that? My first memory of Trav is when he was giving me a shower 'cause he couldn't stand my smell anymore. And after all that—he stayed. I mean… when someone sees you at your worst and stays, you want to show them your best. And… and I think he's seen that. And it was good enough. So, yeah. Trav. Saved my life. Go figure."

They walked in silence for a moment, and Kell said unexpectedly, "It's true. Trav sorta saved us all."

Grant stopped, and they stopped with him, and he stood for a moment and watched as Jefferson and Stevie took turns giving Katy runs on top of their shoulders. She was squealing, and they could hear her screams of "Giddyap!" from across the yard.

"I wish I'd been there to be saved," he said. "Because really? What saved me was dying."

Mackey swallowed hard. He had no answer to that.

"You *will* explain that," Kell demanded.

Grant let out a breath. "So, see, I was going to do this all by lawyer, guys," he said, and he sounded apologetic. "I didn't… I mean, I wanted to see you before I died, but… if you were still pissed at me? I didn't want to know it." He caught his breath, and Mackey saw what looked like a spasm cross his face.

Then he realized—Grant's eyes didn't tear up anymore. This was his voice giving in to tears.

"I couldn't stand it, Kell, if you didn't want to be my brother anymore. Mackey, I didn't think anyone could forgive what I did. So I thought I'd die with the way we used to be, all fixed up in my brain, and then you guys would have to deal with the fallout." The look he gave Mackey was bitter with self-hatred. "You should recognize my methods by now."

Mackey swallowed. "I was pissed," he rasped, "but I didn't even blame you. You got no idea what it took for me to tell the fucking world. And I was pretty sure my mother loved me."

Grant laughed humorlessly. "Mine doesn't. Not anymore. She's said so. But that's okay. See, your mom came in and told me you all were coming, and I realized for once, I didn't have to take the coward's way out. For once I could do things aboveboard, like a man. So I came out to my family—about all of it. About you, about Tony—"

"Tony?" Mackey said, so stunned he didn't even have a chance to be sick.

"We were friends," Grant said quickly. "That's all. But we were friends because we knew about each other—and I should have known. I'm sorry, Mackey. I should have fucking known, but I kept thinking if I could do it, so could he. I used to think he was real brave, remember?"

"We both did," Mackey said numbly, although they'd never talked about it. It had been there in the way Grant had kept Tony off of Kell's radar, in the way he'd been kind.

"I guess nobody's that brave when they think they're gonna be alone forever," Grant said, his voice so bleak that Mackey turned his head and dropped a kiss on his blade of a shoulder, poking the fabric of his sweatshirt up in a tent.

"Yeah," he rasped. "You got that right."

Grant kissed his forehead, and Kell cleared his throat.

"You guys, uhm…."

"Let's get to the barn," Grant said. "I'll rest there, and I need to get this out."

"Like a swing," Mackey said, looking at Kell. Kell nodded, and hell, Trav had them working out enough. They linked arms behind Grant and, very carefully, picked him up in the cradle of their clasped hands.

They didn't talk much, because even wasted away like he was, he was still a grown man and Mackey was still short, but they got him into the barn without too much huffing and puffing, and that was a relief.

They set him on a little throne of hay bales and then sat next to him, one on either side.

He grabbed Mackey's hand, free and clear, and Mackey let him and stroked the skeletal back of Grant's hand softly with his thumb. It was something he'd gotten used to with Trav in the past year, just casually touching someone he loved in public. It was something Grant would never have. Kell looped an arm over Grant's shoulder.

"Lean on me, brother," he said softly. "I'm not afraid of you."

Grant tilted his head so it was on his brother's shoulder, and they sat there for a few moments, the darkness and animal warmth inside the barn sort of a welcome relief from the autumn chill and the hard, bright sun.

"Trav's inside with my lawyer," Grant said. "Mackey, I do hope he loves you, because I'm asking something huge from all of you."

"Like what?" Mackey asked, afraid of the answer.

"I want you to look after Katy—*not*," he added quickly, probably responding to the panic and outrage on Mackey's face, "full-time. Or even most time. But the lawyer is making sure you can take her for up to a month a year. And any time you drop by, my family *has* to let you see her. Officially, you and Kell are her godfathers, but really…." He pulled in a breath and let it out, and the pause was so long Mackey wondered if he was going to finish. "You're her salvation," he said after a moment.

"I don't know anything about kids," Mackey muttered, meeting Kell's eyes. Kell looked as panicked as he felt, which was reassuring. "God, Grant, I can barely keep a ficus alive, and that's because I pay someone to help me!"

"Don't look at me," Kell muttered. "Blake kept killing off the damned fish. I was having Astrid buy them on her way into work so we could swap them out before he saw."

Like a rubber band, Mackey was back into the world he and Kell had left, the normal they had worked hard for—the normal he'd craved as the tour drew to a close.

"Fuckin' really?" he asked, trying not to cackle. "Man, that's hilarious. Does Trav know?"

Kell grunted. "It was Trav's idea. But see!" he said, obviously calling their attention back to Grant. "We're hardly qualified—"

"She'll die here," Grant said soberly, cutting through all their denial bullshit with simple, quiet sincerity. "Like I did. This house will swallow her, and she'll never get out. Just like me." His face crumpled again. "God, I wish I could cry. Fucking radiation— can't even cry anymore, and it would feel so good. But you guys gotta promise me.

You'll come visit. You'll have her over for summer. You'll bring toys. You'll listen to her want to be an astronaut or a cowboy or a poet and you'll let her. Tell her she can go to college or travel to England or play the xylophone or...."

He broke then. Tears or not, his frail body convulsed with sobs, and Mackey and Kell couldn't do anything but hold him, unashamed and unafraid, and shed the tears their brother couldn't.

He couldn't cry for long—it took strength his body didn't have. The sobs eased, and Kell rested his face against Grant's head, rubbing his cheek on the bandana to take some of the wet.

Grant caught his breath and muttered, "Aw, fuck, that hurt."

"Do you want to straighten up?" Kell asked worriedly.

"No." Grant shook his head. "I don't think I can—you may need to prop me up and go get someone who can *really* carry me."

"Get Trav," Mackey said, and Kell nodded. Trav was bigger, and his biceps were cannon-size. He could do it. "You got pain meds? Codeine? A joint?"

Grant let out a shallow breath. "The pot's good, but sometimes it's hard on the lungs, and I left the damned vaporizer inside. Just let me rest. Go get Trav in a sec, but first, Kell?"

Kell propped him up and took off his own sweatshirt. "Here, Mackey. If we shift him to this side, he can lean against the hay bale and I can prop up his neck."

They moved him so he was reclined and more comfortable, but Grant wasn't going to let it go. "Mackey, Kell—please?"

Mackey's brother's eyes were brown. His face was made with heavier lines than Mackey's, the lines of a metalworker or a ditch digger, with thick lips and large ears.

But those brown eyes, plain as mud, were suddenly soft, warm, and kind. In that moment, Mackey saw that all the hero worship he'd given Kell when they were younger had been well placed.

"Mackey?" Kell asked softly.

"Yeah," Mackey agreed. "I'm scared shitless, you know. But if it's all of us—Jeff and Stevie, Shelia, Trav, you, Blake, me—"

"Briony," Kell said quickly, "'cause she's not going anywhere."

"Yeah." Mackey allowed a corner of his mouth to quirk up for hope that Kell and Briony could be family together too. "Yeah. We can give her something, Grant. I promise. *We* promise. We'll give her wings and a sky and a tree if she needs it. Is that what you wanted?"

Grant closed his eyes and nodded. "Yeah," he whispered. "Kell, could you go get Mr. Ford now?"

Kell stood up and pressed his forehead against Grant's, palming his head gently. That was all. No words. And then he slid out of the barn.

"You got your pot in your pocket?" Mackey asked.

Grant grinned a little. "Yup. Lifetime supply—for me, anyway."

Mackey reached gently into the front pocket and pulled out a joint and a lighter. "I was serious," he said, looking at the joint. "About not hating you. Man, I was always afraid this house, it was gonna swallow you up. I mean, we were kids, but we knew. We knew about your folks same way we knew about Stevie's dad—"

"You seen him?" Grant asked, opening his eyes curiously.

"No," Mackey said grimly. "Stevie and Jefferson ain't told Stevie's folks they're here. They don't want Shelia to ever meet them."

"So much," Grant sighed. "So much we all knew but we never talked about. Stevie's dad. My folks. You and me."

"I loved you like my life was your next breath," Mackey said boldly. It wasn't something he'd said, even when he and Grant were stealing the moments that defined them.

Grant opened his eyes and swallowed. "I still love you that way," he said, a corner of his mouth lifting in apology. "That's why Sam hates you so badly. 'Cause when I came out to my family and told them what I was fixing to do with custody, I told them every fucking thing. You, me, being in love."

Mackey made a hurt sound. "I can't…. Trav," he managed. God, not even for this moment could he tell that lie.

Grant shook his head. "You're here," he said. "And I might have gotten over you eventually, but there's no time now. It's okay. You're here, and I love you. And even if you can't say it back, I can finally say it, and that's good too."

Mackey looked at the joint in his hand and sighed. He didn't want it. He didn't crave it. There was a chance he could do this and his enemy might not master him, just this once.

*God, Trav, please understand.* He stood and held the joint to his lips, flicking the lighter and inhaling with his mouth like with a cigar, trying not to hold any more smoke in his lungs than he had to. It tasted sweet, herbal, like medicine. God, it made him queasy.

"What are you doing?" Grant asked.

Mackey leaned over, bracing his hands on the hay bale behind Grant's head, and fitted his mouth to Grant's, exhaling slowly, letting the smoke slip into Grant's body, hoping that this once, the secondhand smoke would do something.

Grant held the smoke, and Mackey took another hit. God, he wasn't sure if he was lightheaded from the weed or from holding his breath, but Grant opened his mouth and let the last breath slip out, and Mackey breathed for him again.

And again.

And again.

When the joint was done, down to the roach, Mackey ground it out carefully on the sole of his shoe and slipped it back in Grant's pocket.

He was buzzing hard from the crown of his head to the soles of his shoes, and thinking rather desperately that he didn't miss this feeling, didn't miss it at all. Not really.

"Feel better?" he asked Grant, his voice far away. He wobbled for a minute and sat down hard at Grant's feet. He rested his hand on Grant's knee and stroked, wanting the high to be over, wanting to be over it so he would know he could be fine without it.

"Yes," Grant said, his voice dreamy. "It's funny. My dad voted against medical marijuana his entire life, but I got sick, and suddenly he couldn't buy it fast enough."

"Yeah?" Mackey said, laughing gently. Yeah, everything was funnier with weed. "How's he feel about faggots?"

"He still hates us," Grant said, but he didn't sound like he particularly cared. "But now that he's bought me all this awesome weed? I don't give a shit."

Mackey laughed some more and slid his hand down Grant's thigh. He was just touching, familiar, and Grant sighed.

"God, Mackey. It just feels so good to be touched. My family ain't hugged me since I came out."

Mackey kept stroking, not trying to arouse, just to touch. He leaned his head back against the hay and closed his eyes. "Well, your real family is here now," he mumbled, sliding his hand to Grant's other thigh. "You'll get all the touch you can stand."

# Ghosts That We Knew

TRAV MISSED his parents with a terrible, sudden ferocity.

He remembered coming out. He'd been so nervous—seriously, who liked to talk to their parents? And he'd already told them about joining the military, and they were so very, very opposed. Liberal to the bone, both of them, they had disliked everything the military stood for.

But they'd ultimately been proud of their son.

He'd come down the stairs of their little Quaker-style house wearing cargo shorts, a polo shirt, and loafers, feeling so very grown-up because he was going to take the car into town and find himself a summer job at a local tourist trap, and because he'd graduated from high school two days before and his little brother still looked at him like he was a god. After pouring himself a cup of coffee, he sat down, thinking he was going to have a little adult talk with Tom and Linda (as he had never called them since), and they… well, listened gravely at first.

"Mom, Dad, I know you have been waiting for me to date, because it's age appropriate, but you should know that there's something about me—"

"You're gay," his mom interrupted practically. "Travis, we've been waiting for you to tell us—it's one of the reasons we were so opposed to the military!"

He stared at them, all of the wind flown from his sails. "But—but isn't this going to be a thing?"

"No," his father said grimly, shaking Splenda on his oatmeal and bananas. "It should never be a thing. The only reason people should worry about telling their parents is so their parents know who they're bringing home. That's polite. Gender expectations may be antiquated, but sometimes they're all we have."

Trav's dad—graying curly hair, stooped shoulders, graying red beard, and horn-rimmed glasses—gave the closest approximation to a growl Trav had ever heard. And suddenly his family was talking politics, which they did all the time anyway, and Trav ate oatmeal and bananas before he went to find his job—and his first lover, the musician on the corner.

Grant's family was nothing like his family.

Nothing.

"Now, Mr. Ford, you surely know we don't plan on letting our son do this to his wife and baby girl."

Travis looked at the paperwork in his hands and at the lawyer who'd handed it to him. "I'm going to scan this with my phone and send it to the boys' lawyer. Then we'll talk."

"It should be airtight," Mr. Reeves said, and Trav nodded.

Harold Reeves was a dapper little man about Mackey's height, with an aesthetic, slightly built body, a brown tweed suit, and a bow tie. He was the epitome of the middle-aged gay bachelor, and Trav wondered if Grant had chosen him with that in mind.

He'd certainly done Grant Adams proud with what he'd planned.

On the one hand, Trav was appalled, because Grant was giving partial custody of his baby girl to a bunch of feckless rock stars who, this time last year, could barely take a dump on their own without missing the bowl.

On the other hand, he was pleased—pleased and honored—because his boys were grown-up, and they were ready. The baby would be an impetus to stay straight. These boys loved each other like brothers—their brother's child would be sacred.

It wasn't full custody, which would have been madness, but just enough. Just enough to make them part of the little girl's life. Just enough to keep Grant Adams alive for them. Just enough to want to be better men for her.

Just enough to remind the boys where they came from, and how far they'd come.

This, he thought as he scanned the documents, could be a very good thing.

There were only three really ugly things in the way.

"I think it's disgusting," Samantha Adams spat. "He did those disgusting things with that Sanders kid when they were in school, and it's one thing when you're kids at school, but it's another when—"

"How did you know?" Trav asked, frowning. "You just said he came out a month ago—how do you know they were together when they were in school? Did Grant tell you that?"

It seemed unlikely. He could see Grant coming out about the affair and even about the little girl's name—which had seemed like a particularly cruel joke until Trav walked into this lovely cream-colored brocaded room with stark green silk bamboo plants on the maple end tables. There wasn't any dust, which Trav was used to in LA, but here, with the horses and the entire backyard being devoted to a farm, the thought of keeping everything free from cloying red dust was terrifying. For the freedom to get dirty alone, that little girl deserved to get the hell out of Tyson, and she deserved a namesake who could be strong enough to carry her away if she wished it.

So he could see Grant telling his family he was gay, and that he wanted his daughter to know Mackey, and to know Kell and the boys he'd called his brothers.

But he couldn't see Grant telling any of them—not his blonde helmet-coiffed mother, his good-ol'-boy father, or his bitter small-town bride—that he and Mackey had fucked away their high school years like too many kids to count.

"He must have," Sam said, looking away. She was wearing a blue turtleneck and dark blue jeans. Besides fake plants and the playpen in the corner filled with toys, he couldn't see any other color in the entire house. The living room was supposed to be arranged into a conversation pit. The effect was ruined by the giant hospital bed placed under the window. The window itself was in a vaulted turret, and it shined down into the room. The light made the bones of the place easy to see. Trav's gaze lingered on that bed in the sunshine, and he swallowed.

"Mr. Reeves, can I see those papers again?"

He took the sheaf and looked through them, looking for Katy's birth date, and his eyes widened. "She was born on the first of June?" he said, to make sure.

"Says so on the papers," Mr. Reeves confirmed. "Why?"

"Because Outbreak Monkey signed with Tailpipe Productions at the end of August."

"I'm sorry?" Reeves looked puzzled, but as Trav looked around the room, Sam glared at him and walked toward the window, folding her arms and turning her back on them all.

Grant's mother, Loretta, didn't meet his eyes.

"Right," Trav muttered, shaking his head in disgust.

"Right what? What sort of judgments are you passing, faggot?" Casper Adams, Grant's father, was a real prize. Trav raked him over, top to bottom, leather cowboy hat, matching shiny boots, and all.

"Nothing you would understand," he said after a moment. "And to answer your question, yes. Yes, I can and I will insist that you honor Grant's last will and testament. I'll get Mackey and the boys to sign that they accept."

"You can't do that!" Loretta said, fidgeting. Trav could smell the old smoke in the living room, and her fingers were nicotine stained. A smoker—not reformed, maybe, but perhaps forced to smoke outside the house. She was dressed elegantly in a daytime outfit of a burnt-orange pantsuit and pearls that would give any woman in Beverly Hills a run for her money—and Trav knew enough executives, male and female, to know this was fact. She'd used enough hairspray to lock a semi into place on the tarmac, and her boobs, butt, and face had all been done with the same X-Acto knife.

Trav's mom was probably the same age. She'd had her eyes done, and she dyed her hair brown like it had been in her youth, but the brittle quality, the so-perfect-it-can-snap thing—that was missing in comfortable, kind Linda Ford, who had always wanted to hug Trav as he was growing up and too old for such things.

"I can," Trav said, looking at the paperwork. "I mean, Grant's wife can withhold Katy from us, but that would mean that the royalty percentage Grant gets from the band would no longer be going to support Samantha but would, in fact, be divided between Katy's college fund and an LGBTQ homeless shelter. Now, you two could take them both into your home and Sam wouldn't have to work to support the baby, and that would be your choice, but you'd never see a penny of that money for support. And Katy can only claim the college money by coming to visit the members of the band. That's a proviso. One way or another, your daughter is going to know the Sanders kids. You can do it this way, let their gifts into your home, let their mother come visit, let them take her for a few weeks a year, or you can spring them on her all at once, when she's eighteen and you don't have a say in her life. It is *all* up to you."

"I can't believe he did this to me," Sam muttered, still not looking at any of them.

"After what you did to him?" Trav snapped, trying to control the aching in his chest. June. The baby had been born in June. He knew the story: Grant couldn't come with the band because he'd knocked his girlfriend up. But the band signed in August. And he knew Grant had instilled the condom habit in Mackey pretty darned securely—probably because he'd been practicing it himself with Sam.

"What's that supposed to mean?" Casper Adams asked, glaring at him. Well, he'd been glaring at Trav and Mr. Reeves the entire visit. Trav was starting to think of it like a sunlamp. He could close his eyes and tan his skin in the joules from that faggot-hating glare.

"That means you should ask your wife," Trav said shortly, and then bathed himself in the glacier that was Loretta Adams.

"I don't have any idea what you're talking about," she said and fixed heavily mascaraed eyes on his face, daring him to contradict her.

"Of course you don't," he sneered. "But even if you did, it wouldn't change that my guys are going to be this baby's godparents—"

"This is *bullshit!*" Oh, oh yeah. Casper was going to try to intimidate him. He stumped forward—he was shorter than Trav by about five inches—and thrust out his chest. "Those Sanders boys are nothing but trash, just like their whoring mother, and if you think we're letting my boy's baby into the hands of drug-addicted, cock-sucking faggots, you got another thing coming!"

"You can do what you wish," Trav said, looking down at him. Of course he'd take the money. Of *course* he'd take the money. "You can keep her here and kiss most of her royalties good-bye to a LGBTQ cause, or you can let her see fresh air and sunlight and honor your son's last request. It is *completely* up to you."

"That money is my boy's!" Casper snarled.

Trav let his temper show. "That money is his because the Sanders kids are generous as *fuck*," Trav hissed. "Their manager and producer both tried to talk them out of that royalty cut, but they said Grant had been there for the beginning—he should see that money too. So this? This is Grant standing up for himself. This is the one thing Grant Adams has ever asked from any of you, and you can either honor it or shit on it, but whatever you choose, it doesn't have a damned thing to do with my boys. They are *good* boys. They are kind and generous and smart. They've been getting their degrees online as we've toured, and adopting causes, and generally improving the hell out of a world that didn't give a fuck about them one way or another—and *your* boy never had a chance to do that himself. And every person in this room is to blame. So you do what you think is right, but you ask yourself: When this is over and they put that kid in the ground, who are they going to be burying? The kid you tried to lock away in this fucking house, or the kid my boys love? 'Cause I'm saying, I've listened to their CDs for the last year, in and out, and I can tell you which boy is going to live forever in music."

That stopped Grant's dad. His mouth opened and closed and his tongue appeared, wetting his thick lips. He closed his eyes and breathed hard.

"I don't listen to rock music," he said after a moment.

"You should," Trav said, relenting a little. "It's as close to your son as you may ever get." He sighed, tired of this place, and he'd only been in there for twenty minutes. "Mr. Reeves, do you have anything to add?"

The lawyer nodded. "Yes, sir, but if I may talk to you privately?"

"God, yeah," Trav said, looking around the living room at the three adults who couldn't meet each other's eyes. "You people deserve each other. I hope it's true what they say—that when you die, you move on to a better place. Because your son deserves a better place than this." They all turned to him, surprised, and Samantha's face twisted. She might be the only person here who would cry for Grant Adams, and she was crying from anger, not from love.

For a scant second, Trav hoped Grant and Mackey were making out, mouths open, tongues down each other's throats, groin to groin. Mackey was usually ferocious, but he could be gentle too. Trav hoped Mackey was giving Grant a gentle blow job, lots of little breaths, lots of reverence.

Suddenly Trav hoped Grant Adams had a little bit of happy, just a little, before he died. "I've got to get out of here. Mr. Reeves, can we step outside?"

"Certainly."

Trav walked into the sunlight on the back porch and let out a sigh of relief. The porch was surrounded by planters, all of them filled with bright off-season flowers that made Trav feel like he was at a gas station instead of someone's home.

"Those people," Reeves said, blowing out a breath and shaking his head. He grimaced when Trav glanced his way. "I'm sorry—that was unprofessional of me."

"But *very* understandable," Trav answered. "What did you need to talk about?"

Mr. Reeves sighed and looked out across the yard. Stevie had the little girl in his arms, but Jefferson and Blake were right over his shoulder, and they were all petting one of the horses. "They look like good kids," he said quietly. "I mean, I follow the papers"—he shot Trav a shy smile—"I own both their CDs, but you hear things."

Trav nodded. "Yeah," he said frankly. "They were a mess a year ago."

"That's what I wanted to talk about." Reeves had brought another folder out, and he handed it to Trav as they stood. "I've got another copy of this—Grant asked that I not show this to his parents, and I agreed. They would use it to make your lives miserable, but it's something your guys need to agree to."

"What is it?" Trav frowned, leafing through the documents. "Is this a—?"

"A drug-free clause," Reeves confirmed. "Grant felt bad about it, but he knew some of the boys had problems in the past, and—"

"It's his baby," Trav said with a tight throat. "It's his baby, and he wants to make sure she's taken care of. And he's not stupid."

"Not at all," Reeves answered.

Trav glanced at him and then took a closer look. Reeves was gazing out, far away, sadness etched in the corners of his eyes.

"You fell for him?" he asked gently, and the lawyer shrugged.

"A little bit. It will hurt when he's gone."

"Tell him," Trav said, closing his eyes against the sun—the real sun, and not the toxic sun of the Adams house. "It will make him happy, I think. His life will feel bigger."

"Yeah," Reeves said before swallowing. "Anyway—are your guys going to balk at peeing in a cup before the little girl comes to visit?"

"For Grant?" Trav half laughed. "They'd bleed in a cup if you asked them. Even Blake, and he just met the guy. That's who they are."

At that moment, Kell trotted out of the barn toward them, and Trav nodded at Reeves in dismissal. He took off at a half jog and met Kell on his way.

"Grant's in pain," Kell said baldly. "Mackey and I were hoping you could do your big bad soldier thing and carry him back."

Trav nodded and handed the folder of documents over. "Do me a favor and make sure these get put in the SUV in the pocket of my briefcase, okay? They're important."

The lines etched into Kell's forehead eased up. "Are they about the baby?" he said hopefully. "Because me and Mackey want to."

Trav nodded, smiling a little, because there was a really pure heart in this caveman, and he was glad he'd gotten a chance to see it. "Yeah. Yeah—get the other folder from Mr. Reeves too—but don't go inside." Trav shuddered. "And for God's sake don't talk to Grant's parents. They're not nice people."

"I knew that," Kell said, not surprised. "It's weird, how you think that stuff is just normal when you're a kid. But then you grow up and you realize it's not normal at all. It's wrong. And you wonder what else you took for granted and need to change your mind about." He shrugged and turned toward the car. "Go get Grant. He's in pain."

Trav set off toward the barn.

He opened the side door just as Mackey was shotgunning his first breath of smoke. Trav paused, stunned, betrayed, paralyzed by the thought of Mackey close enough to kiss, breathing for the kid he'd just been feeling sorry for.

He should say something. He should open his mouth and roar, grab Mackey's shoulder, scream, *You promised!* He'd promised. Promised he wouldn't make a fool of Trav. Promised he'd take care of him.

He should turn around and walk away. Catch a cab to the hotel, never to see Mackey again. He'd done it. He'd done it with Terry, just turned around and walked away.

The thought felt like a shaft of glass through his testicles, ripping up through his stomach, tearing the muscles, skin, and flesh in jagged layers.

He had to grip the doorframe to keep from falling to his knees.

He couldn't do that. Not with Mackey. He could no more walk out on Mackey than he could walk out on his heart if it lay at his feet, still beating.

*I could go down and blow the guy, Trav, and it wouldn't have a thing to do with you.*

Mackey finished breathing, stopped touching his lips to Grant's, and sat down, leaning back and closing his eyes. He was rubbing Grant's legs now, familiarly but not... not sexily.

Trav was holding his breath, or he never would have heard Grant's plea to be touched.

He took a breath and backed up, closing the door to the barn softly behind him. He leaned against it for a moment and dragged in a breath, feeling the fine particulate of grief and his own hypocrisy sand his lungs like metal scrap.

He'd wished Grant could have love again. Wished he could have kindness, could have touch. For a moment, for a hidden, stolen piece of time.

*You always knew Mackey was on loan from his demons.*

Well, this was the last debt Mackey had to pay. Trav had made this bargain without knowing it, the year before, when he'd let Mackey in his bed, made them public, when they'd become lovers. He'd known Mackey had to finish his business, but he'd been willing to take him on faith.

Now he had to have some.

This was not as simple as cheating with a kiss, cheating with a drug. Trav was a grown-up, and he knew that.

He hadn't known that a year ago. A year ago, walking into a hotel room in Burbank, he'd thought everything was black and white, everything was cut-and-dried. A lover cheated, or he loved you. Those things could not coexist.

Mackey loved him.

He knew Mackey loved him.

He knew it in his vitals, deeper than his stomach, or his groin, or his heart. It was in his cells, in his *soul*. Mackey loved him.

What was happening in that barn had nothing to do with Trav. It had everything to do with a kid who would never have a chance to fall in love again, who would never leave the house that had trapped him, a fly in a jar, until his few hours on earth were up.

He thought of Terry again and looked around. Kell was dancing with the baby in the sunshine near the horse pen, crooning softly to her as the guys sang harmony. They were singing, of all things, Harry Nilsson, and he wondered where they'd heard that in their fractured childhood. It was a good song, about a tiny little boat kept afloat by faith.

Trav had to have faith.

He had some time, he figured, so he pulled out his phone and opened an e-mail.

*Terry,*

*I know, we're done talking, and I don't want to get back together. You don't even need to reply to this, but I needed to say it. I was wrong. I don't think we should have been together—but I was wrong to just walk away. You tried to tell me what you were doing with that boy had nothing to do with me and everything to do with something inside of you. I was not the person who would listen to you then. I hear you now.*

*I'm sorry I didn't listen. I hope you're happy.*

*I am.*

*Trav.*

He'd just hit Send when Samantha stalked outside, heading straight for him. He made sure to block the door.

"I thought you were bringing Grant in," she said, her voice plainly unfriendly.

"Grant's busy right now," he said flatly. "I'll go get him when they're ready."

He'd never really thought about heaven or hell—had always assumed demons were figurative, like Mackey's. But the way her face twisted, her forehead furrowed, her lip curled up in a sneer—the way this pretty girl, still in her twenties, could suddenly turn ugly—abruptly made Trav believe in hell.

"You're not even man enough to keep them from doing it in the barn, are you?" she snarled.

Trav's laugh sounded flat and humorless, even to his own ears. "Exactly what do you think they're doing?" he asked. "What do you think he can do? He can barely walk; he's not getting it up in there. They're not having swinging-from-the-rafters monkey sex. They're having a moment."

"Well, I'm going to put an end to that right—"

"No," Trav said implacably. "No, Samantha, you're not."

"You gonna stop me, big man?" she sneered, and he nodded.

"I am. I am, and you're going to let me."

"Why would I do that?"

"Because if you don't, I'll make Grant do the math, and then he'll take Katy away from you for good." He doubted Grant could actually do that, but it was a stall, and he figured that was all Grant and Mackey needed anyway. Besides, somebody needed to say it. Somebody needed to make her see that she'd done wrong.

"I don't know what you're talking about," she muttered. Her eyes cut to the left when she said it, and she took a step back. She was possibly the worst liar he'd ever seen.

"Yeah, you do. You said they were carrying on in school. There was only a little time when Mackey and Grant were in school together—I did *that* math myself. You knew. From the very beginning, you knew about the two of them. And Grant started to get excited, the band was coming along, they had a rep from a record company, and you decided to pull the trump card."

"I really thought—"

"Bullshit!" He was angry—so angry. And she was just a kid. But he had to take it out on someone. *She's just a kid. Just like the boys. God, it's not like they all didn't fuck up.* But that didn't stop him from carrying this through. "You knew. And the one thing—the *one thing*—Grant taught Mackey about the big, bad world was to always wear a condom if it wasn't him and Grant. He always wore a rubber, didn't he, Sam? Always. Until...."

She was openly crying now, and he thought his mother would be ashamed of him. He couldn't fix this in himself. He couldn't. He *was* this man, this angry, bitter man, who saw the waste of Grant Adams and wanted someone to pay.

"Until he thought I was already pregnant," she finished, almost like she was afraid of stopping too. "He wasn't going to marry me," she said apologetically. "He would have gone off with them, would have gone and... done *whatever* with Mackey Sanders, and I'd be stuck here in my house without anything to look forward to but watching my dad get drunk and fuck his secretary. He was supposed to be *mine*!"

"How's that feel, Sam?" Trav asked nastily. "How's that feel, now that he's yours? He's in there with the only person he's ever loved, and it's not you. You're going to walk away from this a very rich woman, and you're going to marry again and probably have more children. And Grant is going to die, and he never got to do a damned thing he wanted. And you did that. I'm sure you're very proud."

"I loved him," she whimpered. "I loved him so much."

And finally, *finally*, Trav could feel some softness in him. "Then don't stand in the way of his last wish," he said, his voice gentling. "God—you took away all his hopes in life. Give him something in death."

She was sobbing too hard to say anything. She just wiped her eyes with her palms again and again, and finally turned away and walked back to the house. Her shoulders were hunched, and she seemed curled in on herself, a smaller, different person in one revelation. She'd just gotten to the porch when Trav heard Mackey's voice.

"Trav? You out there? He's in a lot of pain, man. It's time we get him back into bed."

Neither of them looked undressed when he got there. Mackey turned up an anxious face, looking a little stoned but innocent. He wasn't afraid of Trav leaving him, wasn't afraid what he'd done was wrong.

That right there was enough for Trav to start to let it go.

"Here," he said, finding some of the gentleness he wished he could have found with Samantha. "I'm going to lift you up, okay? Lean your head on my shoulder—that's my boy. I've got you."

Grant's eyes were closed, his face screwed up like everything inside hurt, but once Trav hefted him into his arms, some of that pain eased up. Grant opened his eyes and looked tiredly up at Trav.

"Hope you don't mind if Mackey did a little weed with me, Mr. Ford," he said, sounding truly apologetic. "It was hard on my lungs, and he was sort of paying me back a favor."

"A favor?" Trav asked, that shaft of agony receding, a remembered wound, aching in the rain. "Yeah?"

"From when we were kids," Grant said softly. "It was sort of our first kiss."

"I get it," Trav said, actually getting it.

"You do?" Mackey said hopefully, sounding lost. Well, he hadn't been high in a long time. The comedown was probably a bitch.

"Yeah," Trav said, meeting Mackey's eyes over Grant. "I really do." Big and luminous, and a little bloodshot, Mackey's eyes searched Trav's face hungrily. Mackey loved him. Whatever it had been, it hadn't been betrayal.

"Good," Grant murmured, cuddling almost like a kitten into Trav's chest. "You feel really good, Mr. Ford. Mackey's lucky. I bet you hold him every day."

"As tight as I can," Trav said, resting his chin on top of Grant's head for a moment. God. Twenty-five. This kid had once had so much more living in him. Babies. All of them, babies. "Tight enough to keep him out of trouble."

"Mackey needs that," Grant said, and it sounded like he was falling asleep. His weight in Trav's arms felt heavier, not like he had that much weight to begin with.

"He really does," Trav said. Suddenly he wanted nothing more than to tuck Grant Adams in and hold Mackey tight, so tight, like a tourniquet, so none of this could hurt him, none of this could *touch* him, because if he hurt anywhere near as bad as Trav, it was too damned much.

Nobody got in their way. Hell, the only person in the living room as Trav and Mackey put Grant to bed was the in-house nurse. The guys came in with Katy, who was sleeping soundly on Kell's shoulder, exhausted by the new people and the horses and the pretty day.

The nurse, an older woman who probably did this as a second job, took the baby from Kell and settled her into the crook of Grant's shoulder, making sure the bedrail was up so she couldn't roll out. "He likes it when we do that," she said, smiling softly at them all. "I think that baby's the only reason he's held on so long."

"Say good-bye, guys," Trav said softly. "We'll be back tomorrow, but it's always good to say bye."

They filed by one at a time—a kiss on the bandana, a touch on the hand. Blake, surprisingly enough, bent and whispered something in Grant's ear. Mackey kissed his cheek. And then they left.

The SUV was so quiet on the way back that Debra kept checking the rearview mirror to make sure they were okay.

"I don't know about you guys," Mackey said as they drove through the little strip of town that was Tyson, "but I need a fucking hot fudge sundae after that."

"God, the frostie guy's a mean old bastard," Kell said. "Maybe we can stop and get shit on the way?"

Which was how they ended up eating monster ice cream bowls filled with fudge and nuts and bananas and cookie crumbles at two o'clock in the afternoon, while the smell of ham and potatoes filled the air.

Nobody at the house—not Briony, not Shelia, not Heather Sanders—said a damned word against it either.

# Shadow of the Day

"WHAT NOW?" Kell asked as Mackey licked the bottom of Trav's bowl. God. Pot munchies. It *had* been a long time.

God willing, it would be a helluva lot longer before it happened again.

"Now?" Mackey muttered, smelling the afternoon of sickness and weed and sadness on his clothes. "Now, I take a shower. And then? Jesus, you fuckin' slackers—we ain't practiced in four goddamned days. How you feelin', Briony?"

Briony looked up over the rim of her ice cream bowl. When she pulled it away, she had white streaks all around her mouth. She sucked the last bit of sundae off her tongue and said, "Better—but then, I slept all morning."

"Sorry your mom couldn't come," he said, feeling bad about it. He and Trav had tried.

"I'm a grown-up, and the little kids need her. I'll see her at Christmas. Anyway, what'd you want?"

"Can we do a setup in the garage? There's fuckin' room in there—"

"Mackey?" his mother said, playing with her melting bowl of ice cream. "Do you really have to swear that much?"

"Fu—"

"No, seriously. It's one thing to use it for emotion, but it's like every other word. Do you really need to go to the fucking store to buy some fucking ice cream to fucking eat?"

Mackey took a deep breath. "Mom, I just went to a fucking house of doom to see my fucking ex-boyfriend because he's fucking dying. Yes, and that's why we need to fucking practice, because if I don't get some of this fucking shit out of my chest, I'm gonna *fucking* lose it. Okay?"

Oh God. He'd killed it. They'd been doing okay—they'd been dealing, but he'd just yelled at his mother and brought it all out to the surface and—

"Ah-fucking-men," Jefferson and Stevie said together, their voices coming from low and inside.

"Anything you want on the playlist?" Jefferson asked.

Mackey grinned at him, suddenly loving his brothers so much it hurt. "Rock and Roll Ain't Noise Pollution," he said, "'Badlands,' 'When They Come For Me,' 'Johnny Guitar,' 'We Will Rock You'—"

"Further On Up The Road," Kell added, since it was clear they were doing covers.

Mackey nodded. "Fair enough. Any other requests?"

"Come Out and Play," Stevie said, at the same time Jefferson said, "The Kids Aren't Alright."

Mackey had to laugh. "Offspring it is." It figured they'd both pick the same band.

"Stairway to Heaven," Blake said, and they all met eyes.

"Wish You Were Here," Trav said, and a sigh riffled through the room.

"We'll close with that," Mackey said. They all knew the songs—they were practice favorites. They'd even done some of them on stage. But they weren't Outbreak Monkey songs. Just this once, they were going to let someone else's words, someone else's pain, speak for them. It was pretty damned clear the band didn't have words of their own. That was okay. Sometimes that's what rock'n'roll was for.

He looked up then, conscious that he was a grown-up, and he needed to mend his fences as he busted them. "And I'm sorry, Mom, for swearing at you in your kitchen."

His mom grimaced. "And I'm sorry, Mackey, for picking the wrong way to parent at the wrong damned time. Go shower. I'll let Briony set up the garage."

"Sure thing, Ms. Sanders—just let me talk to Mackey first."

Briony met him in the hallway just as he was wondering if he was really going to need some Motrin for a little bit of weed. No. No, because the hangover, the letdown, was important. He didn't like this feeling. He should remember that.

"How are you?" Briony asked as Mackey grabbed the handle to his door.

For a moment Mackey let his shoulders sag. "Trav ain't talked to me since we left," he said, letting her see it. "I… it's complicated. But I was tender with Grant. Sweet. I think Trav saw. I woulda told him, but…."

"He's not the forgiving sort," Briony said softly.

"I had to," Mackey said, believing that. "God, Briony. It don't matter what we were to each other when no one was looking. He was a boy I grew up with—*the* boy I grew up with. It's…."

Trav walked in, and suddenly Mackey couldn't talk. He had no words. None. He walked away abruptly, heading for the shower.

Ah, God, water was supposed to purify, wasn't it? *Help me, Jesus, wash away my sins, wash away my past, 'cause I wouldn't trade a thing, but it wasn't meant to last.*

He started singing, loud, louder, the rhythm of the water nothing on the rhythm inside him.

*Help me put shit into boxes, help me ship it all away, 'cause I don't want to trade the home I built for the shelter I built yesterday.*

Oh God. God, Trav's eyes searing into Mackey from across the hallway. Mackey didn't know what it meant.

*Help me read the grown-up runes carved in my skin and bone. Help me keep my lover while I learn to stand alone.*

He could. He *could* stand alone.

*Help me make amends, oh please, 'cause it sucks to be alone.*

*It's hard to take the memories, hard to put them on a shelf*

*Even harder when I'm by my fucking self.*

*'Cause I put the dishes with the clothes and*

*Clothes with the magazines*

*And none of the labels I got for shit*

*Are really what they mean.*

*And I'm working hard on frameworks*

*And I'm starting to break a sweat.*

*'Cause every box that I've unpacked is labeled with regret.*

*I'm fucking tired of regret.*

*Break that fucking box, destroy what's all inside.*

*Until there's not another regret to fucking find.*

He screamed the last part, screamed it hard, the melody conforming to the words as he sang. He wanted percussion *here,* and he wanted guitars, both of them, *here,* and he wanted them real, in his ears—

*I need the water off my body,*

*Let it cleanse my fucking* mind!

He stood naked in the shower, panting, barely aware that Trav reached inside and turned off the tap. The shower curtain whisked back, and Mackey realized he was naked, literally, in body and spirit.

Trav handed him a towel and gave him a hand out of the tub. He needed the hand; his knees were shaking.

"What're you doing?" Mackey muttered as Trav wrapped another towel around his shoulders and started drying him off.

Trav closed his eyes and pressed his temple against Mackey's. "This shit in your head, it's here to stay," he said softly. "Give me some time, but don't worry. It's not anything I can't live with."

Mackey closed his eyes, felt Trav's warmth against his face, felt his heartbeat even out a little, and some of the fight drained out of him. "That is so fucking good to know," he said, at ease for the first time since they'd left for Grant's that morning. "Are the guys set up?"

"I told them to give it twenty minutes. Write the song down. I dug out your notebook and everything."

Mackey smiled a little and pulled away. "It'll make a good single before we go on hiatus."

Trav grunted. "It's fucking brilliant, McKay. It's going to make you all a lot of money—but that's not going to make up for what it's going to cost to sing it."

Mackey sighed and shrugged. "Isn't that art?"

Trav grimaced. "Thanks. I'll never envy you again. Now come on out. I dug out some old sweats and stuff. Get dressed."

For over a year, they'd shared a room. Once they had to get dressed in a minute and a half because the hotel had forgotten the wake-up call and their plane left in an hour. Even then Trav had touched his bare bottom in passing.

"Trav?" he asked, grabbing his clothes with one hand and toweling his hair with the other.

"Yeah?"

"If you're not mad at me, could you, you know, do me a favor and rub my ass? Or my back? Or my shoulders? Or—" His voice shook. He remembered Grant's plea.

"What's wrong?" Trav at his back, sliding his hand across his stomach, was enough to make him shake.

"Grant hadn't been touched in two weeks. Nobody hugged him. I don't think he got any before that either. Two weeks, Trav. I shake just—oolf!"

Trav engulfed him, warmth from top to bottom, those big anaconda arms around his shoulders, the hard line of Trav's body along his back, even Trav's chin resting on top of his head.

"Thank you," Mackey sighed, leaning his head on that cannon-size bicep.

Trav's breath whispered in his ear. "Welcome. You can have more after you practice. You need it."

"Yeah. Move, Goliath—time for me to write."

STEVIE DIDN'T have the drum set there, but Briony had brought two drum pads and a keyboard, and then, in a stroke of genius, she scrounged up a couple of pots and boxes, as well as some wooden spoons. Stevie cackled when he saw it, and by the time the guys had tuned their acoustic guitars, he was playing with all the toys, as gleeful as a kid playing rock band.

For all their experience, for all their fame, Mackey had a moment to realize they *were* kids playing rock band.

And that thought made him really fucking proud.

They riffed for a minute, the garage door open so they'd have more room. Mackey kept his guitar slung around his neck, because some of the songs they'd picked had guitar solos, and he missed doing that work. When he wasn't doing the worm on stage, he loved getting a chance to play.

"Stevie, you ready?" Mackey asked, grinning.

In response, Stevie started pounding out the drum riff from "When They Come For Me" on the top of three plastic cat litter boxes. "Try to catch up, motherfucker!" he crowed, and everybody howled.

By the time they reached "Stairway to Heaven," the band was hoarse and swimming in sweat. Mackey would need another shower before he slept, but he didn't care. His body ached because he'd thrown himself around on his mother's driveway just like he would have on stage, and he had the scrapes on his elbows and knees to prove it. He didn't care. None of them cared. Kell, Blake, and Jefferson had done knee drops, and Stevie had sliced his hand open banging on the side of the garage for "Come Out and Play," but none of them were stopping.

Mackey played every song to their small audience—Trav, Shelia, Briony, his mom, Walter, Debra, and a collection of neighbors who had wandered in when the cacophony reached them.

But now it was the second-to-last one, and it was time to settle down.

"You know what pisses me off about this song?" Mackey mused, not really riffing to the crowd but talking to his guys.

"What?" Kell asked, tuning up. His practice guitar was his old Walmart model, and it fell out of tune with almost every song. It was worse because there was frost on the air tonight, and the sky had turned black as they played.

"It's not just women who do this shit. Man, it's fuckin' everybody. Briony? Shelia? You guys hum the flute part, okay? Stevie's keyboard isn't doing the high notes."

"Got it, Mackey!" they said together and lined up behind Jefferson, huddling, their breath coming out like smoke.

Mackey picked out the opening notes, and the entire neighborhood stopped rustling, stopped panting, stopped moving in the reverence that riff inevitably brought.

Briony and Shelia didn't have bad voices, either, and their sweet counterpoint soared out of the garage just like the song said, a bridge of notes, a stairway to heaven.

Mackey twisted a smile at his band and winked. "There's a gay-be who's sure all that glitters is gold...."

Everybody laughed quietly, even people who, Mackey was sure, had no idea who Outbreak Monkey was and that Mackey was talking about himself. That was okay. Trav made the grimly ironic face he wore when he knew Mackey was making a joke at his own expense. Well, fine. Trav didn't have to like his jokes as long as he kept loving Mackey.

The song wailed, soared, exploded, and distilled into the haunting finale. Mackey closed his eyes as the last note died, and his audience, such as it was, let the silence hold.

For a moment in the cold country October in the Sierra Foothills, everything was silver frost and hard, bright gold.

Then the smattering of applause made him open his eyes, and he smiled, his whole body sagging. He was exhausted, he realized. The band probably was too. But they'd promised one more number, and Mackey was going to go over the new song he'd written in the shower.

Well, the song was written down and could wait until tomorrow, but he didn't want to disappoint Trav.

He made eye contact with Trav and knew him well enough by now that he could tell that Trav was about to let them off the hook for "Wish You Were Here," but he didn't get a chance.

A pre-turn-of-the-century Oldsmobile had just parked in front of Mackey's mom's house. The top was burgundy, but the wear from too many autowashes had dulled it, and it was starting to smoke.

It was in almost *exactly* the same condition it had been the last time they'd been practicing at Stevie's house, and Stevie's dad had come home early.

They all knew the drill. Stevie and Jefferson stood up and grabbed Shelia's hand. "Mackey?" Stevie's voice shook.

"We can't do this," Jefferson said matter-of-factly. "We've had our closure—we're not engaging with this asshole now."

Mackey nodded, unslinging his guitar and setting it carefully inside the garage.

"You guys go on in," he agreed. The last time they had done this, the Olds had pulled up and the five of them had simply taken off running for Grant's minivan, instruments over their necks, Stevie's sticks held tight in his hands. Jeff and Stevie had never told them why, but they hadn't needed to know. The fear was infectious—it always had been. The two of them must have stood up to him at some time, because they weren't afraid now. They were just bone-tired.

Mackey understood that. He was tired too. But it was always easier to deal with shit when it wasn't yours.

"Who's that?" Trav asked as a pudgy, balding middle-aged man wearing a cheap polyester suit and a tacky tie got out of the car and strode up. He had a broad, clueless smile on his face, like he didn't see what all the fuss was about.

"Stevie's dad," Mackey told him grimly.

He was completely unprepared for what happened next.

Trav was wearing a soft navy sweater, and he literally rolled up his sleeves with definite intent. Then he hauled ass down to meet Stevie's dad with an expression on his face that Mackey could only describe as murderous.

"Trav?"

"Get out of here," Trav growled, his very presence pushing the older man backward. "You are not welcome here."

"Now, I'm Stevie Harris's father—"

"I know *exactly* who you are and I've got a fair idea of what you've done, and my boys don't need you." Trav poked a sharp finger into Mr. Harris's sternum. "They"—poke—"don't"—poke—"need you!"

"I've got as much right as anyone else to be here!" he protested, and Mackey caught his breath. He'd been afraid of Trav's anger. He should have known. If Trav was ever really, *truly* angry at Mackey, Mackey would have been really, *truly* afraid.

He was certainly afraid for Stevie's dad right now.

"This is private property, and you have until the count of three before everybody on this lawn either calls the police or helps me kick your ass back into your car!"

"He's going to kill that bad man," Blake said at Mackey's side.

"Oh God, Mackey! He hated jail when it was all of us in there." Kell sounded a little panicked.

So was Mackey. "Well, we better make sure he doesn't go back." He'd go with him—hell, he'd help Trav beat up Stevie's dad for *free*—but…. "We don't got time for jail right now. Grant's counting on us. We can't lose time for this bullshit."

"Get ouuuuut!" Trav screamed, flecks of spittle coming from his mouth.

Mr. Harris must have been seven times a fool, because he was still stuttering, fumbling—and then, oh God, he really was too stupid to live. "It's just that, you know, I lost my job and we could use a little bit of—"

Mackey knew where this was going, and he knew what Trav would do. "Stop him," Mackey cried and ran down the lawn to grab Trav's arm as he cocked it back. "We don't got time for this bullshit!" he yelled, hoping to get Trav's attention.

"I will *kill* this guy if he touches one of you!" Trav shouted.

To Mackey's relief, Kell was on his other arm and Blake—brave man—jumped on Trav's back.

"I'll just… you know, I can come back…." Mr. Harris backtracked like a scuttling crab, and Mackey and his brothers just held on to Trav as every muscle in his body fought to either smash the man's face in or wrap his hands around his throat.

"Do it and I'll kill you!" Trav screamed, and Mackey snapped, "Not with witnesses, dumbass!" loud enough to penetrate.

The release of tension in Trav's body was so great that it sent them all stumbling backward, Trav landing square on top of Blake, Kell and Mackey scrambling to the side.

He was small but he was quick, and he rolled, tumbled, and hopped on Trav's chest, sitting with his backside toward Trav's face. He didn't want any of their intimacy done in front of the strangers now watching the show on the frost-crispy lawn as the battered Oldsmobile peeled down the street.

"You can get up now, Mackey," Trav muttered.

"God, please!" Blake groaned, but Mackey didn't believe it.

"Walter!" he called.

Sure enough, the driver—who'd had the day off and spent it hanging out in Mackey's mom's living room instead of the hotel like he'd said—popped front and center to where Mackey was perched on his stubborn-assed boyfriend's chest. "Yes, Mr. Sanders?"

"Could you go to Walmart—it should still be open—and buy one of those big leather bags that we keep in the basement, and bring it here and set it up?"

Walter nodded, as if he approved of this plan. "Would you like tape and headgear and—"

"The whole nine yards," Mackey said, smacking Trav's arm. "Stop wiggling, asshole. I'm saving your butt."

"Blake is kneeing me in the back," Trav snapped.

"Good. If he was in position, I'd let him knee you in the balls. Jesus, you people talk about *my* self-control!"

"I have wanted to beat the shit out of that guy for a *year*!"

In spite of the absurd gravity of the situation, Mackey had to smile. His boys. God, Trav really was proof that God could throw you down a cast-iron jock sometimes, wasn't he? "Well, we've wanted a piece of him for most of our lives. Get in line. We're not doing this now. If we end up in jail, who's visiting Grant?"

Trav's muffled groan of self-awareness had real apology in it. "Aw, fuck. Fuck, fuck, fuck, fuck, fuck…."

"Walter?" Mackey said, nodding.

Walter nodded back. "Back in an hour, Mr. Sanders."

"Use the gas card, Walter!" Trav called, but Walter probably knew that already.

"Okay," Mackey said, standing up and turning around to offer Trav a hand up. "Show's over, everybody. Vamoose!"

The neighbors took the hint—and just the fact that they scattered on command proved to Mackey that this was a much better neighborhood than the one they'd grown up in, not that he needed any convincing.

"You okay, Blake?" Mackey asked, truly concerned.

Blake grunted. "You twisted my knee, asshole!"

Kell helped him up, and he tested his weight on it. "It'll be okay," Kell judged. "Here. Let's go get showers and let Mackey calm Trav down. I don't know about you all, but I could use some boob-tube and dinner." And it was just so normal. Like practicing. Like being together.

"Yeah, that sounds awesome. Go on inside." Mackey checked on Trav, who was looking around sheepishly like he was trying to judge how many people had seen that. "We'll be there in a minute."

"Sure thing, Mackey."

They disappeared, leaving Mackey and Trav out on the lawn in the darkness.

Mackey put his hands on either side of Trav's face, liking the warmth and the stubble, *needing* the contact. "You can't do that," he said nakedly. "You're our rock. You don't get to murder the bad guys in front of witnesses."

"But without witnesses is okay?" Trav asked, and he was his magnificent sarcastic self again. When Trav palmed the back of Mackey's head and pulled him in against his warmth and his protection and his—oh my *God*—smell of sweat and expensive aftershave, Mackey went. Trav's arms around his back, his heat in the autumn cold— these were animal things, like water and food, and Mackey needed them.

"Trav?" Mackey's voice was muffled against his chest.

"Yeah?"

"I really love you. I'm sorry I got high."

"I'm sorry your old boyfriend is dying. I'm sorry you and the guys hurt and I can't do a fucking thing about it."

"You're gonna need to beat up that bag a lot in the next two weeks."

Some of the pent-up tension loosened from Trav's body. Thank God. It was about to strangle him.

"That was brilliant, by the way. First time I've seen you actually use money."

"Well, it's either that or stuff it in a big house and a bunch of show ponies you don't know how to ride."

Trav grunted. "Mackey, do you have a plan for when we leave here?"

Mackey looked up at him and saw that his face was bleak against the moonlight. This time, Trav needed some hope.

"We're gonna go home. All of us. We're gonna go to fucking Disneyland, 'cause Grant never got to go. We're gonna buy a dog—you know that? I want animals in our place, I don't care if we have to pay Astrid extra. And Christmas is coming up. I don't know what the rest of the guys are doing, but I made a promise last year, and I'm keeping it."

Trav's mouth relaxed some. The aloneness eased from around his eyes. "God, I really want you to meet my parents. I think you'd love them."

"I love you," Mackey said again, and Trav bent down and took his mouth, softly.

"I love you too," he whispered when the kiss was over. "And for the first time, I think my folks'll see I mean it."

Mackey pulled away only to rest his head on Trav's shoulder again. They would go inside eventually and realize they were starving. Mackey would shower again, and they'd watch *The Dark Knight* and hoot and holler at the screen. Briony would fold herself just to rest on Mackey's chest while Mackey rested on Trav's, and Mackey would wonder why he'd never realized that women could be stunning creatures, even if you didn't want to bang them. (For one thing, all of that long, soft, curling hair—he just liked to sink his hands in and stroke it.)

She'd sleep in her own room, though, and Mackey and Trav would touch each other softly in the dark, smoothing their hands down bare skin, erections secondary to the contact, to the touching.

Their orgasms would be quiet things, organic, easy cresting in each other's mouths. They were mindful of the others in the house, but more than that. They were tender with each other, easy. Mackey kept hearing Grant's pathetic words about being touched, and he was grateful that Trav had let that happen.

He would never take touching his lover for granted again.

When they were done and he lay with his head on Trav's chest, stroking the fur that traveled to his hard stomach, he wanted to say something important.

"Trav?"

"Yeah?"

"You know when I wouldn't tell anyone I was gay and it was eating me alive, and this thing with Grant was killing me, and all I could think about was my next hit?"

"Yeah."

"That sucked."

Trav's bark of laughter echoed in the quiet room. "You think?"

"But it was worth everything—rehab and crying for months and all that bullshit—if you and me can walk away from this together."

Trav groaned and swallowed him in a hug that was so tight he couldn't breathe. That was okay. Breathing was optional. For the moment, he had Trav.

# Wish You Were Here

BETWEEN TRAV and the other guys, they beat the bag soft by the end of the next two weeks.

They went over to the big, oppressive dragon-house (as Mackey called it) every day after lunch. The guys took turns talking to Grant, playing with the little girl, or playing music. Grant picked up Mackey's tiny, beat-up guitar and maneuvered it around the various tubes and wires in his arm that tracked the pain meds and the fluids that were sustaining him. They played rusty versions of the songs on the first CDs, but only one or two at a time. By the time they finished the second song, he was usually falling asleep, unwillingly, and they would kiss him on the forehead or the cheek, then kiss Katy on the cheek as she cuddled with her daddy, and file out.

That one golden day when Trav saw more than he wanted and less than he'd hoped for, when he'd carried the young man back to his sick bed, had been the last time Grant walked on his own.

He would never leave the bed in the perfectly pristine living room again.

A week after that day, Grant called Trav, Mackey, and Kell in for a conference. Reeves sat next to him, stoic and professional. Only the tight lines at the corners of his eyes and mouth betrayed the fact that Grant was more than a client and that he was mourning what could have been between them.

"I know," Grant said, a tired smile on his face, "you all are tired of the damned manila folders. This one's sort of the last one—" Suddenly he sat up like he'd forgotten something. "You signed the paperwork, right? I mean, that's in. Sam signed off and—"

"It's done, Grant," Reeves said, touching his shoulder gently. "Everybody signed, it's ironclad and airtight. The guys will have a right to be a part of your daughter's life."

Grant fell back against the pillow and sighed. "Okay. Good. I'm tired. I'm forgetting shit. I keep waking up and worrying that my dad's gonna find my stash of weed, and then I remember it's legal now. *Then* I remember I can't smoke it anymore—too hard."

Mackey stroked his hand, and Trav focused on that motion. The skin was pale, dry, like paper, contrasted to Mackey's vital, rough, brown, ink-stained left hand. Trav had seen Mackey walk away from writing at his desk with black smudges from his pinkie to his elbow, and even though he'd wrecked a couple of shirts and one misguided purchase of white jeans that way, Trav had never minded. It meant Mackey's brain was engaged: he was happy when he was writing.

A dark smudge appeared on the back of Grant's hand, and another. Trav found himself hoping they'd stay.

"What'd you need us for?" Mackey prompted. "It's my turn to sing with you. Was looking forward to it."

Grant breathed out. "Mr. Reeves here has my funeral requests. My folks are sort of pissed about them, but I can pay, so it's all right. Reeves wants you to take a look and tell me if you agree to all of them."

"Grant, you really suck, do you know that? Jesus! We couldn't just show up in black suits and let some stranger say shit over you?"

Grant laughed, and it sounded like tattered pages fluttering. "Yeah, well, consider it payback for all the times I kept you from being beat up. You owe me this."

"I don't owe you shit," Mackey said, but amicably, like they were competing over who got the last piece of pizza.

Grant suddenly focused his eyes hungrily on Mackey's face. "You don't," he said seriously. "You owe me nothing. I owe you every good moment I've ever had. I can give you my daughter to help raise, but that's an obligation. I know it. But do this for me, okay? I don't want the black suits and the person I don't know. I want you and the guys. And I don't want to be buried here in the local cemetery in the family plot. I fucking *lived* here. Reeves set up a trust for me—I want my ashes sprinkled in the ocean. I want to be *free*."

Mackey looked up at Trav, helpless in the face of the paperwork in the folder.

"Of course." Trav's voice sounded a long way away, even from his own ears. "I can make this happen."

"But Trav—"

Mackey's shoulder shook under his hand, and Trav knew that this was the thing he could do, the way he could help his boys, the thing he was uniquely qualified to take care of.

"Don't worry about it. It's what I do. I manage."

"Yeah, asshole," Mackey said, keeping that tender stroking of Grant's hand. "We'll do it. In case you were wondering how much you meant to me, I'll tell you right now how much I hate this."

Grant aimed his weary, dreamy gaze at Trav. "I hope you're not expecting flowers, Mr. Ford. Or poetry. Or fancy dinners."

"I know what I'm getting," Trav said sincerely. "Good and the bad, hard and the soft. I know."

"He's amazing, isn't he?"

"Stunning."

"Shut up, both of you," Mackey said thickly. "Now are you going to tell us what you need us to do or not?" He never stopped touching Grant's hand. Trav would have picked up if he left off.

The directions were very specific. Trav was sure he was going to get flack from the boy's family.

He didn't care.

Three days later, it was Trav and Mackey's turn to play with Katy on the little porch. She knew their names by now—all of them. She knew "Tav" from Mackey from Kell from "Bake" from "Tevie" from "Chef," and got excited when they came.

That morning she'd almost fallen out of her mother's arms in her attempt to get to Mackey, and Mackey actually caught her. Trav thought that maybe those few weekends a year, that one month they could leverage for, was going to count for this child. For the rest of the world, Outbreak Monkey was a band, a god, a source of music Trav didn't think would ever dry up.

For Grant Adams's daughter, they were going to be salvation and refuge—real men who would do their human best to share her father with her.

Trav could live with that. Letting her run from him to Mackey and back again was an easy way to spend a half an hour, and he was almost sad when Kell came out, looking strained.

"He's not going to be awake much longer, Mackey. He's asking for his song."

Grant had wandered in and out of consciousness since he'd given them the file with the funeral directions. Nobody said the words "He doesn't have long," but everybody knew.

"Yeah, coming." Mackey scooped up the little girl and started inside. Uncharacteristically he grabbed Trav's hand, pulling him into the room behind him.

Grant's chest hardly rose and fell, and the hush in the room was almost painful. Katy was ready for her snuggle time with Daddy, so Jefferson lifted the rail and settled her at his shoulder, on top of his wasted chest.

Trav had seen pictures of Grant since he'd come to Tyson. The Sanders kids didn't have a lot of them, but every picture they had featured Grant. Their mother had kept a scrapbook, and he'd seen the full lips, the odd nose with almost no bridge, the golden eyes, as luminous in their way as Mackey's gray ones. That beautiful boy bore no resemblance to the wasted frame Trav had seen for the past two weeks. He wondered— did his boys look at Grant and see him? Or did they see what Blake and Trav saw? Did it make it easier to see the illusion of youth and joy impressed on the frame of death, or harder, when the illusion slipped?

He didn't have words for that question.

All he really had was the leather bag and the amp he'd bought from Mackey's old music store. The night before, he'd held the bag and dodged as Stevie and Jefferson had, in an oddly synchronous dance, pummeled it, first one, then the other, their harsh grunts echoing in the garage like song. The night before that, Mackey gave the neighbors a solo performance, all guitar, no words, using the amp. The boys had the tools, but no words.

But Mackey's hands maintained that ever-present smudge that showed he was writing. And the song about cleansing sins was on the top of the practice roster.

Trav found himself praying for Grant to let them go, to *let* go, and do it soon, so his boys had enough of themselves to drag back home and grieve.

Today it looked like God might have visited that little room after all, and Trav might get his prayer.

"Mackey, you singing my song today?" Grant asked.

Mackey grunted. "Yeah. You got anything you want us to sing after? You can fall asleep to it."

"Surprise me," Grant murmured. His eyes were half-closed, and Mackey stroked his hand one more time before picking up the guitar.

Mackey's song about making love in the river shadows rang through the room. The boys hummed the backup harmonies, and Stevie tapped out a sedate rhythm on the side of the gurney. The little room was peaceful, and the window in the vaulted ceiling let in a stream of thin autumn sunshine so pure the dust-motes looked like stars. Grant started out humming the song with the boys, but by the time Mackey was done, he was asleep.

For a moment, Trav thought that was it and the boys would pack up, kiss his cheek, and go.

But there was a weighted pause, and Mackey and Kell met eyes.

Kell opened his mouth this time, and although he didn't have Mackey's tone or his passion, he had a passable voice.

*So. So you think you can tell,*

*Heaven from hell....*

Trav knew the words to this one too. Mackey picked up the guitar, and the clean chords surged in melancholy waves under their quiet voices.

When they got to the part about the two lost souls, Mackey's voice cracked, but his brothers kept up the melody, and Mackey did what he'd done the first time Grant left. He just kept playing, because it was all he had.

Kell was the one who broke the tableau of the dying song. He bent and kissed Grant on the forehead. "Bye, brother. Sing in heaven for us, okay?"

Jefferson and Stevie followed suit, and Blake held that wasted, ink-smudged hand for a moment before kissing him on the forehead too.

Mackey paused at his bedside and bent down, whispering in his ear. Trav heard him, though, because his voice was broken, and whispers didn't come easy.

"Let it go, Grant. Fly. We'll wish you were here."

Trav touched foreheads with the boy he'd hated since he first heard Mackey say his name. "I've got him, Grant. I'll take good care of him. You're leaving him in good hands. You can go now. It's okay."

Silently they filed out.

The next morning Grant's father called and Mackey's mother answered the phone. She came by their room, but she didn't have to. Mackey had heard the truth in the silence, and she and Trav met eyes as he wept silently on Trav's chest.

She told Trav later that it had been the same with the other boys. Kell had known. Blake had known. Briony ran into Kell's room while Mackey's mom tried to get the words out, and Kell fell into her arms and cried like a baby while Blake hugged him from behind. Shelia was sitting up in bed while Stevie and Jefferson wept on her lap.

Cheever had come home the night before, and he stood in the hallway, baffled, while his mother cried. Trav saw him looking into every doorway in wonder, but Trav didn't have words.

He only had Mackey, and the hope that they would get over the crying and start to live.

A WEEK later they stood at a grave and buried an empty coffin while the ashes sat beside Kell and Mackey in a big black urn.

Mackey was supposed to speak, and he glared at everyone from behind his sunglasses as they got out of the car.

"I'll bet he thinks this is real fuckin' funny," he snapped. "Man, he's laughing his ass off in heaven, you know that?"

"I hope so," Trav muttered.

A week—it had taken a week to rush the funeral through, and the boys were strangling and their mother was ready to have them out of the fucking house. Mackey kept talking about home, and Trav did the math. They had two weeks before Thanksgiving and less than a month before they got on the plane to his parents' house—and besides a stop in San Francisco, which he was actually looking forward to, this was the last thing they had to do.

It gave him heart that the guys had bitched about the funeral during the planning.

"Flowers? Roses? Did he really ask for that?" Kell demanded.

Trav shrugged. "It just says flowers."

"Chrysanthemums," Mackey said promptly. "For his eyes."

"Gross, Mackey," Kell muttered, but it was for form. "Daisies, for his sunny personality."

"He will come back and haunt you!" Trav snapped, out of patience.

Kell flashed him a grin just like Mackey's. "I fucking dare him."

"Roses, daisies, and chrysanthemums, because I fucking say so," Trav snarled, putting his foot down.

"And irises," Shelia said, from nowhere.

The boys all looked at her.

"They're pretty!" she defended.

"And those big calla lily things," Briony said thoughtfully.

"Yeah," Cheever agreed, obviously trying to help. "Those are nice. Can we get some of those?"

It was a damned weird-looking arrangement, and it took up the entire empty coffin.

And it made Trav smile. God, it wasn't perfect or ordinary, but it was definitely his people. And it was showy, and that was important, because this wasn't the real funeral—not for Trav's guys. This was a performance piece, a play, and they'd even practiced a little, taking turns saying the shit they most wanted off their chest about Grant Adams and, by association, the town that had twisted them all.

Mackey brought his guitar, and grinned at Grant's parents and Samantha, who glared back. The baby was there, struggling to crawl out of Samantha's arms, and Ms. Sanders was on that like white on rice.

"Can I take her?" she said, smiling into Samantha's eyes. "I'll just let her wander over here while Mackey talks. It's not fun for a baby."

Samantha simply gave her over, and Mackey's mom smiled her son's smile, but untainted by bitterness or guile. "Thank you! It's lovely to hold a baby. It's been so long."

Trav watched the way Samantha looked after the two of them, and then looked over at her parents. He thought that maybe there would be more healing to happen—but that, please God, he and Mackey wouldn't have to be there for any of it.

Mackey looked around at the crowd—the guys from Grant's dad's dealership, what looked to be Grant's relatives including his mostly absent sister, all sitting down in the ordered chairs and looking solemn, and Samantha and her mother and father—and then looked at his phone for the time.

"We about ready?" he asked, tuning idly, and Kell, Jefferson, and Stevie shook their heads.

"You're doing all the hard shit, Mackey," Kell answered, getting his own guitar out of the case. "Are *you* ready?"

"If you drop the fucking song, Kell, I will throw you into the big hole."

"That's not what I'm talking about and you know it. Grant didn't make this easy on you."

Mackey rolled his eyes. "God, ain't that the truth. Didn't make it easy on any of us. Okay, everyone. Whether you're ready for this or not, here goes." He swung to the assembly without ceremony or reverence, and Trav wondered if everyone was as surprised by Grant's edict as he was. *Tell the truth. Tell it unvarnished. Be pissed off if you want. And sing something angry. This isn't the real ceremony. That's private. This is the rock star show. It's all the public needs to know.*

"Grant Adams," Mackey said, and then paused like he was choosing his words. He said Grant's name again, licked his lips, and then, like a cannonball, he was off.

"Grant Adams asked me and my brothers to talk at his funeral. You may notice we're burying an empty casket, which I think is weird and Kell thinks is fucking hilarious, and you're welcome to think what you like, but it's what we're doing. See, Grant Adams and I...." He took a deep breath and met Trav's eyes. Whatever he saw in Trav's eyes must have given him strength, because he kept going.

"Grant Adams and I were in love for five years. We were *lovers* for five years. And we kept that from everybody—from his parents, from his girlfriend, from my brothers. And he let me go, at first because he was afraid of what would happen if he came out and told the world about us, and then because his girlfriend lied and said she was knocked up, because she knew it would keep him here."

Samantha gasped and Mackey rolled his eyes. "Yeah, don't nobody think I can do math or anything. Grant neither. We knew. We figured it out. It was a shitty thing to do, but Grant loved that baby, so he forgave you for it. Don't worry. Anyway, my boyfriend and my brother's best friend felt like none of you knew him. You knew what you *thought* was him. The good boy who stayed home when he wanted to fly, the nice husband, the good father, and maybe he was partly those things—but that was just the outside. That's what you get to bury. Kell?"

Mackey's delivery had been sarcastic and aggressive, and Kell's was not much better.

"We're going to take his ashes to the San Francisco Bay and we're going to throw them in. He's got a boat, and a trust, and a whole thing worked out. Me and my brothers are going to see it, and we're going to ride on the ferry, which he told us was hella fun, and we're going to eat fried donuts at the pier and buy all sorts of shit we don't need and ship it up here to his daughter. He told me once that some of his happiest moments had been in San Francisco. I didn't know then that those were when he was sneaking away to bang my brother silly, but now that I know, I figured you all have to live with that information too. It *should* make you happy that he got some happy, and if it does, then you can count yourself as someone my best friend—my brother—really loved. If it doesn't, I'm going to let you live with that, because it should, and yes, I think it makes you a bad person if you think worse of the dead because he stole him some happy."

"Grant wanted us to sing a nice song and all," Jefferson said, picking up the thread. Even in rehearsals they'd gotten good at picking up the thread when the last person dropped it. Which might come in handy, especially if the crowd turned ugly. "But not here. He wants my brother to play their love song, which I don't know if Mackey will ever be able to sing again after he does that, so it's a big deal—but Grant doesn't want that here. He wants that on the ferry, and I'm sort of looking forward to that. What he wants here is an old Eric Burdon song that I think every garage band in the history of ever has played. Which is awesome. I wish Grant had played this when we were in high school. This would have been a very different thing."

"And by the way," Stevie said, taking his part. That small, subversive smile that he got when he was about to do something evil had crept up. "I know a lot of you are out there judging us, judging this dog and pony show, judging how pissed off we sound and how we're saving the sweetness for ourselves and not sharing. You all ask yourself this. Can I get a show of hands for how many people knew my father was a douche bag who liked to watch little boys undress and touch their asses and beat off while they watched?"

Trav opened his eyes really wide and looked out at the crowd in disbelief. *This* had not been in rehearsal.

To his horror, about half the crowd looked shocked. And the other half looked uncomfortable and guilty. Fucking Jesus, was he ready to get out of this town.

"Yeah," Stevie said, angry. "I sort of thought so. So those of you judging us, you go ahead and judge yourselves, okay? I got no more apologies to make to you people, and neither do my brothers. Blake, you got anything to say?"

Blake glared out at the little group of people and grinned at the few news cameras that had been sent to cover a quiet funeral attended by a rock band.

"Yeah, all. Whoever fucks with my brothers ain't worthy. Grant Adams was my brother too. We're going to let you to your little funeral, the one with the preacher and the service and the empty casket and all, but we've got to catch a flight to Sausalito in an hour so we can go have a day at the pier. You ready, Mackey?"

Mackey grinned at them and screamed out, *"But Baby—"*

*"Baby—"*

*"Remember—"*

*"Remember—"*

*"It's my life, and I'll do what I want—"*

He and Kell strummed furiously, making up in fierceness what they didn't have in electronic sound mixing, and the band, including Trav and Cheever, including the girls—hell, including Walter and Debra, who were taking them to the airport as soon as this was over—all screamed out the chorus.

When they were done, when the last chord echoed through the shocked assembly, Mackey's mom was there with the baby, who squealed and clapped, ready to be delivered to her mama.

Trav grabbed the urn, Mackey and Kell grabbed their guitars, and the whole lot of them strode across the cemetery, got into the cars, and drove away. They would drop Heather and Cheever off back at the house and continue on to the airport, but Trav knew he wasn't the only one to feel that surge, that pressure, that fearful desire to get the holy hell out of this town.

They really didn't have anything else to say at that point anyway. There was only freedom to be had.

# Gives You Hell

MACKEY AND Grant had gotten to San Francisco only a handful of times in their five years together, and they only had one picture to show for it. It had come in the manila envelope, faded and dusty, one of those computer printer deals that wasn't going to last much longer, even if they kept it framed.

This time round, Mackey made sure everyone charged their camera phones. When they got back to LA, he'd make a big collage on the computer, have it developed on photo paper, and have it framed. Trav would commend him for spending his money on something cool, and Mackey would blow him off, but the whole family wanted that picture in the front room.

They were all happy.

They all wore matching tourist sweatshirts *and* bottoms, because their stuff was packed before they got on the plane, and they didn't want to run around the bay in their somber suits and dresses. Mackey left his suit in a pile in a public restroom. He hoped a very small homeless man found it and enjoyed. The sweats looked almost like a uniform, and they'd joked about that a lot—how they should have Outbreak Monkey gear made and wear it in public. Trav had sent the idea to Heath, and Heath had eaten it up with a fork. Mackey said that making money off the idea sort of took the fun out of it, but Trav just laughed. Apparently that made him feel like he was doing his job.

There was a picture of Shelia and Briony coming out of the puppet store with giant, fluffy puppets while the guys all looked on in horror. Briony's was a big fluffy llama, and Mackey found himself oddly drawn to it. He liked touching it, and they kept it in the living room so it could be groped and fondled during television time.

Trav took a picture of Stevie and Jefferson racing each other down the Embarcadero, dodging pedestrians and vaulting over a badly parked motorcycle, their faces so fierce and so free Mackey's chest hurt for the closure they'd found years ago. He finally knew how they felt.

Mackey took a picture of Blake playing a street performer's guitar, looking like he knew the venue well. Blake's eyes were closed, and his thin face looked full and angelic. He made the street performer a lot of money in ten minutes, but the best part was when Mackey showed him the picture and said, "Look at you. You love it. That's the only reason you should do it."

Blake's smile hadn't been captured on film, but Mackey would remember it forever.

They had *all* taken a picture of Kell and Briony standing side by side at the end of the pier, heads close together like they were telling secrets. And they all noticed that when Briony didn't have Mackey by the hand, dragging him from place to place to show him something, she and Kell were walking quietly, holding hands in a whole other way.

And Trav took the picture of Mackey singing "River Shadows" when they were on the prow of the ferry, with what looked like nothing but clear sky and bright bay behind him.

Nobody took a picture of Mackey putting the tiniest bit of Grant's ashes in a baggie, because when they got home they were going to Disneyland, and Mackey was going to bury a little bit of him in a planter at the Enchanted Kingdom, just so he'd be there for the guys.

Kell's pic of the whole bunch of them asleep on the plane, Mackey drooling on Trav's shoulder in the foreground, almost didn't make it into the collage, but then Mackey decided Kell had it right. They weren't always pretty and they weren't always posed. This was them too.

The collage was Mackey's Thanksgiving present to the whole family, since everyone else had helped plan the meal while Mackey was busy writing the new album. He took direction this time. Blake, Kell, the twins—everybody had a note or a verse they wanted to contribute, and he was pretty sure that when they went back to the studio in March, what would come out would be the best music he and his brothers had ever made.

But it was a long time until March. Before that was Christmas, and Mackey was going to meet Trav's parents and his brother and his sister. Briony's mother was going to fly down to LA, along with Heather and Cheever, so Mackey could meet her before he left. More importantly, Kell could meet her and the stumbling, shy progression of what looked to be the smartest thing Mackey's brother ever did could get the parental seal of approval.

And Shelia could plan the special room they were building for Katy, because she was good at that, and she and the boys weren't planning to have babies until after the next tour.

And Mackey and Trav could be…

Everything.

The morning after they returned from San Francisco, Mackey woke up slowly.

He was in bed. At home. Trav was lined up along his back, hard and warm, and Mackey stretched, pushing against that warmth, but not to break away. Just to touch it a little more firmly.

Trav.

Mackey turned lazily in Trav's arms and licked at his neck. They'd showered before collapsing into bed the night before, so he was only a little salty. Mostly he tasted like soap and sleep.

"Mm…."

Trav didn't wake up fast or even in a good mood, most times. That was okay. Mackey could deal with a growly man in the morning. Mackey kept licking, then suckled hard at Trav's nipple.

Which abruptly became hard in his mouth.

Trav groaned and clutched Mackey's head to his chest. "Augh—*Mackey*!"

Mackey reached between them and found Trav's cock through his boxer briefs. Hard and long and thick—Trav had a memorable piece down there, and not just because it was attached to the love of Mackey's life. Mackey slid his hand underneath the elastic and squeezed, stroking long and hard, rubbing his thumb in the thick liquid at the tip.

"You'd better be ready to pony up, McKay," Trav groaned.

Mackey grinned at him, fuck-off-and-love-me, and kissed his way down.

Ah, *God*, Trav tasted good. Mackey wasn't sure if he'd ever really appreciated giving blowjobs before Trav. With Grant it had always been so rough, in such a rush. With everyone else it had always been too fuzzy. With Trav, he took his time, licking the broad head, swallowing it down. The taste of Trav's skin was sweet, and his precome was sweeter. Mackey shoved his head down farther, gagging, not caring, wanting Trav in his throat and his belly, *dying* to be filled.

Trav wiggled, fiddling with something on the end table, and Mackey's hips were abruptly lifted, positioned, until Mackey straddled Trav's head while Trav shucked Mackey's briefs.

Trav's mouth on his cock made him see stars. Just the hot and the wet and the edge of teeth, the sensual scrape, the little bit of roughness; Trav's assertive, no-bullshit blowjob made Mackey move his head faster.

Then Trav penetrated Mackey's asshole with a lube-slick thumb, and Mackey had to stop everything and groan. Trav's cock slid out of his mouth, and he buried his head in Trav's thigh and groaned.

"Oh my God! *Trav*!"

"Move, Mackey," Trav grunted. "Face up, legs spread. Now."

Mackey had never liked faceup before Trav. He hated that people saw him when he wasn't singing, wasn't screaming. Hated that he was bare and out of control. But Trav saw him like that anyway, so Mackey hauled at his thighs and waited, writhing, eyes closed, while Trav spread the lube and stretched him. The burn was delicious, and Mackey's cock throbbed, waiting.

He wanted, wanted, his body aching with it.

Trav made him greedy, made him beg and steal. He'd stolen their first year together, but he figured that now, all his demons behind him, Trav was his rightfully. He'd paid by hard growing, and Trav belonged to him.

And Trav could take him any time he wanted.

That big blunt head stretched at Mackey's entrance, slow and tender, and Mackey opened his eyes and grunted with impatience.

"Hard, fast, and now!" he snapped, but a slow, sweet smile played at Trav's mouth.

"Slow," he breathed, sliding in one burn at a time. "Slow. Easy. Now."

Trav's sepia eyes were intent on Mackey's face, and Mackey—Mackey was losing his mind, writhing under Trav's achingly slow possession.

"You... are... killing... me!" Mackey grabbed his cock only to have Trav knock his hand away.

"Deal, Mackey. You can take it."

Mackey's head fell back, and his whole body shook. Agony—urgency—took over his body, and he needed.... God, he'd thought he'd craved Grant, thought he'd craved drugs, thought he'd craved cocks. What he'd really craved was this. Being possessed, being thoroughly taken over, being owned, body and soul, by someone you owned right back.

He craved Trav.

And Trav was holding out on him.

"Please," Mackey whispered, and Trav fell forward on his elbows, held Mackey's face, kissed him hard. The kiss felt brutal in the margins. Trav nibbled on his chin, down his throat, and Mackey thought he'd die.

"Mackey?"

"God!"

"I really want you!"

"Thank you, Jesus!"

"No, Mackey. Thank you, Trav."

"*Please, Trav, would you fuck me?*"

Mackey tried humping from the bottom, and Trav laughed evilly, thrusting hard and shutting him up.

"You can hang on to your cock now," he rumbled.

Mackey grabbed it quickly, impatient. Greedy.

Trav pushed back up, and Mackey rolled his hips, because, *God*. Let's get this fuck on the road!

Thrust after thrust, Trav pounded away inside him, and Mackey jerked roughly on his own cock. In the end, Mackey was wholly selfish, invested completely in the ache in his ass, in the sparking behind his eyes when Trav hit his gland, in his beating, squeezing self-assault on his own dick.

He was breathless, panting, groaning, *begging* when the moment came. He clenched, convulsed, released, the fireworks behind his eyes all tinged sepia, like Trav's eyes.

Trav let out a grunt above him that probably ripped from his taint to his sternum, and started to pump inside of Mackey like a fire hose.

Ah, yes! Something else Mackey treasured—the slippery feeling of Trav's come inside, sliding out, binding them in a way. Wasn't neat, wasn't clean, it was sloppy and real, and Mackey craved it like he craved Trav's sweat and his touch and the hotness of his mouth.

The kiss at the end went on forever, sweet, infinite, and then Trav collapsed on top of Mackey, resting his head on Mackey's chest, trusting Mackey could hold his weight.

They were breathing too hard to tell if anyone else in the house was up, and for a moment, it was just the two of them. Their room. Their house. Their world.

"Trav?"

"Yeah?"

"I love you."

"Love you too."

"Does this mean we made it? It's all good after this?"

Trav pushed up so he could look Mackey in the eyes.

"There *is* no finish line," he said seriously. "This means we made it over some big stuff. Means the other stuff might not seem so big. But you've seen guys, pros, trip up in concert over a single song they've done a zillion times—"

"Like when Bruce forgot the lyrics to 'Born to Run,'" Mackey said gravely, because it was legend.

"Yeah. My mom told me the trick to staying in love was falling in love every day. Like you do with music. You listen for good music every day."

Mackey smiled a little, ran his fingers through that military hair, grazed those lean lips, swollen from sucking Mackey's cock, touched that hard, square jaw.

"So I have to listen for you every day?" he said, delighted—even more so when he saw what he thought of as Trav's sex flush wash over Trav's cheekbones again.

"You've got to find something in me to love every day," Trav said, embarrassed.

"Yeah, well, you've got the harder job," Mackey said seriously. "I'm a pain in the ass."

Trav laughed softly and ground his softening cock inside Mackey one last time. "I beg to differ," he murmured.

Mackey laughed, because, well, dick joke, and because morning sex, and because their own room and their own home and Disneyland tomorrow and sleeping in, and because....

"Trav?"

"Yeah?"

"Not every day is going to be this good."

Trav kissed his chest. "No," he said softly.

"Let's make sure we remember this one, okay?"

"For how long?" Trav asked, half-playful, half-serious.

"Forever. Until tomorrow. When I fall in love with you again."

It was a deal. They kissed on it. They kissed again before they got up, and again in the shower, where Mackey started singing because that was just what his heart did.

*"It's a beautiful day...."*

AMY LANE is a mother of four and a compulsive knitter who writes because she can't silence the voices in her head. She adores cats, Chi-who-whats, knitting socks, and hawt menz, and she dislikes moths, cat boxes, and knuckle-headed macspazzmatrons. She is rarely found cooking, cleaning, or doing domestic chores, but she has been known to knit up an emergency hat/blanket/pair of socks for any occasion whatsoever, or sometimes for no reason at all. She writes in the shower, while at the gym, while taxiing children to soccer/dance/gymnastics/band oh my! and has learned from necessity to type like the wind. She lives in a spider-infested, crumbling house in a shoddy suburb and counts on her beloved Mate to keep her tethered to reality—which he does, while keeping her cell phone charged as a bonus. She's been married for twenty-plus years and still believes in Twu Wuv, with a capital Twu and a capital Wuv, and she doesn't see any reason at all for that to change.

Website: www.greenshill.com
Blog: www.writerslane.blogspot.com
E-mail: amylane@greenshill.com
Facebook: www.facebook.com/amy.lane.167
Twitter: @amymaclane

# The Johnnies Series

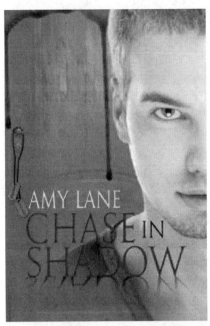

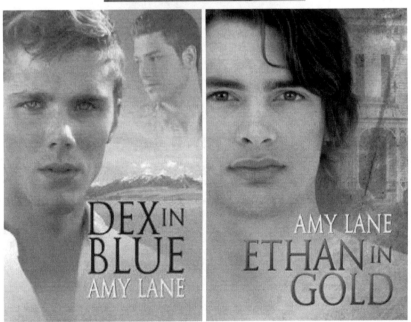

http://www.dreamspinnerpress.com

# Keeping Promise Rock Series

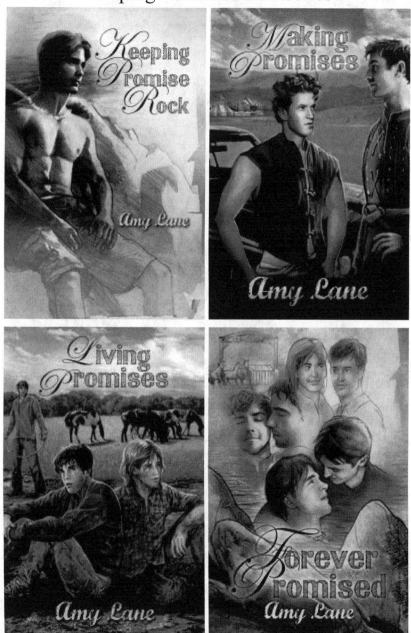

http://www.dreamspinnerpress.com